World Without Duct Tape

World Without Duct Tape

Frances Tucker

Artist Proof Edition
Published by Lulu.com

Cover design by Frances Tucker Jahnke
Copyright 2023

LIBRARY OF CONGRESS CATALOGING-IN-PUBLICATION DATA
Names: Tucker, Frances. Author.
Title: World Without Duct Tape / Frances Tucker.
Description: Austin, Texas : Frances Tucker, 2023
Identifiers: ISBN 979-8-9875042-1-5 (pbk)
ISBN 979-8-9875042-2-2 (hbk)
ISBN 979-8-9875042-3-9 (ebook)
Subjects: LCSH: Science fiction, American –Texas--Austin |
Adventure stories–Texas—Austin | Business Intelligence
BISAC: FICTION / Science Fiction / Crime & Mystery |
FICTION / Science Fiction / Action & Adventure
GSAFD: Science Fiction
Classification: LCC PS3620.U25 W67

For Kit

Table of Contents

Chapter 1: Getting to Work

It happened so slowly that at first she didn't notice, although it was irritating when grocery store shelves were empty and she couldn't find the products she wanted. Poor ordering practices she told herself; or perhaps a glitch in the delivery system. In the end, the decline seemed to appear overnight, but still somehow, it had been hesitant and unconvincing in its approach.

By the time she truly woke up, life as she had always known it was gone. She hadn't been paying attention. All the catastrophe films she loved to watch had not prepared her. Today was the first day of the rest of her life and she could not go back and start over.

The day that it happened, or at any rate, when she realized it had happened, Polly was trudging along a busy frontage road, picking out the larger and more level chunks of concrete sidewalk to step on. It seemed like only yesterday that the Chronicle had published an article about deteriorating sidewalks. How long ago was that? A few sidewalks were repaired and then interest or funds dwindled away.

That's how it is. One's home is perfectly fine day after day, happily ignored and taken for granted, until all of a sudden there is a leak. "Now where did that come from out of the blue?" Next thing you know you are an inch deep in water and have black mold.

What happened was a failure to care about the little things. And there is the rub, because the little things all run together to make the big things, the catastrophes. That is when it all breaks down. That is when it can no longer be ignored, but the little things along the way are difficult to see.

It was a beautiful, cloudless autumn day up above the ground level pollution. Even down here on the ground, the smog was less oppressive because of the bright sun light filtering through. Polly reached the crosswalk and pressed the button. To save money, city government decided to eliminate most crosswalks, but public outcry caused the passing of an ordinance requiring at least one every 5 blocks in areas with high vehicle traffic. Polly remembered when she was still in school walking home with her friends. There had been a crosswalk nearly every block. It seemed crazy now. "Wasteful, I guess," she thought.

The pollution was getting to her. She glanced at her compucell still held in her hand since the last closed crosswalk. That couldn't be right. Had it died again? She just recharged the battery. When was that? There were no functioning crosswalks on this side of the city according to the ubiquitous device.

She pressed the "Press To Walk" button again before noticing a taped-on sign announcing the button "Out

Of Order". This wasn't even her correct crosswalk. The one closest to her bus stop was 5 blocks farther up. It was "Out Of Order" too. Without the crosswalk light, right turning traffic would mow her down before she was halfway across the street even when the vehicle traffic light changed to green. And it would be her fault. Now that the Supreme Court had ruled that motor vehicles were people, with the same rights as people, she would be responsible for any damage that her body might do.

She would have to hire a flit to take her across. Pulling out the comp she had just placed back into her pocket, she tapped in "flit" and a list of nearby cabs appeared. This was going to make her late and cost her an hour's pay as well. Maybe she should just call in sick. She stood there undecided. A bus pulled up to the broken curb on the other side of the street. A few people smiled smugly at her as they boarded.

"What kind of people do that?" she said out loud to the unhearing humans on the other side of the road. "What kind of people are you to take pleasure in someone's distress?" She remembered in school when they studied about Germany and the great wars, how the teacher taught them the word *schadenfreude*, which meant joy in someone else's misfortune. She kicked at a lump of sidewalk. It didn't even have weeds growing up through it. There was just greasy dirt and trash.

"You have to get to work." She bullied herself, but in the back of her consciousness there were rebellious whispers. She tapped the first flit provider from the list on her comp and got an "unable to connect" message. Maybe I should just walk to the next crosswalk she thought and began to move down the street. She couldn't even see the next crosswalk from here.

Traffic was at a dead stop, but she wasn't daring enough to cross through it. She had seen people do that, usually vagrants or students. It irritated her when people didn't follow the rules put there for their own good, but she was beginning to see their point. "People who do those things don't have anything to lose," she lectured herself. Slender fingers automatically, if not autonomously, scrolled through a directory and tapped Binge HR, then typed, "Late to work. Debit personal account." In an instant, a message came back that said in large red print "Accepted*" the asterisk meant that she was on notice to watch this last minute leave taking.

Now, how to get across the street?

When did it get this hard?

People said these were the good old days, meaning that it was only going to get worse. Learn to appreciate what you have while you have it, instead of longing for it after it is too late. Would she be longing for this?"

Horns blared when the traffic did not move. A great river of dirty metal and stinky exhaust created an impenetrable wall next to her as she continued down the broken walkway. At least pedestrians were still allowed along this road. Most thoroughfares had banned pedestrians unless they were on toll sidewalks.

Between the toll roads, toll sidewalks and increasing traffic, companies had begun building their own housing. With employees grouped together, they could be transported to and from work by a company flit-bus. Owning your own vehicle was expensive and time consuming. Still, living in a company building did not allow much freedom. People living in these communities ended up going to the company doctors and buying from the company store located on the first level of their building. God forbid that they should get fired.

"Oof," Polly grimaced as her ankle twisted painfully. Distracted by the sea of automobiles and commercial trucks, she had failed to look down at the sidewalk. "Damn," she cursed out loud and reached down and grabbed the injured joint. She wiggled her foot up and down. High top boots she always wore when walking outside protected her from badly spraining it.

"Okay," she decided, "this is ridiculous. I am calling a flit." With that, she pulled out her comp again and tapped in "emergency flit service". She got a message saying, "Currently unavailable." With a heavy sigh, she continued down the street.

As she approached the next crosswalk, she saw several people standing about. "Good," she thought, "I won't be alone. This one must work." This crosswalk was in front of a huge box-like home improvement store surrounded by a nearly empty parking lot. A bit farther down from the crosswalk stood a group of unskilled day laborers waiting for work. They would be picked up and taken to work if they were lucky enough to be needed. Had they exchanged long-term job security for freedom? Or did they have a choice? She joined the crosswalk group.

"How long have you been waiting?" She asked, in lieu of an introduction.

They all turned toward her. There were three of them, two men and one woman. They looked tired and the day had only begun. A middle-aged man in a slightly tattered, tweed jacket paired with blue jeans and sneakers spoke first. He stroked his closely groomed salt and pepper beard professorially with the attitude of someone used to being in charge.

"Roads are supposed to connect people, instead they cut us off," he addressed her angrily as if it were her fault. Speaking for the group he continued, "we were thinking of going up the way you came, to the next crosswalk. Did you go by that one? Was it working? We can't seem to get a flit."

She hesitated before answering. It was beginning to dawn on her that she was not going to be able to get across the road, and that her employer would have no sympathy for an employee that did not live in company housing; not that employers had much sympathy for their employees anyway. "This is my third stop," Polly replied with distress. "Have you tried any farther down?"

A small, slim woman with smooth, Native-American features and braided, long dark-brown hair streaked with grey spoke up. Her demeanor was calm, almost fatalistic. She carried a large cloth bag that, from the things peeking out, food, water and various cutting and digging tools, suggested a job requiring manual labor. A pair of large clippers sticking out of one side might be garden shears, Polly noted.

"I have traveled the farthest. I came from five stops down and there I was told that even three stops on from that they were not working. This is a very bad day."

"How are people supposed to live like this?" cried the younger man. Slouched shoulders reduced the height of his tall frame. He looked to be in his mid-twenties. A handsome pale face was marred by a flush of rosacea on one cheek. Straw-colored hair partially covered by a vintage, black fedora was too short to be successfully tamed by a sturdy rubber tie holding it back in a ponytail. His eyes were hidden by wrap-around sunglasses.

They all turned to observe him as if for the first time, and then Polly said, "the traffic has not been moving." They were all nearly shouting, although they stood next to each other; so loud was the din of the immobile machines. The only movement in the street consisted of the fumes coming from the cars and the fuming people inside of them.

"I think that, because all the intersections are blocked by cars, the crosswalk light can't trigger. Remember when they were trying to enforce that "don't block the box" rule? It was simple enough in principle and it worked until the driving population doubled and then doubled again," the man in the tweed jacket observed with a frown. "With this many vehicles the intersections are never empty, and who can afford a flit every time you have to cross the street?"

Flits had come from an inventive coupling of next generation drones and backing from Lifft/YUber. They were made specifically to lift a person over an intersection. When first announced, it had been an adventure to fly over a crowded street strapped to a seat attached to a drone, but now it was a necessity. Even so, they were never around when you needed one.

The woman with the single, long braid down her back remarked, "Flit operators do not keep up maintenance on their drones. My neighbor's son might never walk again because a flit dropped him in middle of traffic. He was hit by three separate vehicles before they even realized what had happened."

"Good gracious," Polly put a hand to her mouth to cover her shock. "Even with financial compensation, you can never be the same after an accident like that."

"What compensation?" the woman asked. "It was the fault of the flit operator and he didn't have insurance or any possessions to speak of and he lives in a different country!"

"Look," the young man interjected, "I'm going to miss my class. I paid good money for it and I need the certification if I am ever going to get a job. Do any of you have any ideas that might help?"

"His hair sticks out from under that black hat in a ridiculous way," Polly observed silently. "I wonder what color his eyes are".

He wore dirty blue jeans and a tight, black shirt. They all looked at him and said nothing. No one had any ideas.

As they stood there, unable to think of a course of action, a police drone flew over with yellow lights blinking and a loud speaker blaring. "Pedestrians must not enter motorized vehicle traffic. This street no longer permits crossing by non-motorized vehicles or people on foot. Please proceed to the nearest crossover/under." It proceeded down the street, hovering over the grumbling line of vehicles, repeating its announcement.

"Well, that is that," sighed the woman. She rustled through her bag and pulled out a dried apricot that she popped into her mouth. "Care for one?" she asked the others. They all moved their heads side-to-side to indicate "no" even though they wanted one. She chewed thoughtfully, focused on the delicate texture and tangy, flowery flavor. Then she swallowed wistfully and announced, drawing her chest up as she spoke, "I liked that job." With that, she walked away.

"I wonder what she does," the student mused.

"What right do they have to suddenly close an intersection?" Tweed jacket man exhaled irritably, ignoring the young man.

"I guess they didn't have a choice," soothed Polly, "what with the traffic so heavy."

"Whose fault is that?" interjected the student. "Why don't we have public transportation?"

"That was replaced by corporate mass transit services. If you work for a corporation, they provide transportation to and from work. Since corporations are providing a *free* mass transit service, public funds can be used for other things." Polly was one of the receptionists at Binge, so she could corporate speak with ease. However, the truth was she didn't pay close attention to what she was saying at these times.

"*Other things* like fat bonuses to CEO's and kick-backs to politicians. Anyone can see that it isn't being spent on the things people really need," the student said vehemently.

"Have you noticed all the shortages lately?" The man in the tweed jacket asked, moving the conversation away from what might become a conflict, "I can't find pipe tobacco anywhere and when I went to market for milk last week, they were completely out. No milk mind you! Think about it and where it comes from, maybe one day there will be no milk or tobacco anywhere. What kind of world would that be?"

A huge gust of wind and noise overhead caught the attention of the three people at the crosswalk. It was an army helicopter flying very low, perhaps helping the civil government monitor the traffic situation, Polly imagined. Dust and trash flew up around them and the force of the wind knocked free the "Out Of Order" sign taped to the pole. Underneath, the metal sheath that guarded the wiring was hanging by one loose screw.

Seeing this, the student said, "I might be able to make this crosswalk work long enough for us to get across."

The bearded man cocked his head at the gangly youth. "How do you mean?"

"I am getting my certification in wiring and drone maintenance, traffic drones, you know. There's a simple, button-activated robot inside this pole. It must be disconnected or shorted out." He twisted a few times and then pulled out the screw holding the metal plate. It fell onto the sidewalk and blended in with the rest of the rubbish piled up against the pole.

Polly and the older man stood behind him looking around his shoulders. He was taller than either of them. They couldn't really see what he was doing, but they could tell he was poking around knowledgably inside the cavity that the loose metal cover had exposed.

Finally, he stepped back. They stepped aside and looked at him expectantly.

"Looks easy enough," he said, "I just need some strong, water-proof tape. Like duct tape or electrical tape."

"There's a home improvement store right there." Polly pointed out with excitement. "I'll go get some."

"I'll pay for it," the other man offered. He reached into his pocket and pulled out a cash card. "I should still have enough on this card to cover it."

"I can't believe this," Polly beamed at them as she started walking across the mostly empty parking lot, "working together, helping each other, this is how it should be." They smiled back at her. There was only the slightest shadow of pessimism in their faces.

Inside, the store felt cavernous. The ceiling lights were so high up that the light dimmed by the time it reached the floor. Polly headed for an aisle with a floating sign above it that read PAINT. She passed by the caulk and noticed that the bins were poorly stocked. "Bad management," she muttered.

She passed by the tape section and had to retrace her footsteps. In the bins before her were several sizes of painter's tape, a flimsy paper tape with light adhesion. There was one roll of masking tape in a very narrow width. There was no duct tape. There was no electrical tape. She figured she was mistaken. This was crazy. She carefully read the tiny, printed description on every bin. The bins were there, but there was nothing in them.

"Well, that's ridiculous," she muttered and stormed to the front of the store. There was a row of empty checkout lanes that stretched from one end of the store to the other with no one manning any of them.

Traversing the aisle at the head of the line of checkout lanes, she paused at each to glance down at the register, but saw only empty space. When she reached the last one a door opened and a man rushed out. "Do you need something?" he asked brusquely.

"Yes," she answered, "I need some duct tape. And it is rather urgent."

"Oh," he said dismissively, "that would be on aisle 20 in PAINT."

"Yes, I know where it should be," an edge coming into her voice. "The bin is empty. There are only a few bins that are filled, in fact."

"Yeah, well, we might be going out of business. With traffic so bad, no one comes in. You can buy what's out on the shelves, that's all there is."

"But I need a strong, water-proof, non-conductive tape," she argued. "It's important. It's my livelihood. It is important to the other people at the crosswalk."

"The crosswalk," the clerk exclaimed, "is that what this is all about. You better not try to cross that street. They don't want you to cross anymore."

"That's crazy. Why would that be?"

"Security concerns, is what they told me," he said. "Those of us who have jobs have to maintain security for the sake of the country. It isn't safe on the other side of that street. Until the police get it under control I advise staying put."

"That's ridiculous. I work over there. Don't you even have some duct tape of your own you could lend me?" Polly cajoled, trying to conceal her contempt in vain. She smiled at him unconvincingly.

He frowned. "Look lady, if there is anything else I can help you with I will be glad to, but there isn't any duct tape." He crossed his arms in front of his chest.

"Thank you anyway," Polly grumbled and turned toward the exit.

When she got back to the crosswalk, the two men huddling around the pole straightened up and looked at her expectantly. It hurt to have to tell them that she had been unsuccessful. She gave back the cash card.

"I guess I'll call in sick and get demoted or canned," Polly sighed. "If I still have a job, I'll have to live in company housing."

The student kicked the metal cover that had been leaning against the pole and it clattered across the broken walk. "What good is it to try to do anything? Everything is fucked!" Stirred up dust blew up into his face and he brushed at his eyes automatically, knocking off his glasses. Polly saw that he had soft blue eyes rimmed with red like he hadn't had enough sleep. He pulled himself together and looked at Polly apologetically. "Been nice meeting you," he said, stooping to pick up his glasses. Then he shook the man's hand and left, cutting diagonally across the parking lot. Polly and the man stared after him.

"That's the way they are when they're young," the man in the tweed jacket commented sagely in a distant voice. "He'll be brought to heel like the rest of us."

Polly looked at him somewhat shocked. She wondered what he did for a living, but didn't dare ask. Instead she said, "What will you do?"

"Traffic is light during the night. It's when most service industries move their workers; makes quite a stream, though a bit dangerous for someone alone. I suppose I could cross under the open underpass on the south side then, if a flit doesn't become available. I don't know why I bother anymore."

She was about to satisfy her curiosity and ask him what he did, but he had already turned and started walking away down the sidewalk. "Uh, good-bye," she called after him. He lifted a hand but did not turn.

Polly pulled out her comp and tapped in her Binge HR account. She pulled up her last sick day, accepted it and tapped the YES button for petition to live in company housing. A long scroll of text came up. It was the housing contract. She quickly scanned it. It was a seven year contract. Seven years was a long time. She hesitated, then looked around and sighed. She had to choose one side of the street or the other she supposed. She tapped the green ACCEPT button and then leaned back against the crossing sign.

Chapter 2: Second Thoughts

Heavy clouds of ugly, yellow smoke rolled toward Polly as she leaned uncomfortably against the signal pole. Gasping for breath, she looked up to see a bulky, old-style flit moving across the traffic cloud. It headed for the parking lot behind her and settled onto the pavement. An overweight, middle-aged man emerged. He wore a crumpled coverall with the name Mitchell embroidered across the pocket and carried a clipboard, the kind with a compartment attached to the back. Huffing with the exertion, he came toward her."You call for a chip implant?" He wheezed.

"No," Polly answered, "I called for transportation to work."

"Says here that you need a chip implanted," he countered, looking at his compcell.

"I called for a ride to work," Polly replied uneasily. "Are you from Binge?"

"I am today," he answered. "No chip. No ride."

Polly thought back to the contract she had signed. Of course, she hadn't read the whole thing. Did anyone live long enough to read all the documents that one was required to sign to get through the work day?

"I didn't know that I would have to be chipped," she replied.

"Look lady, I don't have all day. Do you want a ride or not?"

She looked around searching for an out, but all she saw was the endless traffic, the smog and a big, empty parking lot. She didn't want to be here anymore. How bad could a chip be anyway?

"Well, okay, I guess," she breathed, her vocal cords hardly able to form the words.

"Give me your hand then," he scowled. "The one you use least."

He withdrew a small case from the back of the clipboard. He set the clipboard on the ground and opened the case. Inside there was an injector gun and a chip in a tiny plastic bag that looked like it could go in anything, a compucell, a computer, an auto-flit. He loaded it into the injector gun without putting on germicidal gloves. She flinched when he grabbed her hand. She thought she saw the flicker of a smile crease his bloated features as he gouged the pointed end into the space between her thumb and forefinger. Before she had time to complain about his hygiene, he pulled the trigger. A pain shot up her arm and made her shoulder seize up temporarily. She jerked her hand back instantly and violently.

"Oh Hell," the tech protested, "I hope you didn't fowl the mechanism. How does your hand feel?"

"It hurts," she stifled a sob. Her hand throbbed and the joints between the thumb and index finger felt as though they were on fire.

"Fucking dip-shit, signing on at a bus stop," he muttered to himself as he put away his gear, "deserves to feel some pain." He was on his seventh chip for crying out loud and you didn't hear him complaining. The company needed to find some tougher employees.

"Once the chip is installed, I am authorized to take you to your current domicile. I have charged your chip for the convenience of a pickup and chip install," he finished with a false smile. "It activates in 24 hours."

Polly didn't protest. She felt thoroughly beaten. Twenty-four hours until she was housed in an all women dormitory, two to a room and one giant bathroom on each floor. That would be what she came home to after work for the next seven years. What had she been thinking? Her left hand throbbed. "I can't do it. Take the chip out. I'll take my chances here," her brain screamed, but no words came out.

It didn't take long to get back home. Corporate transports could travel short distances above ground, but could also operate on the road and were given the same access to express routes as the police and emergency services.

The transport operator stopped abruptly in front of her apartment house and activated the electric door. She barely stumbled out before he pulled away without a word or backward glance. The broken walkway up to her apartment complex looked quaint and nostalgic in comparison to the sterile, smooth walkways she would be treading from now on. An aggressive weed growing from a gap brushed her leg and made it itch. She made a mental note to pull it before she realized it wouldn't be bothering her any more.

Regret swept over her as she inserted and removed the old-style key card from the slot in the door handle. There was a buzzing sound as the lock released. Polly entered a small corridor with a door on both sides and a stairway at the end. She began to climb the stairs to her 2nd floor apartment. A tear dribbled down her face and she allowed herself an audible sob as she pulled a small, antique brass key from her pocket and opened her front door for the last time.

Pushing a stray strand of hair from her hazel eyes, she beheld in the bathroom mirror a dirty, soot-smudged face with wavy, dark-blonde hair falling to her shoulders. She must have touched something while she was outside. Probably the crosswalk pole. Anymore everything was covered in soot and it hadn't rained all summer. Dish-water blonde her friends called the color of her hair in grammar school, but later in college boys she dated called it honey-colored. Now it might as well be gray as tired and old as she felt. Following a hot shower, the mirror would be too steamed up to bother her, thank goodness.

The hot water handle dropped off in her hand when she turned it, but she managed a quick tepid shower and then plopped down onto her bed. She couldn't get comfortable. Like a bit of food stuck in a tooth, the idea of getting out of her contract had lodged itself in her mind from the moment that she had agreed to it. On top of that, her hand, swollen to twice its size, throbbed relentlessly.

She tapped in "emergency clinic" on her phone and was directed to an online service. There she filled-out a form, submitted it and was put in a queue. She waited 20 minutes before a nurse appeared on the tiny comp screen and demanded to know which hand had been severed. Polly held up a swollen fist.

"That doesn't look severed to me," pointed out the nurse. "Is it the other one?"

"No," said Polly. "I am having a terrible reaction to a corporate chip that was inserted about an hour ago. I need it removed."

"I am not authorized to remove corporate chips. You will have to contact your company for that," the nurse explained without emotion.

"My branch doesn't have a doctor on staff," Polly countered. "I am a receptionist for Binge, Inc. Westside and they are still in the process of creating a clinic and child-rearing facility for my building complex."

"Oh, you don't need a company doctor. We will be glad to do it for you with company permission. Your chip is not functional while your hand is swarming with antibodies, so the company with have to give us the chip code that is tied to your payroll account."

"I just want the chip out. I don't want a chip." Polly reiterated.

"That is illegal," the nurse replied with unmistakable smugness.

"So I need permission from Binge to get the chip removed?" Polly said, shocked. "Do I need a doctor's permission slip and my deceased parent's signatures, also?" she asked sardonically.

"Oh the chip won't be removed. We will treat you with immune suppressing drugs. Some people have to be on them for their whole lives." The nurse said this with malevolent satisfaction.

"That's bullshit," Polly mumbled, a chilly wave of terror passing over her.

"Shall I contact your employer for you?" The nurse asked, enjoying the reaction she was getting from her patient.

"I think I'll try an icepack first," Polly answered and ended the connection.

Ice was a good idea, but where to get it. She was lucky to have a small shower and toilet in her room. It was the only luxury she had been able to afford. She did not have a refrigeration unit.

"There used to be a convenience store behind this apartment and on the other side of the alley. Might as well see if it's still there," she decided and grabbed her purse and key card on her way out.

A large garbage bin next to a loading dock faced the alley at the back of Polly's apartment building and on the other side was a narrow strip of small scraggly trees and weeds. The bit of vegetation did little to block the view of the convenience store. The smell back here was vintage decay and filth. Layers of grease coated everything even though the only greasy, hot food at the convenience store consisted of rotating, light-bulb broiled soy-sausages. There was a black-top parking lot surrounding the building, making it seem like an oasis rising out of a carbon desert. She passed the garbage bin that serviced the store and entered the front door.

"Need some help?" asked the teen-aged clerk when she stood in the middle of the store looking lost.

"I need some ice, but I don't have any way to pay 'cause my chip got infected," Polly's voice trembled. Verging on tears again, she held up her swollen fist.

"Holy crap!" the youth exclaimed. "What happened?" Empathy aroused him from his usual bored stupor. Palming a worn pass card, he used it to release the turn-style door next to the glassed-in counter that he stood behind for safety, and more importantly, for the safety of the money box. His boss had explained to him that if the money was safe, then so was he.

"How long has it been like that?" he asked. When she told him that it had only been a bit over an hour, he looked concerned. "That's some immune reaction. Are you sure that ferry guy used a clean needle?"

"I assumed he would. It is corporate, right? If anyone would have clean needles it would be corporate."

"Yeah, except if the guy is skimming on the side. Sometimes they get paid to infect a new chip with ad bias. If the chip had been handled prior to injection it could pick up all sorts of viruses, organic and digital, neither one too good for humans, if you know what I mean. If your immune system is depressed, you could die, and do you think the corporation would miss a beat replacing you?"

Polly did start crying and once she started it was impossible to stop. She decided to cry until she was a desiccated husk that could just blow away, because she was out of all other options. The clerk, completely out of his depth when it came to tears, stood awkwardly staring at her. Finally he said. "Maybe my grandmother can help. Okay? She knows all about real medicine, natural medicine. We can go when my relief gets here. He's late already. Meantime, take some ice from the ice machine. Just put it back when we leave and I won't have to charge you."

Chapter 3: Margarita

Margarita Perez walked slowly and carefully, less because she was worried about falling than because she didn't know where she was going. When she walked away from the bus stop where the nervous girl had tried to get duct tape to fix the bad wires, she had put effort toward being calm and collected. It was how she coped. The crazier things got, the calmer she became. Inside she felt more defeat than calm, but she refused to follow such emotion to its inevitable conclusion.

She had a 17-year-old grandson to think about and the kind of work you get without a chip does not make you rich. Each paycheck barely covered rent and food. She could not afford to miss work anymore than the others at the bus stop. Mostly, she worked for older couples who needed some landscaping or cleaning. They still used the old technology that enabled payment on an independent card.

Her daughter had been chewed up and swallowed by a maquiladora along the border. The company doctor told her it was an accident caused by a loose bolt on a packaging machine and there was nothing that could be done. Her daughter was responsible for checking the safety of the equipment she operated, the company spokesperson explained. Therefore, they were not liable for injury or death.

That night she carried her daughter's five-year-old son on her back across the shallow water of the Rio Grande River before the corporation could claim him too. The company had presented her with a bill for the handling of the corpse and clean-up of the job site. The manager who handed it to her explained that they could arrange to take the child in exchange for the debt if she was unable to pay it. That wasn't going to happen she assured him. He said that he would come back the next day for payment or the child. This was all completely illegal, but without money or an education, it was beyond Margarita to know that or do anything about it.

Margarita had been born on her parent's farm in a valley surrounded by mountains covered in mist. There were no papers or microchips for a baby born in a one-room adobe hut. When she crossed the border she broke no laws because she did not belong to either country or to any corporation. Her parents told her that she belonged to the land, to the Earth, just like the trees and the sky and that it would take her back in the end.

Now the sky was a foul, yellow-pink color from smog and the only tree in sight was long dead. The traffic next to her was moving again. In the distance she heard a bird cry. It called again and again and then gave up. If its mate answered back it was drowned out by the constant traffic noise.

Margarita's husband went missing when her daughter was thirteen. He had traveled north to find migrant crop work to make enough money to send his daughter to school in the Capitol. Margarita had begged him not to go. "Our daughter is fine where we are," she told him, pointing out that they had three goats, five acres each of corn and potatoes and a good well.

He was not of the land, though. He was from the city. The farm life grew tiresome and boring to him. He did not appreciate the little changes that occurred constantly in nature. A few years in the north and he would come back a hero with money to spare he insisted, ready to retire to a quiet life. If his beautiful daughter did not want to leave the farm then, that would be her choice.

He had not come back.

Part of why Margarita had come north with her small grandson was because she hoped that somehow she would find her husband. That never happened, but watching her grandson grow up was enough in the end. She was not unhappy.

Margarita paid attention and prepared, but today her feet pushed through air thick as molasses as she made her way back to the underpass near her house. This day was not auspicious. First, she had overslept. That meant missing the pre-dawn open transits, the best time to cross the main thoroughfare dividing the city. That had never happened to her before. She was getting old.

She lived close to the south end all-day pedestrian underpass, but today it was closed when she got there.

There had been another murder over-night and it would be blocked off for several hours. Lately, a policeman always blocked the underpass for some reason or other. It was becoming an unreliable entry point to the other side of the city where one could find work, but her grandson was young and able. Somehow he always got through. He would be passing through it on his way home from work.

After missing the early crossing time that morning, she had headed off to a bus stop/crossing light. When the first one was closed for repairs, she shrugged her shoulders and trudged on. It was only five blocks before there would be another. That went on until she had walked several miles without thinking and then she came upon the group at the crossing by that big-box store. By then, half the morning was spent. The open streets would be unbearable after noon.

Cloaked in thought, she hiked back toward the underpass. She had no place else to go. Perhaps she would cross paths with her grandson on his way home from work. She noticed that the police were gone and people were crossing again. "Good," she thought, "Germán will be able to get home without climbing the wall." She decided to sit for a while and wait to walk the rest of the way with him.

Leaning back against the huge, concrete wall that separated the main part of the city from the south end, she popped another apricot into her mouth and chewed. She savored its fragrant, sweet-and-sour flavor. The bitter skin was balanced by soft, sweet flesh, an allegory for the bitterness of her life that had been soften and sweetened by the love she felt for her grandson.

Half an hour passed. It was nearly mid-day and where the sidewalks were bathed in sunlight they were burning hot to the touch. Smog held in the heat and was no good at filtering UV rays. Margarita's implacable demeanor disguised the intense discomfort she felt even in the shade of the great highway; tired bones upon which she rested were hardly cushioned by a thin, folded cloth she pulled from her canvas bag to sit upon. Her chin slumped down upon her collar bone as she dozed off, melted by the heat.

She awoke with a start at the sound of her name and saw Germán coming down the large, open footpath under the road toward her. He was excitedly dragging a woman along by one arm. She held her other arm against her body like an injured animal.

Margarita stood up and called to him as he rushed toward her looking relieved, still tugging the woman along with him. Suddenly Margarita recognized her as the lady at the bus stop. What happened to her hand?

"Abuela," Germán hugged his grandmother and kissed her cheek. "Abuela, this lady needs your help. I hope you don't mind. I told her you could help her."

Margarita touched Polly's hand lightly along the knuckles and Polly winced. "I remember you from the bus stop," Margarita said. "You were not hurt then. How did this happen?"

When she heard the story, she looked concerned. "You need antibiotics. I have garlic, but you need stronger. I can remove that thing in your hand, but without antibiotics you might get a bad infection. You could lose your hand. You need what we call 'free range' doctor; one who does not belong to a corporation or a drug company."

"I just want it out. We'll worry about the infection later," cried Polly. "It hurts. I had ice on it before and it dulled the pain, but I can't bear it now. My hand is exploding."

Margarita and Germán exchanged a serious look. Margarita rummaged through her satchel until she found a small, silk bag. She opened it and took out two, chalky-white pills. "Like Vicodin, take it, here is some water." She handed her the pills and her water bottle.

Polly looked at Germán who nodded. "I told you my grandmother knew about medicine." Polly downed the pills and drank deeply of the water.

"Come home with us for now. I will soak the hand in a solvent to draw out the chip," the small women with the high cheek bones and long braid down her back sighed.

"Will that work?" queried the injured woman.

"That depends how deep. First injection so no scar tissue yet. Soak," Margarita curtly proclaimed with authority. She led the way home, paralleling the freeway for several blocks.

The small, shotgun-style house was almost right next to the giant super highway under which they had met. She sat Polly down at the kitchen table in front of a large bowl of warm water. She handed her a glass of plain water to drink, told her to put her hand in the bowl and left the room.

"Germán," Margarita called softly to her grandson. He came out of his bedroom where he had been splayed out on his bed and followed her into the living room. "Where are we going to find a doctor for this woman? If that chip is traced here we could go to jail. She says we have 24 hours before the company locks the ID. There is no getting it out after that without taking the hand whole or using a corporate doctor. I heard from curandero that barbs attach deep into flesh and only the company can remove. Do not doubt the power of the company," she warned.

"You aren't mad at me for helping her, are you, Abuela?"

"I just worry about you, mijo. We will do what we can." His grandmother patted his hand reassuringly like she always had. It made them both feel better. "This chip business goes deeper than you know, but we will help. We will do it for your mother."

"Are these people with the chips the same as my mother's maquiladora?" Germán asked.

"It is the same, Germán. It is always the same," his grandmother replied with a wise nod of her head. "But now they are nibbling on their own as they think they have already eaten up all of us."

Germán did not take his grandmother too seriously. To her, "us" were the farmers of the land, the country people. Those people did not exist anymore as far as he could tell. How could they know if Binge Inc. was not connected to the maquiladoras along the border? Corporations had many tentacles with which to suck the life from all that they touched. One tentacle did not always know what the other was doing. What if it was Binge that had killed his mother? Had he been thinking of his mother when he offered his help? Should they risk their lives for a stranger? It was a moot question because his grandmother had already decided, but he hadn't thought about the danger to his grandmother and to himself when he had offered to help the woman.

"Germán," his grandmother said suddenly, "I have an idea of what to do for this woman. You will help me."

Chapter 4: Paul and Tom

Paul left the crosswalk in a huff that propelled him through the deserted big-box store parking lot and onto a less congested side street where a small residential area had squeezed itself in between the intersection of two major throughways. Throughway was a misrepresentation of the actual function of the roads, since none of the vehicles were moving. There were no sidewalks, so he had to walk through narrow front lawns full of weeds and broken glass. Parked cars clogged both sides of the street leaving room for only one car at a time to barely squeeze past.

He made his way to a large complex that took up an entire block. It was built to the edge of the street from stark rectangles of variously colored metal interrupted in regular intervals by windows all the same size and shape. The dark jaws of an entryway penetrated one wall and led into the building complex parking lot. It was slightly wider than it needed to be for an automobile by the width of maybe three feet that was delineated by a painted line. Paul walked into the courtyard along this pedestrian path. Inside, two stories of apartments framed the parking area on all sides.

"My view," Paul remarked desolately to himself. He wondered if his performance at the street light had impressed his boss. If the woman had returned with the duct tape he could have fixed the machine, too. Sending her off for it did have the bonus of getting rid of her for a while. The other woman was quiet and kept to herself, but she was observant. He was glad that she had already left when he handed off the information card. He had looked forward to the drama of his first incognito contact, but the job of spy was not as exciting as he had imagined. It was boringly simple to slip the tiny drive to Tom when he shook his hand.

He thumbed the small screen to the left of the door handle and when the green light appeared, entered his one-room apartment. It was called an efficiency apartment because, he assumed, it was efficient to build. The refrigerator was too small to hold anything more than a few beverage bottles and some left overs. There was a built-in microwave oven with a two burner stove above it. A sink next to that was filled with dirty glasses, plates and a bowl. Counter space barely accommodated a chopping board. The one sitting there now was used for cutting tomatoes when he made sandwiches and for citrus fruit. He had a blender that he kept on the kitchen table since there wasn't any space for it elsewhere. In Central Texas a blender was a must for making the de rigueur Margarita.

Besides a rickety chair pushed under the table, the apartment contained a desk with swivel chair and a day bed pushed up against the wall underneath the front window that looked out over the parking lot. On the opposite side of the room, the kitchen table was pushed up next to the street side window. He dropped his tattered black fedora and wraparound sunglasses onto the table before flopping down on the day bed. Automatically, he pushed an unkempt handful of straw-colored hair behind one ear to clear his vision. Flicking on his comp, he thumbed to incoming messages. Sure enough, Tom had already sent him one.

It read: *Unnecessary to complicate situation. What were you thinking when you sent woman for duct tape? This made event more memorable, our faces more memorable. You have failed this assignment. Will read purloined info on drive before deciding whether to retain you in program. Check for message in one hour.*

Paul angrily uttered, "I sold my soul for this?" He lunged off the sofa and began pacing. He wanted to take the info back. He basically sold out a friend to get it. Tom would be sorry if he messed with him. In fact, he would make the "program" sorry if they tried to delete him. Fear and regret fueled a violent desire for revenge that felt out of character with the person he imaged himself to be. The person he had always been. Even so, he began to make plans just in case things went sideways.

§

Again, Tom called for Mitchell to pick him up. Walking along this disgusting stretch of highway was no fun and Mitchell was way overdue. Mitchell worked as a flit driver and copy boy for Binge and just happened to use the cubicle next to Tom's. Somewhere down the line he got suspicious of Tom's activities so Tom had recruited him.

Tom's purported employer, Professional Focus Inc. or ProFo, was housed inside Binge's west-side campus.

On the surface, Tom's job was to tabulate consumer preferences for various products, but in reality he was an industrial spy. Right now he was working for Binge and other manufacturers simultaneously. Not as difficult as it might sound as long as client interests didn't collide.

ProFo was the perfect cover. It bought information from banks and networking companies to repackage for marketing sales. In the beginning it was used for targeted advertising, but eventually political entities had seen the potential for keeping tabs on their populations and thereby influencing and controlling elections. The government always looked the other way in matters of infringement of personal rights. Once corporations were declared people it was all the easier.

When vehicles were given the same rights as people, city life became even more untenable. At the age of 55, Tom could remember better times. If there was any guilt at his part in the undermining of personal liberties, he quickly silenced it by reminding himself that he had a pension to think about.

As the flit approached, he pocketed his comp. Mitchell levered open the side door with a switch and Tom climbed in. "Where have you been?" Then tersely he added, "Never mind for now. Go to the office."

Mitchell had been an uncomfortable addition to his pool of assets. The guy was both smart and slovenly. He was easily overlooked and took advantage of that; benefits for a spy, except Tom didn't trust him like he trusted Paul. Paul was a whiz at electrical engineering, but it was Mitchell who hacked the main server at Binge and found the leak Tom was using to syphon patents. The guy was clever and he liked to drive. For now, he seemed pleased to be added to the payroll, but what he might want in the future was anybody's guess.

The flit rose up over ground traffic and headed off toward the industrial park that housed Binge Inc., ProFo Inc. and Central Government Police Substation 3. The latter was housed rent-free, with the building co-owned by the two corporations that occupied the main building. It was an ingenious plan that provided security services funded by taxpayers. Additionally, the corporations could write off the free rent and look like model citizens at the same time.

Leaving Mitchell to deal with the flit, Tom jumped out at the front doors and took an elevator to the 3rd floor. He maneuvered the cubicle maze to his desk, opened his computer and plugged in the drive. There was only one file. He clicked on it. Columns of 1's and 0's followed by various combinations of letters filled the screen. Tom grimaced. Was this code for a bioweapon? Binge had its greedy fingers into anything that could make money but could he in good conscience be a part of this? Could he pass on technology that destroyed human life? Apparently Paul had succeeded in his first job he thought grimly. "I guess we will keep you a little longer." He copied the file and then picked up his comp to contact his protégée with the good news.

Chapter 5: Polly Gets Help

Polly sat silently with her hand submerged in the bowl of warm water that the woman had stirred white crystalline granules into with a large, wooden spoon. She sniffed it, but couldn't detect a defining odor. She might fall asleep, she thought, except for the throb that radiated out from her palm, which was impossible to close without pain. Still, tension was draining away, soothed by the warm water. The muffled sound of traffic was almost peaceful since it no longer impeded her progress to…..To what? To a meaningless job maintaining a meaningless existence? To consuming and then being consumed?

Once, a blind date told her that our whole purpose is to burn energy or something like that, so that everything can become the same. It had to do with entropy. His point being, he said, was people should have fun while they can. Polly contemplatively reasoned that conversely **not** being the same as everything else equaled living. Living was mostly fun back then. She didn't want to die, but living as she did was not a compelling argument for the alternative. Entropy seemed to be turning the world into one big pile of shit.

"It's all slippery," Polly decided, her thinking enhanced by pain relievers. "Philosophy, Science, Religion, none of them provide enough grit to get any footing."

With the codeine settling a soothing interface between the pain and her direct experience of it, Polly felt more like observing her surroundings. The kitchen was average size, but felt small because of the space taken up by the furnishings. A Formica table with metal legs and border held the bowl where she was seated. Four heavy, wooden chairs surrounded it but there was room for six. A wide opening off to the right led to a dining room. It was filled with another table covered in tools, papers, and an ancient computer complete with a cathode tube monitor and tower containing the drives. A large range and cupboard filled the wall behind her. She half turned to see that the white, porcelain range was tinged with ancient, brown grease that would require a professional detailer to remove. The fancy chrome handles and large griddle in between four gas burners placed it as decades old and an heirloom if it was refurbished. A cupboard next to the range was painted festive aquamarine and yellow. To her left was a large farmhouse sink that any interior designer would covet. Above it was the only window in the cramped room, obscured by delicate lace curtains that had yellowed with age. With the window full open, they hung limp and lifeless in the humid late morning air. Next to the sink was a rusted, white refrigerator that made a constant humming noise, as if to assure that it was still alive. A wood cabinet panel covered one side of the refrigerator and a row of sharp kitchen knives clung to a magnetic knife holder mounted to it. All the appliances had seen better days about 30 years ago. The room's ceiling soared above the modest furniture, allowing heat to rise away from the occupied areas. It was a popular style in Southern houses of the period. Ceilings and walls were smoke and grease stained an uneven light-brownish-yellow. She wondered if the original color was yellow or white.

Directly across from where she sat, a rusty screen door framed a view of a long, narrow, neatly trimmed back yard. The screen door hung crookedly across the opening, supporting the bulk of its weight on the threshold. Wedged between the door and the wall was a polished hardwood buffet that was too big for the space and spoke of better times in the past.

"Ma'am," Germán said as he entered the kitchen from the dining room. He sidled past the hardback wood chair on which she sat and rounded the table to stand in between her and the back door.

"Oh, call me Polly, please," Polly replied. "Did I introduce myself? I mean my name."

Margarita entered the room. "Grandma, this is Polly." Germán formally introduced the two from his vantage point by the screen door. A hot breeze blew across his neck, but couldn't move the damp, dark hair that would soon touch his collar if a haircut was not imminent. "Polly this is Margarita Perez de San Miguel." He bowed slightly. "I am Germán Santos Perez at your service." He aimed a loving smile at his abuela before disappearing out the door.

"You have a very kind grandson," Polly said after the tattered screen door creaked to a partial close.

Perhaps too kind, thought Margarita, then chastised herself, that was the Devil speaking. "He is my world," she answered simply. A dreadful silence dragged on for several seconds before she continued. "I have been both mother and grandmother to him since my daughter died."

"I am so sorry," Polly said. "It must have been hard." Another silence ensued that was less tense. The two women tried to adjust to each other under the stressful circumstances, like two rusted gears meshing, their conversational skills suffering from disuse and neglect.

Margarita sighed, feeling older than her 56 years. "Let me see your hand."

The raw, red opening made by the insertion was visible now that the hand had been soaking. Margarita examined it, turning the hand one way then the other. Polly bravely stifled a sob.

"It should come out now," declared Margarita. "If we wait any longer it will have bonded to your flesh."

"How will you remove it?" Polly asked nervously.

"Please hold this," Margarita replied, ignoring the question. She handed Polly a large magnifying glass equipped with an attached light. From her canvas bag, she removed a sewing kit and opened it. She pulled out a small, sharp knife, scissors, needle and tweezers. She looked at the assembled tools with a thoughtful expression. "I have an idea," she said. "My neighbor still gets catheters in the mail for her son who was injured in a drone accident. She had to sign a contract for a three year supply so she has plenty. Sometimes she sells them on the black market to help pay for them. I tell her you will pay her generously once you can get back to your house for the money. I have a vacuum cleaner," she smiled proudly. "One of my clients gave me her old one. Now if only we had some duct tape."

"Not duct tape again!" cried the distraught younger woman.

"A most important invention," Margarita replied, "but the world will go on without it and so will we." Margarita continued, "These catheters are self-lubricated and covered with antibiotic. The very best. My neighbor will need much money to repay her. Germán has gone to fetch one."

When Germán returned a short time later with a long, tapered tube in a sealed plastic bag, Polly's eyes widened in terror. "You can't put that thing into my hand!"

"Yes, it may not fit and we will have to cut the hand open to get it out," Margarita agreed. While Germán was gone, she had dragged a large, cylindrical vacuum and hose into the tight space of the kitchen. "But look what I found." She held up an old Christmas card. "I wish it was duct tape but if I cut a hole for the catheter and hold it with my spread out fingers it might do the trick."

Color drained from Polly's face and she thought she might faint, but such a blessing was not to be had. Before she could say another word, Margarita plunged the catheter into her tender hand and Polly screamed. The sound was swallowed up by the traffic noise and Margarita appeared only slightly annoyed. The pain did not subside, but Polly did not scream anymore. What would be the point? Was there a point to anything anymore? She thought about asking for more pills but then decided that she might throw up if she took them and make things even less sanitary and more uncomfortable. The pain was unbearable. She was writhing uncontrollably in the hard chair, trying not to move her hand in the process. "Oh, hurry," she whispered. "Please, hurry."

Margarita did not hurry. She had stopped hurrying long ago when she realized there was nothing to hurry to. This was it. She wheeled the ancient vacuum machine closer and unplugging the toaster, she used the freed up outlet to plug it into the wall.

"Does that thing work?" Polly moaned.

"If it doesn't then the catheter was a waste of time," Margarita answered. She smiled, humming to herself as she poked a hole in the card with her knife and fitted it onto the end of the tube jutting from Polly's hand.

Polly thought she might faint from the pain. "Let this be over, please God. Let this be over." She chanted to herself.

Margarita fitted the vacuum hose up against the card and spread her fingers around it to hold it in place. It was not a perfectly tight fit but it would have to do. Germán put his hand on Polly's shoulder and squeezed tightly when she squirmed.

"Better to hold still," he warned.

Polly did not see the wisdom in his words, but controlled her impulse to jerk the catheter out and flee. Her legs were limp beneath her and her instincts told her that she would cause herself even more pain if she moved.

Margarita used her free hand to flip the switch. A great roaring came from the machine and suction pulled at the blood and flesh of Polly's hand. Luckily, it was an old vacuum and the suction was not too great. The card slipped as Margarita held it with her hand causing the catheter to jiggle around.

Polly moaned softly. "Oh, oh, oh, oh," she held on to the sound of her voice to keep from thinking about what was happening. "Oh, oh, oh, oh," she cried more intensely. Tears ran down her hot, puffy cheeks.

Slowly, Margarita began to drag the catheter back out. Polly could feel something move in her hand. She hoped that it was the chip and not some vital organ. Then suddenly, the card gave way to the suction and the machine inhaled with a congested gulp.

Margarita flipped the switch off. "This is more difficult than I imagined," she remarked.

Polly wanted to say something sarcastic, but was unable to under the circumstances. Tears streamed down her face and she rocked back and forth in her chair, her hand plastered to the table with pain, the catheter still projecting from it and dripping blood.

"I could try just with my fingers plugging the nozzle," Margarita suggested.

Polly's face was the color of a white sheet. She swayed woozily in the hardback chair and before she fainted dead away, Margarita pulled the catheter free using a finger to cover the opening at the end of the tube. She doubted it would keep anything captured on the inserted end of the catheter from dislodging, but it was the best option she had. There was nothing at the end of the tube. Blood streamed from the wound. It was going to require surgery now.

"Press on that to stop the bleeding," Margarita instructed. "I will get some gauze."

"Did you get it?" asked Polly weakly.

"Does it feel like it?" Margarita countered.

Polly thought about how it feels when a splinter is removed. There is pressure while it is in there and the sudden relief from the pressure causes a release from the pain, but not the soreness. She wasn't sure. All she felt was unbearable, throbbing pain. This was a bad idea, she thought.

While Margarita was in the other room hunting down gauze, Germán sat down in the chair across from Polly, reaching out to hold the clenched fist of the uninjured hand and asked, "Are you okay?" Polly's pale complexion couldn't get any whiter and her breathing was ragged, but she loosened her fist and let him touch her fingertips.

Before she could answer in the negative, Margarita returned carrying the medical supplies. She gave Germán a wary look, but said nothing. Germán observed the injured woman helplessly.

Polly thought, "What have I done? And what have I done to deserve it." Mustering her courage she spoke out loud, "so we don't know if we got it?" An involuntary shudder passed over her at the thought of that thing, that toxic device lodged permanently in her flesh, but she pulled herself together for the sake of the sympathetic youth and gave him a weak smile.

Meanwhile, Germán's abuela completed the bandaging of Polly's hand and began wiping down the table. "Abuela let me do that," Germán exclaimed belatedly.

"You need to look for that chip," Margarita said somewhat harshly, "and you Polly, must decide if you feel it still."

"That chip? Where do you mean?" Germán asked before in dawned on him and he looked warily at the vacuum. "You mean in there?"

Polly felt her popularity waning. Should she offer to look with her one good hand? She glanced at the wounded hand. Blood seeped through the gauze. It hurt so much. How was she supposed to tell if it was better?

Margarita went to the sink to rinse out her dish cloth full of blood. She had been thinking that maybe the vacuum cleaner idea was not her best.

Germán disconnected the hose from the cylinder that held the bag inside the vacuum and took it into the dining room. He somehow managed to clear a space on the table which he covered with a folded oilcloth. He popped open the vacuum and took out the bag which he emptied onto the protected surface. His abuela had not bothered to put in a clean bag before beginning the operation. Dust billowed up into a cloud before him making him squint his eyes shut and sneeze. When he opened them, he saw an unpalatable pile of dust, hair and lint.

"It is good that the bag was not yet full," Margarita proclaimed from the other room.

"How does this chip look?" Germán asked. He poked gingerly through the dirty mess.

"Like a chip. I don't know," his grandmother answered back.

"It looks like a very small insect." Polly offered. "Like a soldier ant. My parents took me to a park when I was a little girl and the ants wanted our picnic. Most of them were very small but some of them were bigger and they had hard shells and strong jaws to bite with. It is maybe a half inch long, I guess."

"Then I think I got the little devil," Margarita announced proudly. "It got stuck in the catheter, but I couldn't see it because of the blood. It is more cylindrical than a bug is. Look Germán. Bring the magnifying glass."

Germán was all too willing to abandon the dirt pile to do his abuela's bidding. He brought her the magnifying glass with the cord trailing from the handle. Margarita plugged it into the outlet by the sink and a bright light illuminated the small, black object she had placed on a white dish cloth. "It is good I was careful to inspect this while I was cleaning it and didn't throw it away. It does not look much like an ant," she corrected Polly.

Polly and Germán both squeezed in to see what she had found. In the light of the magnifying glass the tiny details made it easy to identify as a chip. "It is not that much bigger than a soldier ant," Germán said. His grandmother flashed him a look of mild irritation.

"I will put some aloe vera on that," Margarita said nodding toward Polly's hand. "There is a plant in the other room. Take the gauze off and wash your hand in the sink with soap and water. Germán, come help me." Germán looked surprised that she would need his help to fetch a plant leaf but he followed her out with a shrug.

Once in the other room, Margarita lowered her voice and nodded to her grandson to come closer. "We need to talk," she whispered. He could tell that her earlier mood had changed. She loved a problem to solve, his abuela, but once solved she moved on quickly.

"This gringa is trouble, mijo, I do not want you to get any more involved with this."

"Mi abuelita, she is no threat. Why do you not like her?"

"It is not that. It is the danger. Perhaps you were too young to remember what happened to your mother."

"I was five-years-old. I remember," Germán replied indignantly. "Is it the chip?"

"Yes it is. If it activates in 24 hours like she says, we should be well rid of her before then. It is dangerous to go against the wishes of a corporation."

"I have a friend who knows about these things, Abuela, perhaps she will help us."

"I do not like what this woman brings. You are young and do not know the strength and stretch of the corporations. I do not care that they are given the power of a citizen of this country; they do not have the conscience of a person. They do not know of the loss of one that is loved. They have no love and the only loss that they feel is of money and power."

"But she is a person not a corporation, Abuela," her grandson pointed out gently. "You have said that we must help each other."

"She is a gringa, Germán. Do not confuse her with your lost mama. She has not known the things that we have known. She has not suffered as we have."

"She is suffering now," Germán replied.

His grandmother favored him with an indulgent grimace before putting her arm around the boy who looked down at her so concerned. She hugged him tightly. His eyebrows knitted together. He was already six feet tall and handsome. He had his father's dark, silky hair and deep-brown eyes. Who could say no to such a face?

"We will help her for now," she decided. "But we must take every precaution. We must try to think like a soulless beast, like this Binge Corporation."

"How can we do that, Abuela, we are not soulless?"

"We must use our imaginations."

"Do you think this Binge could track us here? Is that what that chip does?"

"I do not know, mijo. We must assume that it can and even more."

"This is complicated."

"Do you still want to help her?" asked his grandmother hopefully.

Germán graced his grandmother with an angelic smile. A smile that shone through any veil of misgivings his grandmother felt, the smile that his mother had given him. "Of course, I do! And I have four days off to do it in."

Chapter 6: Pam Needs Paul

Paul's comp beeped for his attention instead of playing annoying, personal music that invaded everyone's air space. Not everyone liked country-western or classic rock or even Beethoven. He prided himself on being sophisticated enough to know this. A beep was neutral territory. So many people weren't as thoughtful as he was.

It was his former girlfriend, Pam. He almost ignored it, but what else did he have to do?

"Pam," he answered, forcing a casual tone that sounded like the exact opposite. "What can I do you for?" Bad choice of phrasing he realized too late.

She chose to ignore the innuendo. "Hi Paul, how have you been?"

"Fine. And yourself?"

"I need to ask a favor," she said cutting short the small talk.

He doubted the favor was that he would give her another chance. She was the one who broke off the relationship after the third date. They occasionally ran into each other at University and were still civil to each other, but that was as far as it went.

"May I ask what the favor is before I agree to it?" he replied.

"Well," she hesitated before continuing, making him wait as usual, "I've been volunteering at an afterschool outreach program for community service credits and also to study large-scale versus small-scale adaptations in education and skills programs for teen populations. It's research for my dissertation." She paused. He imagined her chewing her hair, a nervous habit he had found endearing. "One of my students with a particularly interesting family history agreed to be the focus of my paper." There was another pregnant pause. "He called me today asking for my help, but it's a problem beyond my skill level. I'm more of a soft science person and this is a hard science problem, something that you are really good at."

"Okay, so what is this 'hard science' problem?"

"Can we meet? I don't want to discuss it over the telephone."

One of the many things he found attractive about her was her use of archaic expressions like "telephone" even if they were affectations. Of course he would meet her. "I just finished a meeting and was waiting for a follow up, but if you don't mind a possible interruption we could get together now. I'm not sure what the rest of my day is going to look like, so the sooner the better."

A satisfied smile crossed her lips. "Great. What side of the highway are you on? I have a flit, so I can leave right now to pick you up and we can go to the Student Union and

I can give you the back story. I'll buy you a cup of something."

"I'm at my apartment. You know where that is," he answered, painfully aware that he did not have a flit. He certainly wasn't going to impress her with his financial prowess. At least not yet.

"Great," she said, "I'll be there in a jiff."

"I'll be ready." He clicked her off and saw that he had a text message from his boss. His boss would just have to wait.

He found a comb in his bathroom by the sink and ran it through his wavy, blonde hair wishing he had washed it the night before. His hat would cover most of it anyway, he reassured himself. His skin was pale and of course his rosacea had reared up the night before on one side of his cheek, but he had shaved this morning before meeting Tom at the crosswalk. That was a plus. He peeled off the black, cowboy-style shirt that had been clean this morning but was already damp with sweat and replaced it with a clean, vintage T-shirt advertising a long defunct Punk Rock band called the Skunks. Even though it was autumn, he doubted he would need his hoody, but he grabbed his signature fedora and sunglasses.

Pam didn't waste any time getting to his apartment. He was thumbing through his music files looking for something that said "this guy has class", when he heard a knock on his door. He waited a beat and then opened it.

"Hi Paul," Pam smiled. She was 5'5" but carried herself like she was six feet tall. Her long, blonde hair was loose across one shoulder. She wore clean blue jeans and a tight T-shirt with an iconic design on the front of a woman wearing a kerchief on her head and making a fist to show off her bicep. He recognized it as one of the first girl-power advertisements made during World War II.

"Hey Pam, how you been?" He asked mildly, showing her that he was doing *her* the favor in case she got the wrong idea.

"May I come in?" she asked.

"Oh, sure," he answered quickly and moved out of the doorway, "take a chair." There was a choice between the upholstered, rolling desk chair and the wobbly chair at the kitchen table. She breezed past him. Her scent was clean, fresh and sweet. No standing at defunct crosswalks for her. Daddy had money. Damn, he thought, it was unlikely he would ever have that kind of squeeze.

"So, how can I be of service?" he asked with studied nonchalance.

"Like I said in my message, I want to help a friend of one of my students and I need your expertise to do that. Are you ready to go? We can talk outside."

"Okay, could you be more specific?" Paul said once they were on the walkway heading for the flit. He was relieved to see that it was a commercial hire instead of her personal vehicle. Either she was trying to make it on her own or Daddy didn't have the stretch he assumed he had.

"It's a problem with a chip. A corporate chip. One of those things they use to track and pay their employees. I was hoping you could disable it."

"That is illegal you know." He paused to gauge her reaction, but she just stared at him. "That could get us permanently banned from employment," he added.

"I didn't know you were worried about that. When we were dating you told me that you weren't interested in becoming a corporate lackey."

"Not a lackey. No." He hesitated, "but I'm not sure that I want to go to jail and have all my options closed for good."

"It is a risk," Pam admitted, "a serious risk, but one that I am willing to take for a friend."

And checkmate, he thought. If he said no, then he was not her friend. If he said yes, he could be in hot water with his employer. But his employer was an industrial spy. Surely, that gave him some leverage.

"Show me this chipped person. I can look anyway and maybe advise you about how to handle it. I don't know that I could disable it. Who is it inside?"

"That is the beauty of it. It is not inside of anyone anymore. They got it out."

"Oh, shit," he cursed, "we better hurry then. Once it leaves the body it will start sending a homing signal. You can fill me in on the details later."

Pam instructed the flit driver to drop them at the universal underpass. Neither she nor Paul spoke once in the cab. So much for flirting over a cup of something at the Student Union, he thought. What they were doing could cost them their future hopes of leaving this cramped city or even completing University. University might not be an oasis of green and peace and knowledge anymore, but it was definitely a necessary evil. Nowadays the campus plants and trees were diseased and dying and the no car zones were crammed with scooters, bicycles, vender's carts and pedestrians blocking every artery. Still, completion of a University degree might keep you out of lower tier corporate jobs and start you at least at mid-bracket. High paying jobs in pleasant surroundings could still be had by the clever and well-educated. Why else spend the time and money. But even with an advanced degree, a single suspect word about what they were about to do could severely limit their job future. Corporations owned the world in which they lived, including the Universities, and one did not go against them without consequences.

When the flit lifted after depositing them by the south-side underpass Paul spoke up. "Is this where the chip is? Are we going under?"

"No," Pam replied smiling. She had such a lovely smile Paul thought. "But it isn't far. I thought this would be the best place to go since our destination could be on either side from here. We need to be careful."

"I think the cat is already out of the bag," Paul answered, "but lead on." He was warming up to this adventure. Maybe he still had a chance to impress her, especially if the spy gig worked out. In the movies no woman can resist a secret agent. She had called him for help after all, not some new boyfriend, and this cloak-and-dagger stuff was right up his current alley.

It wasn't far. It was a good thing, too. Even a short walk was laborious because the sweltering afternoon heat and smog were oppressive.

They approached an ancient Victorian-era house nestled almost under the main throughway. Peeling white paint clung to its clapboard siding. In a narrow front yard, fading red antique roses climbed up and entwined the front porch railings, hiding rotted wood and giving the façade a bit of a face lift. Concrete steps led up to a wide porch that was stained and cracked and lined on either side with potted plants. The place had a rundown look but still managed to feel cared for. A white picket fence, sorely in need of painting, separated the sidewalk from the tiny front yard. Pam and Paul opened the gate and walked up to the front door.

Pam knocked on the heavy, eight-panel wood door. Solid wood and probably original to the house she noted. A tarnished, mortised brass latch embellished with scrollwork worn down by time decorated both the knob and faceplate. The knob slowly turned and the door slit open. A section of eye, nose and chin appeared from the shadows within.

"Miss Turner!" a young male voice exclaimed. Beaming, Germán opened the door full wide, "come in."

The two visitors entered the house, a cool and dark retreat compared to the outside. "Please sit down," Germán indicated a rundown sofa covered with a woven blanket. Its pattern of bright red, blue, green and yellow chevrons stood out boldly against the worn, beige carpet and yellowish walls. A table was positioned under the one large window facing out to the porch. It was covered with succulents in clay pots, most notably aloe veras and kalanchoes. The latter showed off orange blossoms scattered amongst their shiny blue-green leaves. The only other furniture in the room was an old rocker made comfortable with cushions at the back and seat.

"I'll get my grandmother," Germán said and left the room.

Paul took off his sunglasses and hooked them over the crew neck of his T-shirt. He looked at Pam, but before they could speak a handsome, middle-age woman appeared from the hallway to the right of the sofa. She and Paul did a double-take.

"You are from the crosswalk!" Margarita exclaimed, "What is going on here?"

Paul jumped to his feet, "what are you up to Pam?" His eyebrows furrowed in consternation and surprise and his eyes blazed.

"What do you mean?" asked Pam, clearly taken aback by his reaction.

"What kind of set-up is this?"

"I told you what kind of set-up it is. I don't understand why you are upset all of a sudden."

Paul tried to relax but did not sit back down. "I met this woman this morning." His mind was racing, trying to figure the angle. Was Pam involved in counter-espionage? He knew her father was a former Binge executive and that Tom worked for Binge right now. Maybe this was a test. Maybe Pam was working for Binge. Was she using their former relationship and his ongoing attraction to her as a tool to penetrate his cover?

Meanwhile, Margarita was parsing the situation. "Please," she said, "let us all sit down and I am sure that everything will be made clear."

Germán had slipped back into the kitchen to warn Polly to stay put.

Paul hesitantly sat back down on the sofa edge as far from Pam as possible. Pam observed him with obvious disappointment. She had started to think she might have been precipitous in breaking it off with him.

"First, let us introduce ourselves. I am Margarita Perez and that was my grandson, Germán, who opened the door. You may call me Margarita. We did not ask to be involved in this, but my grandson has too kind of a heart and cannot let a stray go untended. This is how we are involved. I would like nothing better than to not be involved."

"Oh, mi abuela! Your heart is kind. You are my guide for kindness," Germán interjected from the hallway. He came back into the room. "Abuela, this is Pam, the lady who comes to our school and helps us with our studies. She is going to help me to go to college and get a job that will take care of us both. We will have a flit, so you won't have to worry about crossing the highway. You will fly over it."

"I am not unhappy where I am," Margarita replied stubbornly, and then added. "It is nice to meet you."

"And you," Pam answered. "And this is Paul, who has volunteered to help us with the chip."

Paul said, "how do you do? Pam said you removed a chip from someone? I need to quickly see the chip. I presume that you don't want a tracer targeting your residence."

Margarita scowled, trying to piece together the connections. First Polly shows up and now this man from the crosswalk. She wondered when the self-possessed, professorial man would walk through the door. "Though I did not choose it, we are here now and it is best to help each other. I vacuum it out her poor, swollen hand. She is in the kitchen and I put that thing upon the counter."

"She will need a doctor," Paul said, "and the chip should be put on ice."

"Before we see the chip, there is one more thing," Margarita looked at the young man's face as she spoke to gauge his reaction. "There is someone else here who you met this morning." She hesitated, then rose from her chair and motioned the others to follow her. "People who keep coming together as though by invisible force are guided by the saints. There is one more person here you already know, someone else from the crosswalk this morning. We are now in the hands of the angels."

A cold sweat broke out on Paul's forehead as a chill ran up his spine. Tom! Is Tom here? What did that mean? This was too coincidental. Pam looked at him with a worried expression. His behavior since they arrived had not been what she had expected.

Polly appeared in the hallway. "Hello," she said meekly, swaying against the wall for support. "I'm sorry to have caused so much trouble. I appreciate your help." Her face squelched up with her last few words as she struggled not to cry. "I'm so sorry."

Both Paul and Pam bolted up at once and motioned for her to sit on the couch. Paul forgot his paranoia as she collapsed onto the sofa and obviously fought to regain her composure. They hovered over her, plying her face with tandem looks of concern.

"I'm sorry," she said again, "I'm Polly. And you are Pam and Paul. I heard from the kitchen." A tear escaped the corner of one eye and she snuffled back the moisture that gathered in her nose. "I won't hold it against you if you decide not to help me. I wish I hadn't dragged Germán and Margarita into this, but it is too late now. I just don't know what to do."

At that she completely broke down crying. Germán rushed to the bedroom and returned with a clean handkerchief which he handed to her. Pam and Paul stood in front of her, nervously shifting from one foot to the other. Pam gave Paul a searching look. It was all up to him.

Margarita reseated herself, rocking gently back and forth in her cushioned chair, unfazed by Polly's emotional outbursts. Finally, she said to Paul, "do you want to see the chip?"

He answered in the affirmative and everyone rose and went into the kitchen, the change of venue a welcome distraction from Polly's half-stifled sobs. She followed them as far as the dining room and looked on as they gathered around the counter. Margarita and Germán stood back to let Paul and Pam examine the chip.

"It is there," Margarita said, pointing to a tiny, black object on a white paper towel that lay on the counter next to the sink.

"Hum," Paul muttered, peering closely. The others ranging around him leaned forward. "Excuse me," he shrugged his shoulders and they edged back to give him room. Pulling a pair of needle nose plyers from his jeans pocket with one hand, with the other he picked up the magnifying glass Margarita had laid on the counter. Holding it in his left hand, he carefully lifted the chip toward the lens. "It looks like a D-6 model with modification. This isn't like any biochip I've seen before. I'm not sure that I can disarm it," he said.

There was a collective, apprehensive intake of air. Margarita moved back to the kitchen table while Pam and Germán stood on either side of Paul watching his every move with interest. Polly joined Margarita at the table. Paul set the chip back down on the napkin and pulled a wallet from his other pocket. Inside there was a collection of fine tools neatly arranged and held tightly by elastic bands. He selected a long, thin tubular tool that extended when he pushed a tab forward. As he was doing this, the noise of a traffic drone grew louder and louder. It was getting so loud that he found it hard to concentrate and decided to let it pass by before he continued.

Margarita stood up from her seat at the table, edging past the little group to peer through the kitchen window.

"That is odd," she remarked. "That traffic drone is pointed toward our house. It does not move."

Paul quickly retracted his tool and slid it back into its elastic holder. He closed the wallet and put it and the plyers back into his pocket. Wrapping the chip up in the paper napkin he gestured for Margarita to get away from the window. "Pam," he uttered tensely, "look out the window without letting them see you. Can you tell if that is a corporate drone or a city drone and if corporate, which corporation it is?"

"It's Binge Corp," she said, peering through the lace of the curtain. "Is it because of the chip?"

"I don't know, but it won't be good for them to find us here with a renegade chip."

"You cannot leave that chip," Margarita exclaimed.

Polly was rendered senseless. She visible shook and rocked back and forth, holding onto the counter for support. "I'm so sorry," she cried, "I'm so s-s-sorry."

Germán exchanged a meaningful look with this grandmother. "We could go out through my bedroom window and into Miguel's house through his window and they could not see us from where they are right now."

"I do not want to spread this to Miguel's family," she replied, a hard look on her face. "If they are tracking this, they will see it move. They will follow us wherever we go. Can you prevent it tracking?" she asked Paul.

"I don't know. It would take more time than we have. Do you have an ice chest and some ice? I can force a state of hibernation. At least, I might be able to weaken the signal temporarily, make it harder for them to pick up.

"Yes, I'll get my lunch box," Germán offered.

"What then?" asked Pam.

"Then we follow Germán's plan," Paul answered, giving them all a sober look before replacing his sunglasses. "We all need to get out of here and the sooner the better."

Chapter 7: Teller

Tom was agitated. The owner of the maquiladora that hired him did not accept failure. Success paid well, but there would be no hesitation in using 'extreme prejudice' if things did not go as planned. Gaining one piece of the puzzle was not sufficient and now there was a missing player he had to worry about. If only Mitchell, the flit driver with the other chip, had made the rendezvous this morning, then he wouldn't be in this predicament. Now he couldn't reach Paul or Mitchell.

A message from his new employer instructed him to be at the Regent Hotel, suite 2101, by one o'clock. Every bit of an hour had been squandered in finding a flit to take him there and at double the legal contract price, a price he could scarcely afford. Brusquely pushing past the doorman without glancing at the disapproving glare he knew would be on his face, he entered the lobby.

Once inside he hesitated, rubbing a hand across the bristly fur that sprouted from his cheeks and chin and decided to visit the men's room before meeting with his boss. In his collegiate days, he had looked good with a neatly trimmed beard and mustache, but now that he spent so much time outside his beard was too hot and itchy. The tweed jacket was an affectation he kept to hide sweat stains that were a constant in this heat even though it was autumn for God's sake. He checked his comp and saw that he was late. It was already a quarter past but he scanned the lobby of the hotel for a men's room anyway.

It was hidden under the staircase. There was no attendant this time of day so he had the room to himself. After relieving himself at the urinal, he removed his jacket and laid it across one of the two sinks. He leaned forward across the other sink and stared at his reflection in the mirror. A rather handsome, middle-aged man stared back. Thanks to his Tigua Apache great-grandmother he still had a full head of hair. A strong jaw line held back the sagging jowls he saw more and more among his corporate bosses, besides he worked out and watched what he ate. It helped that he couldn't afford steak and wine for dinner every night. Crow's feet and fine wrinkles along his cheeks and at the corners of his mouth added a rugged, experienced patina.

Carefully washing his hands, he checked his nails in the running water to make sure they weren't hiding any dirt before using the forced air dryer. After drying his hands he turned the nozzle upward to dry the sweat in his arm pits. Satisfied with this make-do toilet, he slipped on his jacket and ran his fingers through his hair. The gray-flecked dark-brown waves were cut close enough to stop them just short of unruly. Exiting the restroom, he checked his appearance in the full length mirror on the wall. "Okay," he said aloud, straightening his back, "let's do this."

The elevator stopped on the 21st floor and Tom stepped out onto a thick, pale-blue, gold and maroon carpet woven into large geometric shapes. This hotel was only a year old so the hallway carpet was still soft and luxurious. He stood in a small foyer that was furnished with a carved wooden table on which sat an intricately filigreed lamp and two old fashioned telephones with numbered dials on heavy bases, the ear and mouth pieces cradled between silver u-shaped metal holders. How they worked in this day and age of everything digital was beyond him, but they looked like they could be used to club someone in a pinch. Several chairs upholstered in gold and blue paisley brocade completed the cozy arrangement.

There were only two numbered doors on this floor and they stood opposite each other. Opaque, handmade glass dotted with bubbly imperfections framed the sides of the doors. On the left, the glass was a dark rose color, streaked with silver, on the right it was navy blue and gold. Tom knocked on the mahogany door framed by the rose glass. A few moments later a tall brunette opened the door.

"You must be Tom," she said in a voice that was soaked in sunny California beach and surf.

"That I am," he answered, "I have an appointment with your boss that I am a bit late for. Had trouble getting a flit."

"Next time, if there is one, you might allow more time for transport," she reprimanded dispassionately. "We have other things to do."

Cheeky secretary, he thought, but lucky boss. "Yes, well, we'll see. Now that I am here, I'd like to get on with it. Where is your boss?" Without the black heels, she would be about my height, Tom assured himself. Her dark auburn hair was pulled back into a tight bun, but would no doubt be lovely loosely tossed against her shoulders. Perfect sun-kissed golden skin stretched across broad, high cheek bones. Full, lacquered red lips the color of ripe cherries glistened invitingly. She wore a simple, tight-fitting dark red dress that matched the color of her lipstick and hung just below her knees. As she turned to walk back into the room, he noticed that it was slit up the back for mobility. Her curvy, voluptuous looks contrasted with a harsh, business-like demeanor.

"Perhaps you would like to take a seat," she gestured toward a group of three overstuffed leather chairs arranged in front of a glass coffee table. On the opposite side was a sofa. He chose one of the armchairs. The large room was filled with light from floor to ceiling windows overlooking the city, a thick haze of car exhaust obliterating the view.

Tom sat down as she strode over to the windows, one index finger pressing into her chin. Looking out, she said, "Tell me if I have wasted my time waiting for you?"

"What do you mean?" Tom replied, slowly changing gears. "Where's Teller?"

"In front of you," she answered irritably.

"You can't be Teller," he blurted out. Teller was a tough, blood-thirsty criminal. Teller ordered people killed if they did not fulfill his wishes.

"You are surprised because I am a woman," she said, still staring out the window. "Why Tom, I thought an educated man like you would be less of a male chauvinist."

"I'm just surprised because I spoke to a man at the factory," he tried to recover.

"My husband was also Teller, but he is gone now. You have the information?" She turned to face him, her look hard and penetrating.

"I do, but...." Tom trailed off.

"There can be no but's, Tom. You were hired to do a job and I expect that job to be done. You **do** want to leave this hell-hole city don't you? In one piece, still breathing?"

"Getting tough with me will not help the situation," Tom said, quickly regaining his composure.

"What situation, Tom? Why is there a situation?"

"It's not really a situation. There was a snafu, a hold up, nothing that another day won't take care of. I have one of the chips, but not on me. The other one was misplaced but I know where it is."

"Another day? How many times have I heard that phrase from people who do not deliver?"

Tom sat still and watched her draw in a deep breath of air as if trying to control her temper. "Do you realize what I am trying to do here? Do you realize how important every single day is? I am trying to save this world, this filthy degraded world we have made. I am on the side of the angels, Tom. I am a savior!"

Tom continued to sit silently, never shifting his eyes from her face. "Do you know what is in the chip that you are to deliver?" she asked.

"I know that it is a DNA code. I assume that it is a biological weapon of some sort."

"Ha," she exhaled. "A biological weapon? Do you watch crime shows? How simplistic. How could a weapon add anything to the biological weapon wielded daily by the people on this planet? Look out the window Tom and tell me what you see."

"I can't see much of anything. The smog is too thick."

"Exactly," she said. "It is too thick to see through. It makes one sick to breathe it. My mother died when I was 12 from lung disease, from breathing this pollution. She lived a healthy life, never smoked and still this world killed her. I could not save her, but I can save myself. I will get what I want one way or the other."

Tom swallowed. His mouth had gone dry. She smiled at him and he squirmed involuntarily on the plush leather armchair. He said, "What is the code for then?"

"It is for a biological generator, Tom. A generator that will save this world, a power source that both stores and creates electricity without polluting the air." A dark cloud passed over her features and she glared, "now that you show up late for our appointment empty-handed, I think perhaps my associates and I would do better to find someone more adept."

Dismissing him with a curt hand gesture, she turned toward a door to the left of the windows. A surge of adrenaline sent a wave of foreboding washing over Tom's brain like a tsunami. It was a dangerous game that he played, Binge against the Teller maquiladoras, but he thought of himself as a flexible spy instead of a double agent. He stole secrets from each of his employers to sell to the other, yes, but the net outcome was a level playing field. If these two chips held the formula for truly clean energy production, then whoever ended up with it could change history.

"Wait," he stopped her, "if you fire me now you will not get either chip. Give me 24-hours to get the other half, the rest of the chemical code that you need to manufacture this generator of yours. I know it would take you longer than that to start over from scratch. I have one piece and I can get you the other one. You need both parts of the puzzle. In 24-hours you will have both pieces. You can save the world."

She hesitated, turning back around. She stared at him without expression. "24-hours, Tom, and this time don't be late. Show yourself out."

He pulled himself out of the chair, "you have a reputation for doing away with people. Can I trust you to pay me when I bring you the chips?"

She narrowed her eyes but said nothing.

He continued, "I'll make copies just in case. If you give me trouble I'll instruct my associates to sell them to the next highest bidder. You may be a savior and all that, but you are still a business woman I assume."

She slid a card from the bodice of her dress and threw it onto the gleaming surface of the coffee table. "This is your money," she said distastefully, "it will be here for you tomorrow. I want your copies, too. Don't double cross me or I promise that you will regret it."

He looked at the card longingly, but dared not grab it. Instead, he went to the door and let himself out into the elegantly appointed lobby and then pushed the down button for the elevator. As he stood waiting for the lift, his comp chimed. It was Mitchell. "It's about time," he said.

"I'm in trouble," Mitchell said, "I think Binge is going to sever my contract." They both knew what that meant. Chips, flit and all paraphernalia and items on his person or in the flit would be immediately confiscated. Binge suspected him of espionage but needed proof to incarcerate or incinerate as the case might be.

"Did they get the chip?" Tom asked.

"No, I suspected something was going down, so I injected it into that girl you left at the crosswalk. Your partner."

"What girl?" Tom asked, his agitation growing like a tumor in his belly. He experienced a sharp pang of indigestion. "And what crosswalk? Where were you? You were supposed to land in that big-box store parking lot and wait for me."

"I thought I was being followed," Mitchell replied, silently congratulating himself for his cleverness. "I saw you standing at the crosswalk but I held back watching for a while in the shadow of the building. I saw you give that woman the handoff and send her into the store. That's how I figured out she was with you. I didn't approach until I received the signal for the implant."

Handoff, Tom thought, what handoff? Oh, the credit card I gave her. Do spies think everything has an ulterior motive or a hidden meaning?

"I figured you didn't want to be seen with me so I kept my distance. You know since Binge is on my heels to fire me." Mitchell kept talking. "After you walked off, I intercepted her message to Binge HR. It bounced off my sponge receiver before it made it to the cell tower and I shut it down. Figured you knew I'd be hovering nearby and would appreciate the help. When she asked for a seven-year contract with suspension of rights, I figured that had to be my signal. Why would anyone do that, right? But I played along just in case there was a monitor somewhere. Read her a contract and then injected it. Has she brought it to you yet? I need my cut. I gotta leave town for a while."

Oh God, thought Tom, where the hell was the chip. He took a minute to collect himself and then said, "Do you know the name of the woman? We have to find her. She wasn't with me. She might be at Binge right now."

"Not with you? I don't understand. You sent her to that store. I saw you give her something. Why would she go to Binge? You think she's a rat?"

"I gave her my credit card. She went to buy duct tape to fix the crosswalk so Paul could get to class since you didn't show up to take him. He's my operative. She wasn't part of this. Do you know her name for God's sake?"

"Yeah," Mitchell replied, "Polly. She was kind of a wimp about the injection."

"Do you know where she lives? We need to go get her now. We have 24 hours before the Teller cartel removes us permanently from their payroll."

"Yeah," Mitchell replied, "yeah, I do, but so does Binge. We can't just drive up and go knocking on the door. Remember, my contract is close to being severed and they might be watching me. Also, I don't have a flit anymore."

"I can get a flit from here. They line up at these high-class hotels like flies at a picnic." He was starting to sound like one of his assets, he thought, instead of a defunct college professor. "I'll pick you up at the usual location. We 'll have to come up with a plan on the way there."

"Sure. I can't do much else until I get some stretch. I need to smooth out of here real soon." Mitchell stated, trying to sound cool.

"If we don't find this Polly, we'll both need to smooth out of here, stretch or not. And please don't try to use slang. It makes you sound like a fool."

"Oh, there might be another problem," Mitchell remembered. "The chip could be corrupted with a Binge taint. If they know I found the chip and they don't find it on me they can follow a residual tracer that's like a chemical fingerprint the injector rubs on it. They will be able to track all the injections that I have made including that one."

"How long do we have?" Tom asked with irritation. When he looked up, the doors of the elevator were open in front of him and he stepped inside.

Chapter 8: Binge Makes Its Move

"We're ready to move out. You lead the way German," Paul ordered. He had a firm grip on the insulated lunch bag that held a plastic bag containing the chip and ice from the refrigerator. Margarita grabbed her carry-all and headed out of the kitchen in the direction of German's room just off the dining area. German had loaded his backpack with some basic supplies which he slung over his shoulder and then levered Polly up from her chair with one hand under her elbow. Pam stood staring out the window.

"Someone is being suspended from the helicopter," she informed them. "They are dropping someone out!" There was a knock at the front door simultaneous with a shadow traversing the screen door in the kitchen.

"Everyone out now," Paul commanded *sotto voce*.

A knock sounded again, this time at the back door and the screen door pushed open admitting a burly man dressed in an army fatigue T-shirt and dirty blue jeans. He wore a baseball cap with the slogan "smoke'm if you got 'm" embroidered across the front. Paul tossed the lunch bag to Pam and slammed the door back into his face. The screen crumpled and the door partially wrenched from its frame, but it barely startled the man. Margarita, Polly and Germán used the moment's distraction to get out of the kitchen and head for Germán's bedroom. Pam edged around the kitchen table as a shattering crash came from the living room. "He's thrown something through the front window," Pam called to Paul. She found herself worrying about Margarita's plants for half a second.

"Paul!" she warned as the man at the back reach around the broken screen door and grabbed Paul's shirt.

"Go," Paul screamed.

There was a magnetic knife holder covered in knives of various sizes screwed onto the cabinet next to the sink. Pam backed over to the window and grabbed a butcher knife. Clutching the lunch bag with her left hand, she used her free one to slice the back of the man's neck. He cried out and let go of Paul. Reaching back to staunch the blood oozing from the wound with one palm, he pushed the screen door back into Paul's face with his other hand, but Paul caught the door and shoved it as hard as he could. The intruder fell backward into Pam's knife and collapsed to the floor, the knife sticking out of his back. Another crash and a loud clump came from the living room, followed by the sound of plants being knocked off the table.

"We have to get out now," Paul huffed, grabbing Pam's arm and dragging her into the dining room. Down the short hallway to the parlor, they saw a man dressed in a black suit pick himself off the floor, being careful not to put his hands on the shattered glass and pottery shards.

Paul grabbed the lunch pail from Pam and swung it over his head and across his shoulder bandolier-style. They ran for Germán's room.

"Shut the door," Paul shrieked. "Is there a lock?"

"No," Pam cried in panic.

"Never mind," Paul instructed, "wedge this chair under the door knob. He pushed a straight back wooden chair over to her. She no sooner got it lodged securely before the handle turned and the door began to rattle.

"Out the window! Now!" Paul ordered breathlessly, holding out his hand to support her. She was limber and fit and made quick work of sailing through the window the others had left open. Paul climbed through after her. One large stride brought them to the window of the other house. He made a cup of his hands for her to step on so she could lift herself through and then he pulled himself up over the window sill after her into a small bedroom.

"We should split-up so we aren't so easy to follow," Paul suggested to the others who were gathered in the bedroom waiting for them. "Polly, you come with me. Pam, go with Germán and Margarita. Get them to safety."

"I can take them to Dad's house, but what about you?" She realized he was protecting her by separating her from Polly and the chip, protecting all of them. Maybe she wasn't in-love with the guy but he did grow on you.

"I'll text you when I figure something out. Just go now." There was a crash from next door. The black-suited man must have broken the chair.

"Out the back! The fence will keep us from sight until we get to the alley,'" Margarita ordered. "We will cross over to the other side of the highway. You two go opposite."

They all rushed out the back door of the neighbor's house. It would have been a great plan except for the helicopter.

As they rushed through the narrow back yard to the alley, they heard the chop-chop-chop of the helicopter hovering over them, a man hanging from a long line trailed underneath. He was about 35 feet up, just above the tree and roof lines. Behind them they heard the man in the black suit making his way through the house with little consideration for the furnishings.

Although the alley was overgrown with weeds and bushes it was not completely obscured from the air. The group hugged the edges for protection, limbs and leaves scratching them as they moved.

"They need a clearing," Paul shouted. "Don't go to the street." He held Polly's arm so tightly she winced. He pulled her down the alley away from the others.

Before turning the corner, they looked back to see Margarita leading Germán and Pam toward the highway where they could access the underpass. She either didn't hear Paul or decided to disregard his instructions, hoping to get lost in the crowd of people who always gathered there. Clearly, it was impossible to get there by staying in alleys and yards.

Just then the man in the black suit appeared. He looked first at Paul and Polly then in the other direction. He hesitated for only a moment before turning to run after Paul and Polly who had disappeared around the corner of a house at the end of the narrow roadway.

Seeing this from above, the helicopter pilot followed Margarita's group. "Abuela, we need to take shelter!" Germán shouted, but Margarita was intent on proceeding to the underpass. Germán put a hand on her back, "Abuela, don't go to the street."

Disregarding her grandson's warning she dashed forward and ran down the side of the road wedged between a solid stream of dirty, gasping vehicles on one side and a solid line of corrugated metal, wood and wire fences on the other. Germán ran after her and Pam was not far behind. "She is in good shape for a middle-aged woman," Pam panted to no one in particular.

The helicopter followed them. Once over the street, the man dangling from the line slowly lowered until he was about 10 feet above them. Cars filling the access road inched along with drivers swerving to get a better view of the dangling man. There was the sound of scraping metal and angry shouts. The helicopter's cable operator let down the line so that the hanging man's heavily booted feet hit the roofs of the automobiles as he hopscotched along the line of traffic. A driver honked his horn and used a hand gesture to communicate his displeasure. Nonplused, when he was about 20 feet away from the group that he was stalking, the man disconnected from the line and landed feet first onto the roof of a vintage deep-blue Mercedes-Benz before rolling onto the hood. He grabbed at the windshield, gripping and tearing off a wiper before rolling off to the side bordered by sidewalk. He was protected by a padded vest and a light-weight helmet equipped with a receiver and mouthpiece. The helicopter continued to follow from above.

They were still several blocks away from the underpass and the man was gaining on them. "Run," cried Germán and he turned to face their pursuer.

Margarita looked back at the sound of her grandson's voice behind her and stopped in her tracks. Pam grabbed her arm and tried to pull her on but she planted her feet and refused to budge.

"What do you want," she shouted at the man who had caught up to Germán.

The man held him with his arm twisted behind. He pulled a gun from a holster strapped to his waist and pointed it at Germán's head.

"Which of you is Polly?" he asked.

"Why do you ask," Margarita inquired stubbornly hiding her fear.

"Look, I'm only doing my job. Polly goes with me and the rest of you can go on your merry way."

"Well, none of us is Polly," Margarita frowned, "so *you* can go on *your* merry way."

"Don't get smart with me lady or you'll regret it," the man replied.

"I always regret meeting your kind."

"Let's not get hostile," Pam interjected. "If you don't believe us, look at our ID's"

The man stopped focusing on the women for a moment and seemed to be listening to a voice coming through his helmet. It was too faint for the two women to hear. He silently nodded then said, "Affirmative".

Abruptly, he let go of Germán's arm. "We will be keeping an eye on you. All of you. If you hear from Polly, contact Binge immediately. It is a matter of national security." He loosed his grip on Germán and then handed him a card that he pulled from his vest.

"Since when is Binge involved in national security?" Pam asked.

He gifted her with a surly smile, saluted and said, "Have a good day." The helicopter which had never stopped hovering over them let the line back down to the ground and the man clipped himself onto it and was lifted away.

Germán ran to his grandmother and hugged her. He looked at Pam and asked her if she was all right.

"I'm fine," she answered, "but I'm worried about Paul and Polly. That man in the black suit must have gone after them."

"We can't do anything for them now," Margarita said. "We should go back to our house and make a plan."

"I'm always up for a plan," agreed Pam. She smiled at the grandmother and grandson who were still holding onto each other.

Chapter 9: The Man in Black

Paul dragged Polly along to the backside of a shopping center. This part of town was a hodgepodge of old houses and small shops squeezed in between soaring condo complexes and desolate mega-food-mart anchored strip malls. The man in black never lost sight of them for long, although he wasn't gaining on them either. Paul changed directions by jumping over backyard fences to take short-cuts and avoid impossible to cross streets. Still they could not elude the man in black. Polly, barely able to catch her breath, held her left side with one hand to massage a sharp, painful cramp that penetrated to her stomach. She pleaded with Paul to stop, but he dragged her on. They entered a sunless alley; graffiti the only bright spots in the otherwise dismal gloom that hemmed them in. Overflowing gray dumpsters stood like sentinels beside small raised loading docks streaked with the remains of leaking delivery drones and dripping trash bags. On the opposite side a tall, corrugated-metal privacy fence prevented access to the backyards beyond.

This was a bad idea, thought Polly. The man in black had rounded the end of the first building and stood at the end of the alley staring at them. Glancing back as they ran, she saw him pull a gun from a shoulder holster he wore under his black suit coat.

"Paul," she gasped, "he's going to shoot us!"

Paul jerked her to the side behind a dumpster, wedging them in between a 2-foot high concrete loading dock and the trash receptacle. He began to swear under his breath.

Polly pulled free from his grip and scrambled up onto the concrete loading dock, flinging herself at the smooth face of the handle-less steel door and banging with both fists. "Let us in. It's an emergency."

Surprisingly, the door swung open. A teenage boy in a dirty, white apron holding a black plastic trash bag said, "Say, whasup? You know you gotta go roun' t' da front."

"We're just passing through," Paul declared as he leaped up onto the loading dock behind Polly. He reached around her and grabbed the boy's trash bag, roughly tugging it and the boy out the door. With one leg across the threshold, he managed to keep the door from closing while he wrapped an arm around Polly's waist and propelled her forward. She twisted in his grip turning toward the boy, who had stumbled across the loading dock and nearly over the edge. He regained his balance in time to see Polly being pulled backwards into the restaurant and the door shutting closed.

They were in the storage area off the kitchen of a Mexican food restaurant. Smells of hot grease and chilies wafted toward them through a sound sea of clattering dishes, rapid conversation and the characteristic polka beat of Norteño music. Two cooks spoke Spanish and gestured at them angrily as they exited the storage room and squeezed past the ovens. Polly smiled politely. Paul nodded and steered them out the swinging doors into the dining room.

They had minutes before the man in black would burst through the kitchen or run around the building. Paul looked frantically left and right for an escape route, but Polly dragged him out the front door toward a city bus that just pulled up to the curb on the other side of the parking lot. "Quick," she yelled, "before he sees us."

They ran across the lot, zigzagging through a maze of dusty, dented and rust-eaten flits, cars and trucks, many with weathered tow stickers attached to the windshields. Nobody bothered to tow anymore. The tow lots were filled to the max with abandoned vehicles. If you didn't have access to a flit, walking was becoming faster and more convenient. Bicycles and land bound scooters were challenged to the point of uselessness by ill-kept, cracked and irregular sidewalks littered with jagged metal and broken glass and of course the streets were packed with vehicles. Still, the only safe way to cross the great streets and highways was in a motor vehicle if you didn't have a flit or a Yooter.

They made it to the bus stop as the driver began to close the folding doors. Paul stepped up first and pulled out his student ID and was motioned on. Polly started to hand over her Binge employee ID badge but then thought better of it. "How much?" she asked

"Credits only," the driver replied coldly. "Twenty creds, one way."

"I..I don't have a card." Polly stuttered.

"No credit, no ride," the driver shook his head indifferently.

Paul handed Polly his credit card with a curt, "use this". She took it apologetically, paid and was allowed to board. Out the side windows they saw the man in black making his way through the desolate parking lot toward the bus. Please don't let the driver wait for him, Polly prayed.

Suddenly the driver lurched forward to take advantage of a tiny break in traffic and almost knocked the two fugitives off their feet. Tires squealed and there was a great cacophony of horns to accompany his action.

"That's awesome. Lucky he's a good driver," breathed Paul, hanging onto the grab bar. There were no available seats so they stood holding vertical bars that ran ceiling to floor next to each group of benches.

Once in traffic the bus ground to a near stop. Polly directed worried, wide eyes toward Paul and they both stared out the window. The man in black had reached the ruined sidewalk and was following the bus on foot. They were trapped like rats in a cage. She saw him smirk and relax his stride.

Paul's mind raced. He was a secret agent for goodness sake; he was supposed to be able to deal with any circumstance.

They had inched their way forward to an intersection, when a helicopter flew over loud and low. Polly started crying silently, one stray tear running down her face. "I didn't know," she whimpered, "I didn't know I would cause so much trouble. I'm so sorry."

"Stop saying that," Paul reprimanded brusquely. "You don't know what is going on. Just stay cool. Look out the window. That's a traffic drone. It isn't after you."

She snuffled back her tears as a loud speaker mounted on the drone warned, "Do not block the intersection. Any vehicle blocking the intersection will be removed by force." Giant pincers hung down below the hull to underline this point.

The bus made a left turn through a gap in traffic when a few timid drivers heeded the warning. The drone flew off and the intersection was quickly blocked again. Paul looked out the window as the bus turned and saw the man in black stop in his tracks to watch them make their getaway. That was the trouble with walking. He was never going to be able to cross that intersection on foot.

"Maybe there are some positives to end-of-the-world traffic congestion," he muttered, but Polly wasn't paying attention. She swished her dress from side to side to simulate a breeze in the stagnant air of the crowded bus. Paul saw a long red mark on the inside of her arm. Her legs were smeared with dirt. Two middle-aged ladies sharing the bench connected to the pole she was clinging to favored her with a disapproving, condescending look. They were dressed for work in identical, button-down-the-front dresses and opaque tights. Their company's name was embroidered across the left-breast pocket.

Polly thought about how dramatically her life had changed in the last 24-hours. Yesterday, she might have been one of these ladies, off to work, dressed in her own style of uniform. Strangely, Polly felt glad she was standing up on the other side of the pole, swinging her skirt as if she didn't have a care in the world. She did not know her future, but at least it was not the one to which these two were headed.

The bus moved along at an appallingly slow pace, but eventually they made it to the next stop and the two climbed off. "We need to move quickly. They'll have a flit after us," Paul warned.

"But where can we go?" asked Polly.

"I need to contact my boss. He'll help us." Paul decided as he pulled his comp from the front pocket of his jeans and pushed a speed dial button.

Tom answered with an exasperated, "Where the Hell are you? You didn't get my message?"

"Oh," Paul replied, remembering the message he received just before Pam arrived, "I was out-of-pocket."

"You'll be out of a job," Tom scolded. "We have a problem. I'm on my way to a Polly Anna's place. She has our other chip and it is imperative that we get it back. Where are you? We'll pick you up on the way."

Paul sighed with relief. "I'm at the eastside bus stop on Palm Street next to a boarded up Walmania Megamart.

It's best if we stay out of sight until you get here. Some man in black is following us. I think he's from Binge."

"Binge? Why do you have a Binger on your tail? What's going on and who is we?"

"I'll tell you when you get here. Just hurry. This guy is loaded and I mean deadly."

"*Carajo*, Paul, you're an intern not a secret agent. What have you got yourself into?"

"We'll be behind the store. Just hover over the area and we'll come out to you." The connection clicked off.

They found a concealed space under a Chinaberry tree that grew out of a crack near a fence pole. Invasive species like the Chinaberry adapted easily to the extreme hot and cold swings of global warming. They were immune to diseases and insect infestation and no birds or bugs ate the toxic leaves and berries. So here it thrived at the edge of a parking lot in middle of a major urban area's perpetually orange glow, in a place that never got truly dark or truly light.

"In the spring, these trees blossom with the most deliciously sweet smell. As sweet as a Mountain Laurel or a lilac but less bubble-gummy," Polly remarked nostalgically. She tucked her dress under her as she sat down on a raised root and leaned back against the smooth trunk.

Paul leaned back on the other side. He took his hat off. Dirty, blonde hair was plastered to his head where the hat had held it tightly. Lifting the front of his t-shirt to show a not-too-flabby belly, he wiped the sweat from his face. He wasn't a weight lifter but all the walking he did kept him from getting fat; that and his student/intern budget.

Polly frowned seriously as she stared at his belly. "Paul, I've been thinking. Why would Binge spend all these resources on a receptionist? I mean they make millions of these chips. It certainly isn't worth this amount of retrieval. I'm sure I will be held liable for the replacement value plus interest, but all this? A helicopter? Trained assailants? I'm not even that good of a receptionist. They might make it impossible for me to get another job, but I just don't see them coming after me to this extent"

"I think you're right," Paul said and hesitated, "by the way, what's your last name?"

"What does that matter?" Polly asked him and then said, "Anna."

"You're Polly Anna?"

"Yes… Why? What do you know about me?"

"My boss wants something that you have, your chip."

"Well he can have it. That takes care of that. Right? We'll be rid of it."

"I don't know. What if those guys chasing us don't quit? What if they want it and if we don't have it they won't believe that we gave it to Tom." Paul worried. He didn't like that a chip had been planted in an innocent person, a bystander. He had not been officially hired yet, as Tom like to point out, so his allegiance was variable.

"You think they would abduct us," she cradled her injured hand protectively. "Do you think they would torture us?"

"I'm just thinking that we should know what is going on before we commit to a course of action."

"You don't trust your boss to protect us?"

"I don't know who to trust. Maybe we shouldn't wait for him. Do you trust Binge?"

"No, but what can we do?"

"I'm going to call Pam. We were going to meet for coffee at the student union. Maybe we should go ahead and do that. It's as good a place as any and I think we can maneuver our way there on foot."

"Okay, and maybe we can find some duct tape at one of these stores. There's a tear in that lunch bag and the strap looks like it is about to go," Polly pointed out. She pushed back her hair wishing she had a broad-brimmed hat to shade her face. The flower print polyester sundress she wore didn't do much for protecting her arms and legs either. At least she had on sturdy high-top boots.

"Do any stores have that stuff anymore?" Paul frowned. "We can check out a few places on the way."

"What did people do before duct tape was invented?" Polly wondered.

"What we're going to have to do," sighed Paul, "since it seems to be a world without duct tape as far as I can tell."

She stripped a branch from the Chinaberry tree and split it down the middle, but not all the way in half, then she slipped it around the lunch bag and wove it up through the strap to reinforce the torn spot. The bag still leaked but Paul could carry it over his shoulder and free up his hands.

"Do you think we should try to find more ice?"

"Yeah and duct tape because I look like some kind of crazy forest nymph with this branch around my arm."

"Okay, a convenient store. At least they should have ice. Duct tape seems to be a thing of the past. Where does it come from anyway?"

"Duct tape farms, I guess," Paul joked acidly, "probably in South America. They cut down the rain forest to grow it." His lopsided smile gave his face a certain boyish charm. He added seriously, "I need to contact Pam and make sure that she made it to safety." He tapped out the number on his comp and when she didn't answer, waited before trying again. Finally he heard Pam's anxious voice at the other end with some sort of white-noise behind it. "Pam, are you okay?"

"We're fine. They didn't bother with us once they realized that Polly wasn't with us. What's going on anyway? We've been sitting around Margarita's house trying to figure out what we should do, but this doesn't make sense. Why are there armed forces out after this woman? She must have done something that she isn't telling us about."

"Listen, can you meet us at the Union? I don't think we should be talking over the air waves. I'm not sure what is going on, but Polly doesn't know either. Maybe if we all put our heads together we can figure this out."

"Where are you now? Should I pick you up in a flit?"

"Would be nice but too risky. You might be followed. Might take us a while but we'll be there."

"Okay. I'll wait," Pam hesitated, "and Paul."

"Yes."

"Be careful."

"Always am," he answered with false bravado and clicked off. He removed the battery from his comp and placed the separated pieces into the opposing pockets of his pants.

"Let's go then," Paul extend a hand to Polly. She took it and pulled herself upright, straightened her dress and then the two solemnly left the comfort of their sidewalk treehouse.

They meandered through the back streets of the neighborhood for a while, cutting through yards and climbing fences. Sometimes vicious barking from an unseen animal would dissuade them from that route and they would take a detour. Eventually, they made it to the main thoroughfare they needed to cross to reach the campus.

"Déjà vu," Polly commented. Paul shot her an irritated glance. By now all the ice had melted down the side of his pants, soaking the battery in that pocket. The chip could activate and signal their location at any time. His other pocket was damp and there was a good chance his comp wouldn't work until it dried out. Polly didn't carry anything except a small shoulder bag. According to her story, she hadn't taken anything with her when she left her apartment except a Binge credit card which was no longer any good. Paul didn't have enough credits for a Quick Flit and a community service flit could take forever or never to reach them.

Polly said, "Give me the chip."

"No, you don't have to do that. Besides, I may be a selfish bastard but I'm in this now just as much as you."

"Paul, I have an idea. Let's go to that convenient store next block over. I'll tell you on the way. You can buy me some chewing gum," she beseeched with a shy smile, "and we'll get ice and I'll carry the lunch bag. That leafy twig strap will look better on me don't you think?" She laughed, "And you need to dry out.

Chapter 10: Pam Has a Plan

While Polly and Paul were threading their way through alleys and back yards to avoid the man in black, Margarita's group went back to her house and gathered at the kitchen table to strategize. Germán offered to sweep up the broken pots and plants in the living room but his grandmother told him to leave it. She needed to salvage plants from the debris and she wasn't up to it right then. There were more important things to do first.

She put a kettle on the stove and lit the gas burner with a match. From a cupboard she removed a tin box and a porcelain teapot decorated with blue dragons. The spout was a dragon's neck ending in an open mouth. She lifted the lid and spooned some fragrant leaves into the basket beneath. Germán and Pam watched silently. The commonplace, domestic movements were relaxing and reassuring. Preparations completed, she sat down at the table and gave the pair a meaningful look. "What do you think is going on?" she asked.

Pam was the first to speak. "This isn't just about breaking an indenture contract. I'm sure of that."

Germán stared pensively across the table and out the kitchen window where Pam had first spotted the Binge helicopter. Now the late afternoon sun turned the sky into a blank, orange inferno devoid of clouds or birds or any signs of life. Feeling the gaze of the women, he drew his eyes back to the table, but avoided their faces by speaking to the salt and pepper shaker. "It has to be something about the chip, right? Unless Polly isn't who she says she is."

"If they weren't after any of us, and we can be pretty sure of that since the man who was chasing us said as much, then it is either Polly, Paul or the chip that they wanted, or all three. Those are the only choices," Margarita continued her grandson's chain of reasoning.

"It has to be the chip," interjected Pam. "Polly is just a receptionist and why would they want Paul. He's still in college. He hasn't even been able to finish his tech certification and he's already 22, maybe 23."

"Yes," Margarita frowned, "I think it must be the chip, but why was it in Polly? Maybe she is more than she appears. Maybe she is a secret agent under cover."

"Grandma, I have known Polly the longest. I met her when she came into my convenient store. She was really terrified. I could not be wrong about that. Either that or she is a great actress or has secret personalities. In school we learned of Occam's razor which means the simplest reason is most likely correct. What is the simplest explanation?"

They all looked down at their laps to think about this until the kettle whistle made them jump slightly in their chairs. Margarita rose from the table to retrieve the kettle and poured steaming hot water into the waiting teapot.

"The simplest explanation is that there is something about that chip. Something other than just a tracking device and as long as it is out there Binge is going to be looking for it." Margarita paused and gave them a meaningful look. "That means that anyone coming into contact with it is not out of danger until they get it back. Polly and Paul are in the most danger right now, but I don't think that we are perfectly safe no matter what that man said. I think they might still be watching us."

Pam nodded vigorously while holding a finger to her lips.

"Do we care if they see us having tea?" Margarita continued with a silent nod to Pam and a serious glance at Germán. She fetched three mismatched souvenir mugs from the cabinet next to the sink. After handing them around the table, she went out the back door and came back in with a large lemon. "I have a lemon tree in the backyard," she explained, going to the counter by the sink. "It blossomed twice this year, but it could not make fruit in the summer because of the heat. The blossoms and most of the leaves fell off and it was dormant, then when the temperatures cooled in the fall it budded out again. It is a survivor like I am." She got a plate and a bamboo chopping board from the cabinet and took a knife from the magnetic knife holder by the side of the grumbling, old refrigerator. She sliced the lemon lengthwise and then each side in half twice to produce a plate of lemon wedges that she brought to the table. She poured the tea.

"That man in black could have planted something in our house after we left!" Germán muttered over his cup in a loud whisper. Both women shot him a warning look. Pam went to the vacuum that still sat in the dining room corner and turned it on full blast. "Or there are listening devices aimed toward us from across the street to hear everything we say," she added in a stagey whisper that they had to lean in to hear over the roaring vacuum.

As if on cue, her comp rang out her latest favorite show tune from an oldies movie she had recently discovered, Judy Garland singing "Somewhere over the Rainbow". She withdrew it from a small bag suspended at her side by a long, thin strap. She started to announce that it was Paul, but stopped herself at the last moment. Instead she told the assembled group, "I'll get that later. Right now I want some tea, but my hands are filthy. May I use your bathroom?"

With a curious nod, Margarita said, "yes, it's off the hall, first door on the right."

"Thanks," Pam said. She got up and passed through the dining room into the hallway and then went into the bathroom and closed the door. The bathroom was furnished with a tall, antique wardrobe closet and a combination medicine cabinet and mirror mounted on the wall above the sink. Opening the closet, she rummaged through a disorganized mess of cleansers, toilet paper and toiletries until she found a hair dryer. She turned it on high and holding it with one hand, picked up her comp with the other.

By now, Paul had hung up and was ringing again. "Paul?" Pam answered. "Where are you? Are you okay? Is Polly with you?" They made plans to meet at the Student Union.

When she returned to the table, both Margarita and Germán gave her a long, hard look. They had heard the hair dryer noise coming from the bathroom and had figured out what Pam was doing.

"I'll help you clean up the living room," Pam said quickly.

Margarita put the dishes in the sink and they all adjourned to the shambles of the living room. Margarita fetched a couple of large plastic tarps from a closet and began to tenderly place the damaged plants on one. She scraped some of the scattered dirt up into her strong, work-hardened hands and covered what was left of their roots. Pam followed her lead while Germán picked up the large pieces of glass and pottery. When they were done, Germán vacuumed up what was left and emptied the full bag into the trash bin.

Margarita spread out the remaining plastic tarp and directed Pam to take the other end and hold it up to the window. Germán tacked it into place. "Not water-tight," he sighed, "but that is the best we can do without duct tape."

"Duct tape isn't the only thing we are lacking," Pam remarked. She lowered her voice to a whisper. "We need to meet Paul and Polly at the campus union. Shall I call a flit?"

No one talked while they were in the air. The flit took them to the nearest landing pad next to the campus and from there they made their way to the large stone building that housed the Student Union. Inside to the right were nooks furnished with over-stuffed chairs and reading lamps. A small coffee shop rented space on the left. It was into this that they strolled and found a table in the far corner.

"We are all in danger now," Margarita said when Pam returned to the table and sat down a cardboard tray supporting three paper cups full of iced, ersatz coffee.

"I miss real coffee," Margarita remarked with a matronly look toward the two young people seated across from her. "I guess this is all you have ever tasted. But real coffee has a smell so earthy and rich. Those coffee disc room fresheners they make do not even come close."

"I've seen what these corporations do," Germán blurted suddenly as if answering a question only he could hear. He seemed lost in his own world. He shrugged away Pam's imploring gaze and sipped his coffee.

"My mother was killed by the corporations," he said finally. At Pam's prompting, he filled her in on his mother's death and he and his grandmother's subsequent arrival into central Texas. "But this is the United States now," he added tilting his head to look into his grandmother's downcast eyes, "surely one does not murder with abandon here. There are consequences."

"There are never consequences for the rich and powerful, *mijo*,"his grandmother said. "There is only the occasional inconvenience."

"Well then, let's make it damned inconvenient for them to murder us," Pam interjected. "I'm not going anywhere."

"How do we do that?" asked Germán.

"I'll get some snacks, I'm hungry, and then we wait for Paul and Polly. When they get here we'll come up with something. Paul is really quite good with technological stuff and I know a few powerful and wealthy people here in Austin. There is always a way."

"There is a way until there isn't," amended Margarita before lapsing into a meditative silence.

More than an hour later, having thoroughly read all the brochures arrayed in front of the stately oak reception desk and having studied their full-color, glossy, photo illustrations in minutiae as if looking for Waldo, the three were restlessly squirming in their seats from lower back pain. They looked surreptitiously through the broad storefront windows of the coffee shop across the lobby at students seated in overstuffed chairs, eyes sunk into their books. When new students passed by, the trio expectantly looked up from their brochures. No one looked back. They twiddled with the empty remains of their refreshments.

Germán broke the silence, "we need to find out what is on that chip."

"I've been thinking about that," Pam replied. "There is every kind of chip reader imaginable in the art library. I wish I could reach Paul and have them meet us there. His comp must be dead."

"The art library has a biochip reader?" Germán interjected with surprise.

"Yes, one of the professors does cyber art, art that is delivered directly to the mind through the optic nerve. The art is stored on a biochip. He creates a limited numbers of images. It's like limiting a run of fine art prints bya destroying the plate. The chip is copyrighted and has a failsafe crash program if someone tries to copy it more times than the limit. One of the big tech companies donated the technology in exchange for advertising rights; so now all over campus you see ads for Mono Company with the art of that cyber art professor. Anyway, now we have brand-new, top-of-the-line biochip readers in the library. In fact, the art library has readers for every kind of port imaginable."

"So the plan is to wait until Paul and Polly get here with the chip, then go to the art library with it and find out what is on it," Margarita summarized.

"That is the plan," Pam stated with satisfaction just as two passersby stopped in front of their table and looked around for empty chairs to pull up. Paul and Polly had arrived at last.

Pam laid out her plan and Paul beamed at her with an appreciation of her intellect as well as other features, until Polly burst everyone's bubble. "The chip isn't in the bag," she blurted.

She had never before seen such appalled faces. "How could it not be?" Paul was the first to say.

Polly shook her head at them before saying, "I'll explain outside."

"Paul, do you remember when we stopped at that convenient store where I got the gum that you used to adjust the crossing light so we could get across the street?" Polly began. "Clever way to ground a wire I think. Gum and paper work like a temporary duct tape," she explained to the group.

"I still had to drag you kicking and screaming through those stopped cars," Paul pointed out, his eyes catching Polly's. They both smiled. Pam knitted her brows.

"It required trusting those drivers behind that lit up signal to pause long enough for us to wind our way through very briefly stopped traffic. Also, I didn't know how long your handmade adhesive would hold," Polly shook her head.

"You had started carrying the bag with the chip," Paul realized. "What happened? How did it fall out of the container?"

"I didn't say I lost it," Polly corrected. "I said that I didn't have it. Remember when I told you I had an idea?"

"That's right. You never told me what it was. I got busy rigging the traffic light and forgot all about it," Paul reflected.

"Then where is it?" interjected Margarita.

"I hid it, at least for a while. We will need to retrieve it before too long."

"You hid it where?" Paul inquired sharply. The chip was his leverage with his boss and with his boss's boss. This was surely higher skill level work than intern-grade. He had meant to ask for a raise when he got the chip in his possession.

"I don't want to put any of you in danger. If you don't know where it is, then you have nothing that they want," Polly replied.

"We have been tainted by it. They will get rid of us to hide their trail," Margarita scowled.

Polly turned slightly green. "I don't think they would do that."

"Where is the chip, Polly?" Paul asked again in a controlled, gravelly voice.

"I hid it in the ice machine at the convenient store," she admitted.

"Polly and I will have to go back then and get it," Paul said resignedly. It would do no good to berate Polly for doing something without telling him. She was so naïve that she most likely thought she was being brave and clever.

"I'm going too," blurted Pam impulsively. "I'll call a flit."

"Germán and I are going back home. They come for us or they don't. Maybe they just watch us. We will wait to hear from you," Margarita decided.

"It is getting late and it has been a long day," Germán rejoined.

"Okay," said Paul, "we'll get in touch as soon as we know what is going on. Be safe." He clasped their hands in a farewell gesture and they departed. Pam thoughtfully used her comp to order them a prepaid flit to take them back home.

Humid, clinging heat enveloped the ensemble as they stepped onto the broad, stone staircase leading out of the Union. A lone fly buzzed around Paul's head and he swatted it away. It didn't give up though. It landed on his nose and when he brushed it away his sunglasses went flying, hit the concrete and cracked across the bridge. He barely had time to snatch them up when Pam called out that the flit was waiting for them in the landing area. Flit traffic was heavy in the evening, which although sometimes terrifying, was also good camouflage. They lifted into the air without incident, but their good fortune could only hold for so long. When they arrived at the convenient store whose ice machine held the safety of their future, it was closed.

"Aren't convenient stores supposed to stay open all the time?" Pam asked.

"Not anymore," Polly replied dismally.

"We'll have to break in," Paul reasoned.

"Aren't there consequences for that kind of thing?" Pam queried nervously.

"Aren't there consequences no matter what we do?" Paul rebutted philosophically.

"How secure are these stores?" questioned Polly.

"If we cut the electricity to the whole store, we would only need to break through the physical barrier," Paul said.

"You mean the back door?" Polly clarified.

"Yeah, I think I can manage that one too. We might even get away if we're fast."

"That isn't an option. We are gone before the authorities show up. Period," Pam said with ardor. "We don't have time for you to do both, so Polly and I will open the backdoor and retrieve the chip from the ice machine. You will watch from outside and make sure we don't get trapped inside."

"I'll need a huge pair of bolt cutters and rubber gloves that go halfway up my arm," Paul told Pam. "As soon as the electricity goes out, you and Polly gain entry and get that chip."

"We'll need a ballpeen hammer for that," Polly said.

"What about picks and bent wires? Aren't those more likely lock pick tools?"

"Pam do you know how to pick a lock?" Polly asked. Pam shrugged and shook her head no. "Me neither, but we have to get the chip so I need a ballpeen hammer."

"Okay, fine," conceded Paul, "but where are we going to get anything?"

"Margarita!" they all three said at the same time.

"I don't think we should go there. I think they are being watched, but maybe we could call Germán and he could bring the tools to us," Pam said. "This store is on the same side of the highway that he lives on."

"Neither Germán nor Margarita can afford a flit to get here. It is too dangerous to try to share the roadways with the traffic on foot at this time of day, so how would they get here? And don't you think Germán might be followed?" Polly pointed out.

"I'll call. Maybe he has an idea. I'll tell him to watch out for someone following him," Pam volunteered.

When his comp buzzed Germán recognized Pam's number. Remembering how she had turned on the hair dryer when she took the call from Paul, he went outside where the traffic noise was so loud that he could barely hear what she was saying. "Pam, it is Germán, are you okay?" he asked.

"Yes, so far I am fine, but we are in a predicament. Can you talk?" She paused, hearing the cacophony of inefficient machines in the background and she smiled a little into her comp.

"Go ahead. How can I help you?" Germán asked.

"We need some tools and we need them delivered," and then she continued to reveal their location and the plan. As she spoke, Paul sidled up beside her to listen. She put Germán on speaker.

"How do you plan to get out of there and where will you go?" Germán asked with concern. "Sounds on the fly. May I suggest a better plan?"

"Sure," Paul shot Pam a concerned look and sequestered the comp. "What is that?"

"You should wait until they open up in the morning. Stay there tonight to make sure the Binge people don't show up, and then when the first employees of the day come in greet them with a request to get your girlfriend's engagement ring out of the bottom of the freezer where she must have lost it getting a bag of ice yesterday. I will come help you since I know that store. I'll bring some food and water for tonight. It will be much easier to evade the police for loitering than for breaking and entering."

"You make sense, I guess. I'll talk to the others. We can't do anything right now anyway."

"Good. I'll be there in a few hours. The traffic will lighten up tonight. Just stay low, find a concealed area and take a nap until I get there."

"We'll stay occupied. A nap will be easier after we have something to eat and drink. Take care walking out there at night. Try to stay away from the streets."

"I'll see you soon," Germán signed off.

Pam snatched back her comp. "You couldn't hear it when I hold it?" Paul gave her a puzzled look and walked over to stand by Polly, but Polly ignored him. Tired, thirsty and hungry they were getting on each other's nerves.

Impending darkness did nothing to cool off the dank, muggy atmosphere that hung physically and mentally over the three would-be burglars. Paul paced in agitation. Pam and Polly slumped dejectedly against the wall in the shadows. It was difficult to see them if you didn't know that they were there.

"So I guess it is plow shares instead of swords," Paul said trying to engage the two women in conversation.

"What does that mean?" Pam asked. "Are we getting farm implements for the break-in?"

Paul hesitated. His eyes traveled across the two glum faces staring up at him, defying him to brighten their mood. "He's bringing food and water."

"Are we laying siege?" quipped Pam, still miffed that Paul had taken over the phone call.

Paul heaved a sigh. "We are going to wait until they open. You heard him."

Polly absorbed this conversation before saying, "it is a better idea. They open at 5:00 AM."

"Then I'll wait. You two don't need to be here," Paul offered gallantly.

"I'm the one who hid it here," Polly said, "I'll wait too. Besides, I don't have anywhere to go."

"You could come to my Dad's place with me," Pam offered half-heartedly. Her dad was permissive, but maybe not completely untied to Binge. He had many holdings. Since she had moved back home after her mother died, she had to consider the hand that fed her and not accidentally bite it. "Or we could all three stay here."

The area was not well lit, so they sat on the dirt next to the dark side of the building and stared at a wire fence covered thickly with vines. In places, the force of the ever entangling foliage caused the fence to tilt and lean toward them in an ominous way. Occasional rustling among the vines suggested rats or snakes or some creature it was best not to think about or mention.

"So the plan is for Paul to say that his sister dropped his girlfriend's ring in the ice chest. What? She was wearing it but it was too big for her?" Pam broke the silence.

"Right," Paul confirmed. "Polly will go to the freezer and find the chip and say that it is a ring."

"You need a ring. In case the clerk takes an interest in seeing it. You can use mine," Pam offered, slipping a ring that looked a lot like an engagement ring from her right-hand ring finger. Instead of a diamond, the central stone was a dark-pink ruby. It was surrounded by small princess cut diamonds and set in rose-colored gold; subtle in design but not cheap.

"Nice ring," Paul commented, an edge in his voice. "When did you get it?"

Pam shot him a startled look and shrugged. Before she could explain, they saw Germán riding a hover scooter called a Yooter up the street. He had a large pack strapped to his back. "He's here," Pam announced with relief.

Germán propped the Yooter against the fence and unslung his backpack. He distributed granola bars and a canteen that they passed around. Not much of a supper but better than nothing. Polly's stomach growled loudly enough for everyone to hear and Germán offered an apology. "Sorry I couldn't bring more, but this was all we had that was portable." He added sheepishly, "I have a bag of potato chips, too."

"Maybe we **should** break into the store," Polly suggested over a second loud growl from her stomach, "just for some food."

There was a rumble of thunder in answer and lightning suddenly streaked through the orangey-pink overcast of the city's night sky. "We need to do something other than stay out here all night," Pam remarked.

Before anyone could address the issue, a flit approached, hesitated and then parked in the empty lot in front of the store. The little group realized that they were standing out in the open for anyone to see. It was too late to sink back into the shadows. "Should we separate in different directions?" Pam asked softly.

"It's too late for that," Paul said. "Act casual."

A man exited the flit cab and stood there staring at the group, his hands on his hips. "Well, Paul," he said, "have you been evading me? Perhaps you would like to introduce me to your friends."

Polly gasped when she recognized the man from the crosswalk. "Paul, do you know this man?"

"Let me handle this," Paul said tersely. "Tom, you know Polly. This is Pam and this is Germán, friends of mine. Pam, Germán this is Tom, my employer."

"Your employer?" Pam and Polly blurted in unison their eyes meeting for a moment. They all shook hands.

Germán looked at him suspiciously and nodded.

"So what are you all doing here?" Tom asked casually with a tense smile that was anything but friendly.

Before the others could speak, Paul replied. "Waiting for you to rescue us, I guess. It's been a long day. If you could take my friends to Germán's house maybe you and I could go somewhere that is not out on the street in the rain to talk." An isolated drop or two of rain fell and another roll of distant thunder heralded more.

"Sure," Tom said, "as long as Polly comes with us." He opened one arm out toward the open door of the flit and nodded in a genteel manner. "Be my guest."

Pam looked questioningly at Paul and he shook his head slightly. Germán and Polly caught the gesture. Polly clutched Germán's sleeve and spoke to him in a whisper, unconsciously leaning against him for support.

"You are not abandoned. Don't despair," Germán advised as he helped her into the flit. Paul and Pam entered after her. Tom sat next to Polly, facing them on the opposite bench. They fastened the seat belts and the driver started the propeller. Polly thought resignedly about the consequences of her actions. Her head sagged forward from exhaustion so that her chin nearly touched her chest. The fact that the chip had been removed and was no longer in her possession was surely in her favor. Or not.

Tom ordered his driver to take Pam home then head for the Binge Campus. They got out in front of the semi-dark building. The three of them ascended in an elevator to the 3rd floor where Tom told his two hostages to sit on a couple of upholstered office chairs wedged in front of his desk. Tom stood blocking the entrance to the cubicle and stared intensely into Paul's face. Finally he asked, "Where have you been?"

"It wasn't easy to shake the guys tailing me," Paul kept his voice steady and his eyes unsheltered. "How did you find me?"

"You disabled your comp, so we had to use eyes on the street," Tom explained. "I sent an alert over the security web and it was a coincidence that a Binge security guard who was meeting his son for lunch at the University Union saw you there and contacted me. As you were leaving the building, a bug tracker attached itself to your hat. Couldn't have done it without the hat. You didn't notice a thing."

He looked at Polly. "You have given us quite a scare. You received the wrong chip so we will need to remove the one in your hand now. It is possible to replace it," he paused, "or perhaps you do not need to sign a contract. There might be a freelance position available working with Paul. You would, of course, get a company flit when you needed one. No more worries about getting to work. And in your new chip you'd have a company card, acceptable legal tender in multiple markets."

Polly frowned, narrowing her eyes to slits. "Nothing is free I'm told, everything else has a price."

"In my experience," Paul interjected, appreciating Polly's sly humor, "nothing sometimes can be very expensive." Polly released her frown and favored Paul with a Mona Lisa smile.

"Is the chip still in your hand?" Tom asked, irritation penetrating his tone. When Polly hesitated Tom added. "There is a technician in this building if we need to call for one."

"No technician," Polly's bandaged hand flinched. "I don't have the chip anymore. I got it out and...and destroyed it."

"You did not destroy it," Tom said, "you better not have." His lips were set tightly together, his fists clenched. "Binge will be very unhappy if you destroyed it."

"It's not destroyed," Paul broke in, "I can get it for you but it will take some time."

"How much more time do you need?" Tom inquired with a menacing look.

"24-hours," Paul answered. "I'll bring it to you here in 24-hours."

"I no longer trust you to keep your word," Tom said.

"What do you mean?" Paul demanded angrily. "I found Polly for you and I'll get the chip."

Polly shifted uncomfortably. "I guess I can't trust anyone." She glared at Paul. No, no she thought fighting back tears, Pam and Margarita and Germán were not part of the Binge web. She could trust them; because the alternative was not trusting anyone and she didn't think she could live that way. "I have no money for a flit and I doubt I have a room anymore since I am unemployed."

"There is a converted storage room with two cots and a working sink, restrooms on either side. You can spend the night in there. Both of you. I'm not paying for a flit until it takes us to the chip. It's late, so we'll start in the morning. Do you want me to get you something to eat from the vending machine?" They both shook their heads no. "Suit yourself. We'll write up a new contract tomorrow, once the chip is in my possession. You will both have plenty of money for living expenses then, right?"

He flashed an insincere smile before herding them to their storage room accommodation down a wide hallway floored in brilliantly waxed, 12-inch square, black and white vinyl tiles. The storage room was large for storage but small for two cots and a sink. Two thin blankets on top of a flat pillow sat neatly folded into a single pile on each cot. The cots were arranged in an L-shape around the large sink. Space on the side of the sink not taken up by a cot was filled with cleaning equipment, a mop, dust mop and broom.

Catching a quizzical look from Paul, Tom said, "For lab workers. Sometimes technicians are here all night on call-in shifts." There was a brief pause before he continued, "we'll all go together tomorrow to get the chip. No one is going alone. I'll sleep in the boss's office. He has an oversized leather sofa that is a little cushier than these cots. Don't try to leave without me. Security has been informed that you are not to leave the building." He left the room, shutting the door behind him.

Polly immediately grabbed the door knob, jerked the door back open and then closed it again. She slouched onto the cot at the far end and laid the pillow next to the sink. "Why did you tell him you would give him the chip?" she asked.

"He was testing you. You hesitated when you said it was destroyed. It was pretty obvious that you were lying."

"Should I believe him about the job, the new contract?"

"I don't know," said Paul, "I'm not officially with the firm yet. I'm on an internship. What choice do I have? If I don't turn over the chip, then the last year of my life was a waste. I've done things I'm not proud of to get this position."

In response to Polly's appalled look he added, "Nothing that bad."

"I'm going to the restroom," she announced. "You do what you have to do. I'm too tired to care. Tomorrow is another day."

Chapter 11: Night and another Day

Night did not lie peacefully across the restless city but pressed down upon it in a swollen, suffocating mass. Lightning and thunder troubled the darkness and the air grew more humid, but no rain materialized. Nor was there a peaceful sleep to be had in Margarita's shattered home.

Tired as he was, Germán found it impossible to relax. He dragged himself into the living room to stare at the plastic stretched over the broken window. Mottled red and yellow light strobed upon the semi-opaque window covering in a steady beat dictated by endless traffic. Eventually the muffled noise of passing cars and transport trucks lulled him to sleep on the sofa.

He awoke to a gray dawn, the air no cleaner because of the drizzly morning moisture. Storm clouds had produced nothing more than heavy dew. The soothing patter of shower water coming from the single bathroom made him long for the comfort of hot water on his tired muscles. He would have to wait for his grandmother to finish, so in the meantime he went to the kitchen to make coffee.

His comp sang out "Los Ojos de Pancha" as a chicory and coffee mix dripped black liquid into a carafe. It was Pam. "I'm coming to the restaurant around the corner from your house," she announced. "You and Margarita join me if you like. Breakfast is on me. We need to talk."

"Okay, we can be there in maybe 45 minutes," he estimated.

It was a small, TexMex diner with a dedicated local clientele. Pam slid into a window booth that was vacating as she walked in. The upholstery was red-vinyl embossed with a leaf pattern; a patina of grime filled crevices in the design for contrast. Carved initials textured the sticky table top. A harried busboy came over and pushed the litter of dirty plates and glasses into a gray, plastic tub and then disappeared without wiping the table. Once the waitress took her order of ersatz coffee with ½ real milk, she made her way to the lady's room. Margarita and Germán were walking through the door when she came out and she gestured to the empty booth. When the waitress brought Pam her coffee, she ordered soy-chorizo, potato and egg tacos for the three of them and two more coffees.

"We should go directly to the convenient store," Pam said after a sip of the hot drink. "Then we take the chip to the art library as planned."

"Yes, that was the plan," confirmed Germán.

"Was? Have you changed your mind?"

"Well, no, but what do you think this Tom fellow is planning to do with it?"

"We'll know better once we see what is on it."

"Do you think that it's safe to know what is on it?" worried Margarita. She looked with concern at her grandson seated across from her.

"Safer than not knowing, knowledge is always useful."

Tacos brimming with juicy sausage, fried potato cubes and melting cheese product arrived just in time to quiet the growls from their stomachs, which had begun to inform them that coffee was not a substitute for food. They concentrated on devouring the greasy, dripping meal without further conversation. Tiny recycled-paper napkins, singly dispensed from a metal container, did not sufficiently manage the spill-over. When they were finished, there was a pile of them by each empty plate.

When the waitress came by with the pot to refill their cups they waved her off and she immediately presented them with the check. Pam pulled out her credit card. "Pay at the register," the waitress informed her and proceeded to the next booth.

After Pam paid and returned to the table, Margarita said, "Germán, you go with Pam. I know I cannot talk sense to you. I have things to do here. *Ten cuidado, mijo.*"

"**Siempre**, Abuela, I am always careful," Germán took his grandmother's hands into his larger ones and tenderly kissed her forehead.

Judy Garland belted out a tune before they made it to the door and Pam answered her comp. It was Polly calling from the convenient store.

"Change of plans, Germán. Polly is at the store. She needs a lift. Maybe we will have the chip to decipher sooner rather than later. But she sounds like she's in bad shape and wants to go to my house."

"I'll stay here with my abuela then and talk to you later. Thanks for breakfast."

§

While Germán was falling asleep to the sound of traffic during the previous night, Paul and Polly fell asleep to the hum of office machines. Tom planned to be at the convenient store before it opened. He woke them up before dawn and ushered them toward the doors to the stairs.

"I need to use the restroom," Polly informed him.

"Me too," Paul chimed in.

"All right," Tom agreed with a suspicious frown, "just don't take too long."

"And I need some tape to fix my sunglasses. Do you have any duct tape here?" Paul added, holding up his damaged glasses.

"No duct tape, and our office tape doesn't stay stuck either as I discovered. I almost lost my watch." He pulled up one sleeve and displayed an old Rolex wrist watch that was tied on with braided string. "String chafes a bit. I tried to fix my leather wrist band with that transparent tape. Didn't work. Not a substitute for duct tape, but there's a ball of string on my desk. Help yourself. I'll call for a flit and meet you both out front."

"What are we going to do?" Polly whispered as they retraced their steps. "I'm not giving that man my chip."

"It's not your chip," Paul answered.

"It was injected into my hand." She held up her injured limb. Without the bandage, he could see that it was red and swollen.

"I'll ask him for some antibiotics," Paul said.

"I'm still not giving it to him."

"We don't have a choice," Paul reasoned.

"We do if we think of a plan," Polly said stubbornly.

"I think we should give him the chip and be rid of it," Paul said.

"Whose side are you on?" Polly sneered.

"I'm on my side," Paul answered sharply, then backed down a little. "Look, I'm on your side too, but I don't think this chip will do either of us any good. If we take him to it, we can be rid of it and go on with our lives. He said he would get you a better contract and you need medicine."

"Now that the chip is out of my hand, Binge has no control over me. I may be out of a job, but I have my life back. I might take the route that Margarita took. Work without a contract. We could misdirect him. Make sure that he doesn't find the chip at the convenient store, and then slip off with it ourselves."

"Do you really think we could give him the slip? I don't."

"Well, I'm going to try."

"I will pretend that I don't know where you hid it, but that is as far as I go. Remember, he is my employer."

"I'll think of something. Just don't give me away," Polly said as she opened the door to the lady's room. "Oh, do you still have your comp? I want to check in with Pam. She said she might be able to put me up for a few nights while I get my life back together."

Paul pulled the separated screen and batteries from his pockets. "You know how to put it back together?"

"I think I can figure it out." She shot him an offended half smile, palmed the separated parts of the comp and disappeared inside the lady's room.

Outside Tom paced back and forth in front of the building's large glass doors and windows. Every three turns he stopped to either look across the parking lot to the street or into the quiet lobby of the building. Occasionally he struck the back of his hand against a pants leg in frustration. Gray light filtered through the heavy clouds providing a dingy backdrop for morning traffic blocking the entrance to the parking lot. The sky was still mostly vacant in the nascent dawn.

The flit arrived before Polly and Paul. Impatient, Tom was about to head back into the building when the elevator opened and they both appeared.

"It's about time," he huffed and directed them to get into the cab. He gave the driver the address for the convenient store and they flew off over the stalled traffic below into increasingly dense traffic higher up. No one spoke.

"I hid it in the ice maker," Polly admitted once they had landed. Tom told the flit driver to wait.

"Then let's go get it," Tom said as he turned and headed into the store.

The clerk was busy cleaning the Slurpy machine and didn't seem to notice them enter. Polly made her way to the ice maker at the rear of the store. Tom trailed at a distance, browsing through various items as he strolled down the aisle, intending to distract attention from Polly. Paul pretended to shop for snacks near the front of the store, standing in the line of view between the attendant and the ice machine. It felt like a sting operation, like actual spy work Paul thought, his adrenaline rising. Was Polly going to try something or had she given in to the inevitable?

She was taking her time. Tom gathered a few breakfast snack items in his arms, hesitated, put them back and went to the door for a basket. As he walked back to the snack aisle, the clerk finally looked up and nodded his head once in greeting. "I hope you don't want a Slurpy," he said cheerfully.

"No, no, just some breakfast, thanks," Tom replied.

From his elevated position on top of a stool positioned to allow him to peer down into the slush machine, he saw Polly at the back of the store. "Customers aren't allowed to get their own ice," he announced.

"Oh, so sorry, I thought there might me some ice cream inside," Polly explained.

"Ice cream is in the freezer up front," the clerk pointed out.

"Oh, excellent. Tom, would you buy me an ice cream for breakfast?" she asked and headed back down the aisle toward the front of the store.

"Of course," Tom answered, bowing with exaggerated generosity.

After paying for the food they went back outside and stood on the sidewalk to sort it. Polly handed Tom a chip wrapped in plastic.

"Well," said Tom admiring his prize with satisfaction. "Is this it?"

"As far as I know," Polly answered. Tom gave her a questioning look so she added, "I'm sure it is."

"Just in case there is a problem, you had better accompany me while I check to see its contents," he decided.

"I've had enough," Polly suddenly cried, throwing her ice cream bar to the ground. "I need a bath and some real food and…." A damn broke and tears streamed down her cheeks, "I'm not going anywhere, do you hear, I…I…" The words were drowned out by her howling sobs. She jerked away from Tom's restraining hand and covered her eyes with one arm, wiping her nose on her bare skin.

The front door of the convenient store opened and the clerk looked out. "Are you okay, Miss?"

"I…I need to use your comp, if you don't mind. I know you probably have rules against customer usage, but I really need your help," Polly sniffled.

"The store has a courtesy caller you can use," the clerk replied, casting a warning glare Tom's way.

Two cars pulled out of traffic and into the parking lot. The clerk continued to hold the door open and Tom, worried more strangers would come to her aid, had no choice but to let her go. He flashed an angry look at Paul, pushed his lower jaw out and dropped the corners of his mouth into a deep frown. He needed to leave to check the chip before high tailing it over to Veronica's. Could he trust Paul to keep an eye on Polly for him or was Paul going rogue? Was Paul making a deal with Binge behind his back?

Paul watched his employer weigh the situation, taking care not make a suggestion that might benefit Polly or him. He had to appear unbiased and unconcerned. If Tom sensed anything amiss he might call in reinforcements.

He knew one thing. He knew that Polly was stubborn and would refuse to go anywhere until Tom and the flit were well gone. Inside the store she was relatively untouchable. It was a smart move. Was this her plan? But hadn't she already given up the chip?

Inside the store, Polly called Pam. Pam picked up on the second ring, "Polly! Are you okay? Is Paul with you?"

"We're at the convenient store," Polly said. "Could you come get me?"

"Sure, of course. Germán and I were planning to go there right now. You said me. What about Paul? Is he alright?"

"Paul is here, but I don't know for how long. Tom might take him with him."

"Tom is there? Did you give him the chip?'

"Pam, I really need you to come as quickly as possible. We can talk when you get here."

"I'll be there in ten minutes."

"Okay, I'll be waiting," Polly said and disconnected.

Outside Tom's comp chimed. He checked to see who it was and then grimaced. It was Veronica. "I have to take this," he told Paul. "You go inside and keep an eye on Polly. I don't trust that woman."

"Your time has run out," Veronica informed him hotly.

"You gave me until this afternoon," Tom reminded her. "But don't worry. I have it."

"Then come directly here," she ordered.

"I haven't had a chance to check the contents," he replied.

"We can check together. Where are you? I'll send a flit."

"That won't be necessary, I have one waiting."

"You have twenty minutes." She hung up.

When Tom reentered the store, Paul was staring out the large display windows lost in thought. Polly was nowhere to be seen. "Where's Polly?" he asked.

"She's in the back," Paul answered.

"Keep an eye on her. I'm not done with you yet," he warned. "I have to go somewhere right now. I'll see you later. Come to the office this afternoon, you and Polly. We can discuss our further association then."

Tom marched back to the parked flit and got in. "Regent Hotel," he told the driver, "but I need to make a stop on the way. Go back to where you picked me up." The gray sky reflected his mood as the flit lifted from the parking lot and headed back to Binge. Rush hour was in full swing and the flit lifted slowly to avoid the Lifft/Yuber low flying auto-flits, a more economical if more dangerous choice of taxi. Comp apps could locate the nearest stand and a card swipe activated it until it was swiped again to deactivate. A step above lift-drones, they were mostly self-operated and were required to fly below the various commercial and personal flits soaring above the buildings. Their safety record was dubious at best but safety issues could not quash their popularity which was fueled by convenience and cheapness. Generally, they were only used for short distances by office workers and laborers. The young and nimble preferred Yooters which skimmed over perpetually stalled traffic and impossibly rugged sidewalks on a stream of forced air and magnetic repulsion.

Tom hurried up to his office/cubicle. This was the information that would buy him out of the corporate world and into an early retirement. He planned to leave the city and move to a reasonably-sized town where the air was breathable and traffic so light that it never blocked the intersection. He wondered if such a place existed.

In spite of Veronica's impatience, Tom wanted to be prepared before he saw her again. He plugged the chip into his computer's universal slot. Prohibitively expensive for a private user, it conformed itself to accept most peripheral drives and cards and it could translate any computer language. Only huge corporations like Binge Inc. could afford them.

The screen filled with a spreadsheet. Tom tried to understand what the numbers and names arranged in columns side-by-side meant. Why were there names? Was this after all a bioweapon? Why was his name on the list? And there was Pam's name and, "Oh Hell," he proclaimed out loud to the padded cubicle wall in front of him. "It's the chip from Paul's comp."

He sat back heavily in his swiveling, rolling office chair causing it to glide back away from the desk before he stopped it with his feet. "Polly!" he exhaled and then bent his face into his upraised palms. So much for early retirement, he would be retired all right. Retired to a cremation furnace, his ashes added to all the other pollution in the city air.

Chapter 12: Between a Chip and a Hard Place

Sulking silently, Tom sank low into his chair and stared for a few minutes at the nubby fabric of the padded, gray cubicle wall. There was no time to try to find Paul or Polly and the real chip. He would have to make do.

"Buy some time," he mouthed the words out loud as if to convince himself. How could he buy enough time to hunt down the real chip that, according to Veronica, was going to save the world and as a bonus save him from Binge and ProFo?

He looked up to see Mitchell from the next cubicle peering at him over the top of the partial wall. Mitchell was a Binge flit tech but he helped Tom when there was enough money involved. Mitchell's looming presence made the tiny cubicle feel unbearably claustrophobic. "Can I help you?" Tom queried edgily.

"How's it going?" Mitchell asked.

"Fine. Fine," Tom returned begrudgingly, and then looked expectantly into his associate's fleshy face. "Mitchell, do you still have those chips confiscated last month?"

"Yeah, I scraped the last one this morning. I was going to turn them in on my way out this afternoon."

"Could I have a copy? It would help me with a new project."

"A copy of those? They are a total wash. There is nothing of value there, but sure, if I can help you out. And you do still owe me for the last favor I did for you, remember? What are you going to do with it?"

"That is yet to be determined," Tom replied cryptically

"Right. I'll be back with a dupe in a minute." Mitchell slid back down into his cubicle. For a large man, he was surprisingly agile. He popped up a short while later with the chip. He handed it over to Tom with a flourish and said, "A chemical equation for the cure to cancer."

"Great," said Tom, "I just hope all bio-equations look alike."

Back at the hotel, Veronica opened the door to let him into her hotel suite. She wore beaded leather sandals, blue jeans and a soft mulberry T-shirt that caressed her curves. No longer was the suite immaculate and impersonal. Papers and notebooks littered the coffee table and surrounding floor. There was a machine on the desk with multi-colored wires that protruded from one side and disappeared off the edge. It was linked to a printer on an end-table that had been moved next to the desk. The kitchenette countertop held an assortment of take-out boxes, empty beer bottles, dirty coffee cups and grimy, partially-filled glasses of soda water. It appeared she had been busy brain-storming with her staff, but he saw no one else in the apartment now.

"Have a seat," she motioned to a clean spot on the sofa. In spite of her hard-hearted business woman manner, she moved with grace and ease. There was a softness about her that belied the no-nonsense policies she instigated in her dealings and which he knew of by reputation.

As soon as he sat down she demanded to see the chip. From his tweed jacket's inner pocket, he pulled out a small, hard plastic case. She grabbed for it hungrily and once it was in her possession she opened it immediately. She took the twin set of chips to the machine on the desk and inserted one. Tom followed her and stood behind her just close enough to see the computer screen. The same series of numbers and letters and bars covered her screen that Tom had seen on his own when he looked at the first chip. It was genetic code.

She stroked some keys and pressed a button then smiled in his direction, "I'm sending this to my experts. Please wait for their reply." She paused. When he didn't move she pointed to the sofa. "Over there."

Tom shifted uneasily, but did as asked. He wasn't going to get away with the fake information. If only something would prevent her from looking at the second one. She might be satisfied for now with what she had and let him leave.

Ten minutes passed. Tom watched Veronica softly pad like a caged tiger around the room several times before ending up at the floor to ceiling windows. She stared out at the shrouded, smoggy city below, streets like clogged arteries. If only she could put them on a healthier diet, a diet of bio-created energy from tiny carbon-dioxide eating creatures.

Her comp bleeped and she pulled it from the back pocket of her jeans. "Sounds like you did well, Tom. This could be lucrative for all of us. I see no problem in making a fortune while I save the world." She chuckled with unfettered glee. "Let's just look at the other one." Long, perfectly manicured fingers worked the controls to eject the one chip and insert the other.

"Wait," cried Tom, beads of sweat suddenly sprouting across his forehead, "that isn't the right chip." He ran his hands through his thick, wavy hair, his dark eyes trying to penetrate her expression of dissatisfaction.

"How can that be, Tom? Did you lie to me?" She moved about the room, a sinuous snake sizing up its prey.

"Not exactly, I just found out before I got here," he projected his sincerity. When all else fails, go for the truth.

"You came here with a fake chip hoping you could pass something over on me," Veronica stated bluntly, her face grim, eyebrows furrowed.

"Yes, but not in a sinister way, I was hoping to have the real chip before you were inconvenienced," Tom looked beseechingly into her angry green eyes. He could see she wasn't buying it.

Unexpectedly she softened. "Binge knows that I might be involved with the disappearance of their chip. They think that I hired one of their employees to work for me under-cover. They would like to know who it is. Little do they know, right Tom?" She stood directly in front of him with an unmoving gaze. "Professional Focus, Inc. is contracted with Binge, isn't it? Do they know that you will work for anyone? With money that is."

Tom gulped and said nothing. He thought she might spit in his face, but she turned away to go back to the view out the window.

"Their severance pay can be brutal," Veronica warned menacingly.

"I shall have to forgo severance pay then," he replied bravely.

"I might be able to protect you, if you bring me the other chip. And I would be willing to add enough creds to your account so that you could retire. Now doesn't that sound preferable to the alternative?"

"That depends on the alternative," Tom answered.

"The alternative is death, Tom. I thought I had made that clear."

"Death from you or from Binge?" Tom asked in a faltering voice.

"Take your choice. We may be smaller, but that doesn't mean we aren't deadly." She qualified, "metaphorically speaking, of course."

"Of course," Tom said, "but I need more time if I'm going to get this chip that everyone wants."

"Understood."

"Then we have a deal." Veronica offered her hand and they shook. "Now, how do we find it? I intend to assist you so that there can be no more problems."

"Transfer half of the funds to my account now," Tom bargained. "Once I see them I will share with you everything that I know."

Veronica slanted a tiny smile his way but agreed. She transferred funds and he checked his comp to make sure they had made it before he said, "there is a convenient store where Polly stashed the real chip in an ice machine. I was watching when she retrieved it or pretended to. She's already been there so I don't know if that means she has it, she stashed it somewhere else or it is still in the convenient store. Or," he paused to scratch his head, "or, Polly never had it."

"What do you mean?" Veronica asked.

"I mean that I have not seen the contents of this second chip. There was an early player. It is possible that he has it."

"Great," Veronica exclaimed. "Who knew that saving the world would be such a bother? Where to first?"

Tom waved his comp at Veronica. "I'd like to take a good look at that convenient store. But first, I have to text my operatives." Veronica gave him a questioning look, so he explained, "I need a status update."

"Do it on the way." Veronica picked up a large, black nylon satchel and declared that she was ready to leave.

Tom stood up and followed her through the door. In the lobby of the hotel, Veronica quickly got the attention of the concierge and ordered transportation. Moments later, the doorman informed her that her flit was waiting.

During the silent ride to the convenient store, he wondered if it was the money or the person that drove people's willingness to give Veronica everything that she wanted. She certainly was the product of privilege. Things seemed to magically happen in her favor. He could not remember a time, ever, when a flit happened to be waiting right when he needed one.

The clerk smiled as Veronica entered, not even noticing Tom trailing behind her. "May I help you with anything?" he asked.

"I need some ice," she answered.

"Sure, I'll get it for you."

"I'd prefer to get it for myself. I am picky about my water products." She graced him with a pout.

"Of course," he told her.

Tom wanted to pipe up with the rule about customers not being allowed to get their own ice, but stopped himself.

Veronica spent an indeterminate amount of time, which might have been a decade or two, before returning to the front of the store with a bag of ice. "Let me get that," Tom offered.

"Thank you. I will."

The clerk took Tom's card without taking his eyes off Veronica. She turned and left the store, leaving the bag of ice on the counter for Tom to carry.

Once back in the flit, she glared at the ice. "Why did you bring that in here, although ice is preferable to this dirty, clinging heat? How do you stand it?" She did not hide her irritation. "At least on the border the heat is dry. It cleanses the soul."

"I take it that you had no luck?"

"You are absolutely prescient," she said, "where to next?"

"I need to contact my assets. They might be reluctant to meet a stranger, so perhaps you should return to the comfort of your hotel and I will keep in touch as things develop."

"Don't try to lose me, Tom. I will find you."

"I would never do that. You have my retirement in your hands. Do you think I would do anything to jeopardize that? You might have noticed the intolerable conditions in the city."

"I'll meet you for dinner at my hotel tomorrow. Make it seven o'clock? That gives you more than 24-hours to work with your associates. I expect a full accounting. Oh, and dinner is on me. The least I can do after you bought me that lovely bag of ice." She instructed the driver to return to the hotel.

Upon arrival, she coolly exited and said, "Take the gentleman where he needs to go and charge it to my card." She left the ice melting on the seat.

Tom had the driver take him to Margarita's house. He poured out what was left the dripping bag of ice under a bush by the front porch before knocking. Margarita cracked the door and peered out. Reluctantly, she widened the opening to admit him.

"What do you want?" She asked bluntly.

"I'm looking for Paul. Or Polly," he said.

"They aren't here," she answered.

"Do you know where I could find them? It is rather important."

"Why is it important?"

He hesitated, then said, "Because all our lives depend on it."

"How do you mean?" She asked unfazed.

"They have information that is important to some powerful people."

"What information?"

"I'm not sure. I've only seen half, but from what I've seen, it could be the solution to all the things wrong with this world."

She gifted him with a long silence before sighing. "You think that chip will save the world? I think you want to save yourself."

He delved into her expression. Her dark eyes flashed with an intelligence that made him uncomfortable. She saw right through him. "May I sit down?"

"Help yourself." She motioned to the sofa and seated herself in the rocker without taking her eyes off of him.

"I'm sorry if we got off on the wrong foot," Tom continued. "It is just important that I contact Paul. He's not answering his comp. I'm worried about him and Polly too."

"You were with them when I saw them last. Why would they be here?"

Putting his head into his hands, Tom's mind raced. How was he going to get these people to cooperate? Why should they?

"I'm worried about your grandson," he said. It worked to get her attention. Alarm briefly lit up her eyes.

"You leave my grandson alone."

"I would never harm him or you," he patted the air with his hands in a calming gesture, "but there are others who are not so compassionate. Corporate people."

"I should have known that you are involved in corporation dealings. What is going on with this chip? Maybe if you are honest with me then I will be honest with you. But do not even think of involving my grandson in anything." Daggers of lightning flashed from her eyes, Tom squirmed uncomfortably. It is always the quiet ones who end up being the fiercest, he thought.

"You tell me what is going on and I will tell you where Polly is," Margarita decided. "Come into the kitchen and I will make tea."

Chapter 13: Paul Tries to Help Polly

When Paul entered the small office and break room of the convenient store, he saw Polly seated on a tattered chair behind a desk littered with snack food wrappers and sales receipts. Listlessly she stared at an advertising poster of Mr. Popper popcorn adorning the wall. Bits of twigs were entwined in her dark, blonde curls tumbling in a tangled mass against her shoulders. She had lost her hair tie some time during the previous day's adventures. He fought an impulse to pluck the debris from her hair and comb it with his fingers. Bruises and scratches covered her bare arms and legs. Her sundress had lost its sheen and appeared ready for a good laundering that included a liberal dose of stain remover.

"Did you call for a ride?" Paul asked gently.

"Yes, Pam is on her way."

"Good. Do you have a place to stay?"

"What do you think?"

"I'm guessing, no."

"I don't even have any clothes. Everything I own is at that apartment."

"Well, Tom said that he was going to help you, right? Maybe Pam has some clothes she could lend you in the meantime."

"I guess." She moved her eyes from the poster and looked up into Paul's face. "Tom didn't get what he wanted."

"What do you mean? I saw you give it to him."

"I didn't find the chip. That was the chip from your comp."

"Oh great, my comp is dead now. That's just what I need."

"I'm sorry. I didn't know what else to do."

Paul furrowed his eyebrows. She looked way too pathetic to rebuke. Possession of the chip was a mixed bag, but in the end it had value they could barter. After giving it some thought, he said, "That *was* pretty clever." For a second, Paul wondered what it would be like to work as an agent with Polly. Tom thought she had promise. Or was that him trying to sell her a line. Correct that, sell both of them a line. He was beginning to realize how little he could trust his boss. "Look... they sell disposable comps here. My boss transferred some funds into my account this morning so I'm going to buy us both one. I think we should stay in touch until this situation is resolved."

"Yeah, right, until I give you the real chip." She was miffed but then did an about face. "Paul," she spoke sadly, a solemn expression pulling down the edges of her eyes, "do you think I'm holding out on you?"

"I haven't thought that for a while. I think you're a person who desperately needs a friend."

Polly's expression lightened. "Are you my friend?"

Paul answered with some reserve, "I guess I could be."

"We meet again," Pam appeared in the doorway and leaned one hand on the frame. For a moment she observed the frazzled duo. "You look like you had a tough night. Am I dropping you at your place, Paul? Polly, you can come home with me and freshen up. Did I mention that you both look like crap?"

"Thanks Pam," Paul grimaced.

"Thanks Pam, that would be great," Polly bestowed a weak smile on her benefactor.

"Before we leave, I need to purchase something," Paul said and left for the store interior to buy the temporary phones.

After dropping off Paul, the flit gained altitude and headed for the less populated hills west of the city. Pam lived in a sprawling mini-mansion on a five-acre hillside that commanded a view of the lake. The house was a two-story, sided in native limestone with an iconic red-tile roof and long porch overhung by a balcony. Outside, the style was native-TexMex ranch wannabe manor house. Inside, imported marble and granite floors were laid in intricate patterns throughout, with real hardwoods upstairs. The ceiling in the entryway rose up to a mezzanine that provided entry to a long hall lined with rooms.

Pam led Polly up the stairs and down to the last door. "This is my room," she said, "you can shower in there." She pointed to an attached bathroom. "I'll leave you some clean clothes on the bed. I'll use one of the guest room baths." She pulled a t-shirt, underwear and a pair of shorts from a drawer. "I don't know if you can wear my underwear," she said with a calculating glance at Polly's bosom, "but, you're welcome to try."

"I really appreciate this," Polly said, before wearily heading into the bathroom. Pam gathered up some clean things for herself and left as soon as she heard shower water splashing.

When Polly came out of the bathroom wrapped in a bath towel, Pam was sitting on the edge of the bed filing her fingernails. "Hey, I put your clothes in the washing machine."

"My undies, too?" Polly asked with a frown.

"Yes," Pam looked up and smiled disarmingly. "So you won't have to wear my undies. I know they would be too small. Don't worry. Yours will be ready in no time. Meanwhile, relax. If the shorts and t-shirt don't fit, you can wear this robe. Come fix your nails with me. Dad is having a guest for dinner and wants us both to attend."

Polly took the robe into the bathroom to exchange it with the towel. When she returned, Pam asked her if she needed to borrow her curling iron or a blow dryer. "I usually let it dry naturally," Polly answered. "By the way, I never gave your ring back." She set it on the dresser.

"I almost forgot about it," Pam said. "A gentleman gave that to me before leaving for South America. Last I heard he had met a Brazilian. Oh, well. Anyway I need to do something with my hair. Do you mind if I leave you for a while? The television remote is on the dresser or you might want to nap. We could both probably use one of those. I'll bring your clothes when they're ready. Dinner is at seven, but Dad wants us downstairs for cocktails at six-thirty."

As soon as the door closed, Polly lay back on the bed and closed her eyes.

When she opened them again, her clothes were laid out on the bed next to her. A large, antique wall clock pointed to six o'clock. Quickly dressing, she combed her hair with Pam's brush and borrowed eye liner and lipstick from one of the drawers in the bathroom vanity. According to the image in the mirror, she was presentable if not overly so.

Pam was downstairs in the living area looking sleek and unblemished by the events of the previous day and night. She wore a short, pink, cotton dress speckled with tiny flowers. Her ballet-style slippers were also pink and contrasted harshly with Polly's boots. Polly was by no means chubby, but next to Pam's tall, lean, muscular frame she felt that way.

"There you are," Pam exclaimed. "I wondered if you would wake up in time. Veronica just arrived. Dad is showing her the view from the terrace out back. Shall we join them?"

"Uhm, sure."

A small, wet bar served the outside patio and Pam proceeded over to it. "What will you have? Dad whipped up some killer margaritas, but there is also beer and soft drinks, scotch and cognac."

"A margarita sounds great," Polly said enthusiastically, "no salt."

"Good, I'll get us both one."

Equipped with their drinks, the two circumnavigated the pool and spa to join Pam's father and his guest.

"Dad, this is Polly," Pam said.

"Polly, welcome to our humble abode. Let me introduce Veronica Teller and you can call me Bob."

"How do you do, Veronica? I hope you will excuse my presence. Pam sort of rescued me yesterday when I got evicted from my apartment."

"Do tell, what happened to cause that?" Veronica asked pleasantly.

Pam and her father flashed each other a look that Polly caught out of the corner of her eye. Pam interjected, "no need to go into that right now, huh Polly? Let's keep this a happy occasion. Aren't these margaritas yummy? I'm famished. Shall we go in for appetizers?"

Dinner was served on a long table situated near panoramic windows that looked out over the terraced pool area and beyond to a view of the lake and Texas hill country. Food was typical Texas fare consisting of smoked brisket and sausages, pinto beans with cilantro and jalapenos, mixed-greens and tomato salad, coleslaw and potato salad. Polly's mouth watered from the smell of the smoked meats as soon as they walked back inside the house.

"What kind of business are you in?" Pam asked Veronica.

"I have a few factories. I do outreach for venture capital funding, but I'm also an entrepreneur."

"Providing money for businesses?" asked Polly innocently.

Ignoring Polly, Bob interjected to explain to Pam that he and Veronica were thinking of going into business marketing a revolutionary new kind of energy. Pam shrugged off the slight to her guest and turned to her father. "Terrific," she said, "when will this new energy be going on the market?"

"That's what we were discussing before you two arrived on the terrace," her father said, magnanimously including Polly. "There has been a problem getting a chip that contains the final piece of the design."

Polly's mouth was full of sausage that she quickly swallowed to keep from spitting it out. When Bob noticed her discomfiture she managed to sputter, "I understand that you work for Binge, Bob."

"Not anymore," said Bob, looking fully at her for the first time. "I own stock in the company now, but I was the Chief Financial Officer there before I took early retirement."

"Oh," said Polly, "and are you an entrepreneur now, also?"

"Of sorts. I do a little exploration for Binge now and again and if something comes up that sounds interesting I might invest some of my own money. What do you do Polly?" Bob asked with feigned interest.

"I worked for Binge, but not anymore."

"Really, what a coincidence. And might I ask what position you held?"

"I was an industrial spy," Polly said surprising even herself with this revelation. Why should she tell these smug, self-important people that she was a receptionist?

"A spy?" interjected Veronica who had focused her attention at the word spy. "Are you Polly Anna by any chance?"

"Isn't this auspicious," blurted Bob, relieved that Polly could bring something interesting to the dinner chitchat. "Do you two know each other?"

"As a matter of fact, that is my name," Polly verified, ignoring her host and staring pointedly at Veronica. "Why do you ask?"

"I have a friend who is looking for something you might possess. It could be lucrative for you. This is indeed a pleasure. We should talk."

"Would that friend's name be Tom, by any chance?" Polly asked.

Before Veronica could answer, Bob cut in. "Hold on both of you. What's going on? I suddenly feel left out of the conversation."

Polly favored him with a smug look. Welcome to my world, she thought. She said, "I really can't talk about it right now. If you will excuse me, I think I've had enough. Dinner was divine. Thank you so much for having me, Bob. Veronica." She actually curtsied before clomping out. Once out of sight, she ran up the stairs to Pam's rooms, locked the door and pulled out the little comp that Paul had given her. "Paul," she panted, still catching her breath.

"Polly?" He answered with concern. "Where are you? Are you okay?"

"I don't think so. Can you get a flit and come pick me up? I think I might be in trouble."

"I might be able to. Where are you? I thought you were going to spend the night at Pam's."

"So did I. That's where I am. Something came up and I get the feeling that I might be in trouble. Do you know someone named Veronica Teller?"

"Doesn't ring a bell, why?"

"Because she knows Tom and she's heard of me. I think the chip that is now missing was for some new technology that will revolutionize the energy industry and Pam's father is in on it."

"Does Pam know about this?"

"Pam? What does that matter? Look you and Pam can deal with your relationship later, right now I need help. You said that you would help me and I am counting on it. I don't think I am safe here."

"Surely they won't try anything with Pam there. Even if I can scrounge up enough credits to take a flit out there to get you, it would take at least an hour, maybe longer. What will you do in the meantime?"

"I'll pretend to be sick and lock myself in the bathroom. Just come. And hurry."

"Okay, I'll be there as soon as I can. Don't go anywhere in the meantime."

"Yeah, right. Like I have anywhere to go. Hurry!" She disconnected.

No sooner did she hang up than there was a knock on the door. "Who is it?" she called.

"It's me, Pam, and this is my room. Let me in."

What could she do? The bedroom was on the second floor and with the high ceilings that meant a 12 or 15 foot jump from the window onto a hard surface below. She wasn't about to attempt that. "Okay, just a minute," she said and hid the comp in her bra between her breasts. Luckily, they weren't the little athletic size that she had envied since puberty and with a little jiggling and adjusting it wasn't too obvious what was buried in her cleavage. She bent over to tie her shoelace and it dropped out onto the floor. How did women do this? She had seen it done in the movies many times and they made it look seamless. Then she thought of her high top boots. She unlaced the top and positioned the comp between the tongue and laces. It was painfully uncomfortable. Finally, she stuffed it down the back of her panties just above her buttocks. She checked herself out in the mirror, moved it more to the center so the lump was at least symmetrically positioned and opened the door.

"Polly, what is going on? You had no right to bring German into this mess with you. So it turns out that you're an industrial spy using innocent people to get what you want?"

"Pam, I am obviously not a spy. Really? I don't know why I said that. But your father is in on this with Binge, him and that Veronica lady. Don't you see? I wasn't going to tell them the truth."

"What is the truth, Polly? I believe I deserve to know. After all that I've done to try to help you."

"Yes, well, I appreciate the use of your laundry and the meal, but I have to go now."

"I thought you didn't have anywhere to go."

"If you must know, I've called Paul to come and get me."

"Paul," Pam frowned and looked thoughtful. "How is Paul going to get you, he doesn't have a flit and I doubt he even has the creds to rent one. I'll tell you what. Let me take you to Paul's. We can all discuss this together."

"I don't know. I already called him. He might be on his way here already."

"I'll call right now. I can borrow Dad's flit. Mine is getting an upgrade and won't be ready until the end of the week. Let's just call Paul on my comp and see what he says."

"Okay," Polly agreed reluctantly.

Paul answered on the first ring and Pam told him that they needed to get together to compare notes. Paul told her that he would wait for them at his apartment. When

Pam asked her father for the keys to his vehicle, Bob agreed with the caveat that she drop off Veronica at her hotel. Polly was feeling like a pawn in a game of chess where she didn't know all the rules, very like she played chess in real life.

Once they were airborne, Veronica turned to Polly who was seated alone in the back seat and said, "I must admit, you are smarter than you look. What did you do with the chip?"

"Thanks for the compliment, you really shouldn't have. I don't know where the chip is and if I did I wouldn't give it to you. You might want to learn to be more persuasive. Insults don't work for me."

"I can be very persuasive if that's what it takes. Are we bargaining?"

"No, and for one last time, I don't know what happened to it," Polly replied, anger taking control of her voice.

"Just to let you know," Veronica continued, "my partners are not patient and they are used to getting what they want."

"Is that a threat?"

"Take it as you will. But let me add this, you were the last one to have it so you are the one responsible for its return."

"It was injected into my body," Polly shrieked. Pam winced, but said nothing. "I didn't ask for it or asked to be involved in any of this. I was just trying to get to work."

"That may be, but it is of no consequence now. You can have the same deal that I offered Tom. Get the chip for me in the next 24-hours and I will see that you have enough money to live on for quite some time. We might even find a job for you with our organization."

"Look, lady, I have no money, no job, no transportation, no clothes other than what I have on my back, how could I possibly get you your damned chip?"

"As they say, not my problem. And let me just add, if you don't bring me the chip, you might also have no life."

"I already don't have a life," Polly exclaimed.

"You are still breathing, aren't you?" With that Veronica turned back around in her seat and dead silence reigned between the passengers for the rest of the trip to the hotel.

After dropping off Veronica, they were soon at Paul's tiny apartment seated on his wobbly kitchen chair and day bed. Paul sat on the rolling chair he used at his desk and listened as the women filled him in on the latest happenings. "Do you think this technology was invented at Binge?" Paul asked.

"It might have been. Binge is certainly interested in getting possession of it. But Dad's retired and Veronica isn't working for Binge and she also wants it. We can't be sure how many players are going after it at this point," Pam said.

"That could be a good thing," Polly decided. "They might get in each other's way and leave us alone."

"Oh, I don't think they are going to leave you alone," Pam smirked. "You were the one who lost it."

"Okay," Paul remarked, "that wasn't Polly's fault. She thought she was doing the right thing when she hid it. Putting it in the ice maker was a good idea on the surface of it. Right? It kept them from tracing us or finding it."

"Polly, do you think it could still be in the ice maker, somehow? Did you search everywhere? Could it still be there? After all, you were the only one who looked for it. And you were the last one to have it," Pam said.

"What are you saying Pam? Do you think that I am holding out on you and your father?"

"I don't like that tone," Pam cast an angry gaze toward the woman seated across from her. "I am the one who came to everyone's aid, remember?"

"Yes, I remember," Polly said.

Paul contemplated the two women. Sitting so close to each other their differences were striking. Pam presented a composed demeanor, a pretty portrait in pink dress and slippers. Her hair was neatly combed and her eyes were dramatically made up like she was going to a party. While Polly had made herself presentable, her hair tumbled chaotically around her shoulders as if she had forgotten to comb it. She wore little makeup, if any, and the combination of her high top hiking boots paired with a sundress was jarring. Still Polly was pretty in her own disheveled way and she held her own when climbing fences and outrunning guard dogs.

"Look, you two," Paul said, "we need to work together. I believe Polly. If what you told me is true, it sounds like it is her life on the line here."

"You think they would kill me?" Polly gasped making her chair wobble.

"I'm sure they would just torture you," Pam said leaning back on her arms. "What would be the point of killing you?"

"Comforting," Paul gave Pam a dark look.

Miffed, Pam sat upright and continued, "Well, what do we do? It seems to me the easiest solution to everyone's problem would be to find the chip and give it to my dad and let him handle Binge. Or do we plan to strike out on our own and bargain with it ourselves. Dangerous, but perhaps lucrative."

Paul pointed out, "I think that it is up to Polly. She is the one being threatened. What do you want to do Polly?"

"I want to stay here tonight, if that's okay with you Paul," she stuck out her lower lip obstinately. "Pam needs to get her father's flit back to him. Don't you Pam? Maybe we could meet in the morning and make a plan then."

Pam wriggled uncomfortably as her mind raced but could come up with no alternative. "Yes, that is probably best," she said searching Paul's face for emotion.

Staring at his lap, he didn't catch her gaze. He was struggling with the idea of Polly spending the night. Truth be told, he had never had a woman sleep over in his apartment. Even lovers would have a hard time sleeping on the day bed together, so someone would have to spend the night on the floor. Still, she had nowhere else to go. He could hardly send her back to Pam's house after finding out that Pam's father was after the chip, too.

"Let's meet for breakfast," Pam suggested. "I can pick you up and we can go to that place over by Margarita and Germán's place. They could join us or maybe we could check-in with them after."

"Sure," Paul agreed. Polly was quiet but nodded her assent.

"Good," Pam continued. "I'll be here around eight-thirty or nine."

They stood in the doorway watching Pam return to her parked flit. As it lifted into the grey of the dusk sky, Polly turned her face toward Paul's. "Do you have a T-shirt I could sleep in? I had better save this dress for going out. It's the only one I have."

"Sure," Paul said. "You can sleep on the daybed tonight. I have a sleeping bag in the closet." At least the floor is dry and smooth, he thought. It will be better than camping out on the damp, lumpy ground.

Chapter 14: Saving the World

By the time Tom and Margarita finished the pot of tea, they were speaking more civilly to each other. Still, Margarita didn't trust him and he knew it. The newly rehung kitchen screen door banged open and Germán tramped into the room, a backpack slung over one shoulder. Mouth agape, he stood motionlessly staring at his grandmother's visitor and the tea things on the table.

Gathering his wits with some effort, he went to his grandmother and kissed the top of her head. "Abuelita," he said tenderly before tersely nodding to Tom.

"Germán," Tom said gregariously, "your grandmother and I have been talking about saving the world. Apparently, I am most interested in the bit directly surrounding me. Your grandmother, on the other hand, wants to save the whole thing. At least until the sun swallows us all back up."

"My grandmother is a complicated person," Germán remarked.

"Yes, but considering the reality of the situation, what is truly possible," Tom continued, "when you think about an individual's longevity?"

"Longevity! Whose longevity are you talking about? Are you threating us?" Germán bristled.

"I was thinking about my longevity. Why would I threaten my partners?" Tom smiled and sarcastically twisted the ends of an imaginary long-handle mustache like the villain in a melodrama, a gesture lost on his deadpan audience. Germán was such a teenager. So passionate, so sure of what was right and what was wrong. Life is simple when you're young and know little.

"I am not your partner!" Germán adamantly shook his head in horror.

"You could be," Tom said, "and we might save the world, too."

"Hmmff," Margarita interjected her feelings on that topic. She addressed Germán. "I agreed to help only because they threatened his life, mijo. He says he must give them that chip in 24-hours or they will kill him. And you know that they would do it, Germán. Can we feed him to the maquiladora; the maquiladora where your mother died? This maquiladora now belongs to this Veronica."

"Grandma, do you know what is on that chip? It might be the technology that could save or destroy the world. It is more important than a single human life." Germán looked defiantly at Tom.

"Germán," Margarita frowned, "do not misjudge the importance of each life. We do not get to pick and choose the life we are responsible for sometimes." The good-humored jab at her grandson whose upbringing was foisted on her when his mother died and his father disappeared was lost on the boy, who scowled down at the floor, but Tom picked up on it.

Margarita continued speaking. "He says that he works temporary for Binge, but he did not know about the attack on our house. This Veronica, who owns the maquiladora, she says she wants to change her company for good. He wants it for her to do that and so she will not kill him. But he fears Binge would destroy it so they can continue polluting and they might kill him, too. Who knows? Life is cheap for the maquiladora. But it is Binge that chased us. I would not give it to either one, but I cannot let them kill someone either. Or hurt you, mijo."

"If you trust him, grandmother, you are taken in. You are a saint and an angel but perhaps you do not know a snake when you see one, living in the city so long now."

"A snake is only bad when it bites you," Margarita shot back, irritated by the condescending tone of this last bit. She loved him dearly, but sometimes he sassed her. At these times, she thought of how she had carried him away from the maquiladoras, away from the mutilated, dead body of his beautiful mother to relative safety and prosperity in the north. But here there was no custom, no family. The city's culture was bad for him.

"And to prevent a snake bite, stay away from snakes," Germán spat back with a meaningful look at Tom. "The future of everything is at stake. It can't be a choice between a maquiladora and Binge. I want another choice and I'm going to find one." Germán stormed through the doorway at the end of the dining room and into his bedroom, the room they had all traipsed through a few days ago running from the man in black. His broken door knob wiggled loosely in his hand when he twisted it. Once inside, he pulled over his desk chair to hold the door closed, and then he flopped down on the bed and closed his eyes. It was late morning and he already felt like he had put in a full day's work and then some. With the facility of youth, he fell instantly to sleep.

Margarita half apologized, "My grandson has more ideals than experience. He has great passion like his mother."

"Quite understandable after what you have been through," Tom assured her, "the damage to your window, disruption to your life, the fear and anxiety. You are owed compensation. I would be glad to look into that for you."

"Do not misunderstand me because I excuse my grandson's manners to a guest in my home. He sees more black and white in the world because he is young. He thinks evil is like an infection, one touch and it spreads into your whole body."

"So I am infected," Tom surmised.

"You have touched evil?" asked Margarita.

"Haven't we all?" Tom countered.

"There is a difference between naughty and evil," Margarita clarified. "There is a difference between holding on and brushing past it."

"Perhaps I am recovering from an extended touch at this point," Tom decided, "if you consider what is done for self-preservation as a kind of tarnish that can be wiped away instead of an incurable disease. I have not purposely tried to hurt anyone. As I told you, I operate an undercover quality control operation for multiple companies. At present, the needs of some of these companies have collided."

"Germán told me that you are an industrial spy. It must be a serious collision for you to be threatened with death," Margarita stated bluntly.

"One might call it serious. If all goes well, I could take early retirement. If it goes badly," he paused for dramatic effect, "I could take early retirement."

"Come back this evening when Germán is rested," Margarita sighed as if at the inevitable. The man seemed sincere about being in trouble, and she couldn't help but feel compassion for his situation. Still, Germán knew more about him that she did. "Perhaps after he sleeps, he will be willing to talk to you," she added.

"I'll do that," Tom replied, pushing away from the table and heading toward the door. Margarita followed. Lightning appeared in the north and a breeze stirred the tops of the few scrawny trees dotting the street. "It might actually rain," Tom commented as he passed through the door. Pausing at the top of the steps, he turned and said, "I'll be back around seven. Do you think Germán will be awake by then?"

"I don't think he will be able to sleep for long," Margarita assured him. "He is too agitated by this chip business. He will see you this evening."

Tom wondered where Germán had been. Could he have been out helping Polly? He rubbed his eyes wearily. What now? Was Germán keeping something to himself? Where do young people go? To work. To see friends. To a convenient store for a Koffee and a donut. The convenient store. Tom felt a flush of inspiration transfuse his body; it might still be at the convenient store. If Polly hid it there once, then she might just do it again. Maybe she never retrieved it at all. But how to find it?

His comp jangled and he checked the message. It was Mitchell.

"I have something that you are going to want to see," Mitchell said.

"Where are you?" asked Tom.

"At the office, I need to put in some hours."

An hour later, Tom and Mitchell sat next to each other at a table in the breakroom. "I have what you need," Mitchell said in a low voice.

"And what is that?" Tom asked blandly.

"I have a copy of that chip."

"You... have a copy," Tom repeated slowly as he tried to wrap his head around this new information.

"I know you want to give it to Veronica," Mitchell said. "But don't you think we should give Binge a chance to bid on it. It seems only fair all the way around."

"We would have more bargaining power if we had both copies," Tom suggested with a shrewd sideways glance at his companion. "Binge and Veronica both have the first half of the formula but Binge wants to suppress it and Veronica wants to use it. Binge doesn't want anyone to know about it. If Binge can't obtain all of the stray copies of the formula through us, they'll pursue a different avenue and they'll cover their tracks. We are tracks."

"What if we sell half to each and let them duke it out with each other?" Mitchell proposed.

"As bad as it may be; I see no other recourse than to sell to Binge. Veronica might threaten my life, but she will be going back to Tijuana soon. The only reason Binge hasn't permanently deleted me from the payroll already is because I promised them the purloined chip and any copies."

"You think you can find the original chip?" Mitchell asked without sympathy.

"I have someone on it," Tom answered. "We'll find it. Besides, that chip is only half of the formula. Veronica already has the other half. My operative lifted it directly from the Binge research and development lab. Let me see what you have on your copy."

Mitchell chuckled, "Would you know it if you saw it?" Then he scowled, "Seriously? You already gave Veronica half of the formula. Did you even make a copy?"

"No," Tom lied, "but Paul might have. We should get in touch with him."

"Did Paul steal the other half for you?" Mitchell asked suspiciously.

"Why do you ask?

"I need to know that I can trust you, and if there is other involvement, that I can trust them too," Mitchell retorted.

"Forget about Paul. There are two sides to this issue," Tom sighed resignedly, "are you looking to get rich or do you want to stay alive?" Without giving Mitchell a chance to answer, he continued, "both would of course be great, but in a pinch staying alive is my priority. To do that I might have to come up with chips for both Binge and Veronica."

"So what's your plan?" Mitchell asked after some thought.

"We check your chip first. If it is the one they want then we decide how to leverage it. But keep this a secret for now. If necessary we will have to find a scapegoat to buy some time."

"Could we throw Paul under the bus," Mitchell chuckled.

"So you are on board with the scapegoat idea?" Tom frowned.

"Sure, do you want to get some dinner? I'm starving. It's almost seven and I had an early lunch."

"Seven," Tom declared. "I have to be somewhere, but let's meet after. Why don't you grab dinner and then give me a call. We can go look for Paul together."

"Okay," Mitchell said with a meaningful gaze. "Don't forget that I'm the one with the chip." He pushed himself back from the table and ambled out of the room.

Tom followed but instead of returning to his cubicle he hurried downstairs, punching in an order for an auto-flit as he went. These were more available and less expensive than a flit-cab since there was no driver involved, even remotely. Auto-flits could be set to go to any of a number of pre-programmed designations. One strapped into a seat hanging from the bottom and the flit dragged you through the air avoiding obstacles using echolocation like a bat. It did not shield the passenger from the elements, but it was relatively safe and it was cheap. Also, there was an auto-flit stand in front of this complex.

It was a short distance by air to Margarita's place. The breeze created by the moving conveyance was pleasant if he kept his eyes closed, not only to keep the bugs and debris out of them but also to shield his view of the hair raising turns and leaps the drone did to avoid traffic. He unstrapped on the sidewalk in front of Margarita's house and leaned the auto-flit against the fence. Grandmother and grandson were seated next to each other on the porch swing. They watched him open the rickety wooden gate and come up the short walk to the steps. "Evening," he said.

"Germán will talk to you now," Margarita stated coolly. She gave Tom a long, hard, enigmatic look before rising and going to the front door. "Talk out here," she ordered as she opened the door. Mouth-watering aromas of hot grease and yeasty bread wafted out before she closed the door behind her.

How many days since I've had a decent meal, Tom thought. The past two days had been stale granola bars and that awful convenient store burrito he had to throw away.

"Grandma said I have to talk to you," Germán broke the silence. "That is the only reason I am doing it. If you are going to try to buy me then forget it. I don't want anything from you."

"I was hoping you could help me find Paul and Polly. You're mistaken about me, you know. I'm not some ogre out to take anything I can get. I just don't want anyone to get hurt," Tom laughed self-deprecatingly, "especially me."

Germán did not appreciate his sense of humor and showed it. "What do you want with them? I know that you tried to force Polly to go with you at the convenient store where my friend Ted works. He saw you."

"Your friend Ted? The butt-in-ski clerk?" Tom asked knitting his eyebrows together. "Look, I can see that you are a gallant young man, but I did not take Polly anywhere she didn't want to go. I gave them a place to stay for the night."

"So you admit it."

"Yes, of course," Tom rolled around his argument in his head before speaking in a quiet and firm voice, "Germán... what do you want out of life? We all want something. It is what keeps us going, right? But to have it, that would be totally different, what then? What do you want Germán? And what will you do once you have it?"

This kind of conversation made Germán uncomfortable. It reminded him of school and he squirmed in his seat. "Right now I want you to go away," he said defiantly.

"Look Germán, if you and your friends are in possession of that chip you are in a lot of danger. There are at least two major and as many minor players after it. Some of them will stop at nothing. I can't allow you and your grandmother to endanger yourselves. Get it for me and I will take care of it." Tom added, "in a way that will keep you out of harm."

"In a way that will line your pocket," Germán countered.

"At the moment my pocket has a big hole in it, this is true. But this is only partly about me. It is also about Polly. She was offered a salaried position with flit-pool access. What other opportunity does she have?"

Before Germán could answer, his grandmother opened the front door and leaned out. "Dinner is ready," she told them. "Mr. Tom can stay.

"Thank you. I would be delighted," Tom accepted. At least she didn't call me Uncle Tom, he thought. The swing jerked about as Germán rose to go in. Tom steadied the motion and slowly rose to his feet. "Germán, if you'd rather I didn't stay. I wouldn't want to make you uncomfortable."

"Hmmf," he snorted, "it's her food."

"Very gracious of you then," Tom said and followed him into the kitchen, where the table was set for three. The yeasty smell came from a platter of warm whole-grain pita bread drizzled with olive oil. Next to that was a large, ceramic bowl of steaming pinto beans laced with cilantro, onions and garlic and pickled jalapeno. A jicama, avocado, tomato salad and goat cheese completed the meal. "This looks wonderful," Tom exclaimed as he seated himself. "I can't remember when I last had a home cooked meal. You were kind to invite me," he beamed sincere appreciation.

"It is before the evening meal that we pray together as a family," Margarita said and she dropped her eyes as she folded her hands and bowed her head.

Chapter 15: Mitchell Plays All Sides

Back in the sky on the auto-flit after a wonderful meal, but little helpful information, Tom risked a slit-eye view of lightning forking to the ground in front of him. He made a mental note to bring goggles next time he took an auto-flit. Unusual dampness accompanied the wind. Stray gusts blew the drone sideways or backwards suddenly and if it had been rush hour he might have hit another vehicle. By now it was after 10:00. After all, he did stay and help with the dishes. It was the least he could do for the pleasure of their company and that homemade meal. Uncharacteristically thoughtful of me too, he ruminated, maybe he was getting old. Now he headed back to the office to meet with Mitchell over the Paul situation. Mitchell needed to feel that he could trust Tom and Paul. Tom knew for sure that he did not trust Mitchell. Still, if Mitchell had the chip, what choice did he have?

Things were becoming complicated. He needed a win-win-win plan, but how was anyone going to win with Binge destroying the last hope of cleaning up the world? What was the deal with Binge? Did they actually think that they could turn around a ship as big as planet Earth in a few years? Had they heard of the Titanic? Last minute turning doesn't work.

He had always worked with those in power and felt sorry for the underdog while being glad it wasn't him. Then he met Margarita and Germán. He started feeling that he could make a difference. For some reason he started wanting to make a difference, too.

The brightly lit parking lot held only a few flits this late in the evening. No people were about as Tom replaced the auto-flit in the stand and slotted his payment card through the reader. He was thinking about the Binge situation when he drew near to his cubicle and saw, standing like sentries in front of the opening, Mitchell and a man he thought he had seen before at Binge, an executive of some sort. The man was tall and slim with a full head of thick, white hair styled to appear rugged and slightly unkempt.

Mitchell introduced everyone. "Tom, this is Bob. He is interested in helping us find the missing chip."

"Terrific," Tom said, glancing surreptitiously at Mitchell. Mitchell knitted his eyebrows and shook his head almost imperceptibly. Tom took that to mean that Bob didn't know about the duplicate. Yet another player? He let Mitchell take the lead.

"Shall we go inside and talk to Tom for a minute, Bob?" Mitchell queried, leading the way to the elevator. "I could get you a snack or a beverage from the break room."

"No thank you. I just left a supper engagement. Too bad you weren't there. I had the company of three lovely ladies who had some interesting things to say."

"Good to know, good to know," Mitchell muttered rubbing his hands down his pant legs. They always got sweaty when he was in situations like this. Perhaps a bit of sugar would pick him up. He'd only grabbed a convenient store sandwich to eat at his desk for supper since Tom had left him in the lurch. He meant to open the chip while he ate, but an online gaming group he played with was logged in and he never got back to the chip. "I'm going to grab a candy bar," he told the two men, "do you want anything Tom?"

"I'm good," he replied and took a side seat at one end of the long table. Bob sat down across from him, leaving the spot at the head of the table for Mitchell. "How do you know Mitch?" Tom asked.

"I used to be the CEO in charge of sales for Binge International. Mitch worked on a few special assignments for me here in the States. Recently he contacted me about an interesting discovery."

"What discovery might that be?"

"Perhaps we should let Mitch tell us when he gets back."

At that moment, Mitchell sauntered back into the room munching a peanut caramel candy bar. There was a bag of pretzels stuffed into his jacket pocket. He plopped into the vacant chair between the two men, leaned back with exaggerated ease and smiled. "Have to keep my blood sugar level," he stated. "Now what were we discussing, Bob?"

"You have a chip that I am interested in obtaining," Bob answered. He gave the obese man a look and then clarified. "Not the kind that you eat."

Mitchell shrugged. He had learned to ignore rude comments by people who thought they were better than him. He was about to show this little group who was really in charge. "There seems to be a lot of interest in this chip. Are you asking for yourself or for Binge?"

"I have retired from Binge. I am in venture capital now. This is an investment opportunity."

"It truly is," Mitchell laughed, exhibiting the contents of his mouth. Tom turned his face away.

After a moment, he looked back toward the sprawling heap of a man sitting at the head of the table and said, "Please catch me up, Mitchell. What exactly do you have? Are you in possession of this chip?"

"I believe I am," Mitchell managed to mouth through his last bite of candy. "And Tom, Bob here is willing to make it worth my while. Shall we take a look at it?" They followed Mitchell to the chip reader that he kept in his cubicle. Mitchell made copies of everything that passed by his desk, as well as anything else of interest that he could get his hands on.

Neither men were scientists, but they knew what they were looking for. Mitchell's copy might very well be the real thing. Before he inserted it into the reader Tom stopped him. "We should take this to Veronica. I won't be able to tell if it's real. What about you two? It could be a fake cure for cancer as far as I would know." He gave Mitchell a meaningful glance.

"You have a good point. So you also know Veronica," Bob said with interest. "We shouldn't be too hasty about going to Veronica," he continued, "Veronica has henchmen that could take it and then dispose of us just like that." He snapped his nicely manicured fingers. It is what he would have done when he was in charge at Binge.

"She might dispose of us if she doesn't get what she wants," Tom agreed. "Her husband laundered money for the cartels. I'm pretty sure that she is still on good terms with them. But she is honest in her way. I think she would compensate us."

"You know a lot about her. Are you working for her?" Bob queried, his eyes searching Tom's face.

"I work for the highest bidder, Bob," Tom answered frankly.

"Now what," he thought. He had the copy that he had made before giving the first chip to Veronica. If this was the other half, then Veronica and the original inventors would be the only ones in possession of the complete formula. Had the inventors disappeared to a tropical island paradise or to an unmarked grave? Somehow it seemed a bad idea to let Mitchell and Bob know that he also had the first half of the formula they were missing.

Unlike the first part of the formula which was created in the Binge laboratories, the second part was strictly garage outsourced. Binge had put a stop to the tests when they realized the potential of the new energy source. It was Binge's parent company, Omni Oil and Gas, or OOG who had made the call. Keep it in your back pocket, they told Binge and get rid of the developers after you secure their research. If the world was going to be saved, it would be saved on their terms after they made a windfall from the remaining fossil fuels.

"So how do you intend to use this," Tom asked Bob. "Even if this is the correct formula, it's incomplete. It clearly references previous chemical equations. Unless you have a line on the scientists who created it, what good does it do you?"

"It does one very little good as it is, you are right. I am hoping to arrange a buyer. Of course, something this valuable will command a high price. There will be plenty for all of us. For Mitch and me anyway, I am not sure what you bring to the table, Tom. Mitchell, just why were we waiting for Tom?"

"Tom knows where the original is. Our piece will be more valuable if it is the only one."

"Polly," Bob said to everyone's surprise. "I should have locked her in her room."

"Mitchell, could I speak to you in private outside? Bob, do you mind waiting for us in the conference room." Once in the hall, he turned angrily to Mitchell. "Why did you bring him into this? What purpose could it serve?"

"I work for him," Mitchell answered. "I'm like a double agent."

"So you work for Binge and you work for Bob and you work for me. That's a triple agent. Who don't you work for?"

"I don't work for Veronica," he paused dramatically, "yet."

Tom squirmed uncomfortably and hoped that Mitchell didn't notice. He began to think that Veronica was the simplest and most sincere of the lot. He certainly didn't want Mitchell or Bob preying on her. He found her first. "So what is your plan? What is Bob supposed to do?"

"He is buying the copy if you can find the original. You and I then split 50-50."

"What is Bob going to do with it?"

"You'll have to ask him. I don't care."

Tom rubbed his temples. He felt a migraine coming on. "I'm going to the Boss's office for a nap. It's been a long day. I'll call you later." He trudged off toward the back end of the building, stopping at the water fountain for some water to wash down the two headache pills he pulled out of his vest pocket. His boss's office was the only cool, dark place in the forever amber twilight of the building's interior.

Chapter 16: A Restless Night

"Are you asleep yet?" Polly pushed the covers down and pulled herself up higher onto the pillow. "Does it seem warm in here?"

"No more so than usual," Paul lay on the floor staring at the ceiling with his hands cupping the back of his head. This was the first time he had really observed his surroundings. Popcorn texture in the low ceiling trapped every dirty bit that had floated in the air for the last decade, adding an overall dingy vibe to the cramped accommodations. The furniture appeared to have been rejected by a second-hand store. From this angle, he observed that one of the legs of his chair was held together with a splint of wood and twine. His table was scarred and gouged and leveled with bits of folded paper. The kitchen looked like it hadn't been cleaned in weeks, but then that was pretty much true. At least he had visited the laundry recently so he had clean sheets to put on the daybed before Polly tucked in.

"You would have fared better at Pam's place," Paul remarked. "Maybe we can figure out someplace better for you to stay tomorrow."

"It isn't your problem," Polly replied. "I'm sorry to put you out like this. I really don't mind taking the floor."

"I like the floor," Paul lied.

Polly smiled.

"What do you think happened to the chip?"

"If I knew I could buy my way off your hands," she said.

"Hey, really, I don't mind you staying. I just wish I had a better place to offer you."

"Paul," she ventured.

"Yes?"

"I guess it isn't any of my business, but...you and Pam. I don't think you should be worried about impressing her so much. You have tons of potential. You have a college degree and you're very good with technical things. If she can't appreciate that, she isn't the one for you. That's all."

"I have a degree in math. It's pretty much worthless unless I apply it to an industrial use. Companies want applied science and all my experience is theoretical. Great for coming up with the next breakthrough idea, but those are few and far between and I haven't had one. That's why I'm taking tech classes. I figured I could work for Binge in research and development. You know, work my way up. You can't blame Pam for dumping a loser. You've seen what she's used to."

"Don't call yourself that," Polly turned onto her side to look down at him, but he continued to stare at the ceiling. "You are anything but. You are my knight in shining armor." Embarrassed silence followed before Paul spoke up to change the subject.

"We should get some sleep. Tomorrow let's go back to that store and talk to the clerk. Maybe he found the chip. If we could get that chip we could barter it for what we both want."

I wonder what that is, thought Polly and she turned onto her side facing the wall. Neither one found it easy to fall asleep. They both lay silently thinking. Everything had changed. They would rise and wash up and drink coffee substitute and eat breakfast, but that would be the end of the familiar. Polly would not head off to work answering questions and smiling at customers and Paul would not worry about passing his skills test so he could get a decent job and make something out of himself. Their paths had been permanently altered and the future no longer seemed apparent. How different might it have been if that store had been stocked with duct tape and Paul had fixed the crosswalk? Polly would have made it to work and Paul to his class, but would that have been much better?

When Pam got back home her father was on the couch nursing a scotch and soda. He stared out at the view of colored lights reflecting off the surface of the water. "Oh, good, you're back. Come sit with me for a minute I want to talk to you. Do you want something to drink? There is some of that Pinot left in the fridge."

"No thanks," she said suspiciously. "This is a surprise. I can't remember you ever waiting up for me to get home when I was a teenager."

"Well, you're all grown up now aren't you? And you turned out all right."

"Thanks Dad," she sat down next to him. She turned out fine thanks to her nanny, teachers and the maid looking after her. Her dad had taught her an invaluable lesson though. Never say anything you don't have to. She held her tongue and waited.

"I haven't been completely honest with you," he continued. She was hardly surprised by his confession. "I am not exactly retired. I made some unfortunate investments and entailed some debt. You were not a cheap child to bring up, you know," he added, deftly shifting the blame. "So Binge has given me an opportunity to get back what I lost and then some if I come through for them regarding this chip deal."

"You want me to help you get the chip," she stated flatly.

"You don't need to get it, but if you could find out where it is," he paused, letting the ice cubes in his glass clink together before taking a sip. "Binge has deep investments in oil and uranium. This new technology has the potential to change the entire energy industry and the power structure of corporations in this country. And it isn't only Binge; our government is concerned as well. Third world countries could become independent of US aid and then who knows what might happen. That flit you drive, the clothes you wear, even your comp are affordable because of labor and materials generated by other countries, most of them poor with plenty of cheap labor. Because we are on top, we can import all those things at a reasonable cost. If our position should change, *your position* in the world would change also."

He paused. He had educated her at the best schools and she wasn't stupid. She was his daughter after all and probably already knew all this. "I know you are into bleeding heart stuff, helping the less fortunate, going into schools to tutor, which is all fine and dandy, but think about if the tables were turned, if you were the one needing help. I don't want that for you."

"I already said that I would help find the chip. I have been helping Paul and Polly for the last two days. If your Binge buddies hadn't chased them away, Paul would have the chip right now. And Polly would still be here if Veronica hadn't scared her off," instead of with Paul she thought. "Anyway, I'm having breakfast with them in the morning and we are going to figure out what happened to it after Polly hid it in the ice machine. You already know that she couldn't find it when she went back there the next day."

"Yes, yes, that's good. But what I am trying to tell you Sweetheart is that Binge doesn't want the chip per se. They want it destroyed or at least buried. That technology could change the status quo. It could change how *we* live."

"Oh," Pam suddenly understood, feeling dense that it had taken this long for her to see what was going on. "Oh, Dad, you can't really be helping them do this can you? Are you that broke? Have you been outside lately? The air is nearly unbreathable. Traffic is literally impassable. No matter how much money you might lose, you can't really want to help them destroy the world."

"It's the world or our lives. And yes, I put us before everything."

"We still have to live in this world."

"I'll tell you what. Find that chip and Binge will give us enough money to move to wherever we want to go. We could go someplace remote if you like, just the two of us. You always complained that I never had time for you. Well, I will finally have all the time you want. We could fish and play tennis all day long if you like, fishing for me and tennis for you. What do you say?"

She looked into his eyes, but they were focused on a future that did not exist. He never did look her in the eye, she realized, even when she was a little girl. She loved her father in spite of everything, but she didn't want to spend her future with him. She was certain that he felt the same way. What could she say? That there wouldn't be any fish anymore, that there wouldn't be any place to go that wasn't contaminated by human pollution beyond remediation. If she did that, he might turn on her. She wasn't at all sure how deeply his paternal bond went, but she guessed about skin deep. She decide to do what he had taught her to do, don't give anything away.

"And what about Veronica? What is her play?"

"I was trying to figure that out. I'm not sure. If she gets to the chip before us we'll deal with her then. So you're in. You're going to help me?"

"I'll do what I can," she said, giving him a peck on the cheek. She rose from the sofa and headed upstairs.

"Oh, by the way, I'm going back out for a while. An associate I'm thinking of doing business with might need a few drinks to loosen up and give me information than he might not have been forthcoming with so far."

With a concerned expression, she turned to look back at her dad. "Good luck with that." She paused and then added, "Please take a flit cab home. You've already had a few drinks."

Chapter 17: Until Tomorrow

Back in her hotel room Veronica could not rest. Born to parents who both worked but still came up short on the rent more times than she liked to remember, she resented those who had it easy. This Bob and Pam had it easy, just a couple of Binge shills. Not so easy for her. It seemed like from the moment she was born she was struggling to get to the place she was now.

Her best option for future financial security in high school was cosmetology. It was either that or flit mechanic. There she discovered she had a knack for nail design, so she worked her way through community college and university painting amazing nails by appointment only.

Upon graduation her best job offers had been as a secretary for either a real estate agent or for the CEO of Teller Enterprises. She took the latter. One thing led to another and before the end of her second year in that position she was promoted to wife and potentially owner should something happen to her husband. He had not been an easy husband. It was a rocky ten years. Now that he was dead and she was rich, she wanted life to be easy for a change, and meaningful.

So when she had a chance to make something of herself, a mark in history even, she wasn't about to allow some over-the-hill businessman get in her way. She wasn't where she was by being dumb. There was more going on here, more than just a misplaced chip. Why was Polly reluctant to turn it over? She had certainly been offered hefty compensation. And what was Bob's angle? When he contacted her in California he said he wanted to create a partnership to manufacture a revolutionary new product in her newly acquired maquiladoras. He needed financial backing. She was furious when she found out that he didn't have the chip in his possession and that he was colluding with Binge Inc., her rival.

Polly was the key to everything. If she didn't have the chip then she knew where it was. There was no way that she lost it. If she didn't know what was on it until now, she did know that it was valuable, otherwise Binge wouldn't have sent their goons after her. No one was so stupid as to think that a receptionist's service was worth that much trouble. Bob and his daughter were either hoping to gain her confidence so she would hand it over to them or they thought that she would eventually lead them to it. So she needed to steer Polly away from them and into her own helping hands. She picked up her comp to give Pam a friendly call.

"Veronica?" Pam answered. "Did you make it back to your room alright?"

"Oh, yes, of course, sorry to bother you. I hope you weren't already in bed."

"No, I was reading. I'm taking graduate classes, a seminar course this semester. It's pretty dry, so I'm glad to give it a break. What can I do for you?"

"Lucky you. I didn't make it to graduate school," the slightest bitterness tinged her voice. "I called to see what your plans are for breakfast. Maybe you and I could grab a bite, my treat. I don't know where the locals go in this town and I'm tired of the same bland hotel restaurant food."

"Well, actually, I was planning to take a couple of friends of mine to breakfast."

"Oh, I would be happy to buy everyone breakfast. You know, I hope that we can be friends. Your father and I are planning to work together and I would like to get to know you better."

"I hadn't realized you and Dad were that close. Tonight was the first I heard about this new business venture," Pam disclosed touchily.

"Probably better let your father fill you in on the details. I didn't know that he hadn't already. So about breakfast, do you want to pick me up or shall I come by your place and get you?"

"I guess I could pick you up at your hotel. I'll be there sometime around nine. I'm stopping by Paul's first. Polly is staying there and I told them we would all get together at breakfast."

"Oh, so I get to meet Polly's boyfriend."

"He isn't Polly's boyfriend," Pam snapped. She caught herself and added, "He's doing her a favor is all. What's your room number? Shall I come up and get you?"

"I'll come down to the lobby and wait for you in the coffee shop. I appreciate you letting me tag along. I hope I'm not getting in the way of a threesome."

"You're not," Pam assured her brusquely. "I'll see you a little after 9."

"I'll look forward to it."

Veronica chuckled to herself as she laid her comp on the coffee table and headed off to take a long, hot shower or maybe a cold one to offset the heat. The heat and gritty humidity seemed to follow you inside, and then there was the storm that never made it past the horizon. Before stepping into the shower, she set her bedside alarm clock to 7:00 AM in anticipation of an early rising.

§

It was the wee hours of the morning when Tom emerged from Binge Westside. A slight breeze from the north moved limp, humid air through his shaggy head of salt and pepper hair. In the distance he heard rumbling. Lightning forked across the horizon and he decided not to take the drone again. He was standing at the curb lost in thought when Bob and Mitchell appeared having come from Dempsey's Dive a few blocks down the street.

"Oh Tom, I'm glad you're here," Bob effused, swaying slightly. "Mitchell here says that you know someone close to Polly who might help us find her."

"I might," Tom shot Mitchell an irritated look wondering what the two of them had been doing besides drinking. Bob was probably pumping him for information.

"We'd like for you to look for her tonight," he added.

Tom blanched. He felt protective of Polly for some reason and he was pretty sure that she would be with Paul. He definitely had to protect Paul for his own sake.

"Weather is acting strangely," Tom pointed out. They all looked at the lightning that illuminated the horizon. "I better wait until daylight."

"That storm has been threatening since the beginning of autumn," Bob said. "There isn't enough ice left in the Artic to force cool air down this far south. Need that cold air before this humidity will turn into rain."

"Yeah, I think I heard something about that in elementary school," Tom noted acidly.

"Can I give you a lift?" Bob asked, pointedly turning away from Tom. Mitchell shook his head no.

"I need to follow up on a few leads," Tom addressed Bob who slowly turned back toward him. "I might be able to obtain what you are looking for more quickly if I had transportation." He stared down at the pavement thinking. "Do you have any contacts here at Binge? Maybe in transportation? I'd need a heavy duty flit in case the weather gets worse. And," he added looking up, "I need to go on my own."

"If you can fly a helicopter you can borrow mine," Bob slurred. "I have time lease access to choppers at the heliport behind this building."

"I served in the Air Force," Tom said, "helicopter evac. I can stay here tonight and leave first thing in the morning."

"Then I will expect to hear from you tomorrow evening. Perhaps we can take care of business over dinner at my club. I will bring someone who can verify what is on the chip," Bob proclaimed gregariously.

"I'll take good care of your helicopter," Tom assured him. Tomorrow evening at dinner was when he was to meet up with Veronica and give her the second chip, but he didn't mention this to Bob.

"It's not mine," Bob lifted one side of his mouth in a half-smile. "Don't think I would lend you anything that belonged to me personally. Anything happens, I'll say you stole my card."

"You're all heart," Tom remarked, taking the plastic rectangle Bob pulled from his wallet.

A gust of wind nearly ripped it form his hand. The heavy air blew hot one minute and cold the next much like this investigation. It all depended on direction. Tom closed his fingers over the card and shoved it into his back pocket.

Chapter 18: The Storm Breaks

Polly slept lightly. Just after midnight she rose from the daybed and quietly slipped into the bathroom with her dress in tow. When she came out Paul was awake. "What are you doing?" he asked.

"Oh, you startled me," she exclaimed, stopping mid-step to look down at the young man still lying supine on the floor. "I'm going home. I need to get my things. I need to figure out what to do and I can't live my life going from house to house sleeping wherever."

"You aren't afraid of Binge?"

"I was afraid that they would take away my life, my livelihood, my home. Guess what? They already did. I have nothing to lose anymore. I might as well use up the rest of my rent while I try to decide what to do with the rest of my life."

"How will you get there?"

"I can walk. Take a bus if I can find one. It's the middle of the night, the one time when it might be possible to get across the streets."

"I can't let you go by yourself. Give me a minute and I'll go with you."

"You don't have to do that Paul. Besides, you have to be here for Pam to pick you up for breakfast. I don't want to interfere with your life any more than I already have."

Paul was silent while he thought about breakfast with Pam. He was looking forward to seeing her, but he would like to see her from a position of power. He would rather be picking her up for breakfast and taking her out. She would never look twice at him until he could show her that he was a good catch. Although, thinking of relationships in that way reminded him of fishing and that resulted in being eaten or mounted and hung over the fireplace. It was the undersized ones that were thrown back and lived to see another day.

Polly moved toward the door to let herself out. "Wait," yelled Paul, "just wait until I get my pants and shoes on, will you? I volunteered to help and the job isn't done."

"I'm sorry I'm a job to you," Polly muttered under her breath.

If Paul heard, he didn't let on. He rummaged through his closet for his canvas messenger bag to hold a flashlight, communication device, and other urban survival essentials. Just in case. He slung it over one shoulder. "I'm ready," he proclaimed.

They walked by the side of the residential street in silence for a while before Paul spoke up. "Polly I know that you are hiding something. I wish you would trust me. I *am* on your side."

Polly looked at him surprised and nervous. "What is it you think I'm hiding?"

"I know that the chip has to stay cool or it will send out a locating signal. I know that if it had sent out a locating signal already nobody would still be interested in you."

She silently apprised the lanky man strolling beside her before speaking. "Okay, you're right," she said, deciding to trust him. She needed to trust someone. "I moved the chip when we went back to the convenient store with Tom. It's in the ice cream freezer. I put it there when I picked out the ice cream Tom bought me for breakfast."

Paul ran his hands through his hair. He had forgotten to put on his hat in his rush to get dressed before Polly took off without him. "Okay, okay. Listen Polly, we have to go there and get it. Someone from Binge or whoever is working against them is going to find it if we don't move it. The convenient store and you are their only two leads."

"I want to go home. I'm tired and I want to change clothes," Polly insisted.

"I know you do," Paul placated. "But Polly, do you want Binge to get that chip? Or Veronica? How do you think Germán would feel if the maquiladoras profit from this technology? I don't see that we have any other choice."

"I thought you wanted to give it to Tom. Isn't that your job?" Sarcasm sharpened Polly's tone.

"I did, but I don't anymore. I don't care about my job with Tom."

"That doesn't make sense. Why would you change how you feel all of a sudden? Are you doing this for Pam?"

"I don't even know what Pam wants. She lives with Bob now and if he gets the chip what then? Honestly, I don't know if we can trust Pam."

Polly's face relaxed into a tiny smile that Paul missed because he was looking at the skyline. She was surprised that Paul's words gave her comfort and pleasure. After all Pam had been nice to her and had tried to help her. Pam was not the same as her father even if she did live with him. And Pam was helping Germán.

Inky red-tinged blackness lit up orange from forked lightning off to the northwest. A cool breeze blew across their heat-flushed faces and Polly looked up too. As they both stared into the darkness around them another streak of lightning lit the sky, but this time it was accompanied by a peal of thunder.

"Gosh," Polly exclaimed. "Do you think that it really might rain?"

"I think it actually might," Paul confirmed. "Well, what do you want to do? Go to your place, back to my place or take our chances that we aren't made of sugar and head for the convenient store?"

"I am definitely not that sweet. Of course we're going to the convenient store," Polly replied. "We might as well. Neither one of us has any sense when it comes to doing the right thing. How come we got stuck with a conscience?"

"We're not the only ones," Paul remarked drily. "Margarita and Germán seem to know the difference between right and wrong. And" he added thoughtfully, "I'm not sure about Pam. She might be all right after all is said and done."

As they altered their route and headed in the direction of the store, it started to sprinkle. At first the moisture felt cool and refreshing after the days of heat and humidity, but then it began to rain in earnest. Paul counted the seconds between lightning sightings and thunder claps. They were getting closer together.

"If we're struck by lightning, we won't be able to save the world," he pointed out.

"True," Polly agreed, "and I'm getting soaked." Steady, gentle rain spattered down driven by a cool breeze out of the north.

"Yeah, the one time I leave my hat at home I could really use it." Streaky locks of sun-bleached hair funneled the light rain into his eyes and down his cheeks onto his T-shirt adding moisture to his sweat. Polly's longer locks clung to her shoulders and down her back doing nothing to shield her from the chilly, wind-driven sting of the raindrops.

After a particularly loud Earth-shattering clap of thunder, Polly remarked. "This is dangerous, Paul. We have to find shelter. How far is the store?"

"Still several more blocks, but I don't think we have a choice. There aren't any other public shelters closer, and my apartment is at least as far if not farther."

"Well, let's hurry," she said, walking faster. A lightning bolt struck a tree just a block in front of them. The ground shook and Polly literally jumped, splashing water as she landed. It was deafening. All the hairs on their bodies stood up and adrenalin rushed through their veins. She grabbed Paul's arm and pressed her body against his. He encircled her with his other arm, pulling her close for a few moments as a branch split off a live oak tree and fell crashing to the pavement. She pushed her face into his chest and he felt her trembling. In spite of the rain and the cold, they stood like that a few moments longer.

Pulling away, she tilted her face to look up into his. Rain blurred her vision and she had trouble keeping her eyes open, but she saw that he had his closed. When he opened them their eyes met. They stood transfixed, enclosed in the momentary warmth of each other's arms until another clap of thunder brought them back to their senses.

"Come on," Paul said, taking her hand and dragging her forward. "I just hope they're open for a change."

"Oh, Paul," Polly asked wide-eyed in spite of the now torrential rain, "what if they aren't?"

"We can't always have bad luck," he answered. "Besides, I have a feeling that our luck is going to change."

Toes squished inside water-logged shoes. There was no use in avoiding the puddles even if they could. The sky broke open above them and rain seemed intent on driving them backward, but they leaned forward into it and trudged on. It stung Polly's cheeks and bare arms and legs that were already covered in cuts and bruises.

Finally, Paul said, "I think I see it up there. Do you see the lights?"

"I guess so," Polly answered, squinting.

"Let's hurry," Paul urged.

"Oh, I thought I'd take my time. You know, enjoy the journey."

"Smart aleck, you better be careful. There's a creek behind this store that I could drown you in. I bet it has water in it with all this rain."

"What? That ditch I saw the other evening? That's a creek? I thought it was an open sewer."

"That's just what it's used for."

A vein of white lightning traced a jagged line in front of them followed by an immediate clap of thunder. "That's close," Paul remarked. "Look, that's the store up ahead." Then the lights of the entire street went out and they were left in utter darkness. They turned in a circle to see the extent of the affected area. It was dark as far as they could see, not the usual colorless gray but inky black. Behind the building they saw in front of them as their eyes adjusted to the new dark was the sound of rushing water.

This time it was Polly who grabbed Paul's hand and began dragging him toward the entrance to the store. The parking lot had filled with shallow puddles that they splashed through splattering cold, muddy water onto their legs.

Polly pounded on the door of the building and then pressed her face to the glass to see in. It was impossible to see anything in the complete darkness of the storm and power outage. When lightning lit up the sky she thought she noticed movement inside and began to pound harder. A beam of light struck her face.

The door opened and they were ushered in by the clerk that had been there the day Tom had brought Polly and Paul to find the chip. "Thank goodness you're open," Polly gushed.

"Not really open," the clerk said, shining the flashlight on them, "but I can't let you two drown, I guess. Don't I know you?"

"We were here yesterday," Paul said.

"That's right. You're the girl that man was bothering out in the parking lot," the clerk realized. "You used the comp in the office."

"Thanks for coming to our aid," Polly said, "again."

"Anytime," the clerk smiled at her then nodded to Paul. "You two not know about the flash flood warnings? This store is in the flood plain. Owner called me in to put sandbags by the doors. They aren't much use though if the water gets really high."

"What about the ice cream with the power out?" Polly cried.

"The ice cream? You're worried about the ice cream?" The clerk observed the dripping, shivering girl with disbelief. "That's right. You had to have ice cream the last time you were here."

"No!" Polly exclaimed trying to recover from her slip, "I mean yes, I hate to see ice cream go to waste."

The glass doors of the convenient store rattled from the ferocity of the wind. Rain slammed against the windows. "Help me with these bags, would you," asked the clerk. "Grab one of those flashlights off the shelf and some batteries."

"Polly you dry off, the bags are too heavy for you to lift," Paul said.

The clerk took a long look at the trembling, wet rag of a girl before him. "Take some clothes off the rack," he suggested. "They're novelty clothes and tourist garbage but at least they're dry."

"Thanks," Polly said with a shy smile that Paul found irritating for some reason.

When Polly came out of the back room where the employee bathroom was located, she wore an embroidered dress of pastel blue, light-weight muslin overlaid with a soft, gray fleece hoodie. On the back of the hoodie were the glitter embedded words, Austin and Music Capital of the World. She looked like a down-on-the-ropes country and western singer. Her damp hair was curling fetchingly across her shoulders. A pair of rhinestone bedazzled flip-flops had replaced the dirty, wet boots she had worn for the past two days. If she tried, she couldn't have look more innocent and adorable in the eyes of her two companions.

The store clerk projected a welcoming smile to her from across the room where he was sitting on a stool next to Paul, who sat on a sandbag. "You look amazing," he said. She beamed. "Take my chair," he offered getting up and bowing. Paul glared at her and she gave him a frown.

"At least someone is a gentleman," she commented.

"You might notice that I don't have a chair to give up," Paul pointed out. "You are welcome to share my floor."

"I'll get a chair from the office," Polly said.

"Definitely more comfortable. I should have thought of that," the clerk agreed dashing off in front of her to retrieve it.

"Well, it looks like you made a conquest," Paul remarked coolly.

"What is your problem," asked Polly. "You should be happy that he let us in."

"We should have gone back to my place," Paul muttered.

"It was mostly your idea to come here," Polly remarked, miffed. "I think that it was a good idea. With the electricity off for who knows how long, that chip could start sending out a signal. This might be the only chance we have to retrieve it."

Paul had borrowed a dry T-shirt from the racks but was still wearing his wet jeans. His feet were bare because there were no flip flops in a size 14.

"Go ring out those wet pants and blot them dry with some towels. Maybe your mood will improve," Polly suggested.

"My mood is fine," Paul said grumpily and then headed toward the bathroom to dry out.

The store clerk, whose name was Ted, returned with a rolling chair and a small portable radio. "It's a NOAA emergency broadcasting radio," he explained to Polly. "It works on batteries but also has a crank generator. The owner of this place is a survival freak."

"Can't you just check your comp?"

"Well, yes, but I might as well save my battery juice. Who knows how long this storm will last."

"Are the sandbags part of his survival plan? Maybe he could have just located outside the flood zone."

"Yeah, this store has flooded before."

He switched on the radio and after tuning past some static hit upon the right channel. "This is a NOAA emergency broadcast," informed the mechanical voice from the radio. "A flash flood warning has been issued for the following counties." A long list of counties ensued. "If you are in any of these areas take shelter on high ground and do not try to cross rising or standing water. Heavy rain coming down 6 or more inches per hour is expected through the morning. Rain totals of up to 18 inches or higher could fall in some areas within the next 24-hours."

Ted switched off the radio. "It looks like we won't be opening the store today. Good thing there are more sandbags in the back room. When your boyfriend comes back from the powder room he can help me with them."

"He's not my boyfriend," Polly corrected.

"Oh, I see. Who is he, friend or family?"

"He isn't family," Polly said.

"So are you attached?" Ted queried.

"I am entirely unattached," Polly frowned down at the floor. "So unattached I might as well be floating out there in the torrent." Struggling with her emotions, she looked up at the clerk. Poor guy, she thought, none of this was his fault. "I'm sorry. I didn't mean to bring you down. I lost my job and my home a few days ago and I guess I'm feeling a bit sorry for myself right now. It has nothing to do with you and I shouldn't be laying it on you."

"Whoa," he exclaimed. "I'm sorry. Did it have anything to do with that man that was trying to get you into the cab in the parking lot yesterday?"

"Kind of," she confirmed.

Before Ted could pursue the conversation further, Paul appeared. He was still damp but no longer dripping wet. "I could use something hot to drink or alcoholic," he announced.

"Help me with some more sandbags first," Ted ordered. "It looks like we are in for a real flood. That creek in the back floods at the suggestion of rain."

Wind howled against the large picture windows at the front of the store causing the glass to shudder in the frames. Ted and Paul hurried to get sandbags from the storeroom. Polly patrolled the perimeter looking for leaks.

"Should we tape something over these windows?" She called to the men.

"I don't know what we could tape over them that would do any good. Besides, we only have scotch tape," Ted answered back.

"I thought your boss was a survivalist," Polly remarked. "Isn't duct tape what they use to seal gaps in windows and doors?"

"If it's toxic gas," Paul chimed in, "not water."

"Well they go nearly to the floor. If they break, not only water will be coming in, but also broken glass, wind, rain, who knows what else."

"She's right," Ted said. "Let's get some food and drink and hole up in the office. It's a few steps higher than the main floor and it has only that one window high up on the wall. We can still see out if we need to but it should be safer."

"How long is this storm going to last?" Paul asked, once they were supplied and comfortably ensconced in the office. "I heard you listening to that radio while I was in the restroom but I couldn't hear what was said."

"What time is it?" asked Polly. "Do you think Pam will try to pick you up for breakfast Paul?"

"It's six," Ted said looking at his comp. "It's been raining for three hours." He turned the radio on. "The following schools have canceled classes today as severe storms continue to pummel the area." A list of school districts and colleges followed and then areas where tornadoes were likely. "Storms are expected to continue through the day and into tomorrow fueled by gulf moisture and a slow moving cold front followed directly by a tropical storm off the coast of Mexico that just passed over the Yucatan peninsula and is reforming as Hurricane Katia.

"It's early to call her. I'm going to try to get some sleep. It's been a long night," Paul announced and poked around the room for some place comfortable. Polly found a couple of unused sandbags in one corner of the office where she plopped down pulling the hoodie over her head and closed her eyes. Ted staked out the padded rolling chair. Paul sat down on the floor next to Polly.

He must have nodded off, because he woke up with his head in Polly's lap. A hoody from the clothes rack in the store was draped over his upper body. When he stirred, Polly woke up too. Dim light came from the window high in the exterior wall. He checked his comp for the time and jumped when he saw that it was nine already.

"What time is it?" Polly asked.

"Nine," he answered. "I better call Pam." When he tapped in the number he got an unable to connect message. Water raged outside the building, but the walls stood solid since they were made of concrete blocks. "Wake up Ted. We should check on the front."

Polly gave the chair in which Ted was sleeping a little push and he opened his eyes. "What's happening?" He asked groggily.

"Come on. We're going to check out front. The window in here is too high up to see much," Polly explained.

"Yeah, Okay."

Polly led the way, exclaiming in alarm when her foot made a splash as she stepped down into the merchandise area of the little store. "We're flooding!" she cried and turned back toward the others.

"This store tends to flood," Ted reminded her, staring out at more than an inch of water spread across the floor. "It isn't bad yet, though. The sandbags aren't foolproof, you know, they just help keep the worst of it out."

This was not comforting for Polly to hear.

"Let's eat something," Paul chimed in to change the subject. "Does your boss keep a camp stove here? We should cook up some sausages since the electricity is out and they're probably going to go bad."

"He does," confirmed Ted. "I'll get the stove and you two can rummage around for food. We should eat those bananas by the cash register too. They don't last in the heat."

Polly began to shop, picking up an insulated lunch pail in which to put her items and then went to the ice cream freezer. She fished around underneath some quarts of ice cream in the far back corner then grabbed a Fudgesicle. She placed it and a small plastic baggy into her pail. "Want some ice cream," she called to the others. They both replied in the negative. When she turned around, Paul was standing behind her.

"What's that?" He asked suspiciously.

"A Fudgesicle," she answered.

"Not a good idea for breakfast," he remarked knowingly. "Why don't you wait until dinner? The freezer will probably stay cold enough for that long."

"I guess you're right, but in the situation we're in do you think it matters? It might be best to get it while I have the chance."

"You have a point. It's up to you after all."

Ted called from the office for them to bring the food. Paul grabbed a basket and filled it with milk, orange juice, sausages, a carton of eggs, bread and disposable plates, cups and cutlery. Polly added olive oil and butter to her lunch bag and followed him up the two steps into the hallway. On the office desk a camp stove was already turned on and a skillet sat on one of the burners. They put down their containers of food next to it. Polly offered to cook, but first she put the melting ice cream on a plate so she could eat it with a spoon while she stirred scrambled eggs and sausage together in the skillet. "Paul, would you mind to cut up a banana onto my ice cream? I forgot and I don't want to stop stirring these eggs or they'll stick."

"If I must," he said. "I can't believe you are eating ice cream before eggs."

"If I am going to cheat on my vow to avoid sugar, it must be chocolate and preferably in the form of ice cream. Today I feel like I could use the energy and if we don't make it through this ordeal then I don't want to go down thinking of cold, creamy chocolate with regret, I want to think of it with satisfaction. Besides, I don't think the ice cream is going to last very long without refrigeration."

When the food was ready, they all ate and drank in silence. With full bellies, they went to their previous areas and tried to fall asleep again. Only hunger and discomfort had awakened them from the fatigue of staying up all night in the first place, but now they could only lay still. The wind and the situation did not let their minds rest. Steady pounding rain and howling wind brutally whipped the exterior of the building keeping them on edge.

Polly was the first to give up trying to sleep. She tiptoed into the store to check the level of the water. It was full daylight outside although it was as dark as a full-moon lit night. Water sloshed against her ankles in a disturbing way. She made her way over to the large display windows to see how high it was in the parking lot. Shockingly, it didn't look like the parking lot anymore. Dirty brown water rushed to an unseen ocean by way of the shortest route. A large tree branch swam slowly into a car and they both began to move off toward the road or what was now a river. The force must have been terrific to push such heavy objects. The water outside was higher than the water in the store. She wasn't sure how high the building went before the windows started so it was difficult to gauge. Rain poured down onto the city as if it was a pool beneath a waterfall.

Turning back to alert the others, she saw them standing in the hallway at the top of the three steps leading down into the main part of the store. Polly addressed Ted, "your boss can't expect you to stay here in this. He will alert the authorities to send help won't he?"

"I doubt they have resources to airlift everybody who's stranded," Ted replied. "Maybe we should stock up the office."

"The office," Polly exclaimed in horror. "I am not going to get trapped in there by water with no way out. Is there a way to get up on the roof?"

"That would be a bad idea," Paul interjected. "Not only would we be exposed to the cold and the rain, but there is danger of lightning or blowing debris hitting us."

"I didn't mean go up there now," Polly said with a frown. "I mean is there a room that has access that we could hole up in. I'm not staying in a room that we can't get out of."

"It's a flat roof," Ted stated. "There isn't an attic. HVAC people use a ladder on the outside to climb up there. Don't worry, Polly. You would fit through that window in the office. I would get you out." He paused. "Now, since we're stuck here together with nothing else to do for now and I've rescued you twice, do you mind telling me what is going on. Why are you two here? Again. I don't believe that you were just strolling by when it started to rain. Not at almost three in the morning. Why was that man trying to get you into the taxi and why didn't you do anything about it?" This last was directed at Paul.

Chapter 19: Veronica and Pam Have Breakfast

Usually a rainy night made for great sleeping weather, but this storm was anything but peaceful. No gentle patter lulled the senses; instead, the rain beat against the tile roof like artillery fire. Safe and warm as she was, the storm could still touch her with sound. Howling wind and pummeling rain shredded sleep and left her tossing and turning.

Pam knew that it was low income families living in the flood plain where land prices were cheaper that she should worry about on a night like this. She had spent a summer working with a state senator on a campaign to buy up land in flood plains to repurpose into parks. Her father had indulged her naiveté, smiling over supper when she described their efforts and telling her that he was proud of her interest in government. Meanwhile, he had partnered with local builders to create a subdivision in an undeveloped area within the flood plain and made a tidy profit by selling all the units to unsuspecting people, most of them 2nd generation immigrants who thought they finally owned a piece of the American dream. That dream would turn out to be a nightmare if they couldn't afford flood insurance or they became trapped and drowned when the waters rose.

She was awake when her alarm sounded the next morning. She didn't know if she had slept. The rain hadn't let up. Watching the news on the wall screen in her bedroom while getting ready for her breakfast appointment with Paul, Polly and Veronica, she was glad that her flit was back from the repair shop. It would be difficult if not impossible to get a cab on a day like this. She almost called off the breakfast because of bad weather, but her desire to be the one to find the chip overcame her apprehension. She checked the time and was surprised by how late it was considering the darkness outside. Putting on jeans and a French sailor's T-shirt with a low boat neck and blue and white horizontal stripes, she pulled her hair back into a jaunty ponytail. It was no use trying to do anything nice with it on a day like this. If her dad was up, she hadn't seen him, so she left a note on the kitchen table.

In the mud room, she doffed a peacock blue London Fog rain coat and a pair of olive drab rubber boots. Thus stylishly attired she headed for the small heliport off to the side of the house where her flit sat next to her father's bigger one. For a minute, she thought of taking his, thinking it might fare better in the wind, but she didn't know what his plans were and didn't want him to have to drive hers.

The electric motor started up without hesitation and the flit rose easily through the rain. It was small but had a lot of horse power. Once in the air, there was only a little difficulty with veering from the occasional gusts of wind. The storm had settled into a steady rain. The wind of the night before had died down.

Water stood high in the parking lot in the middle of Paul's apartment complex. She revolved a few times looking for a place to land that wasn't inundated. Finally, she set down on top of the building. Highly illegal as it was to land on top of a building with no heliport, she figured she could get away with it on a day like this. Her four-seater fit nicely between two HVAC units leaving only enough space on one side for her to slip out.

Water splashed her rubber boots when she stepped down from her vehicle. She sloshed over to the roof access door, which she knew was never locked because Paul had broken the lock to tinker with the HVAC unit one evening when she was with him. He was a genius at fixing things. If only her father would give him a chance, he could be an asset to their new business. Maybe he could become successful enough to deserve her.

She smoothed back her wet, wind-blown hair before she knocked at his 2nd floor apartment door, hoping she didn't look like a drowned rat. There was no answer even when she knocked again more loudly. Where could he be in weather like this with no flit of his own? She peered through an opening in the drawn curtains, but the gloom inside was worse than outside. There was no sign of light or life. She thought of breaking a window to get in. She could tell him that it was like that when she got here. What if he was sick? Or worse, what if he was in there with Polly and too busy to answer? She could ask the manager to let her in, tell her it was an emergency, but what if she noticed the flit on the roof?

She checked her comp for signal but there were no bars. Come to think of it, there were no lights on at all in this area. Maybe they had evacuated the residents and he had no way to contact her. She liked this explanation best. It was late and she still had to pick up Veronica, so she gave up on Paul and returned to her flit. The wind picked up as she started to lift off and the flit pulled to the left. Her left skid dinged into the side of the HVAC unit. Bad luck for the residents, but if it was damaged, Paul could probably fix it.

The Regent Hotel had a large heliport for flit parking and valet service if you didn't want to park yourself. Pam did not wish to park herself on a day like this. She handed over the keys and the valet opened an umbrella to escort her into the covered portico. Once inside, she went to the coffee shop to look for Veronica.

The coffee shop was crowded. She wouldn't have been able to find a seat if Veronica hadn't wrangled a window booth. She was staring into the plate glass lost in thought when she saw Pam's reflection walking toward her.

"Hi. Where are the others?" Veronica asked.

"Paul wasn't at his apartment. I don't know what happened to him. With this weather I'm thinking that he might have gone out and then was unable to get back."

"And no Polly either I take it," she didn't try to hide her disappointment. "I was thinking we might have breakfast here, as sick of this place as I am. The concierge said flooding has closed down most of the town. Would you like some coffee or tea?"

"I'll order some coffee if it's real when the waiter comes by, thanks. Good idea. I've never seen so much rain. It doesn't let up."

"There's more moisture in the atmosphere because of evaporation caused by global warming; which underlines the importance of that chip getting into the right hands. I don't know what Binge wants to do with it, but I intend to change the world for the better," Veronica stated defiantly.

"The world may be tired of us changing it," Pam suggested.

"You think we should leave it as it is?" Veronica smiled humorlessly.

"Do you plan to include my father in your business of bettering the world?" Pam asked pointedly.

"If he has the chip," Veronica stated.

"And if he doesn't?"

"He's an investor, right? He wants his money to do his work. How interested is he in creating something new from the ground up? He seems a little long in the tooth. I see him as ready for an easy retirement," she hesitated, "but you, I might be interested in working with you."

"With me?" Pam was surprised, but as soon as the idea sank in it rolled around pleasantly in her mind. A waiter stopped at their table with a pot of ersatz coffee, filled the cups that were already on the table and then took their breakfast order.

Pam took a sip and sighed, "I miss real coffee. My dad used to get it for me when I was an undergraduate student. I made it every Saturday for my sorority."

"You would be able to buy yourself real coffee or whatever else you desire if we market this new product successfully. I could use someone like you. I like the way you handle yourself. You're educated. You apparently like helping people and your father told me that you speak Spanish. My factories are in Mexico on the border next to the United States. I need a vice-president to act as a representative and liaison between me, the workers and the government. If you bring me that chip, I will create an energy source that will end coal and oil dependency once and for all. How would you like to be responsible for stopping climate change?"

This Veronica is shrewd, thought Pam, her eyes traveling down to the table. She has very nearly enlisted me in her plan before I've had my second sip of coffee or whatever this is. I had better watch myself with her.

Veronica looked questioningly at her breakfast companion. "Perhaps if I told you my vision you would be less hesitant."

"By all means do," Pam perked up. "With this many people ahead of us, I doubt we will be getting our eggs and bacon any time soon."

Veronica observed the wet landscape barely visible through the foggy window. Her face floated superimposed, blurred and faded on top. She turned and drank some coffee before speaking.

"First, I will make cheap, clean energy to not only power my plants, but to sell. This will eventually replace all the old polluting modes of production. My energy plant will not only produce more power, but will actually clean the air as it does. If this power source is what I think it is, it will out compete so called clean electric energy too. There will be transition, of course, as industries must change and retool but in the end everyone will win."

"Sounds like a terrific dream," Pam agreed. "Tell me, what do you make in your present factories?"

"I own a franchise to make Dubois flits and various flit parts. We also have an apparel factory with its own shoe division. We created a new brand that will soon be a popular seller. It is already successful in Mexico and the Southern United States. I plan to launch it in major cities of the USA and Canada within the next two years." Veronica obviously relished talking about her empire.

"Extremely impressive," Pam admitted. "But just what would a vice-president for this company do? I have no expertise in any of those businesses other than that I drive a Dubois coup, a closed-cabin four-seater parked outside."

"I am aware of the model," Veronica replied coolly.

"You sound rich enough. Why go to all this bother for a patent that hasn't even been tested?"

"I believe I just told you why. I am certainly not going to change the world with car parts and clothing."

"Changing the world is that important to you?" Pam said. "I still don't see what I would be doing as a vice-president other than selling out my own father."

"Sometimes people are mistaken. It is a common human fault and we are all subject to it at some time in our life. I promise you that your father will not be hurt by my possession of the chip technology. Accept the vice-presidency and you can reward your father's help any way that you choose."

"And if I am not your vice-president?"

"Then it is every woman for herself, right? If you should get the chip before I do, we can negotiate."

This vice-president thing sounds bogus, Pam thought. What's to keep her from taking the chip? If we find it together, who is to say she won't forget about helping my dad and me?"

Veronica turned back to the view outside the window to give Pam space to think. A few minutes later a waiter brought their food and they tucked in, enjoying the food in silence. Rain poured down the window, which was only partially shielded by a deep casement with a jutting ridge across the top. The ridge angle created optimal passive solar benefit in the form of shade from the southern sun and on a day like this, it sheltered the window from most of the rain. All the big, progressive businesses had already started turning to more renewable and less polluting forms of energy use. This type of building was encouraged by recent law suits that put pressure on business to clean up its act. In fact, preventing such law suits against her companies was a compelling reason to find the chip and complete the design. She had already hired five top scientists who were standing by on call right now, each one an expert in the separate fields of computer programming, engineering, applied chemistry, applied biology and mathematics. If this woman sitting across from her could find that chip, then she would be happy to meet all her demands. She would be a fool not to take me up on my offer, thought Veronica.

Pam felt pressure to give Veronica an answer. "I don't see a problem with us working together," Pam said. I don't see many options, she thought. There is Binge on one side and the maquiladoras on the other and here I am stuck in the middle. Dad would tell me to play it by ear, so that is what I will do for now. No sense in choosing sides until push turns to shove.

The waiter brought their bill and Veronica signed it to her room. "I don't want to waste time, storm or not, where do you think Polly is?"

"So you are sure that she is the key," Pam stated.

"I am sure she has some information pertaining to the subject," Veronica replied.

"Then let's start at that convenience store she called me from," said Pam. "We can take my flit." They moved off to the concierge desk and asked for the valet, since his station was empty.

"I am sorry. There is no valet service at present. The national weather service has recommended all air traffic be grounded until noon." He added sarcastically, "Perhaps you haven't noticed the storm outside."

Both women thanked him with a dirty look and proceeded into the lounge area of the lobby. Veronica found an as yet unoccupied corner that boasted two high-back, padded chairs narrowly separated by a small table. "Will this do for..." she glanced down at the comp she carried in her right hand, "an hour-long wait?"

"Don't you have a suite here?" Pam inquired.

"I have one that I have been cooped up in for a week; at least this is a change. Shall I order some drinks brought to our little table here?"

"A Perrier with a slice of lime on the side would be nice," Pam said.

"I'll get two. Wait here until I return."

She already sounded like a boss or else always sounded like one, observed Pam as she watched her walk back into the restaurant with a confidence that belied the flip flop sandals, jeans and loose, semi-transparent muslin shirt. Suddenly there was a loud boom of thunder, the lights flickered then came back on. People shifted uncomfortably for a moment, but did not appear to worry that anything was amiss. Pam palmed her comp and Oodled Veronica Teller while she waited. It looked like the family owned a string of factories along the border; a few were flagged for human rights violations and unsafe working conditions. There was another earth shaking peal of thunder. Lights flickered again and then went out. The lobby was now lit only by comps. As people moved about, more alarmed now that the lights did not come directly back on, the light of the comps moved and flickered like giant fireflies. Pam wondered if Veronica would still manage to bring back two sparkling waters. She seemed like the type to demand what she wanted no matter the inconvenience.

Veronica did return about fifteen minutes later with two glasses trimmed with lemon wedges and a plate of cookies. "They were out of limes," she apologized.

"You are amazing," Pam approved, taking her glass. "So what is the plan, assuming that we work together?"

"You have to realize that without that chip we have nothing. I still have my factories, but I am afraid that you and your father will be left to take care of yourselves. I know that your father made some bad investments and needs this money to repay loans." She shrugged off Pam's astonishment. "I do my homework," she explained. "If we can patent this process and it works as well as my scientists think that it might, none of us will have to ever worry about money again."

"I'm listening," Pam slumped back into her chair.

"I think that Polly is the key to finding that chip. My detective has traced her steps from the moment she called an online doctor about an inflammation to her meeting with Tom Blanche. He is an industrial spy hired by Binge, but also an associate of one of the creators. When the two chips disappeared last month, Binge asked him to investigate the disappearance. Seems they were part of a design initially developed by two Binge scientists, a husband and wife team. When Binge suddenly defunded the project, they couldn't give it up and continued to work on it weekends at home in their free time. It was their pet project."

"Imagine their surprise to find out that Binge knew what they were doing. And they were even more surprised when a police raid removed their computers, personal notebooks and recorded discs. Promptly fired, they disappeared without a trace. The final genetic code and essential process information was not on any of the confiscated items."

"At first Binge executives nearly broke their arms patting themselves on the back for their quick action, thinking they had stopped the research before it amounted to anything, but then a dark cloud appeared." Veronica waved her hand in an arch to represent the cloud. "The oil and gas subsidiaries were not happy. They told Binge that the formula was still out there. It was up to Binge to get rid of it or at least bury it for the present. Binge was ordered to find it and destroy it if it couldn't be suppressed."

When Veronica stopped talking, Pam said, "so Binge will destroy it if they get it?"

"That is what I'm afraid of. I have hired a man to keep that from happening. He has two assets; one of them is called Mitchell and the other Paul."

"Paul!" Pam exclaimed. "Are you talking about my Paul?"

"I believe so," confirmed Veronica. "I am not sure what Polly's connection is to Paul. Maybe you could tell me."

"I wish I knew also," Pam acknowledged. "She certainly seems attached to him. Can an asset have an asset? I don't know. I thought I knew everything there is to know about Paul, but he has begun to surprise me."

"Not necessarily a bad thing in a boyfriend, I imagine," Veronica suggested. "I guess I should tell you that the last place that my detective saw Polly was at Paul's apartment. And that was yesterday evening after I left your place."

"She wanted to leave last night. She felt uncomfortable after being pumped for information about the chip by you and my Dad. I dropped her off there."

"That is very liberal of you, but letting her out of your sight was not so smart," Veronica pointed out.

"I had little choice in the matter. She called for Paul to come get her."

"I see," said Veronica. "This may be more difficult than I had hoped. I thought that you had the inside line on the Polly and Paul duo."

Pam grimaced before stating firmly. "I accept the position of Vice President and I will find that chip for us."

A waiter came by to remove their empty glasses. "Would you like another?" He asked.

"Shall we order a bottle of bubby to celebrate," Veronica asked her new VP. She ordered, then turned back to Pam. "Let's plan."

As they decided their next move, the rain tapered off to a steady light downpour. The waiter delivered a lukewarm bottle of local Brut in a bucket of half melted ice just as Veronica's comp buzzed. She checked to see who it was and frowned. "You'll have to drink that by yourself

I'm afraid. Something urgent has come up. I'll keep in touch." She smiled as she pocketed the comp and headed for the front doors of the hotel.

Left alone, Pam's mind wandered back to a date she'd had with the captain of the football team in high school. There had been a dance and he had invited her. Afterwards they got burgers at the local teen hangout where every girl there shot surreptitious, envious glances her way. She reveled in the glory and was walking on air by the time he brought her back to her door. Then he curtly said, "Well goodnight," and that was it. She was left mid-pucker. It turned out, he had broken up with his girlfriend the week before and she was a last minute fill in. He didn't even notice her the next day when they passed in the hall.

"Am I still going to be Vice-President tomorrow," Pam pondered, leaving the bottle of wine untouched as she headed for the door to call for her flit. "Or will she forget all about asking me?"

Chapter 20: Rising Water

"So you have the chip right now?" Ted asked after Polly recounted the events leading up to their appearance at the store earlier that morning when she moved the chip from ice freezer to ice cream freezer. Paul narrowed his eyes to telegraph his displeasure at her disclosures, but she pointedly refused to look at him.

Polly smiled and said, "Who else would have it?"

"Sounds like there are a number of players and it hasn't been in your possession this whole time. Have you checked to see what is on the chip that you have now?"

"It's not like I carry around a chip reader. Do you?"

"Good point. I think that is the first thing we should do when we get out of here."

"What makes you think that you are coming with us when we get out of here?" Paul asked.

"I guess that's up to Polly," Ted smiled at her and she blushed.

Paul experienced an unexpected rush of adrenalin that made him want to punch Ted in the face. It wasn't like they were romantically entangled, he reminded himself, but he did have a sort of brotherly bond and so was obliged to protect her against forces for which he felt partly liable.

Wind pounded and rain pelted the little building which had become an island in the midst of a swirling brown current. Knowing that this was a flood plain and that the waters were not unusually high for a 100-year flood was no solace to the trio trapped inside. That the owner built his shop out of concrete and cinderblocks was little solace either.

Ted's job, besides the obligatory sandbags, was to remove the goods on the lower shelves to higher spaces. He had moved a few things, batteries, flashlights, some clothes. With insurance reimbursement the owner might actually make money off this storm.

The electric outages and computer cell tower failures had been an unexpected consequence of the storm; and because Ted had stayed late the previous evening, he had been unable to charge a rent-a-flit to his boss before the communication systems crashed. That was why they found him there. Or so his story went. Paul was suspicious of everyone right now, except maybe Polly. Events had revealed a depth of character rarely evident even after a long acquaintance. Sure, she was no superwoman, but when things got tough she didn't run from her portion of the fight.

Polly had lain down on a sandbag bed behind the desk. Paul watched her trying to get comfortable and mulled over why she chose to be so trusting of this new guy. Margarita and Germán were to be trusted, of course, they had proven themselves to be good and proper people during the initial chip removal. Then there was first contact, Polly's first association with Germán at the convenient story seemed random. It was unlikely that Margarita and her grandson were anyone other than who they said they were. Not so much so with this new guy, thought Paul. Ted was suspiciously right on target, ground zero so to speak. And now he was cozying up to Polly.

"So you know Germán?" Paul asked in an effort to draw him out.

"Germán?" repeated Ted, taking time to consider the question as if sorting through a whole list of acquaintances with that particular name. "Do you mean the Germán who occasionally works at this store?"

Paul was surprised. "When did he work here?" he asked. "I thought he worked at the store on the other side of the highway."

"Usually," Ted acknowledged, "but he and I know each other from school and sometimes I cover for him and other times he covers for me."

"Would he have keys to this place and the code to disarm the burglar alarm?"

"I don't know," Ted answered looking troubled, "it's possible. Why do you ask?"

"Because if we find a chip reader when we are released from this flood apocalypse, and then we find that Polly has a bogus chip, what next? That makes you and Germán the only ones with access to the original that Polly left in the ice machine. So in that case one of you must have the chip or a good clue as to where it might be."

"I thought Polly left the chip in the ice cream freezer," Ted said.

"That was later, when Tom came here with her. Before that it was in the ice machine."

"I didn't know that she put something in any freezer until now," Ted pointed out, his voice changing to a higher octave. "Polly just told me. And I work in a store. We have customers in and out all day."

Paul smirked. "So a customer could have found it? That seems unlikely. "

Before Ted could answer, Polly called from behind the desk for them to "lay off". Paul turned around and went out the office door into the narrow hallway, mumbling something about checking the flood level.

"Paul is a good guy. He's my friend, Ted." Polly remarked. She sat upright on her sandbag and sweatshirt nest, only her head was visible above the pitted wood surface of the desk.

"You've made yourself comfortable. How's your hand?" Ted asked trying to turn the topic of conversation.

"Much better, thanks. Pam's dad had some antibiotics he was prescribed but never took. Apparently, rich people can just call their doctor for a prescription. It's called concierge medicine. The swelling is almost gone. See." She held up her hand and laid it upon the desk top for him to examine. He lightly ran his fingers over her knuckles, afraid that the least bit of weight might give her pain. Their eyes met for a long second.

"I trust Paul and Germán," Polly said looking deeply into Ted's gaze. "I don't know how I would have managed alone. Be nice to Paul."

"I didn't say that you should be alone," Ted stated, pulling his hand back.

"I'm sorry," Polly replied haltingly. "I should have stayed with Pam and kept you and Paul out of it."

Polly removed herself from the floor to stand behind the desk. She clenched her fist. "You weren't at Pam's house with her father and this Veronica woman. You don't know what kind of danger I might have been in. Maybe I am too sensitive, but it felt like swimming in a pool of sharks."

There was a short silence before Ted inquired softly, turning his head slightly to avoid looking directly at her. "So, are you interested in Paul? It seems like he has a thing for this Pam."

"You come straight to the point, don't you," she said, glancing away.

"I just wonder how well you know Paul. I vouch for Margarita and Germán. Good people as far as I can tell. But who else would you trust with this chip information? Let me see, there is Tom and Pam, both interested in obtaining the chip for their own reasons. There's Bob." His dark brown eyes searched her face. "How do you feel about me?" he asked. She crossed her arms in front of her and lifted her chin, but averted her eyes. "Which side am I on? Am I on your trust list?" he probed.

She offered a tiny smile, but chose not to answer.

"You have known Paul, what, all of 48 hours," Ted prompted.

"He helped me when I needed help. That's enough for me. Besides how long have I known you, 24 hours?"

"So I am on your trusted list," Ted tried to confirm.

"Of course, dummy," Polly replied. "Why would I tell you about the chip in the freezer if I didn't trust you?"

"Oh, that's good," Ted sighed.

"And I've spent two nights with Paul so far and he has been a perfect gentleman," Polly proclaimed. "One night at Binge locked in a broom closet with guards everywhere and tonight. Besides, I might have ended up indentured to Binge if not for Paul and the others. I don't care if he's training to be a spy."

"He's training to be a spy? That's interesting," Ted's face tightened and Polly bit her lip.

"How do you think he became involved with me?" she laughed. "I might become a spy too. My days as a Binge receptionist are over."

Paul came back into the office. "It's going to be in here soon," he warned them. "I think we should push the desk next to the wall to stand on when we push Polly out the window."

Polly shuddered and her eyes widened. Paul looked over at her with some concern.

The men moved the sandbag nest behind the desk over toward the closed door that led to the hallway. Then they lifted the desk an inch off the floor in preparation for moving it.

"Wait," cried Polly. They abruptly put it down. "Turn it so the desk drawers are facing out. I can open them and use them as steps to climb up."

Ted did as he was told and backed up. The two of them turned the desk with Paul moving backward, nearly tripping over a sandbag.

Polly began to pull open the drawers. "Let's empty these," she suggested. When she opened the top drawer, a flare gun caught her eye. "Well," she exclaimed, picking it up by the bright orange handle and holding it above her head, muzzle pointed at the ceiling. Ted reached toward it but she drew back. "I'll keep it safe," she assured him.

"Do you know how to use it?" Ted asked, shrugging.

"This must be the safety," she lowered the gun to point it toward the floor before sliding a tab forward and backward. "And this is the trigger," she moved her index finger to the lever that would release the flare if they should need rescuing.

"Don't forget that it is also deadly," Paul warned.

"Deadly," Polly repeated. "I didn't think of that. I'll try not to kill either one of you, no matter how much I want to." She tucked the flare gun into the oversized kangaroo pocket of the most recent sweatshirt she had *borrowed* from the convenient store's stock. This was a large gray pull over hoody with one big front pocket that bore the emblem of the University of Texas Super-Schools, UTSS in burnt-orange and black. "Okay, help me with the rest of these drawers," she ordered.

The two men pitched in on either side and there was no longer space for Polly to do any good, so she gladly gave way and let them finish the job. Soon they had opened all the drawers and found little of interest. The desk was less sturdy with the drawers open so they decided that Polly would have to get up on the desk without stairs. It did provide a broad surface for one person to sit or stand on, possibly two people, but definitely not three. Paul and Ted looked at each other with the same thought. Only one of them would be helping Polly through the window and the last person was on his own.

They decided to stock up on provisions before they sandbagged themselves in. Paul took off his shoes and went into the main area of the store, feeling his way slowly so as not to injure his bare feet. He filled his messenger bag with cellophane sacks of peanuts and raisins and plastic bottles of water. At the last minute, he threw in a flashlight and some extra batteries. Polly followed him to the dried fruits and nuts aisle and filled her pocket in a similar fashion, but with more variety. She grabbed almonds and cashews, dried apricots and prunes; then seeing that there was no room left in her pocket, she took an insulated lunch bag from a display and slung its strap over her arm and across her chest to create extra space for a few bottles of water. There was still room in an outside pocket for a flashlight. Ted filled a Styrofoam cooler with juice and beer. Thus equipped, they returned to the office and watched through the open doorway as water slowly seeped over the hallway tiles.

It was impossible to be comfortable in the claustrophobic confines of the tiny office with the threat of death inching its way across the threshold. Polly sat in lotus position on top of the desk. Flanking either side, Ted and Paul were seated on chairs. "Should we check to see how high it is outside?" Ted finally said.

"Take off your shoes and your pants," suggested Polly.

"He can roll up his pants legs," Paul countered.

"Not that you would catch cold, as stuffy as it is in here." She had removed her sweat shirt, and having tied it into a bundle, held it in her lap next to the lunch bag.

"If I don't come back, go on without me," Ted said gallantly as he removed his shoes and socks and rolled up his pants.

"We certainly will," Paul assured him.

"You're only going to the other room," Polly said. "I doubt anything will happen, but Paul maybe you should go with him. Watch out for rats floating on debris or sea serpents," she added helpfully.

Ted sloshed through inch deep water to the end of the hall where the steps down into the main part of the store were located. He eased first one foot and then the other into the deeper water. It covered his knees and slowed his progress around the counter and over to one of the large display windows. Paul followed on his heels before veering off to inspect the aisles for anything they might end up needing.

Outside the afternoon sun, dimmed by heavy clouds, leaked a faint white light instead of its usual red hot brightness. The gray light bleached the color out of everything, softening ugly buildings and parking lots into a good backdrop for an old 1930's Film Noir movie. Swirls of murky, trash-filled water flowed past the window and from inside it was like looking through the glass in an aquarium, dark and alien. Water outside was waist high for a tall man and Ted was of average height. If the window broke, they would have to get out of there. Polly was right about that.

Thunder boomed as Paul stood in the aisles away from the windows. If not for the lightening visible through the huge windows fronting the building, it would be total blackness inside. Thunder rolled across the sky causing a vibration that rippled the standing water. It was followed by a flash of bright light.

He broke out of his reverie. A steady beating rhythm ratcheted louder and louder above the noise of rain, wind and thunder. Is that a helicopter? A real helicopter, more powerful than a flit, something like the military might have? He shredded his way back through the slowly rising water to the hallway to tell Polly. In light of recent events, he wondered what was in store, rescue or capture.

As he headed for the stairs up to the hallway, there was a boom and blinding flash of light and in the next instant he was thrown hard backwards by a rush of water. Dirty liquid filled his mouth and nostrils. Pressure not there a moment earlier pulled at him and he realized with horror that the plate glass windows at the front of the store had given way. He struggled to find the surface. Polly's flare gun must have gone off.

Meanwhile, Ted slowly sloshed his way back to the steps circumventing the toppled shelves. Polly was already there with a flashlight. "Ted! Are you okay?" she shrieked.

"A little wet and scratched up, but I'll survive," he answered gallantly. "A window broke and there was a flash of light. Luckily I was in the corner next to the wall. A bunch of shelves fell over."

"Where is Paul?" she cried, panicked.

"I don't know," stammered Ted, "he was looking in the aisles before that window broke."

"Paul," they both yelled into the dark. Polly's flashlight beam searched the top of the water.

When the loud, bright boom happened, Paul had stumbled and crashed into some shelves. His leg got stuck in the disrupted metal framework tumbling down on top of him. He twisted and writhed to free himself. "Why did Polly fire that flare gun?" he thought in irritation that quickly turned to panic. He needed to breathe, but something was holding him below the surface of the water. Using both hands, he pulled on his trapped leg but it only caused pain. He sensed the air above him just beyond his reach. His hand broke the surface trying to pull the air down to him and he thrashed about to no avail. He wanted to call out for help but his mouth was filled with water. When he passed out, his hand was the only part of his body escaping the dark, wet grave closing in around him.

Chapter 21: Flight

Tom slept through the morning hardly aware of the storm outside. Nobody had come in to work to wake him up and the heavy concrete building blotted out the howling wind and driving rain. His boss's over-size, over-stuffed leather sofa made a comfortable bed.

He was sure he had only dozed off for an hour or two until he saw the wall clock. The digital clock displayed 10:30 in numbers that pierced the dark interior of his make-shift bedroom, but he knew that couldn't be right. Nobody was here and he could see that it was still dark outside. He rose from the couch and shuffled stiffly to the large windows spanning one wall. It wasn't the darkness of night that he was experiencing; instead, dark-violet clouds had extinguished the daylight and filled the heavens with an endless supply of water to empty onto an already drenched landscape. It could be suicide to take a chopper up. He would have to be on his toes. He headed for the break room and made a pot of what passed for coffee. There was a bean and cheese burrito in the refrigerator that someone was probably going to have for lunch today, but it looked like lunch was canceled so he microwaved it and then filled his mug with the fresh brew. By the time he finished a second cup of coffee the rain had eased up, so he splashed water on his face, grabbed his things and headed for the heliport.

Sliding Bob's key-card into the slot at the gate, Tom accessed the tarmac. Lined up before him were three small flit-copters and like a mother hen guarding her chicks, a beautiful red and white vintage Sikorsky MH-60T Jayhawk. With a rush of adrenaline he bee-lined over to the Jayhawk and opened the cabin door. He had trained on one just like this. If anything could navigate the storm it was this baby. He strapped himself into the pilot's seat and then froze. What was he doing? How likely was it that anyone would be out looking for Polly in this weather? Of course, that was his advantage. Still, he wasn't likely to find a place to land at the convenient store.

"Do you know the way to San Jose," sang a muffled voice from his left interior jacket pocket. It took him by surprise and he jumped a little. "I have to change that ringtone," he muttered, taking it from his pocket and unlocking it with a touch of his thumb. The screen displayed a short text with an attached map. A red teardrop pulsed rhythmically over a location in downtown Austin. The text showed that it had been sent hours earlier but final transmission had been delayed by the malfunctioning cell towers. He tapped the teardrop with his index finger and an address appeared. It was the convenient store where he last saw Polly. "Got you," he gleefully exclaimed. "Yes!"

With no more thoughts of personal safety, he checked the altimeter and fuel level and went over the standard pre-takeoff check list. "You have been well maintained," he told the machine before slowly opening the throttle. When he was at the proper RPM, he pulled up on the collective, then depressed the left pedal and cyclic to lift the helicopter off the ground. Reflexively adjusting and synchronizing the cyclic and pedals, he nosed the helicopter toward the direction indicated on his phone. A transponder signalling its location to any other flying machines in the area switched itself on once the helicopter was in motion. Days of control towers manned by humans were long gone. "Just like riding a bike," he assured himself with pleasure. It felt good to be in the driver's seat again. The powerful machine cut through the rain and the wind with ease. Now where was he going to land? That was going to be a problem.

When he reached the location indicated on his phone, he hovered for a minute and then began to circle above the building like a vulture. Down below, hidden inside the partially submerged Quicky Picky was the answer to his dreams, the gateway to his future. How to get at it without killing himself in the process was the problem. He intended to snatch it out of Polly's pried open hand if it came to that. If Paul got in the way, he would make short work of him. Still, as close as he was to his target, he would have to land in order to get it. The parking lot was filled with water and debris. He couldn't tell how deep the water was, but he could tell that it was moving and that there were things in it that were moving also. It was a search and rescue helicopter, but it wasn't immune to moving water any more than any ordinary vehicle.

"Can't keep circling," he chastised himself and he pushed down on the collective to hover a dozen scant feet over the building while he searched frantically for a place to set it down. It was then that it happened. The helicopter drew in a bolt of lightning. For several critical moments, he was blinded and a sharp ringing in his head blotted out all other noise. The hardened electrical system took the blow like a veteran, but the shock sent a shiver through Tom's spine and caused him to push down on the collective. As he frantically adjusted his pressure on the pedals and cyclic to compensate, there was a tremendous crash.

He managed to pull the big machine back up into the sky. Thankfully the giant rotors kept turning. He hovered over the building while he assessed the damage. One of the skids had hit the HVAC unit that sat on top of the store. A trickle of sweat from his forehead found its salty way into one eye and he used a clammy palm to wipe it away. Gently, he maneuvered to the front of the building. A piece of the roof's railing had broken loose and crashed into one of the windows. He could see the flood waters rushing into the store and a flicker of light inside.

Chapter 22: Tom to the rescue

"What happened?" Polly gasped as water rose higher on the floor where she stood in the doorway to the hall. Ted pulled her back protectively. She shrugged him off and went to the desk for a working flashlight. Flicking it on she handed it to Ted. She gazed in horror at the deepening water, now well over the tops of her shoes. "Paul!" she called, sweeping the light back and forth over the gloomy surface of the dark water.

Ted stood transfixed at the end of the narrow passage holding a solid beam of light on top of the black water that was halfway up to the ceiling in this part of the building. His flashlight illuminated a terrifying scene of destruction where the water surged in through a shattered plate glass window. Boxes of cereal and household items from the toppled shelves floated along with organic debris and trash from the empty parking lot like a flotilla of boats on a stormy sea. Bobbing lifelessly amongst them was a solitary hand, but it was lost in the swirling motion of the incoming flood.

"Wait," Ted called, noticing an organic shape amidst the boxes. "What's that? He's here!" He waded toward the hand while keeping the beam of light focused on it. "Shine your light on his hand," he ordered Polly, who was trailing after him. Reaching deep into the cold, swirling water, he followed the arm down to the large shelf pinning Paul's body to its watery coffin. Dipping both arms into the maelstrom, he struggled to lift the shelf enough for Paul to free himself, but Paul failed to make use of the opportunity.

"Help him Polly," Ted cried, panting with exertion. "He isn't moving."

Polly dropped her flashlight and submerged herself next to her trapped friend. She tugged on his arm with all her might until his body moved toward her, and then she reached an arm around to the opposite shoulder while grasping beneath his armpit to get a better grip. She pulled as if her life depended on it, not just Paul's. Ted pushed on the shelf in the opposite direction.

There was a mighty splash as Polly rose up above the surface of the water and fell backwards with Paul held firmly in her arms. Ted dropped the shelf and moved swiftly to assist her, but they both disappeared as quickly as they had emerged.

"Polly!" Ted called.

"Here!" Polly gurgled as she resurfaced. "He isn't moving!"

Ted rushed to pull Paul's shoulders and head above the water. His head lolled forward lifelessly as Ted and Polly dragged him back into the shallower water of the hallway.

"Elevate his torso so I can turn his head to the side," Polly instructed. Ted stripped off his sweat shirt and stuffed it under the supine man. Water poured from his mouth when she rotated his head. She turned it back to the center, pinched his nose and blew into his mouth. She repeated with deep, forceful breaths three more times. "It's not working," she screamed. "Ted, do you know CPR?"

"I...I don't think so. Maybe. What if I break his ribs?" He responded. "Don't you?"

"Press on his sternum," she ordered with exasperation. "Hurry!" She was holding his head. She turned it to the side again and then back when no more water came out of his mouth.

Ted hesitated, but finally moved into position over the drowned man and began pressing the area she indicated. "I don't think it's working," he said. His eyes met hers over the motionless body.

"We can't let him die. We just can't. Can you get him into the office?" Polly implored. "We need to get him above water, on top of the desk or the sandbags."

"Okay," he agreed.

Ted was not a big man. Paul was lanky but tall and outweighed him by at least 20 pounds if not more. With his adrenalin rush dissipating, it took all his will power to lift Paul's torso and begin dragging him backwards toward the office door. Cold now and dripping, Polly followed in his wake.

Somehow after what seemed an eternity they made it into the office where Ted stopped to catch his breath in front of the desk. "Polly, can you lift his feet?" He panted.

"I'll try," Polly was struggling to keep from crying. Why did she find tears so consoling at times like this, times when she wanted to be strong? She was strong. Yet she had to force herself from giving in to a compulsion to splash down in a heap onto the drowned floor and cry like a baby. "I've got them. Tell me when to lift," she managed to reply.

"Okay, let's both lift on three," Ted instructed, "one, two, lift!"

They both heaved with all their might. Ted's half of the body cleared the sides of the sturdy desk but Polly was unable to follow suit. Paul's unconscious body hit the edge with a bruising crack; his legs dangled off into the water at an awkward slant. Ted tugged him over onto his side to keep from losing him altogether. Polly heaved his legs up with all her might, high enough to clear the edge of the only place above water left in the building.

"He looks blue," she shrieked. "Ted, do something."

Exasperated, he took out his frustration with a mighty slap to Paul's back. Amazingly, Paul coughed and water streamed from his mouth.

"Paul...Paul... can you hear me," Polly murmured, her mouth next to his ear. His eyes fluttered open and he coughed again in her face. Jumping back and then laughing, she wiped her eyes with the back of her hand. "I thought you had died," she smiled with relief.

"You can't get rid of me that easily," Paul managed between gasps for air. Ted helped him sit upright, but he was weak and leaned heavily on the other man. It wasn't until then that they all heard the unmistakable sound of the chopper outside.

Polly climbed up on top of the desk next to the revived man and stood on tiptoes to look out the small window. Sure enough, a rescue chopper hovered over the parking lot outside. "They've come!" she shouted in excitement. "We're rescued!"

Paul pulled himself heavily to his feet and Polly gave way to let him see out. "She's right," he verified. "There is a chopper out there. We need to let them know that we're in here. Polly, where is that flare gun? Is that what caused the flash?"

"No," answered Polly pulling the gun from the pocket of her sweatshirt and handing it over while Ted looked on from below. "Wait you two," he exclaimed. "Are you sure they are here to save us?"

Polly glared at her erstwhile protector. "Why else would they be here Ted? Do you know something you're not sharing?"

"No, I just wonder how they found us. Do you have the chip?"

"Right now I want to be saved and I think Paul will agree. We don't know how high these waters will get and the roof is too dangerous in a storm. She paused, "how **did** they find us anyway?"

Paul interjected, "she's right. We need to get to safety first. Then we can sort out the rest." With no more ado he pointed the flare gun out the window away from the helicopter and pulled the trigger. A thin streak of light traced through the gloom and exploded ultimately into a brief and hopeful display of explosive color. The helicopter acknowledged with a dip then turned its opposite side to the window. A cable lowered from atop the door on that side.

"They saw it!" Polly shouted with delight, staring out the window. Ted and Paul glowered suspiciously at each other.

"I'm going to break out that window so you can get through, Polly. It doesn't crank open wide enough for you to get through otherwise. Do you think you can reach the roof from the window?" Paul asked.

"I think so," Polly affirmed. "What about you? Are you going to be able to get out through this small of an opening?"

"Don't worry about that now. Ted and I will manage. What is there around here to break the window with?" he asked Ted.

"There's a tool box in that cupboard," Ted said indicating a metal cabinet, and then slogged through the rising water over to the opposite wall.

He opened the door with difficulty. The tool box was heavy so he unlatched the lid and hunted through the contents where it sat. There was a ball-peen hammer inside that he thought might do the trick. Quickly he brought it over to Paul. "Will this do?"

Wordlessly, Paul took the tool from him and waited for Polly to climb down from the desk. He motioned for them to get back. The first swing smashed the window and shattered glass everywhere. Tapping the head of the hammer around the inside of the frame, he broke loose the jagged pieces still clinging to the edges. Ted came up behind him and offered a rag that he used to clear away some small shards. When done, he spread the rag across the window sill. Finally satisfied that the opening was large enough for Polly to fit through safely, he turned back to his two companions who stood knee-deep in the dirty flood water filling the interior of the building.

Outside, the helicopter hovered a scant few feet above the roof on the side where the window glass had been. A cable terminating in a padded harness dangled just beyond Polly's grasp. "I can't reach it," she cried.

"Yes you can," Paul insisted and he pushed her farther out the window, her bare legs wrapped around his head and supported by his shoulders. His line of sight was obscured by a view of her panties.

"I've got it," she finally cried triumphantly. Holding it for support, she pulled herself up through the opening and stood precariously on the window sill while she slipped her head and shoulders through the straps of the sling and slid onto the seat. Paul's hands clasped her ankles to keep her steady. "Give me your messenger bag. I can take it now so you aren't encumbered," she yelled back to Paul. He hesitated, but told Ted to hand the bag out to her and once she had slung the strap over her head the cable slowly lifted until she disappeared from the limited view of the little window.

"You're next," Paul motioned to Ted who stood transfixed, mouth agape. The view of Polly's sprawled legs struggling through the window had completely filled his mind for the moment.

Finally he said, "No, it's my store. You go ahead."

"It's not like you are the captain of a sinking ship, Ted," Paul protested. "You're shorter so I will be able to get out on my own more easily. Besides, you saved me from drowning. I owe you."

Ted gave him a strange look, but climbed up on the desk and began to shimmy through the small opening. Once the cable was dangling by the window, Paul grabbed his feet to anchor him while he snatched it in close enough to get into the sling. Long minutes later, it was Paul's turn to be pulled up into the hovering helicopter. The rescue continued without incident and all three strapped into their seats. Paul took the co-pilot's seat next to Tom. "Nice flying," he shouted.

Back at Binge headquarters, Tom brewed some hot whatever-passed-for-coffee and passed out towels he found in the custodian's closet. Polly fretted over Paul a bit, getting him some ice wrapped in one of the towels for the bruise on his thigh. Tom rummaged through the storage closet until he found some clean janitor's uniforms for the waterlogged trio.

"How did you find us?" Paul asked with an accusing glance toward Polly.

"Why are you looking at me like that?" Polly asked with a frown that caused her eyebrows to crunch up and wrinkle her brow. Paul was reminded of an enraged kitten.

"You know why. Maybe you would like some ice cream with your coffee?"

"I don't like your tone, Paul," Polly replied. "And after I bothered to save your life. Maybe I **would** like some, topped with whipped cream and a cherry. Would you like to get it for me?"

Ted interjected, "what is up with you two? Who cares how he found us. Can't you be happy we're safe?"

"Are we safe?" Polly asked Tom.

"Ted, could you check on the coffee? I'd like a few minutes with these two," Tom replied.

"Sure," Ted caught Polly's eye. "I'll see if the vending machine sells ice cream while I'm at it." Paul rolled his eyes.

When they were alone in the conference room, Tom closed the door and sat down opposite them. "Where is the chip?" Tom said without preview.

"You mean the chip that was stuck into my hand?" Polly held up her bruised and still swollen extremity? "Why don't you ask your company?"

"Binge isn't my company," Tom assured her. "But that chip does belong to me and I need it back. Whatever it takes," he paused dramatically. "So I would think long and hard about what you are doing."

"Don't threaten her," Paul blurted out. Polly gave him a surprised look.

"Look you two," Tom said in a reasonable voice. "I know you think you are saving the world. Or maybe you think you can feather your nest with this information, but believe me all you are doing is dragging yourselves into something way over your head. Something that is dangerous for all of us."

"I am pretty sure we know how dangerous possession of that chip is," Paul said.

"Okay," Tom continued, "if you don't have it on you, can you tell me where you last had it?"

"What makes you think we don't have it?" Paul asked.

Tom sighed and tried to relax his neck muscles before the migraine came back. Stringy, uncombed hair and matching heather-green jumpsuits lent the two young people standing before him a sense of recalcitrant innocence. Tom flashed on a vision of fraternal twins stubbornly united before a disapproving parent. He sighed again audibly and stretched his neck to one side and then to the other.

He decided to play on Paul's obvious affection for the girl. "Look Paul," he said, "I know you don't want anything bad to happen to Polly." He was rewarded by surprised concern on Paul's face followed by anger.

Polly interjected, "I might have turned off the locating app, which means it could be anywhere. I could have thrown it away," she paused, "into the flood waters."

"Why do you think I was able to find you?" Tom countered. "I'm not playing with you and I don't want anything bad to happen to you. The people who want that chip will stop at nothing to get it. Your life is at stake."

Polly just sneered at him. Paul was shaken but perplexed. If the chip had been frozen until the towers went dead it hadn't sent the signal. With the towers down, it didn't matter if there was a signal since it wouldn't be broadcast. And if Polly really didn't have the chip how did Tom know where to find them. Who or what had sent it?

Ted opened the door and peaked in. "Do you need more time?" he asked meekly.

"No," Tom said grumpily. "We were just getting nowhere."

"What's the problem?" Ted asked innocently.

"These two won't listen to reason," Tom answered. "They think they can beat corporate America."

"Well, if anyone could, it would be Polly," Ted smiled disarmingly at the scruffy vision of feminine charm before him. Her disheveled appearance was strangely appealing. "What can I do to help?" Polly was not immune to a compliment and smiled back appreciatively. "How about I get us all some hot coffee," he suggested and backed out of the room.

"You don't understand that I am on your side," Tom wheedled. "Like I was telling Margarita and Germán, we can't stop the big oil conglomerates on our own. I've come to believe that trusting Veronica to do the right thing is our only option. The problem is how can we do that without getting murdered by Binge? We need the chip for barter."

"Polly, just give him the chip," Paul sighed with exasperation.

She favored him with a look of contempt and turned to Tom. "What makes you think that I have the chip?"

Paul interjected before he could answer. "Seriously, Polly. You took it out of the freezer like I told you not to. How do you think Tom found us?"

"If it was in the freezer when we left, it's gone with the flood waters," she answered irritably. "I saw the entire front of the store disintegrate as we were pulling away. I didn't take it out of the freezer. I don't know how Tom found us, but I'm thankful that he did."

"Polly this is above our pay grade. I think it's time to let the professionals take over, don't you? Besides, what are you going to do with it? I saw you take a plastic bag out of the freezer."

"Is that what this is about? Why didn't you just ask me what I had? Do you want to know what it was?" she asked, disappointment lacing her words.

Tom wriggled uncomfortably. As if on cue, Ted entered with a pot of coffee and four mugs on a tray. "If you want cream or sugar you can go look for some in the break room," he said. "I think there are some packets of something on the counter. I didn't look in the fridge."

"I would be afraid to look in that fridge," Tom favored him with a tight smile. "Thanks for the coffee." The little group poured themselves mugs and sat back in their chairs, momentarily concentrating on the warm, fragrant brew. Polly held hers up to her face but didn't drink. She seemed lost in thought.

Silence enveloped the room as the tired foursome drank and stared down at the table in an exhausted trance. At last, Polly got up and went to the window. "The rain has stopped." It hadn't actually stopped, but it had slowed to a sprinkle and the clouds had thinned in places allowing an uncharacteristic golden glow to lighten the sky. Turning back to the huddled group, she said, "tell me we don't have to spend another night in this place."

Chapter 23: Pam Makes a Conquest

Mitchell heard Tom and the soggy trio coming off the elevator, but decided to remain quiet and see what they were up to. Luckily, they went into the conference room where he kept a bug hidden under the table. After listening in on their conversation for a few minutes, he realized Tom wasn't getting anywhere with Polly and Paul was clueless. Indeed he held all the important pieces in this game of espionage and it was time to play them. He messaged Veronica to meet him at a nearby tavern. If she wanted his copy of the chip, she could buy him dinner first.

As soon as the rain ended, the sun shattered the remaining clouds in its glistening, white-hot brilliance. The air was clean and fresh for the first time he could remember. He was already sweating from the walk of a few blocks, which made him scurry all the faster into the eternal dusk of Dempsey's Dive. Familiar smells of stale beer mingled with weeks old grease and just a trace of urine. Jukebox music droned country classics in the background. As he shuffled quickly over to his favorite booth, Willy Nelson crooned "love is like a dying ember, only memories remain". Cracked vinyl upholstery and a perpetually sticky table welcomed his heavy frame with nostalgic comfort invisible to the occasional customer. This Veronica would meet him on his turf.

She was there before he could finish his first beer, strolling in like she owned the place. He waved her over. She slid in, touching the table lightly with the tips of her fingers before pulling them back in distaste. "Nice place," she didn't smile.

"I thought you'd like it," he answered expressionlessly.

"You have something for me," she didn't waste time. In the background, Johnny Paycheck broke out into a challenging "take this job and shove it".

"Have a beer and we can discuss it," he suggested.

"I don't think so," she parried.

"They make a great burger," he enticed.

"I already ate," she replied.

"Well I am as hungry as a horse."

"I think you mean you could eat a horse."

"I'm not particular," he said.

"I can see that," she drew her purse in close to her body as if she was getting up.

"Wait," he held up his hand like a traffic cop. "Buy me a burger and I will tell you what I have."

"I really don't want to watch you eat. Are you that hard up for cash?"

"Do you want the chip or not," he countered.

She had to think a minute. Was saving the world and her factories worth spending another minute with this guy? Finally she shrugged, "order your burger, but this better be good." She put her purse on her lap.

"I have the code that you are looking for. We just need to agree on a price and it's yours."

Okay. I assume you want more than a burger and beer, but remember that I already have half of the code and I have people working on the other half. The deal is off if this isn't what I'm looking for or if someone else beats you to the punch."

"They won't," he answered smugly. Veronica wondered about his assurance but displayed no emotion on her face. She had learned to present a poker face during the long years of her marriage.

The waitress, a middle-aged, stout woman wearing a too-short skirt that accentuated varicose veins and thick, heavy thighs came for their order. Mitchell added fries to his request of a double meat cheese burger with the "works" and another beer; Veronica asked for bottled water. The best they could offer was filtered tap water in a plastic bottle. When the waitress asked if she wanted a glass and ice, Veronica declined. "Bring it unsealed," she instructed. "I prefer to take the cap off myself."

"I will give you the same deal I offered Tom," she said as soon as the waitress left, "enough money for you to retire."

"I'm not interested in retiring," Mitchell countered. "I want a percentage."

"A percentage of what?" Vanessa frowned. Who did this fat little man think he was and how much could he know? He certainly didn't know with whom he was dealing. "Do you know what it is I am looking for?"

"I know enough to know it is worth more money than you can offer me in one lump sum."

"In that case what am I doing here? If you wish to use the code yourself then go right ahead. I assume you can pay for your own burger." She scooted out of the booth and headed for the door without looking back. As she opened it she heard the waitress ask Mitchell, "Does she want the water to go?"

She had the flit driver wait for her and he hovered down when he saw her leave the building. He released the automatic door latch and she jumped in. As soon as they were aloft she pulled her comp from her bag. "Where to?" he asked. She tapped a short text into the device and waited. After a few seconds she said, "Head over to Binge, it's a few blocks to the north. You can wait for me in the parking lot." It was time to use pressure and she knew just where to apply it.

Mitchell was chagrined that his luncheon had not gone as planned. The least she could have done was pay the check. Instead, he was left to take care of the bill for both his lunch and her water which she didn't even drink. What was he going to do with a bottle of water? He certainly wasn't going to leave it. After all, he had paid for it. He was so angry that he didn't tip the waitress. Then as an afterthought, suddenly feeling generous, he decided she could have the bottle of water for her tip.

He knew just what to do. Outside on the steaming sidewalk he pulled out his comp and punched in a number. He couldn't wait for a text and he was pretty sure the person on the other end would pick up. It was a call that could have only one meaning. "I've got it," he said into the speaker. The voice on the other end told him where to go. "Don't thinks so. You can come and get me," he said with a trace of belligerence. He gave directions to his location and then disconnected.

Traffic was strangely light since the flood. He wondered what people were doing to get around. Come to think of it, Dempsey's was unusually empty. Sweat dripped down into his eyes from his forehead and he wiped it away with the back of his hand. The intense humidity made him feel woozy. He concentrated on how to handle the deal he was about to make. His shirt was drenched with sweat now but he didn't dare go back into Dempsey's after stiffing the waitress. In retrospect, he figured he shouldn't have taken out his frustrations on her, but it was too late now. Better to wait a few weeks before going back. Maybe she would be gone by then. Waitresses didn't last long there. His mother had been a waitress there.

Finally a flit pulled up to the curb. The door slowly levitated open on pneumatic cylinders like an injured bird wing and the driver called out his name. "Where are we going?" he asked the driver with a nervous edge as he got in. He either didn't hear him or ignored the question. They headed for the less populous west side. Abjectly staring downward, he saw the stark, desolate concrete of the inner city recede into an increasing green of live oak and ash juniper. Soon he would be rich and live in a place like this. He relaxed back into his seat.

The flit let him off in front of a rambling, ranch style mini-mansion. He hesitated before approaching the door, wiping his sweaty palms on his wrinkled, no-iron polyester pants. He quickly tucked in his shirt wishing he had worn a belt and pressed the door buzzer. He was about to press it again when he heard noises inside and a young woman's voice call out, "I'll get it."

She had long blonde hair pulled back in a loose ponytail. Either she was wearing her boyfriend's shirt or the current style was big and plaid. Shorts, he assumed she was wearing, were hidden beneath its tails and her feet were bare. She smiled a welcome and invited him into the foyer. "I'm Pam, are you here to see my Dad?"

He had forgotten all about why he was here for a minute. She was just the kind of girl he had always dreamed of but who had never looked at him even once. When he was rich, he would have a girlfriend like this, a real down-to-earth beauty, not a stuck-up bitch like that Veronica.

"Mitchell," Bob appeared from the terrace, a tall, chilled glass of something wet in his hand, "come out to the patio. I see you met my daughter. What can I fix you?" Mitchell stole one last glance at Pam as she disappeared up the stairs and followed him out.

"I'll take a beer," Mitchell said. Bob snatched a local craft brew from the bar refrigerator. They sat down at a glass table next to the spa. "Nice place you have here," Mitchell commented before taking a swig. He surveyed the view over the end of the vanishing edge pool. Living in the city, it was hard to imagine any trees still existed. A breeze blew up from the canyon ruffling what was left of his hair. He pushed it back across the bald spot on the top of his head and behind his ear. His damp shirt felt clammy and uncomfortable.

"So you have something for me?" Bob got down to business.

"That depends on the price you are willing to pay," Mitchell replied craftily.

"I would have to make sure it's the real thing first," Bob said.

"Would you know the real thing if you saw it?" Mitchell smirked.

"I doubt either of us has that kind of expertise, but I know someone who does. Shall I call her?"

"Her? Aren't you working for Binge? I didn't know they hired women for tech jobs anymore. Last I heard they had cleansed their top echelon creative and administrative staff after that rape case. Said it was to make sure there was no temptation in the workplace. Women only in reception and secretarial, men only in technical and administration. Of course, they might have a contract worker of either sex," Mitchell stated knowledgeably. "Could this she be a contract farmer?"

"I am working for whoever pays me," Bob smiled toothlessly, "just like you. But my associate is a woman named Veronica."

Mitchell physically flinched at the name, but Bob ignored it.

Pam had walked out onto the patio unobserved by the two men. She meant to interrupt to ask if Mitchell was planning to stay for supper, since they were eating early today. Cook didn't like surprises. Overhearing Bob mention Veronica, she froze in her tracks. If Mitchell delivered the chip, where did that leave her deal with Veronica? Her mind raced with options. She had to get that chip away from this monstrous man. But how? She needed to buy some time.

Breezing out onto the terrace in view of the two she beamed her most welcoming smile. "I hope you are staying for supper? We're eating early this evening. I already told Cook to prepare an extra setting. It would be nice to have a new conversant at the table, no insult to your always interesting conversation Dad, but we do spend most evenings alone lately." She floated over to her father and gave him a sideways hug and a tender kiss on the cheek. He hid his surprise at her sudden friendliness with the practiced ease of a diplomat.

"Yes, we would love to have you stay. We can check out your copy after supper. I'll give you a tour of the place. Cook makes a wonderful beef stew and bakes fresh, homemade rolls that will melt in your mouth. Nothing special mind you, but delicious."

Mitchell had not been thinking about food for a change, but at the mention of stew and melting hot rolls his mouth began to salivate. Having more time to look at the girl was icing on the cake. He could worry about the money later. "I'd love to. Thanks."

"I'll just go up and change into something presentable," Pam smiled. "You two have another drink and enjoy the environs. I'll come and get you when dinner is ready." She tripped lightly back into the house with both men watching her retreat.

Once in the privacy of her bedroom, she punched in Veronica's number and waited for her new employer to pick up. "I've got it," she blurted.

Veronica needed no explanation. "Where are you?"

"I'm at home. This guy Mitchell is here and he says he has a copy."

"Does he have it on him?"

"I don't know. He is going to stay for supper. I'll try to get more information then. He seems easily distracted by me, so I can use that. Shall I call back after I find out where it is?"

"No. You shouldn't have called me in the first place. Binge could already know. I'm sending some of my staff to keep an eye on the house. I will come to you. Keep any information you obtain to yourself until you give it to me in person."

Pam thought back to the Binge helicopter and the chase. They hadn't been interested in her then, but if they thought she knew something it would be a different story.

"I can do this," she encouraged herself with tamped down enthusiasm.

Choosing a shimmering, pale pink, almost flesh-colored silk dress suspended by spaghetti straps and boasting a plunging neck line, Pam quickly dressed for supper. She selected a delicate gold pendant necklace and pearl earrings from her jewelry box to adorn it and then slipped on matching silk slippers. She eyed the ruby ring thoughtfully, but didn't put it on. The reflection in the mirror confirmed that she looked stunning. Her blue eyes shone back at her and her cheeks were flushed with anticipation. Unconfined by a hair tie, her wavy, blonde hair softly caressed her tanned shoulders. "Time to Mata Hari this Mitchell guy," she told herself with a grin.

Even her father inhaled audibly when she walked out to the patio to call them to the table. "You look beautiful, darling."

"Thank you Dad. I thought I would dress up since we have company."

Mitchell was speechless, his mouth slightly agape. Finally he managed to stammer, "Yes, lovely."

They sat down to a rather homely meal considering the fine place setting and the elegant dress of the hostess. Pam served the wine, a rich, smooth California cabernet sauvignon before taking a seat across from Mitchell. "So," she said wiggling cozily in the padded dining room chair so that he could get a glimpse down the front of her dress, her cleavage enhanced by a push-up bra that glistened with tiny rhinestones sewn to the edge. "What business are you in? something terribly interesting?"

Mitchell forced his eyes away from the mesmerizing twinkle and tried to gather his wits. Bob had never seen this side of his daughter and sat back in his chair to enjoy the show. He might as well have been on another planet as far as Mitchell was concerned.

"I...I'm in the computer business," Mitchell managed to spit out. "But I'm segueing into my own business. I'm thinking of becoming an entrepreneur like your father here."

"How interesting," Pam replied sounding insincere even to herself, but Mitchell didn't seem to notice. "Please, tell me more."

Mitchell smiled with self-importance. "Well, I've discovered a new energy technology, something that could revolutionize the world. I am in the process of finding a distributor, which is why I sought out Bob. I may be working on it with Binge."

"Oh, Dad, you didn't tell me that you were working with Binge again," Pam said turning to her father who was sitting at the head of the table.

"Didn't I?" he said cryptically. "It must have slipped my mind."

"Well, I must know everything," she beamed. "What is this new technology? Do you have anything with you that might illustrate the process? I am simply fascinated with technology. Once upon a time I dated a computer whiz."

Mitchell felt challenged. He took a huge gulp of wine. Pam refilled his glass which was nearly empty, although she and her father had taken only a few sips of theirs. "I'm something of a whiz myself," he admitted raising his eyebrows for emphasis. "I might have something I could show you right now."

"Could it really be this easy?" thought Pam. She smiled her most alluring smile and bent forward again. Sweat broke out across Mitchell's brow and he blotted it with his napkin. Pam forced herself not to grimace.

Cook created a welcome distraction by appearing at the end of the table with a steaming pot of stew and a basket of rolls. She ladled the succulent concoction into the large, flat bowls at each place setting and set the basket on the table. Her scowl implied that this was not her usual duty. Luckily, the heavenly aroma of the dish caught Mitchell's full attention and he totally ignored the sullen service. Conversation ebbed as the diners buttered the hot rolls and tasted the soup. Mitchell almost forgot Pam in his appreciation of the fine food. Dempsey's Dive would never be the same. This beef literally melted on the tongue and the flavor defied his limited vocabulary. Cook went back into the kitchen and returned with side salads of mixed greens dotted with sautéed shrimp which she placed next to the bowls of stew. "There's only ice cream and strawberries for dessert," she stated before stomping back to the kitchen.

"That will be fine," Bob assured her retreating figure. "Pam will serve it." He turned to his guest and explained that it was the maid's day off. "Normally, she would serve when we have guests."

"Of course, no problem," Mitchell replied, as if he understood the various duties of household servants. "It's really good," he called after the cook who had already disappeared.

Pam removed the dishes when they were done and told them to stay seated while she got the ice cream. Pushing open the kitchen door with her shoulder, since her hands were full with the tray of dirty dishes, she saw that Cook had cleaned up and left them to deal with the rest of supper. Pam popped out the kitchen door which opened to the side of the house to make sure she was gone. She had hoped she would stay late so that she could take care of the dessert, but no such luck. She turned to head back in when she heard the unmistakable vibration of a chopper in the distance coming closer and closer. Where they lived it was unusual to hear choppers in the evening. At first, she was curious and stood calmly looking up for it to appear in the still, darkening sky. Then a shiver ran up her spine and she dashed back into the house.

"I think we need to move or something," she exclaimed to the two men at the table. They were finishing off a second bottle of wine, a mellow Santa Margherita Pinot Grigio.

Her father didn't understand what she was getting at. "To the patio for dessert?" he asked.

Mitchell, who decided he liked drinking wine better than beer produced a relaxed convivial smile and agreeably concurred. "Any place you like."

"No," Pam's frustration spiced her words, "out of here. They're here. Binge. They're here to take the chip!"

Mitchell wondered how she could know that Binge was after the chip. He hadn't produced it yet. But then her father was a Binge executive, maybe she knew more about Binge than he did. "Perhaps they would like to get in on the bidding," he said casually.

"I think they will more likely take it," Pam replied tersely, unable to maintain her femme fatale act any longer. "Do you have it on you?"

Mitchell was taken aback by her sudden change in attitude. He stuttered out an affirmative before thinking about the consequences. He was going to have to trust them. They didn't know where on him, after all.

"Then we need to get out of here right now," Pam ordered. "They don't know that you have the chip on you, but they know that you can lead them to it. Give it to me, Mitchell, and I'll hide it for you. Dad, you and Mitchell leave in your flit. I think they will follow. I'll head out into the woods. These guys are not the kind of trackers that will be able to follow me for long in this area." She held out her hand to Mitchell.

He hesitated then said, "how about if I go with you and your father takes off in his flit to lead them away?"

"Because you could never keep up with me. No offense," Pam answered with gritted teeth. "You are going to have to trust someone. Either Binge or me. You better make up your mind or it will be too late."

Mitchell looked to Bob for support but he just shook his head. "It's up to you," he shrugged his shoulders in supplication. "I can vouch for my daughter's integrity though. She is certainly more trustworthy than I am. She is always trying to help the underprivileged and volunteering and voting liberal."

Now the sound of the helicopter blades cutting through the air above the house was loud enough to dissolve any doubt about location. Mitchell desperately wanted to escape this lovely dream turned nightmare, but it was too late. He couldn't just pull the chip out of his pocket. He had hidden it well, perhaps too well. He had injected it underneath his skin.

Chapter 24: Polly Rides a Yooter

Tom went to his cubicle leaving Polly, Paul and Ted in the conference room. He was getting too old for this. The tension between the three young people could be cut with a knife and he didn't think it all had to do with the chip. He thought briefly of his dinner with Margarita. Calm and patient, she refused to play games. She knew where she stood in the scheme of things. Once this mess was over, he wouldn't mind seeing her again. Maybe she would like one of the old Austin places where they served good TexMex and local musicians played soft, comfortable country and western for tips and beers.

When he received Veronica's text, he messaged her back to meet him on the 3rd floor at his cubicle. They could confront Polly together. Meanwhile, he looked up the location he had in mind to take Margarita and checked out the menu.

In the conference room, Paul paced the length of the table and then back. "Polly, I know you have the chip. Stop trying to pretend that you don't. Can't you see that I am worried about you?" She was so stubborn and impractical. She had not bothered to find a comb for her hair and the green overalls were way too big. It made her appear all the more vulnerable. Why couldn't she see that he wanted to protect her and appreciate him for it.

"I told you that I don't," she glared at the tall, rather awkward man who towered grimly over her. The green jumpsuit closest to his size was short in the arms and legs. His rosacea had flared up again and one side of his face along his jawbone was a raw, red color. Even so, his bright blue eyes flashed when he was angry and his straight classical nose and square jaw line made for a rather handsome visage. Even the dirty blond hair seemed to add to his attractiveness rather than detract from it. She was glad he didn't have on that old black felt hat.

Ted spoke up to get her attention. He was the opposite of Paul; shorter, with a perfectly clear complexion, dark brown eyes and silky black hair. He had an ease of movement and a charming way of knowing just the right things to say. She gravitated to the calm, self-possessed demeanor he projected. He liked her, so it was hard telling her, "Polly, I called Tom. Before the computer towers went down I left a repeater signal. It must have been stored until a tower came back up to send it. It was when you both first showed up. I didn't know if the signal got through, but aren't we all glad that it finally did?"

"You called Tom!" They both said it together. Paul halted mid-step. Polly jumped from her chair as if she had been electrocuted. They waited expectantly for him to continue.

Finally, Paul asked in a tone that said he already knew, "are you an operative?"

"I was… kind of," he admitted soberly. "Tom contacted me after the incident in the parking lot. He didn't want me to think he was some kind of masher and he didn't want me to contact the authorities. He offered to pay me for information. He said that you had lost your job and he was going to try to get it back for you, Polly. I couldn't tell him much, but I said that if I saw you again I would call him." He looked at Polly hopefully.

Paul caught Polly's eye. She looked confused and worried. Did she believe him? If so, could he have taken the chip? Polly said she didn't have it. Or was she lying.

"So you have the chip?" Polly asked.

"No, don't you have it?" Ted appeared flabbergasted. He looked at Paul imploringly and Paul looked down at his shoes. He had retrieved them and put them on wet before the flood waters began to fill the building. They were soaked and he realized now that he had left muddy, wet footprints wherever he walked. No one seemed to notice or at least they didn't say anything.

They were surprised when the door opened and a woman wearing bedazzled flip-flops, fashionably faded jeans and a semi-transparent, loose fitting, embroidered shirt that only someone with an athletic build could pull off entered. Behind her followed Tom. "We meet again," she said to Polly and held out her hand.

Polly stared at it as if it was dripping with putrescent slime.

"This is Paul," Tom cut in, "and Ted."

"How adorably dressed you all are in identical outfits. Are you in a club, like the Girl Scouts? Or did you all decide to join the custodial staff?" Veronica jibed.

Ted blushed, "nice to meet you," and he offered his hand. He had never seen anyone so attractive and self-assured. Veronica took his measure before moving on to Paul. Paul mumbled something unintelligible.

"Well is this a shell game? Do I guess under which green jumpsuit I will find the chip?" She clasped her hands together and held them to one cheek, smiling coyly. "Perhaps you would like to share the reward?"

"What reward?" Ted blurted out before being silenced by a dour warning on Tom's face.

"Let us stop playing games, shall we?" Veronica cast a serious gaze over the assembled party. "I want the chip. If you have it you are wise to give it to me now and I will compensate you generously. If you lie to me, I am not responsible for the measures that my associates will take."

"We don't have it," Polly stated fiercely. "If I did have it, I would not give it to you. That damned chip has caused me nothing but pain and misery and I have already lost everything." She stomped her foot.

Veronica laughed out loud, before lowering her head in the posture of a bull before charging. "You still have your life. You still have your friends."

Polly inadvertently looked at Paul and Veronica did not miss the gesture.

"I am wasting my time. Perhaps Paul will come with me. Would you like that, Paul? When you have the chip for me you can have him back. My associates will not be happy if I come back empty handed."

"You can't do that. It's kidnapping," Polly cried.

"He is coming of his own free will as my guest, right Paul? Or would you rather Polly comes instead. I feel that she will be able to find the chip more easily than you. You see, I think that she has known where it is all along."

Ted looked thunder struck. "Do you know where it is, Polly?" She just glared at him.

"Tom, you can't let her do this!" Polly exclaimed.

"It will be alright, Polly, nothing will happen to Paul," Tom soothed without much conviction.

"You will find us at the Regent Hotel when you are ready to do business. Until then, I will take good care of your friend." She paused, "Just don't disappoint me." Opening the conference room door, she gestured Paul through before her.

Once they were gone, Polly turned angrily to Tom. "How could you let her do that? You know he only went to protect us!"

"To protect you," Ted corrected. "She might have taken me". Disappointment laced his words.

"Well I don't have that chip. So what are we going to do now?" She glared at Ted and wondered how she could ever have found him attractive.

"I think you have a pretty good idea about where it is," Tom answered.

"I might, but I'm not sure, and I don't trust either one of you," she exclaimed vehemently.

"You don't have to trust us, but you can. At least you can trust me," Tom said. "I did save you today." At that, she favored him with a sulky half-smile.

"What have I done?" Ted asked bewildered.

"You gave away our location!"

"I saved our lives, too," he rebutted, "by giving away our location."

"Anyway, I need your help. I don't have any money and I need some clothes. Tom, could you take me to my apartment so I can get my things? Do either of you have a place I can stay for a while? And please don't offer me the custodial closet."

Ted started to speak, but Tom cut him off. "You can stay at my place. I'll sleep on the sofa and there's a lock on the bedroom door. We'll drop Ted off on the way. I still have Bob's key card to the parking garage. Paul will be okay until tomorrow. Then you have to find that chip, Polly. These people mean business."

After dropping off Ted and stopping by Polly's old apartment so she could pack a bag, they dropped the flit back at Binge headquarters and took a taxi to Tom's apartment. He lived in a high-rise building near the university campus where he had been an English professor. Bookshelves crammed with weighty volumes lined the walls and piles of books and papers littered every flat surface. The place had a dusty, slightly moldy smell. An oriental-style carpet covered the floor and was held down by a large, ornate wooden desk and chair on one end, a sofa and floor lamp on the other. A tiny kitchen opened off to one side and next to it was a closed door that Polly assumed led into the bedroom. Dust motes danced in the light coming from a single window behind the desk, as if enjoying one last breath of freedom before joining their fellows on the carpet and other surfaces.

"Nice place," Polly politely remarked.

Tom rolled his eyes. "I'll put on the kettle for some tea. You drink tea?"

"How are you going to sleep on this sofa, it isn't even full-sized?" She called from the living room, moving a stack of papers so she could sit.

"Don't worry about it. Just tell me where that chip is. I don't think Veronica is bluffing. Paul is in real danger if we don't show up with the goods."

He banged around in the kitchen looking for some bread or cookies to serve with the tea. There was some clabbered milk in the fridge and a half bag of Scottish shortbread cookies in his cupboard. Ants swarmed the sugar bowl but thankfully had yet to discover the cookies. He pulled out a small tray leaning vertically against the microwave and on it arranged two cups with saucers and a plate chaotically heaped with the cookies. When the kettle whistled, he lifted it from the burner and poured hot water over tea bags into the cups, securing the string with one finger as he poured. Tiny roses decorated the outside and inside border of the fine porcelain china cups and the matching saucers that cradled them. The tea set was all that was left of his failed marriage, if you discounted the acrimonious words from their final days that lodged forever in his mind.

"Here we go," he announced, cheerfully setting the tray on top of a flat stack of papers on his desk.

Polly looked sullenly at the offering, but roused herself to extract a cookie and began to nibble. "I think Germán might have the chip."

Icy dread raced down his spine as he thought of Margarita. "Germán! How did Germán get it? Did you give it to him?"

"I told him where I hid it."

"Oh, God, do you know what danger you've put Margarita and Germán in? Don't tell anyone else. Not until I come up with a plan. Not anyone!"

"Who am I going to tell?" Polly asked on the verge of tears. "Should we go over there?"

"Let me think," Tom said sipping his tea and staring out the window at the bleak cityscape. "I can't risk calling them," he finally decided. "Get your hand bag. Do you think you can manage a Yooter? I don't dare call for a flit. It could be traced. But there is a Yooter stand in front of this building and I happen to have a gift pass in my desk."

"A gift pass?"

"Yeah, an untraceable pre-charged credit card."

"Couldn't you just use it for an auto-flit? The kind without a driver." Polly asked nervously. "I've never tried riding one of those things but I was never very good with a skate board when I was a kid."

"You'll be fine," he assured her, "just don't let go of the handle no matter what. There is a gyroscope built into the thing so that it doesn't turn upside down. Or if it does, it will right itself again. We don't have time to go looking for an auto-flit and because of the automatic tracking device built in, it might be traceable. They're equipped with cameras to ID user for insurance purposes."

"Yes and not being upside down permanently will surely make it a cinch to ride," she said with a tang of sarcasm. "Are we going to Margarita's?"

"That's the plan unless you have a better one. We need to know for sure if Germán has that chip. And I would like to talk to Margarita about our next move. She would never forgive me if something happens to her grandson. She might blame me for getting him involved, even though it was you." He gave her an accusing glare and she slit her eyes back at him. "I have some trainers you can wear. Anyone can ride a Yooter with trainers on. You better change into some shorts or jeans."

The trainers were old, smelly, red, rubber half-shoes that attached to the Yooter with powerful, tiny suction cups like geckos have on the pads of their feet. The front part stretched over the toe end of regular shoes. Grips around the heel completed the package, holding your feet firmly to the top of the board. They appeared to be way too small for Tom, but expanded in a one-size fits all fashion. Polly wrinkled her nose in distaste, but slipped them into her bag and followed the former professor out the door. He grabbed a set of ear clip communication buds from his desk drawer on the way.

"We're lucky I live so close to campus," Tom commented, affectionately running his hand over the fossil-embedded wall that enclosed the west side terracing. "There's a stand just over there. Here, put this in your ear so we can talk to each other. They're set to walkie-talkie mode. Just speak in a normal voice and I'll be able to hear whatever you say."

He passed his gift card through the slot on each of two Yooters at the end of the stand and helped Polly position the trainers onto the cruising board. Holding the Yooter for her, she jammed her feet into the toes and heels. "It's really easy," he instructed, "just twist the left handle forward to rise up and backward to lower. The right handle is for speed."

"Where's the brake?" Polly asked apprehensively.

"There is no brake," Tom chuckled. One side of his mouth lifted in what Polly interpreted as condescension. "Just stop twisting the right handle and it will stop. It's no harder than driving one of those handicap carts at the grocery store. It just has two other directions."

"I actually drove one of those once when I sprained my ankle."

"Good. I'm glad to hear you already know how to do it," Tom declared.

"I ran into an end display. One of the cans fell on my knee and I barely managed to limp back out of the store. I didn't even get my groceries."

WORLD WITHOUT DUCT TAPE

"You'll be fine," Tom reassured her doubtfully, his confidence changing into a worried frown. "Look, we'll take it nice and slow and I will be right here by you."

Tom lifted his Yooter a few feet off the ground and gave her an encouraging smile. Following suit, she balanced precariously at first, and then tipped over horizontal to the ground. Her hips sagged in slow motion until they touched the paved walkway before the machine managed to right itself. It made a grinding sound Tom had never heard one make before as gears and levers struggled with the unusual strain. She fell over in the opposite direction as it righted itself but stopped short of horizontal this time and it slowly righted itself again. Inhaling in deep, quick panicked breaths, she glared at her instructor. "I told you I couldn't do this."

"Of course you can," he insisted doubtfully. "You just need some practice. We'll cross over onto campus and you can practice without worrying about the traffic."

She looked off to her side where the traffic was close enough to crush her head if she leaned too far over in that direction. This was just as dangerous as she had thought. "Okay," she agreed reluctantly.

Tom led her up and down the sidewalk of the main mall. Students scrambled to move aside as she wobbled past them on the hovering skateboard. Eventually she gained confidence in the gyroscope system that prevented her from tipping over and was able to turn and move forward with a minimum of awkwardness. Nearly an hour had passed and they were both ready to move on.

"How do you feel about heading out to the street?" Tom asked.

"I'll try," Polly replied bravely.

Slowly Tom led the way forward and Polly followed. By the time they had gone a few blocks she was feeling more confident. It was kind of fun gliding along above the broken pavement, the wind blowing her hair off her sweaty neck.

When they came to the first traffic crossing, Tom twisted his handle forward and his Yooter lifted up a few inches above the cars filling the street. He glided just above them until his Yooter settled down onto the opposite sidewalk. "Give it a forward twist to boost your speed before you jump," he called back. Traffic was even worse now on streets that hadn't been torn up by the flood. People were literally jamming their cars into each other. A pedestrian or bicycle rider wouldn't stand a chance, while Polly floated over the angry, grinding, crowded roadway with a forward twist of her handle. Polluted air made her eyes water and her breathing labored, but otherwise she was enjoying the ride.

Tom waited for her to pull up beside him on the other side. "Let's take side streets," he suggested and Polly nodded her approval. "We'll go left at the next block."

They had turned and were proceeding down a less congested residential walk when Polly called out. Tom let go of the forward handle and waited for her to catch up to him. "We're being followed," she informed him.

Tom looked around and saw an unmanned drone hovering behind and above them. "Probably an advertising drone," he said.

"I don't think so," Polly stated. "It turned off when we did. Aren't they banned from residential areas? Someone is watching us."

"We can't have it following us," Tom said. "We'll have to try to lose it. We might have to dump these Yooters and walk."

"It might be too late for that. Tom, look," Polly nodded toward two auto-flits approaching from behind the drone. The men driving them were wearing similar equipment to the men who had chased them in the helicopter at Margarita's house, military-style gear that no civilian would have. Tom hadn't been there but he recognized the insignia on their helmets.

"They're from Binge," he said. "Follow me. It's time you earned your pilot's license for real." With that, he pushed his throttle forward. Polly matched his speed without thinking. When she wasn't worrying about falling, her balance greatly improved. She had other things to worry about now.

Chapter 25: Time for Dessert

"You put it where?" Pam demanded again as if she hadn't heard the first time. "What were you thinking? You don't have a wall safe or safe deposit box? Why on Earth would you put it there? How could you put it there?"

"I have experience with self-injection," Mitchell answered sheepishly. "There wasn't time to get a safe deposit box. Besides, how safe are those anyway?"

Pam dropped her face into her hands in despair. "Well there is no chance of out running them." She looked out the big window at the front of the house and saw the chopper landing on the lawn. It was a small two-seater with a pilot and one other person inside. Not what she expected.

"Someone is getting out," her dad observed and they all watched unable to move or think of anything else to do.

Veronica stepped out of the cabin, hair whipping about across her face as the rotors continued to swoop around and around. Bob and Pam sighed with relief.

Mitchell anxiously stated the obvious. "It's Veronica."

"Why is she here?" Bob queried suspiciously. "Does she know you're here?"

"No," Mitchell exclaimed. "I came here in good faith to bargain with you."

"Good," Bob said, "then don't tell her you have it."

"She might already know," Mitchell admitted. "I already saw her about buying it."

"Oh…..and when was this?" he asked. "Oh, never mind. It doesn't matter. Why didn't she buy it from you? I know that she is interested in obtaining it."

"She didn't want to pay my price," Mitchell answered.

"And how much is that?"

"A share of the profits."

"Well," Bob smiled slyly. "I think I can arrange that. Don't tell her where it is and we can work out the details after she leaves."

Pam went to the front door to open it for their unexpected guest. "What's going on? I thought you were just going to keep an eye out for Binge," she whispered.

"Good to see you again also," Veronica said. "My, don't you look lovely this evening. Am I interrupting something?"

"Not at all, come in," Bob called from the living area. "You're just in time for dessert. Pam was going to the kitchen to bring it out. Come join us."

Pam left the door open for Veronica to enter and turned toward the kitchen with a disgusted expression on her face. She hated it when her father treated her like a child or even worse like the help. She left the swinging door propped open so she could hear the discussion in the other room while she dished up bowls of ice cream and spooned the sliced berries on top, but the conversation was polite and uninformative.

Everyone was seated on the L-shaped sectional when she returned so she put the tray on the large, square coffee table in front of it and took a chair across from them. Only Mitchell reached out for the food and then hesitated. "Please," she said, "help yourselves. It is ice cream. Don't want it to melt." Obediently they all took a bowl.

After savoring the sweet treat for several minutes, Veronica was the first to speak. "So you are now trying to sell your copy to Bob. Is that so, Mitchell? You know that he has already approached me." She turned to Bob who was seated between her and Mitchell.

"I just learned that before you arrived. You know that Binge will not allow you to gain access to this information Veronica. They empowered me to retrieve it and they are sparing no expense. They aren't interested in obtaining a copy without the original. They want them both. I don't believe that you or I are immune to the measures that they are willing to take in order to get them."

"I know how Binge operates," Veronica assured him. "They might not be as powerful as you think. Besides, do they know about this copy?" She looked past Bob to gage Mitchell's reaction to this question.

Mitchell sputtered for a moment, his mouth full of ice cream. "I assumed that Bob was their spokesperson."

"Well then," she sat back into the plush sofa cushions, setting her bowl down on the shiny surface of the table where it would leave a water mark. Pam knew the maid would be furious and quickly slipped a napkin under it much to Veronica's amusement. They caught each other's eye and Pam flashed an angry frown her way that had nothing to do with the table. "Bob are you the spokesperson for Binge?"

"I might be," Bob said mysteriously. "If you mean have I informed them of the location of the copy, then no. Mitchell and I were just discussing terms. Right, Mitchell?"

"Er..Uh...yeah," Mitchell muttered. "Bob here is willing to offer me a percentage of the profits."

"Oh, really, Bob, how nice, since if Binge gets hold of it there will be no profits," Veronica pointed out.

"What does she mean, Bob," Mitchell asked in surprise.

Bob adjusted his sitting position while Pam, frustrated at being left out of the discussion, blurted, "Because Binge is going to destroy it."

"Pam," her father cried.

"Tell him the truth, Dad," she uttered quietly.

"Yes, Bob, let's hear the truth," Veronica agreed.

Mitchell stood up suddenly and scanned the party in dismay. "What is going on here?" He realized that he had told Bob where the chip was hidden. If Binge wanted to get rid of it, they could do it without removing the chip. He felt very vulnerable all of a sudden.

He sat down with a heavy thud. "I...I...I put the chip under my skin," he admitted to Veronica. Pam rolled her eyes and her father smiled enigmatically.

"Sit down Mitchell. You are not going to die just yet," Veronica reassured him. "Remember that I want the chip to use it, not to destroy it. Perhaps you would like to rethink our earlier conversation. Let's all go back to my room and continue this discussion there. Paul is no doubt getting lonely." She smiled at Pam. "I am sure that he would enjoy the company. And we can come to an agreement on price. I do not intend to cheat my associates. After all, Pam is working for me now."

"Is that true Pam?" Her father looked at her with shock. "When did this happen?"

"Dad," Pam placated. "I can't live under your roof forever. Veronica offered me a position with her company and I accepted."

"She is my new Vice-President for International Relations as soon as she signs a contract," Veronica clarified.

"When were you going to tell me," Bob asked angrily.

"It just happened this morning, Dad. I was going to tell you, but then Mitchell showed up and I didn't get a chance. Don't be angry with me. It's not like I am going behind your back. I'll be able to take care of you now."

"I don't need taking care of," he fired off before turning to Veronica and saying, "fine let's all go to your place and hash this out. I'll take Mitchell and Pam in my flit since it looks like your transportation isn't equipped for extra passengers."

When they arrived, Paul was sitting comfortably on an overstuffed chair with one leg dangling over the arm. He was staring enraptured at his comp screen while tapping rapidly. Veronica had arrived ahead of them. She opened the door to her suite to let them in and then checked the foyer before closing it again. Inside, an armed guard appraised the new arrivals with a menacing glare before disappearing into one of the two bedrooms.

"Pam," Paul said looking up.

"Are you winning?" She asked, an annoyed edge in her voice.

"Always," he replied closing his game and putting the device into his pants pocket. He was wearing loose fitting cargo pants she had never seen before and a soft, clean T-shirt, pale blue with no slogan. His hair was damp from a recent shampoo. Veronica apparently had taken charge of her ex-boyfriend like everything else. "You look nice. Are you going out?"

"I already did. I'm here," she replied trying to give nothing away.

"Bob, Mitchell," he addressed the other two arrivals. Where was Polly, he thought to himself. As long as she was safe so was the chip. "So what's the plan? Are you here to ransom me?"

"Don't be dramatic," Veronica broke in, "we are all here to discuss the situation and resolve it for the best possible outcome."

Mitchell was sweating profusely. Why had he injected himself? He felt feverish. Had the needle been clean? He couldn't remember where he got it. Sometimes disreputable dealers will reseal dirty needles and sell them as new, but he was usually careful about where he got his. He had been in such a hurry to hide the damned thing he had grabbed a needle from one of the other driver's packs.

"Are you all right, Mitchell?" Bob said. Veronica looked at him suspiciously. Pam noticed the sweating and stepped away from him and closer to Paul, a look of distaste on her face. No sense in trying to seduce the man at this point.

"What's wrong with you?" Veronica asked.

"Nothing," Mitchell wheezed, "I need to sit down." He took a position in middle of the sofa. Pam sat on the edge of a chair next to Paul. Veronica pulled out a chair from the bar and Bob did the same. They sat in a semi-circle staring at the distressed man.

"He injected the chip," Pam explained to Paul.

"Where is the injection, Mitchell?" Veronica asked sympathetically. "I will call my doctor. You seem to be having a reaction. You're going to need antibiotics."

"M…My belly," Mitchell whimpered pulling up his shirt to display a red, swollen area next to where his belly button was buried in folds of fat. Pam wrinkled her nose. She felt embarrassed for having flirted with such a person, someone who would cave at one word from Veronica without so much as an attempt to fight. Surely she wasn't his only option for treatment. Now he might as well hand over the chip to her free of charge. "Call him," Mitchell cried pathetically.

"Her," Veronica corrected, tapping in a quick text. A few moments later there was a soft buzz and after checking the message she announced to the group that the doctor would be there shortly. "While we are waiting shall we discuss terms?" She smiled like the Cheshire cat from Alice in Wonderland before sliding off her stool to fetch drinks from the refrigerator in the kitchenette.

"As you know Mitchell, I'm not willing to share profits, but I am willing to make your life easy from now on if you have what I am looking for. Pam is getting a hefty salary as my VP. Bob, she can throw you a bone or two from her new position. She has expressed a desire to bail you out from your current debt and I see no reason why she won't be able to do so. As my VP she will receive stock options and considerable political currency. A few strings pulled here and there and I am sure Binge will see fit to drop any financial hold they have over your retirement package. They need my connections to the Mexican cartels to ensure their products flow smoothly back and forth over the border." She paused to give the assembly time to process this information. Bob looked stunned. Pam sat up straighter on the arm of the chair a smile forming at the edges of her mouth.

Veronica continued, "I don't care if I have the original or the copy as long as it works. Once we remove it and verify that it's what I am looking for I will give you 10 million creds, Mitchell. That should keep you in double cheeseburgers and beer for quite some time. It might have been more if you had not caused me all this trouble and expense. You are lucky to come away with your life at this point. My body guard could do away with you and say you were attacking me. When it comes to the police, they will always believe the money. Face it, nobody here cares what happens to you."

Mitchell looked at the faces encircling him. Only Paul seemed not at all interested, he had resumed playing his game. Pam and Bob could have been vultures ready to digest some road kill. He vowed never again to be taken in by that innocent, blonde, blue-eyed girl-next-door ideal he had sought all his life.

"Okay, fine," Mitchell agreed grudgingly. "Get this thing out of me and give me a shot of antibiotics and it's yours for 10 mil."

"Terrific," Veronica sat back on her stool contentedly, "I am tired of this town. The border may be dirty and hot but it is far more interesting."

Chapter 26: The Chase

"Follow me. We'll see how serious these guys are," Tom said into his ear phone after a quick glance back at the two Binge musclemen coming toward them on auto-flits.

"Oh, they're serious," Polly stated, "and they're armed."

Tom didn't address that fact but took off at a fast clip with Polly tailing close behind. He hung a sharp left at the next corner to retrace their route.

"Where are we going?" Polly called into her device.

"Back to campus," Tom replied. "I'm banking on knowing that terrain better than these goobers."

"But I don't," Polly said in dismay. This Tom ignored. The Binge thugs were gaining fast. Auto-flits were the faster vehicle, but they had one disadvantage. They maneuvered automatically while the Yooters were controlled by the driver.

By the time they reached campus the auto-flits were flying almost directly over them. Attached to his helmet, one of the men had a loud speaker on which he addressed the fugitives below. "Stop your vehicle and we will not hurt you. You are under suspicion of purveying stolen property.

Surrender now and Binge will not charge you. Continue to flee and you will suffer the consequences."

Neither Polly nor Tom was fooled by this olive branch. They zigged in and zagged out of the crowds of students. A few auto-flits were hovering above the sidewalks and "traffic free" roads of the university. Venders filled any open space. The bell tower chimed the hour and suddenly the buildings lining the walkways disgorged students by the thousands. Polly was pushed sideways and Tom lost sight of her.

"Where are you?" He called into his ear clip.

"I'm here. I don't see you. I'm going to try to lose this guy. I can still see him above me but I'm not sure that he can see me." Trust in the force, she told herself, and the trainer shoes. She twisted her left handle forward and began to rise over the rush of students into plain view of her Binge pursuers.

"There she is," one of them shouted so loudly she heard him without the advantage of a megaphone. They both aimed their flits in her direction, forgetting all about Tom.

When she saw this she took off at top speed which was way slower than the flits, but they had meandered off in the wrong direction when the students crowded out of the classrooms so were not as close as they had been. Tom started to move toward her, but she used her ear clip to tell him not to. "I'm going to lose them. You go warn Margarita and Germán. Get them away from their house, somewhere safe. I'll meet you there."

"Where will that be?" Tom grunted, thinking it was a bad idea to leave her but not wanting them to go after Margarita while he was chasing around the campus.

"Take them to the Art Library on campus." In retrospect, the hour or so of practice on campus had given her a pretty good idea of where the main buildings were located.

Now the two flits were in hot pursuit. Polly crouched back down into the rush of students but that didn't fool them this time. Already the crush of people was thinning. Polly trailed a group over a tiny bridge spanning a rocky creek. It was usually dry, but since the heavy rains rushing water filled its banks. Live oaks clinging to the cliffs above hung complicated webs of branches over the water. Taking a sudden right turn she dipped down into the cool recesses of the channel, ducking to avoid one low lying limb and began to skim over the water. It was tricky maneuvering. Large boulders of granite and limestone exposed by erosion lined the sides, trapping her in a narrow gully.

The auto-flits refused to fly that low so the men hovered above and kept her in sight. She had to think fast. They were faster but she had more maneuverability. How could she use that to her advantage? Well, she thought, she was using it right now by following this stream, but she couldn't lose them because they could follow her higher up. She needed to find a tunnel or covered path. Farther in toward the center of the city Waller Creek was diverted into a storm drain. She could lead them there and they would have to follow her in on foot or station themselves one on each side of the openings. If they followed on foot she would have the advantage on the Yooter. If they split up, then there would be only one to lose when she made her break.

Looming ahead she saw the giant, black, toothless, concrete mouth of the drain. The creek cut its own direct path to the dammed up section of river called Lady Bird Reservoir, so she had made quick progress through the congested city. Seeing she was headed for the tunnel and unwilling to leave the comfort of their vehicles, the two auto-flit drivers split up as she entered the tunnel. It would be difficult to wade through the fast moving, dirty water on foot. It was going to be a waiting game; one that had to go in their favor.

The entrance to the tunnel faded into the background as she moved ahead into the darkness. An initial wet, musty odor gave way to deeper, nastier scents of urine and feces. Fetid dampness clung to her skin like an ancient decaying shroud. The Yooter automatically turned on navigational LED lights that illuminated oily water covered in a floating litter of plastic bottles, food wrappers and worse. Slimy, dripping walls closed in on both sides overhung by a low ceiling that nearly touched her head. She dared not stay in the dark for long or her battery would go dead. She shivered to think of the platform that suspended her above the filthy ooze losing power and sinking down into the deep sewage water below. Turning back around, she stopped short of the entrance and leaned out over the handlebars to peak at the sky. It took a minute for her eyes to adjust. Harsh mid-day light washed over her face and she squinted up to see if the auto-flit driver could see her. In the bright sunlight one back lit flit circled above. She slipped back into the shadows and switched her Yooter to idle to save the battery, and then she waited for the other driver to reach the lake where the tunnel fluid exited into the drinking water of the city.

A splash resonated out of the gloom at her rear. She jerked and pushed her feet off to one side as she turned to look. The Yooter dipped her sideways and dangerously close to the murky water beneath. She grabbed her bag with one hand to keep it from dipping into the water, letting go of the levitating handle. "Never let go of the handle," she remembered Tom's warning. The Yooter sank down a few inches until auto-glide took over to keep it from touching the surface. A big, fat rat swam by inches from her bare arm. If she had still been wearing a dress the skirt would have made a convenient ramp for it to climb up out of the disgusting water that flowed through the drain. Luckily, she had changed into jean shorts and a tight T-shirt. She pressed her bag against her side to keep it from falling in. Unscathed but unnerved, the Yooter righted itself and she crept closer to the entrance to peak out at her pursuer. Whatever else was in the tunnel behind her was better left undiscovered. It was time to attempt her escape.

She zoomed out into the open, catching the driver off guard. His hesitation cost him valuable minutes. She had a slight lead. She aimed the Yooter back toward campus, targeting a direct route to the huge and complicated Business Building. This building had sustained numerous additions, so that it was a conglomerate of different styles connected by a maze of overpasses and tunnels. Native limestone, carved stone corbels and red clay tile roofing fronted half of the building, while on the other side of a plaza the other half was red brick. A glass overpass connected the two. If she was to lose her pursuer this would be a good place.

Instead of following the creek she took the sidewalks, hovering over cars and cutting corners through parking lots, yards and alleys. In order to keep her in view, the Binge henchman had to fly high and broad. His compatriot was nowhere to be seen. She assumed he had radioed that she was coming out. He could appear at any moment. She needed to lose this one before that happened. It would be nearly impossible to give both of them the slip once they synchronized their search.

Nearing campus, the road broadened with bus and bike lanes. A series of law offices fronted with tiny manicured lawns made it even more open. The auto-flit was right above her now. Seeing his chance, he descended toward the pavement. Polly twisted the forward lever hard but it was already at full speed. Still, the automatic controls wouldn't let him hit her from the air. How did he expect to stop her?

No sooner than she thought this than she saw his intent. He swooped in to land in front of her. She looked right and left for an avenue of escape. To her left were throbbing, mechanical veins of traffic sluggishly moving forward. To her right, short brick and stone walkways pierced neat little landscaped lawns of businesses and art galleries converted from single family houses that had lined the street 100 years ago. If she crossed over traffic, she would be up against impenetrable walls with no gaps between. On that side, newer businesses formed a continuous façade that opened directly onto the sidewalk. Escape would be almost impossible. Her only choice was to try to lose him by dodging between the shops to her right.

She made her signature hard right turn, toppling over into an acute triangle with the ground and nearly smashing her head into the corner of a law office before the Yooter straightened. The flit driver reacted instantly and was hot on her tail. Behind the converted houses a narrow alley accessed garbage bins and cramped parking spaces. She turned down the alley in the direction of campus, the flit following her above the rooftops.

As she was nearing the end of the alley, a garbage truck loomed into view. She twisted hard on the levitate handle but it was too little too late. At the last minute she let go of the accelerator and in what felt like slow motion, crashed headlong into the windshield of the truck with only slightly less momentum than full speed. The Yooter's top speed was 20 miles per hour but she had managed to hit the metal frame of the windshield with the handlebars. Her body followed, squashing up against the glass like a splattered bug.

The scooter slid off the front of the truck and thudded to the ground in a disjointed heap; the driver, who had been barely creeping forward as he entered the alley, ground to a complete halt, engine idling as he leaped from his vehicle. Polly laid in a crumpled heap on the dirty asphalt.

"*Carajo*, are you okay," he asked as he helped her to her feet.

"I'm fine," she answered grumpily, a thin stream of blood oozing from her knee and one elbow, her already injured hand was scraped and bruised. "Could you see if my Yooter still works?" She limped over to the scooter lying on its side a few feet away, shaking her hand to relieve the pain.

"You need me to take you to a doctor? Is anything broken?" He asked anxiously.

Up above them, the auto-flit was circling. It had ignored instructions to land. That was the problem with these automatic machines; they had minds of their own. The accident had put it into emergency avoidance mode and it was everything he could do to keep it from flying away entirely.

The garbage man picked up Polly's Yooter and bent the handlebars back into a close approximation to their original position. With one enormous, booted foot he steadied it and gently twisted the hand grips. It rose up off the ground and then forward a few feet. He turned the handlebars to the right and then left to make sure that it could still maneuver. Meanwhile, Polly pulled a hanky from her leather handbag to tenderly blot the blood from her wounds. After thoroughly soiling it, she bound it around her injured hand.

"It has some scratches but otherwise it seems okay," he told her. "Looks better than you. Sure you don't need to see a doctor."

"No thanks," she said scowling, irrationally irritated by his kindness, "what about your truck?"

"Oh, my truck has seen much worse," he assured her. "Besides, it belongs to the company. You only cracked the windshield so I doubt anyone will notice."

"Well, thanks again, now if I can slip past your truck I'll be on my way."

"I think there is room on that side," he said pointing. "Be careful now. I think someone should look at that hand."

"They already have," Polly answered, causing the kindly man to squint in puzzlement. Then he shrugged and after she narrowly passed by the driver's side of his truck, he climbed back in to continue his route.

Polly glided past a parking garage and entered the southern edge of the campus with the Business Building in sight. The auto-flit continued to follow up above, but he didn't try to confront her again. Now he seemed content to see where she was going. Perhaps he was waiting for reinforcements.

Rebuffing the wide classical stone staircase at the front, she rounded the building to enter via the competing façade facing the next street over. The building was so large it took up the entire block. At the last minute, she hung a hard right and slipped under the glass overpass leading to the plaza that separated contrasting building styles. Her body tilted at right angle to the ground and she scraped her already injured elbow across the rough concrete before the Yooter slowly lifted her upright again. This time she used the pause in forward momentum while it righted itself to jerk free of the trainer shoes. Feet free, she propelled the scooter toward the great glass doors of the building. With one foot on the ground she twisted the lift lever forward to gain height and skidded up the stairs, pushing off against every other step with her foot. She was expecting to jump off at the last minute, but as if by magic, the massive glass doors opened as she reached the pinnacle of the staircase and she smoothly sailed into a cool marble foyer.

"That's quite an entrance," Ted remarked when she had glided to a halt.

"Ted," she exclaimed. "What are you doing here?"

"I might ask you the same thing," he said smiling.

"I'm being followed by a couple of Binge goons. You opened those doors just in time. Strange how you're always there when I need you," she remarked, a suspicious glint in her eye."

"I'm taking a class here."

"You're a business major?"

"You sound surprised."

The auto-flit driver was caught off guard by the move. He instructed his aircraft to land, but the automatic control system did not respond. It began to circle, signaling to its operating tower for instructions. To avoid collision, auto-flits could only land in certain designated areas on campus.

"I have to get out of sight," Polly said with a nervous glance outside.

"Follow me," Ted instructed, "it's easy to get lost in this place. But you better leave the Yooter. They aren't allowed in the buildings."

Chapter 27: The Meeting

"I need a disguise," Polly decided and Ted agreed. Luckily, there was a little gift shop attached to one side of the building. Since the plaza with its towering glass walls and views from the walkway over the street attracted lounging students and their visiting families, little gift stores and refreshment stands had proliferated at this location. Ted bought Polly an oversized burnt-orange hoody in his size, a pair of flip flops and a box of X-large Band Aides so she wouldn't bleed on the new sweatshirt. Transformed, she tied her bootstrings together and attached them to the small, leather satchel she wore slung bandolier-style across her chest and hidden under the sweatshirt. During the creek chase she had been glad she didn't wear flip flops. "I keep letting you dress me," she remarked with a shy, appreciative smile.

He looked at her appraisingly and said, "Perhaps someday you will let me undress you." Surprised by his forwardness, she jerked her head back queasily like from a bad odor and he forced out a quick laugh, "just kidding of course." Her expression changed to doubtful consternation. For now she was stuck with the guy.

"I never could walk in flip flops, but you're right, the boots were a dead giveaway. I haven't seen one pair since I got here. We shouldn't leave by the same way that we came in. You said you know the building? Which exit is closest to the Art Building?"

Ted gave Polly his pile of books to carry to further add to the disguise and they made their way over to the Art Building, passed through it and crossed the street to the Art Library. They didn't see anyone patrolling the sky as they crossed over. Inside, Tom was waiting at a table with Margarita and her grandson.

"What's Ted doing here," Tom asked suspiciously.

"He helped me avoid the auto-flit driver and bought me this disguise," Polly answered, shrugging off the hot sweatshirt and handing it over to Ted.

"You certainly are Sir Galahad aren't you," Tom smirked.

Asked how he happened to be on campus at such an opportune moment, Ted explained that he was being groomed to manage some of the Quicky Picks. The corporation was paying his tuition.

"That's nice," Germán grunted, "you never said anything about that to me."

"You never seemed interested, compadre," Ted reached over to jostle Germán's shoulder in a brotherly gesture of friendly condescension. Germán pulled away with the slightest of motions.

"Anyway, we need to find the chip and we were waiting on you to get here before we decided our next move," Tom addressed Polly. After he said it, he had second thoughts about including Ted.

He was worried about Polly. She appeared even more beat up after her chase with the Binge auto-flit drivers than she had after her run in with the flood waters.

Germán and Polly's eyes met. "What does Polly want to do," Germán said.

"It is worthless without the other half. I don't see that we have much choice. I guess we have to make a deal with Veronica. Binge is just going to destroy it," Polly decided.

"I won't let the maquiladoras have it," Germán vehemently proclaimed. "Not after what they did to my mother. Never."

"Germán," Margarita roused from her meditation. "Not all maquiladoras are the same just like not all people are the same. This Veronica might be able to use this to change what they were in the past."

Tom appreciated Margarita's calm, sagacious acceptance of the situation, but Germán glared angrily at his grandmother. She wrinkled her brow.

"We might not need Veronica if we can find an interested third party," Tom remarked sitting back in his chair, arms crossed across his chest, a strange smile passing over his lips.

"You sly dog," Ted cut in delightedly. Polly's opinion of him was beginning to change and not for the better. "Who do you have in mind?"

"Germán said that it is up to me," she reminded everyone. "I think Germán and I should decide what to do with it. We want it to be used to free everyone from the corporations. Cheap, free energy anyone can use with a little effort; personal power stations to provide enough energy for everyone to live comfortably without polluting the world and exploiting each other."

"That sounds nice," Tom said, "but what about your job, my retirement, Ted's.... What do you want out of this anyway, Ted?" Before Ted could answer he added, "To paraphrase Machiavelli, a free and fair world is one I would like to live in, but it is not the world that we do live in. Power wants power and it is power that is in charge. Power does not share."

Ted blurted out, "I want the same thing that you all want: a nice pile of money and to do something to save the world at the same time. It sounds to me like Veronica is our best bet."

Everyone had to admit that money is nice, even Margarita, and if one could get rich saving the world that would be fine. But was it really that easy? Something inside Polly told her it wasn't and she could see that Germán was thinking along the same lines.

Tom's comp sang its oldies tune and a few heads turned to give him a dirty look. Sheepishly, he pulled it from his pocket and checked to see who was calling. It was Mitchell. What did he want? "I have to take this," he told the others, "I'll be just a minute." He went into the hall and stood out of view of the glass doorway and interior windows of the library.

"Mitchell," he said exasperatedly. "What do you want?"

"I'll tell you what I want," Mitchell cried into the speaker. "I want out of here. They are getting ready to cut me open. They have Paul hostage. They told me to call you if you want to be here when the deal goes down."

"Who is we, Mitch. Who else is there with you?"

"Veronica and Pam. They've gone into business together. And Bob is here. I don't know what he wants. Are you working for Binge or for Veronica? She wants to make a deal. She wants to take the chip out legally."

"How legally? Where is the chip? What do you mean take it out?"

"I implanted it," Mitchell shamefully admitted. "They want me to sign permission for their surgeon to remove it in case I die. Can you come over to Veronica's room? I'm not feeling too well. I didn't have anyone else I could call. And Paul wants you to come get him. Veronica won't let him leave until she has the chip."

Well that is just great, Tom thought. "Okay. Let me wrap up what I'm doing. I'll grab a flit and be there soon. Tell Veronica I'm on my way. Don't sign anything until I get there."

"Hurry," Mitchell whimpered before disconnecting.

Tom leaned against the cool plaster of the wall for a moment collecting his thoughts. It seemed Veronica didn't need the master copy after all. Unlike Binge, she didn't want every copy as long as she had both halves. She would worry about the loose ends later. He couldn't leave Paul out in the cold even if he could care less what happened to Mitchell. There goes my farm in the country with Margarita and a couple of goats, he thought as he slowly reentered the library.

The group at the table looked up expectantly. "There's been a change of plans," he told them.

Ted was the least troubled by the news. He shrugged, got up to leave and told them he would keep in touch. No one seemed to care, though Polly said good bye and thanked him again for helping her. Germán refused to acknowledge his good-bye, choosing instead to stare moodily down at the table. Polly reached out a hand to touch his in commiseration, before announcing that she would accompany Tom. Tom was surprised but did not say no.

Margarita gently nudged her grandson from his chair and with an enigmatic nod to Polly and Tom who stood at the end of the table announced a desire to go home and forget this chip business. Tom offered to call her a flit, but she refused, saying they would find their own way. Then Tom insisted, Margarita resisted and finally Polly said they would drop them off on their way to the hotel and that was that.

A muscular man armed with a pistol in a shoulder harness opened the door for them at the hotel. He disappeared into one of the bedrooms. The scene in Veronica's hotel room could have been taken from an action/thriller movie. Mitchell lay on the couch, his stomach exposed, raw and bleeding at the injection site, perspiration beaded across his forehead. His eyes were glazed and unfocused. The air smelled of desperation; sweaty, confined humans trapped together for too long. Veronica stood by the floor to ceiling windows staring out at the smog smothered landscape animated by a trickling line of traffic moving from one side of the city to the other. From the 21st floor, the creeping line of cars and trucks slithered forward in a slow, undulating, snake-like motion. Flits and auto-flits zoomed by like flying insects, irritating and obnoxious. She resisted the urge to reach her hand out and swat them away. She had paid extra for the view, but in retrospect the view of impenetrable smog on the lower floors might have been more relaxing.

Polly had been worried about Paul ever since he was taken captive. Now, seeing him sprawled across an overstuffed chair intent on some video game, she wanted to kick herself for her concern. He barely took his eyes off the tiny comp screen to grunt hello, although he might have paused for one second upon seeing her. Actually, he looked better than she had ever seen him. In contrast she probably looked worse. Obviously, he hadn't been suffering.

Bob and Pam were seated on stools at the bar. Icy drinks clinked in their hands as they observed from their seats like spectators waiting for the next event. "Hi Polly," Pam greeted her suspiciously; "I don't know why I am surprised to see you here. You do like to tag along, don't you?"

Paul looked up at this to gauge Polly's reaction, but Polly said nothing. She merely found a vacant chair and sat down near the supine man on the sofa. Tom stood next to her protectively. Paul went back to his game. With peripheral vision, he observed Pam pull a strand of her hair into her mouth to suck on.

Finally, Veronica turned to address the assembly. She was all poise and business even barefoot and in blue jeans. "I guess you are wondering about how much each of you will benefit financially now that I have the other chip. Please be assured that you will be compensated according to your contribution. As I believe I have made clear, I am not Binge and my maquiladoras will use this technology to create goods that can be produced without harming the environment to the extent that it has been savaged in the past. That said; I am a businesswoman. I will make decisions based on the bottom line and I will employ whatever means I deem necessary to do so."

Polly reacted with disgust, but Paul continued ignoring everything to focus on his game. She noticed the leg he had swung over the arm of the chair began to jiggle. Whether because of his game or the conversation she couldn't tell.

"I'm the one with the chip," Mitchell broke in, "I'm the one who should be compensated."

"Indeed, and you shall be, but these good people have also contributed. I would like for all of us to leave as friends," Veronica responded. "Have you opened it yet? Can you verify what is on it?"

"Friends might be pushing it," Polly interjected, ignoring the wheedling protestations of the man on the sofa.

"Oh yes, you are the one who held the strings until now, but as you see the tides have turned. Perhaps you will not receive compensation," Veronica menaced.

"I cloned it," Mitchell redirected the conversation back to him. "It's software that creates an identical copy without opening it. With everything password protected anymore, I don't have time to open everything that I copy."

Paul looked up with a troubled expression but said nothing.

"Let's get on with it," Pam urged. "Tom, tell Mitchell to sign the release so Veronica's doctor can operate."

Just then there was a tap on the door and Veronica padded across the carpet on bare feet to answer it. She had discarded her flip flops as soon as she entered the room. The doctor came in and surveyed the situation.

"Good thing I brought antibiotics, that man has an infection," she said pointing to Mitchell. "Are you allergic to any medications, sir?"

"No," Mitchell moaned, "I need something for pain."

"Very well then, read and sign this document and I can begin treatment."

Mitchell indicated Tom with a nod and said, "Give it to him first."

When Tom gave his approval, Mitchell glanced at it, winced and signed. "Something for the pain first," he demanded.

"Of course," she said. "I will give you an intravenous cocktail of pain reliever and inflammation reducer and we'll use a topical for the insertion site." She opened her bag and pulled out a couple of hypodermic syringes with needles already attached. They had been prefilled. After rubbing both places with some alcohol pads, she injected one into a vein in his arm and the other into his stomach next to the insertion site. "There," she said with satisfaction, "I bet you feel better already." Mitchell sighed with relief and his eyelids drooped.

Twenty minutes later, the doctor removed a sterile cloth from her supplies and laid it out on a small table Veronica had brought out from the bedroom. She placed her scalpel and medical tweezers on the table and some gauze to swab up the blood.

Polly watched mesmerized. Paul had put away his game to observe the procedure also. They glanced at each other as the doctor began the surgery. Paul knew Polly was remembering how different her extraction had been. This surgery did not require the use of duct tape substitute or a vacuum cleaner.

The surgeon deftly cut into the fatty tissue and after a few minutes of digging grasped the chip firmly between her tweezers. "It was lodged in fat," she told the assembly, "a little slippery, but easier to remove than when it's in muscle." She dipped it into a small bowl of non-corrosive cleanser that Veronica had provided and then into another clean, dry bowl. "And that is that," she said. "I'll give him a shot of penicillin and he is done. If there are any complications you know where to find me. He might want to take some ibuprofen for the pain, but he shouldn't need anything stronger.

"Do you want me to clean up those cuts? They don't look deep enough for stitches but you should disinfest them and cover that one on your elbow," she said looking at Polly. Somehow, Polly had already rubbed the Band Aides off her arms but she wasn't bleeding at the moment.

"Thank you, doctor. We can take care of it. You know where to bill me. I'll walk you to the door," Veronica decided for Polly. She picked up the bowl with the chip in it as she moved across the room.

Mitchell was passed out snoring, a large Band-Aid plastered to his exposed stomach.

"You have what you want. I guess you don't need us anymore. I'll take Polly and Paul and get out of your hair," Tom suggested. At least he had been paid for the first chip. It wasn't enough to retire on but it would keep him solvent for the time being.

"Yes, I do appreciate what you have done, but perhaps Polly should stay until I see if this is the real thing. You may take Paul if you like." Veronica stood in middle of the room tenderly holding the small bowl with both hands.

"I'm not leaving without Polly," Paul declared. Pam looked up at him in surprise and flashed a scowl toward Polly.

"You have no right to keep me here," Polly stated with trepidation.

"Wait until I check the contents. If it's the right information, I have no further need of either one of you. You can keep the clothes as my gift, Paul"

Paul wriggled uncomfortably inside the gifted clothes, running a hand across his chest as if wiping off dirt. Veronica chuckled and walked over to the chip reader/sender she had used to check the contents of the first chip. As she pulled the tiny information storage device from the bowl to insert it, there was a knock at the door.

"Stay put everyone. Dr. Pat must have forgotten something." She casually opened the door.

"Ted!" Polly exclaimed. He pushed through the doorway followed by two large, helmeted men holding machine guns pointed down at the floor. They both wore black Kevlar reinforced uniforms with the Binge logo emblazoned across one front pocket. "What are you doing here?" she finished.

"They were waiting for me when I left the library," he explained sheepishly to the ensemble.

Tom muttered something about knowing that he couldn't be trusted.

The bedroom door opened and Veronica's bodyguard came out holding a Glock pistol. The muzzle was pointed forward and his finger was on the trigger.

Looking surprised at the combined fire power of the intruders, he gently placed the pistol on the floor at his feet and raised his hands.

Veronica bit her lip and said, "You can let these people go. They're only in the way. I have the chip in this bowl." She held up the chip for Ted to inspect. He nodded and the two men motioned everyone but Veronica, Ted and the bodyguard out the door with a wave of their guns. Bob wanted to claim responsibility for finding the chip but Ted silenced him with a nod to one of the armed men, who immediately pointed his weapon directly at the chagrined businessman.

The ousted group all looked at Veronica and then at Mitchell who was still out cold. "Please, take him with you," Veronica implored.

Paul and Tom shook Mitchell until he moaned and opened his eyes. "Hey when is the doctor going to operate," he asked groggily.

"We're moving to a different location. You're on pain medication. Try to stand up because I don't think we can carry you," Tom said. They all filed out. Mitchell leaned heavily upon Tom and Paul until they got him into the elevator and propped him against the wall.

"What happened?" He asked. "Where is my money? Is the chip out?"

"You were robbed Mitchell. No one got anything," Tom said.

"I knew I couldn't trust that Veronica woman."

"It wasn't her. It was Binge." Tom explained what had happened while they descended to the lobby of the hotel.

Debouching wordlessly, Pam and her father went directly to the concierge booth to order transportation. Tom helped Mitchell to a chair in the lobby. Mitchell could fend for himself, but he felt a responsibility to the two young people he had involved in this mess. "Polly, where will you go?"

"I don't know," she said distraughtly. "We need to get the original."

"Polly needs to clean her wounds," Paul said. "She's been through enough. Let's take her to my place and then you and I can go see Germán about finding the original." He was looking at the cuts and bruises on her arms and legs. He couldn't remember ever seeing her when she was whole and happy. It had been like this since they met, one incident after another. None of this was her fault.

"Thanks Paul," she smiled up at her rescuer. "I should probably go back to my apartment though."

"I don't think that's a good idea," Tom said grimly. "You can stay with me until I find a better place for you. Maybe Margarita will be able to help."

"I guess I better go with Tom," Polly conceded, "but first we should go get the master chip." They looked at her expectantly. "Don't be mad at me. I'm pretty sure that Germán has it. I told him where it was when we were all planning to break into the convenient store that night."

Tom moaned as if in pain. "I need to get you to my apartment before I do anything else. You've had enough fun for one day. You're starting to leak." Tom gestured to her arm where a trickle of blood oozing from her elbow had crossed over onto her wrist.

"I have a handkerchief," Polly proclaimed pulling it from her bag. It was already blood stained. She awkwardly tied it with one hand around her arm. "What is it now?" she asked in bewilderment. They were watching dumbfounded still trying to think how to keep her from accompanying them.

"We aren't going to convince her," Paul said. "Let's all just go and get this over with. But what was in the plastic bag that I saw you take from the ice cream freezer?"

"Oh, that, "Polly said, fishing around in her purse, "here." She handed the bag to Paul who could clearly see a chip inside. "It's a replacement chip for your phone. I picked it up when we were raiding the store for supplies. I thought I should replace the one I gave to Tom. With all the flooding, I put it in a plastic bag for safekeeping. I didn't want to say anything in front of Ted until I had the money to pay for it, but under the circumstances of the flood and all the other things we were taking; I didn't think it would matter if I grabbed a phone chip. I had it in my hand when I was searching through the ice cream for the chip."

"You should have said something earlier," Paul cried in exasperation.

"It was never the right time," Polly explained calmly. "I didn't want to talk in front of Ted. And then you drowned. And then you were being a jerk."

Paul ran his fingers through his hair in consideration of pulling on it. Tom smiled and shook his head before saying, "Shall we go now? I can give Paul his original phone chip back once this is all settled. He'll have a spare for our next adventure."

"The way things have been going, that's not a bad idea," Paul sighed in resignation as the trio headed for the hotel exit. "I should start carrying a backup."

Chapter 28: Veronica Almost Wins

After the room cleared out, Veronica appraised the two Binge armed men. With the room emptied, they allowed their gun barrels to sag toward the floor in a less threatening manner. Ted, Veronica and Veronica's bodyguard were seated before them on the sofa.

"I'll make a deal with you," Veronica said. "Leave now without the chip and I will hire you as factory guards for my Tijuana plant at twice what Binge is paying plus benefits."

"Easy for you to say with guns pointing at you," the taller of the two guards sneered.

"You only think you have the upper hand," Veronica warned. "What you don't know is how many armed personnel I have in that other room waiting for my signal." She waved an index finger toward the door to the second bedroom. "Do you really think I would be so unprepared? I come from Juarez. The cartel financed my husband's first factory." She paused for dramatic effect to let this revelation sink in. "I am not going to give up this chip, especially not to a mere pair of armed thieves."

The tall guard glanced nervously at his partner. "Why would you offer us money if you could just take it back from us?" He asked.

"Do you think I want a blood bath here in my room? Do you think Binge does?"

It made sense and Binge wasn't that good of an employer. They were on contract and didn't get any benefits. Besides, they hadn't called in yet, so Binge didn't even know that they had found the chip. They edged over to a corner as far from the trio on the sofa as was possible. Keeping a wary eye on the sofa, they conferred quietly.

Ted took this chance to whisper to Veronica, "Do you really have people in that room?" She gave him a cold look and said nothing.

The two men came back over to face Veronica. "We want a contract signed and delivered right now."

"I'll print one out," she agreed. "Now if you will please put down those guns. They make me nervous."

She was a shrewd and fearless business woman despite her soft exterior, Ted noted. With cool grace she rose from the couch and went to the printer. In a few minutes, the contracts were placed before her new employees and all parties signed in the appropriate places.

"No," she told them peremptorily.

"What?" The taller man exclaimed, suddenly worried he had laid down his gun too soon.

"No, you will not know whether I had armed soldiers in that room or if I was bluffing. You didn't call, you folded. The men smiled their acquiescence. Their new boss was clever and beautiful. "Roger, get one of the credit cards from the bedroom please." The bodyguard picked up his gun and left for a moment to retrieve the card for her. "I will give you money for travel to Tijuana and a week's pay each to get settled. Report to this woman at the Very Goods Factory when you arrive and she will instruct you in your new job. According to your contract, you have three months of probation before your benefits kick in and a permanent contract goes into effect." The bodyguard came back with the card and she handed it to them along with a business card on which she wrote their supervisor's name. "Good bye now and welcome aboard."

Once the door closed behind them, the bodyguard disappeared back into the bedroom. Ted turned to Veronica and asked, "Do you have anyone in that bedroom?" She laughed but refused to say. Then he asked, "Do you need a manager for your warehouse or an administrator? You know I am taking business classes. I'm pretty good at accounting already."

She surveyed the job candidate with curiosity. He was about 20 or so years younger than her and well put together. His silky, dark hair and smooth skin were appealing and he was young enough that his body had not yet gone to fat. They were both about the same height. She might have considered him for a position if he had been trustworthy, but he seemed willing to turn on his friends and that was the one thing she could not tolerate. The guards were just hired goons, free agents, but Ted had cultivated relationships and turned on them. He might be useful while she was in Austin but she was not going to take him to Juarez or Tijuana.

"I will consider it," she said putting him off. "Now I must check this chip. I just paid a lot of money for it. You may stay a while if you like. I was going to order room service and my bodyguard likes to eat by himself. Why don't you look at the menu while I work?"

Ted picked up the menu on the coffee table and Veronica slipped the chip into the reader and turned on the computer next to it to send the information to her brain trust on the border. At least one of her experts was required to be on call at all times while she was away. She smiled over at Ted, her green eyes slanting seductively as the corners of her mouth lifted, and asked if he saw anything that looked tempting. He said yes and then looked down at the menu. She went over to share the menu and they decided on the T-bone steaks with baked potatoes and mixed green salads, then she went back to the computer. He was just picking up the hand piece that connected to the hotel switchboard when she let out a shriek.

"It's destroying itself," she cried panicked. "It's a failsafe copy. We have to get the original before Bob. If he gets it he'll give it to Binge and they'll destroy it. Roger," she called and the door to the bedroom swung opened immediately. "Call a flit and make sure that you're armed."

"I don't think Polly has it," Ted blurted. "I think she gave it to Germán. They acted like they were sharing a secret when I was with them at the library. I know where he lives."

Veronica's expression became predatory but no less attractive. "Don't get in my way and don't question anything that I do," she ordered. "You'll come with us." Blood surged through Ted's veins as he nodded agreement.

Chapter 29: El Rancho

"What next Dad?" Pam asked as they finished a late dinner. She hated seeing her father so glum.

"I'm done for if I don't find that chip. The original is still out there somewhere," he said.

"I've been thinking about that," Pam said. "If Polly doesn't have it and Ted doesn't have it and Paul doesn't have it, then that leaves only one option." Her father perked up expectantly.

"Yes, go on," he prodded.

"Then that just leaves Germán. He was at the convenient store that night we were going to break in to get it. He's the only one left and I know that Polly trusts him."

"You were going to break into a store? Really Pam? What were you thinking? If you'd been caught…" He gave her a look she couldn't decipher. Was it tenderness for her or concern for his reputation? He continued after a reflective pause, "Well, what are we waiting for? He was one of your outreach students wasn't he? So you have his address?"

"Don't you think we should call first?"

"This is no time for etiquette. Let's take my flit. We can apologize for the intrusion when we get there."

They were a bit ahead of Veronica and her accompanying duo, but Germán wasn't home.

He had decided it wasn't safe for his grandmother to stay in a house with no front window to keep out intruders. They had packed their belongings days ago and found alternative lodging. Margarita had given Tom directions, so he ordered a flit at the hotel to take the three of them to the country.

It was a nearly two hour drive even in a flit. Air traffic was heavy until they reached the edge of the city. For Polly and Paul this was a new experience. The air began to clear as the buildings fell away behind them. "You've never been to the Texas Hill Country?" Tom asked. They shook their heads no.

Paul said, "I thought only rich people lived out here."

"Not this far out," Tom said.

It was not much of a house. There was a one-lane dirt road leading up to a tiny clapboard cabin with a rusty tin roof hidden among ash juniper and live oak trees. The entire cabin was hardly bigger than a single bedroom efficiency apartment. Leaving the cab, they stepped into thick weeds at the verge of the road. Polly inhaled a perfume of rich green foliage and flowering plants.

"This is out of my range," the sullen flit operator informed them. "Unless you want to pay for me to wait, I won't be coming back."

"We'll take our chances. You can go," Tom said as he swiped his card, making sure to give the driver only the minimum tip.

"It's beautiful," Polly gushed and then sneezed. "My eyes are itchy."

"Too much clean air," laughed Tom.

Paul looked uncomfortable, but lifted his chin and trudged ahead of the group to the front door. Germán opened it before he could knock. "Our first guests," he greeted them excitedly, "come in."

"How did you ever find this place?" Paul asked. "And why would you move out here? Are you afraid of Binge?"

"Anyone would be afraid of Binge," Margarita answered for him, "but that is not why we chose this place. It belonged to my late husband. Germán has inherited it."

"Seriously," Tom said, "that's great. And you just found this out?"

"Several weeks ago," Margarita confirmed, "at first we thought it was a scheme to steal from us, a scam, but then a lawyer informed us that it was for real and since we did not want to stay in the city anymore, we came to look at it. Please find a seat while I get everyone drinks."

Germán took a seat on an unopened box while the others sat down on an old dusty sofa that must have come with the house. "I am a land owner now," Germán beamed, before adding more seriously, "What is going on with the chip?"

"Veronica has a copy so she is no longer looking for the original. Our only concern now is Binge. They want to destroy all copies. Veronica talks tough and I am sure that she is to a degree, but I don't think she would go in for cold-blooded murder. At this point, she is in just as much danger from Binge as you are," Tom said.

"What can we do?" Margarita asked wrinkling her eyebrows in concern. "Will they find us here?"

"Binge will surely find you eventually," Tom confirmed. "I don't think this chip is worth our lives. Perhaps we should try to make a deal with them."

"I will not deal with Binge or anyone," Germán insisted vehemently, "I intend to use that information to help people. Once it is made public, Binge will have no more reason to pursue us."

Polly spoke up, "You're right. We should open it and put it online. What do you know about the inventors, Tom?"

"They were a young couple working out of their garage who had become disillusioned with Binge. Mitchell got hold of it somehow. He was my asset at the time and Binge had hired me to find out about what kind of research the developers were doing and to steal anything I found. As Binge employees, anything they came up with even in their own time was officially Binge property, so technically it wasn't stealing. As far as Binge was concerned, the inventors were doing the stealing. I sent Mitchell to check it out and he said he'd had luck and to meet him. I told him I had to pick up something from another asset first and that

I would text him when I was ready. He was working undercover as a Binge driver at the time. Apparently he got paranoid when he found out what they were working on and was following me, trying to decide on his next move. Of course he made a copy. He copies everything. When he saw me at the crosswalk with Polly, he thought she was my asset and that's why he approached her after we all left. Also, he thought Binge had eyes on him and didn't want to approach me directly, or maybe he didn't want to give it to me at all. I don't know why he injected it into your hand Polly. It fit his cover, I guess, as a Binge driver. I'm sorry about that," Tom eyed her sheepishly. "I suppose he was afraid that Binge would find out he had it before he could leverage it. He thought it would be safely tucked away in your hand. He didn't expect you to take it out on your own."

"We should talk to Mitchell. What happened to that couple?" Polly asked shrugging off his concern.

"So you know where this chip is," Margarita asked passing out glasses of water.

"It's in the refrigerator," Germán told his grandmother. "It had to be kept cold, Abuela. There weren't many options. Polly told me she put it in a freezer at the convenient store and for me to go pick it up as soon as possible. She said that she would try to keep the corporations and bad guys off my trail."

"We can take it back to my place," Tom suggested. "Do your neighbors know where you went?" He asked Margarita.

"No, of course not," Margarita replied. "I do know that we are in danger. I said that we did not know for sure where we would go, but that we could not stay in a house without a window. They didn't ask too many questions."

"I wish one of us had a flit," Tom mused. "If someone puts in the time and effort they'll be able to track us here eventually. Taxi drivers keep a log of all their pickups and deliveries."

"We have a pickup," Germán interjected.

"Pickup?" Tom queried.

"Yes, I borrowed a pickup from my friend. That's what we used to get out here. It's parked out back."

"Now I wish we hadn't left Mitchell to fend for himself in the lobby of that hotel. We could use his help to find out more about those two who invented this process everyone is so excited about. I'll text him now and try to set up a meeting. He likes this bar a few blocks away from Binge. Could you three meet him there and see what you can find out. Offer him money. That usually does the trick. He wants a share of the profits from the chip.

"Not the bar, tell him to come to my apartment," Paul suggested. "That's where my computer is and I think Polly should clean up. She needs to wash those cuts and she can shower and change clothes at my place."

After filling a bag with fresh ice to keep the chip cold, they followed a path of crushed weeds to the back of the house. Tom exclaimed when he saw the pickup, "that's a 1953 Chevy. That thing is an antique."

It was hard to tell what color it had been since it was mostly rust colored now. Polly thought it might have been dark green and it was so old it had developed personality. Round headlights looked like wide-open eyes and the five-tiered thick chrome grill reminded her of the mouth of a smiling or hungry God or krill filtering teeth of a sea creature. There was a hump where the engine was sheltered under the hood. She was curious as to why they had put so much metal in the front. Tom told her that it was for protection and decoration; when these cars ruled the roads they traveled very fast. The windshield was divided by a metal strip down the middle. There was only one big bench seat for passengers and the cargo bed behind the cabin had been made over with plywood. Inside, candy and potato chip wrappers littered the floor; some might have been as old as the truck. There was no air conditioning and the windows no longer cranked down. It wasn't just because of traffic and Binge spies that Margarita and Germán had done their moving at night. After sunset they didn't have to deal with the addition of solar heat.

Germán instructed Paul to turn on the ignition. It didn't start immediately, but once the engine turned over, the cab filled with a wonderful fragrance of fried chicken.

Polly licked her lips and asked, "Is Margarita cooking? It smells so good it's making me hungry."

Germán laughed, "That's the fuel. My friend's family owns a restaurant and he gets the used cooking oil from his mother. He is something of a tinker. He made over the engine so it burns the leftover grease from the kitchen."

"I hope the tank is full," Polly said. "I don't know where there is a grease station."

"We'll be fine. These old trucks have huge tanks and this one has two. It holds a lot of fuel and refined vegetable oil gets better mileage than regular gas. Probably only works out if you own a restaurant, but it is non-polluting."

"We won't all fit in that cabin," Tom pointed out. "I'll stay here and keep Margarita company." Behind his back, Germán and Polly gave each other a knowing look.

Luckily, the side vents still opened allowing some air to circulate through the interior of the cab. There were stars visible through the windshield as they made good time going back into the city. Polly and Paul couldn't remember seeing stars before except in magazines and on the internet. The engine's rumbling and the friction noise of the tires passing over the black top traveled through the frame of the vehicle in a constant lulling vibration. It was difficult to make conversation over the noise and exhausted from the day's activities, Polly's head began to sag against Paul's shoulder. Her eyelids grew heavy and she was soon sound asleep. Hot and sweaty as it was, Paul didn't disturb her.

As the trio drove the truck back into the city, Veronica's group had made it over to Margarita's previous abode just in time to encounter Pam and Bob. "What are you doing here?" Pam asked with surprise.

"I might ask you the same thing," she countered.

"We thought Germán might have the original. Did Binge get your copy?'

"Copies are no good as it turns out."

"I see. So you came to the same conclusion that I did. Germán has to be the one who has it," Pam said with satisfaction.

"Yes, that is my conclusion. Are you still working for me?" she added.

"Of course," Pam said, "as long as you're paying I'm working. What's the plan, boss?" She motioned toward her father. "Dad is coming along as my assistant." Bob pinched his lips together, but chose to remain silent. He was getting too long in the tooth for these cat and mouse games, but if one of them should drop the ball, so to speak, it wouldn't hurt to be close by to pick it up.

"The plastic window covering was loose so I took a look around inside. There's no sign of life or the chip. Let's canvas the neighbors to see if they know where they went." Veronica motioned for Ted to come with her. "You two take the other side of the street and we'll meet back here," she instructed.

Chapter 30: Password Retrieval

It was close to 10:00 PM when they entered the city. Polly woke up feeling dirty and sticky and more crumpled than ever. There was a drool mark on Paul's shoulder where she had been resting her head. She didn't say anything hoping he wouldn't notice. Paul stiffly scrunched up the arm next to her and leaning out over the floor, shook it then rotated his shoulder. He clenched and unclenched his fist to stimulate a return of circulation.

"You should have woken me up," Polly said, feeling guilty.

"I'll get my feeling back in a minute," he assured her. She frowned in embarrassment but said nothing more.

"I've been thinking," Germán said, "if we do open this chip, what then? It is only half of the formula. Only Binge and Veronica have the other half. That means we either destroy it or barter with one of them. If we destroy it, we would be destroying any chance we have for creating a clean energy source. If we barter with them where does that put us? We would be no better than Mitchell or Veronica."

"Or Tom?" Polly added.

"Tom isn't so bad," Germán decided. "My grandmother seems to like him." Paul and Polly shared a smile at that.

"We haven't opened the chip yet," Paul pointed out. "Let's see what's on it before we decide if we're going to be good guys or bad guys."

Traffic was thickening, but uncharacteristically yielded right of way for the aromatic truck. Some people on the sidewalks stared at it hungrily. Whether out of respect for its vintage looks or because they were stunned by the smell wasn't apparent, but it made Polly nervous. Businesses shut down because of the flood, relieved some of the traffic congestion, too. Instead of a snow day people were taking a flood week. It was still slow going but at least they were moving. The night was young so Polly suggested they stop for some fried chicken. Germán proposed that they go by his friend's restaurant for food so they could return the vehicle and they all agreed.

After a more than satisfying meal of chicken, hush puppies, Cole Slaw and mashed potatoes that the owner insisted was on the house, Germán told them he was going to stay to help his friend clean up in the kitchen. Paul called Mitchell to tell him they were on their way to his place and to meet them there. At the last minute, Germán brought out a to-go-bag of chicken for Mitchell.

Paul's apartment was a quick two mile walk from where they were. A lot had happened since their last walk together. Neither one felt talkative, but they were both thinking about how many adventurous miles they had traversed since they met only a few days ago. This sedate stroll seemed mundane in comparison.

Polly felt like taking a nap after eating the heavy meal, but by the time they reached the apartment she decided a shower would be even nicer. Paul wanted her to thoroughly clean all the cuts and abrasions on her arms and legs before they became infected.

She was coming out of the steamy bathroom wearing a clean T-shirts and gym shorts when Mitchell arrived. "Am I interrupting something?" he smirked.

"A good night's sleep," she replied, "but I'm not sure I would know one if I saw it at this point." Paul surreptitiously glanced at the drool stain on his shirt but made no comment.

"Polly is between apartments," Paul explained. "Tom said that you might help us for a share of the profits. Did he call you about what we want?"

"Yeah, the names of the inventors of that bio-engine," Mitchell confirmed. "Since I missed dinner, I distracted myself by looking through the computer records at Binge for other information about them, too. I found their résumé and a transcript of some of their podcasts."

"Podcasts," Paul expressed excitement. "That might work. You need a password to open a podcast account. It might be the same one they used on the chip. We might be able to con a tech support person into giving up the password if we can answer the security questions correctly. Oh, and we brought you food." He pointed to a grease soaked bag on the table and Mitchell bee-lined to it without another word.

"This is good," he finally uttered through a crunchy mouthful of the savory food.

"I'll check Teeter," Polly offered. She sat cross-legged on the sofa bed and intently tapped on her comp in an effort to avoid watching Mitchell eat. "Paul, are you checking LinkIn?"

Mitchell had brought his laptop as instructed and opened it awkwardly while he devoured the last of the meal. He wiped his greasy fingers on his shirt. Paul opened his computer on the table next to Mitchell and was attempting to stay far enough away from the man so that chicken breading didn't foul his keyboard. "Just opened the app," he confirmed.

"Hey, she has a cat named Polly," Polly proclaimed proudly. "Maybe I can find the name of her first pet. It looks like they like to vacation on the beach. There are a lot of beach photos."

"Great Polly," Paul suggested gently, "but maybe wait to tell us what you find until we finish our searches." He was feeling anxious and claustrophobic sitting so close to Mitchell and it was hard to concentrate.

"Oh, sure Paul," Polly said without rancor, "we should write down what we find out to share when we take a break."

Paul brought out some scrap paper and pencils for everyone. Some questions were quickly answered using résumés and LinkIn accounts: mother's maiden name, elementary school, high school, 1ˢᵗ job, birth place and birthday. Some were more difficult: favorite food, favorite teacher, 1ˢᵗ pet, 1ˢᵗ car, favorite book and favorite vacation spot. It was the last category of questions that it was up to Polly to find.

Mitchell discovered that the podcasts were hosted by her so they assumed that she set up the password. That narrowed their search to one person instead of two. Hopefully, the online questions would allow for at least one mistake.

Mitchell found the answer for "my favorite teacher" in an essay the company required in addition to the résumé. It was titled "Why I Want This Job" and it credited a high school teacher who had been instrumental in her choice of careers. It was the class where the two inventors met.

From the photos on Teeter, Polly surmised that their favorite vacation spot was Jamaica. They liked going up into the Blue Mountains to get away from the heat and humidity at the beach and they both liked to smoke marijuana occasionally. It had to be Jamaica.

At last they were ready to try to get the password. The only two questions they had no likely answers to were: 1ˢᵗ pet's name and favorite food.

"Let's hope they don't ask those," Paul said, "but if they do, then guess."

"Am I making the call?" Polly asked with reluctance.

"You are the trained receptionist," Paul said. "You are better at talking to people. And remember, it's a she's password."

"Oh, yeah, right, that makes sense," Polly frowned. "Well here goes," and she tapped in the numbers that Mitchell wrote down for her. In a few minutes she was connected to the Podcast help desk.

An answering machine told her to press one if she was having technical difficulty with the broadcast function, press two if she wanted to cancel, three if she needed help with her password, or four if she wanted the menu repeated. She pressed three. "It's not a human," she stage whispered to the two men hovering over her. They looked at each other unsure if this was a good thing or a bad thing. "Forgot password," she said loudly and put her comp on speaker mode so they could hear the conversation.

"You need help retrieving your password. Press one if this is correct. Press two if you wish to return to the main menu," instructed the helpful robot. Polly pressed one. There was a brief mechanical pause. She imagined she heard the sound of gears meshing and slots opening and closing, but of course a modern computer would not make those sounds.

"Please state your name," it instructed. Polly gave the name of the female inventor. "Welcome, Sally Meadows and thank you for using our service. To confirm your identity we need you to answer a few questions. Are you ready? Please say yes or no."

"Yes," Polly said.

"Okay, please tell me your mother's maiden name." This was an easy one that Mitchell had found on an ancestry search. It had cost a few creds to join the service but it looked like it was paying off.

"Thank you. Please tell me the name of your favorite teacher." They were right about that one.

"Good. And one final question. Please tell me what is your favorite food?"

"Oh, shit," Polly cursed quietly turning her head away from the speaker. Mitchell and Paul gave each other a worried look. Paul shrugged and mouthed, "Sushi."

Polly almost said it, but hesitated. She hated sushi. Those poor, over-fished tuna were beautiful, iridescent giants of the sea. The vegetarian version was called a California Roll, but who would choose that as their favorite food? She didn't have any idea what Sally Meadows would love eating. Then without thinking she blurted out, "fried chicken."

"Your password will be emailed to you. Please allow several minutes for it to process," the machine informed her. "Email," she repeated looking anxiously at Mitchell and Paul who were shaking their heads no. "No wait," she ordered, "speak to a representative."

At first it did not acknowledge her request and she moved her head side to side for the benefit of her audience. Mitchell shrugged nonpluses, but Paul rolled his eyes up to the ceiling, jerked his head in exasperation and rubbed the back of his neck with one hand. Then the machine processed her request and the mechanical voice said,

"Please wait why I connect you to the next available operator."

"We're in," Polly said. It was a few minutes before a human voice introduced himself as Jack and asked how he could assist her. "Hi Jack," Polly said lightly, "I was hoping you could give me my password verbally. I just left my job and I was using that email address and now I can't access it anymore. I had no idea they would cut me off so quickly. My podcast goes on, well, right now and I forgot the password. I already answered all the security questions."

"Just a moment," Jack said. "You are Sally Meadows?"

"That's right. I did have a personal email account, but I haven't used it in so long I am locked out of it too. I should write these things down." She rattled on breathlessly, being obnoxiously long winded so he wouldn't want to keep her on the phone longer than he had to. "I think I must be off by one letter because I was sure that I knew it. It only gave me three tries and my new keyboard is so small I might have made typo's. Or maybe I type too fast for it." She paused long enough to catch a breath and chuckle self-deprecatingly. "My computer usually remembers me so I don't need to use any passwords, but it died yesterday and I'm on a new one today. It doesn't know anything." She finished with a coquettish laugh.

"I see you answered all the questions correctly, so there shouldn't be any problem. Are you ready to write this down?"

Paul scrambled over to the table to grab a pencil and paper. "Yes, go ahead," Polly said. She repeated it out loud so Paul could write it down.

They had a password. Now to see if it worked on the chip.

Chapter 31: Tom and Margarita

"This place is nice, but what will you do out here?" Tom asked Margarita as they enjoyed an iced hibiscus infusion on the front porch of her new abode. She brought her rocking chair from inside to sit on and Tom had one of the hard-back chairs from the kitchen. They had enjoyed a burning, orangey-red sunset through the branches of the trees in the front yard earlier and now the stars had appeared. The air was still and hot but it wasn't dusty, since the soaking rains of the flood had packed down the dirt road that led to the house. They had been sitting there for hours listening to the calls of the crickets and night birds.

"I've thought of buying a few goats and some chickens. Maybe make artisan goat cheese. Put in a vegetable garden and some fruit trees. There are 20 acres and it is not too far from Austin. Germán could sell at the Farmer's Markets. I like the country life. It is peaceful here and the air is clean."

"You lived next to the freeway, so just about anywhere is going to be more peaceful and clean," Tom commented with a tang of sarcasm that he wished he hadn't given in to. Why did he care where she wanted to live? "Of course, this place is especially nice," he added, trying to make amends.

"There are some old oak trees here," Margarita said, "but the land is not so good. It is very rocky and the top soil is mostly caliche. Good enough for goats though and we can make soil for the plants."

"I always thought I might retire to a place something like this," Tom admitted. "It seems awfully isolated though. If we do find a way to sell the chip without giving in to Binge or the maquiladoras, would you still want to live out here?"

"This is not the end of the world, Tom," she looked at him questioningly, "there are electricity, internet and television. What is it that you would miss exactly?"

"I'm not much of a cook," he admitted. "I like to go to a bookstore or library when the mood strikes. I even go out to the theater on occasions. And when I go to those places, I like to walk or Yoot without having to put much thought or effort into it."

"You are a city boy," she said. "My daughter's husband was a city boy also. He wanted more than nature and his own two hands could provide. I like the nature better than the city."

This conversation was not leading in the direction Tom had hoped to take it, but he didn't know how to turn it around. There was nothing wrong with the country and being stuck out here with Margarita would not be a bad thing. Still he had not thought out what living outside the city meant. It had always been a pie-in-the-sky retirement ideal that he never imaged actually happening. If he wooed this woman as he was tempted to do, he wouldn't even need the money from the chip to have that option. Now he wasn't sure that he wanted it after all.

They sat quietly contemplating the distant hum of traffic on the highway that was miles away. Not far from where they sat, a bird called plaintively and rustled the branches of the trees. Harsh mechanical music broke their reverie and Margarita began to rock in agitation. It took Tom a moment to realize what it was.

"It's Paul," Tom announced, then said into the air over the flat surface of the comp, "Hi, how's it going?"

"We have a password," Paul told him. "What do you want to do?"

"I don't know if I can get a taxi out here, but I'll try. Stay put and I'll call you back."

He tapped in his location and searched for a nearby service. There was a bus that stopped by the highway. It was five miles away. He could get a taxi from town but the charge was doubled since it was considered a two-way trip and it could be traced. If he started walking now he might make the last bus of the evening. If he missed it, he could call for a taxi at the bus stop.

"I need to go back to Austin to help Paul. They have a password that might work. I want to be there in case there are problems and I'm not sure how trustworthy Mitchell is."

Margarita nodded and rose from her seat being careful not to spill her half-full glass. Tom followed her back into the house with his glass, rinsed it and set it on the counter.

"Thanks," Tom said, their eyes met and held for a moment.

"Be careful," she said.

"I will," he assured her, touching her hand tentatively. He didn't know why but he timorously added, "I'll be back. Will you be here?"

"Where else would I be?" she smiled giving his hand a little push as she did so.

He had only walked about a mile when some teenagers in an old-model flit sedan hovered past him, then reversed and asked if he needed a ride. It elevated with ancient fan-blade technology and with his extra weight it barely floated above the road, but they managed to get him the rest of the way to the bus stop. It was a good thing, since the last bus for the night pulled up a few minutes later. Maybe luck was on his side for a change.

He took a cab partway to Paul's because he didn't want to leave an easy trace. Better to be safe. Walking in the city, he became acutely aware of the difference between the city air and that at Margarita's. It had a dirty, sticky feel. It smelled like petroleum and human excrement and, maybe he was imagining it, greed and desperation.

Polly was asleep on the sofa bed and Mitchell and Paul were playing a card game at his wobbly kitchen table when he got there. At the sound of the door closing behind him, Polly sat up drowsily and smiled. She wiped the sleep from her eyes and combed her hair with her fingers.

"Hi Tom, Margarita didn't come?" she asked casually, like they were a couple. He shook his head.

"I brought a chip reader peripheral from the office in case we need it." Tom offered.

"I've already got an adapter on my computer," Mitchell remarked dismissively.

"Well, let's find out what we've got. Will we be able to copy it with the password?"

"Probably not," Paul answered. "It has to be downloaded to be opened. Once it's downloaded it can be manipulated to a certain extent; maybe posted to a website but probably not. Failsafe prevents it from being copied to a flash drive or other external device and as soon as the chip is removed the program downloaded to the computer will be wiped away. A certified copy would have to come from the mainframe computer with the original program on it. An original downloaded from a mainframe with the correct password won't have the failsafe bug, but copies of it will; which means when you open them they self-destruct. You remember the artist who used it to make signed copies of his work. Failsafe keeps anyone from copying those official copies. It's state-of-the art sophisticated software."

"So if we get the password wrong the chip won't destroy itself like Veronica's did," Polly said.

"More likely it will lock down permanently. Maybe the inventor has a key, but it is unlikely that it will be as easy to figure out as the password," Paul explained. "Once we get it open we can copy down the formula on paper. I don't think it will let us move it to a website, Germán, like you and Polly were hoping. Failsafe is specifically designed to prevent plagiarizing digital artwork. I don't know much about it other than that."

"I'm ready," Mitchell stated sitting back in his chair with his arms crossed. "Put it in."

Paul went to his tiny apartment fridge and pulled out the chip in its protective plastic covering. It was wrapped in thin, stretchy plastic that entombed it in multiple layers. He turned the tiny parcel over in his fingers to find the edge of the film. It was difficult to pry loose. Slowly and carefully he unfurled it. It wanted to stick to itself again and his fingers felt large and clumsy as they struggled to retain mastery. Finally, he freed the chip and handed it over to Mitchell.

"Give me the password," Mitchell ordered. Paul handed him the paper and Mitchell typed it in at the prompt. They communally held their breath as they all stared at the screen. "It didn't work," Mitchell stated glumly.

"What now," Paul put his face in his hands in weary frustration. Tom and Polly exchanged concerned looks. Mitchell threw his hands up in the air and pushed back from the keyboard.

Polly said, "At work we were told to change our password every three months. Nobody could ever remember what their password was. A colleague of mine suggested I change one letter each time. He added a number or alphabetical letter to each new iteration of his password and it worked for him. I tried it and it worked for me too. These inventors aren't super-human; they probably had the same problems regular people have. Maybe we could try adding a number or letter to the password."

"That's a good idea Polly," Tom beamed at her. "But how do we know which iteration they were on and how do we know if they did it alphabetically or numerically?"

"I would try numbers first, then the alphabet. We have to start at two don't you think?"

"Okay Mitchell, add a two. Do you agree Paul?" Tom asked.

Paul shrugged and rolled his shoulders, "They were inventors and programmers. It's hard to say. They used math to come up with their bio-engine, but programmers use language too. I guess if Polly thinks we should start with two, let's give it a try."

Mitchell typed in the new password but his finger hovered hesitantly over the enter button. He tilted his head back to take in the tense group gathered around him. For the first time in a long time he felt like part of the gang, like he had just as much to lose or gain as anyone else. It was a good feeling. He wondered how his life would be after the next moment. He always thought it was about money, but now he wasn't so sure. He pressed enter.

The program opened. "We're in," he stated gleefully. Polly gave Mitchell a delighted squeeze to his shoulder then put her arms around Paul's neck and hugged him before jumping up and down for joy.

"Hey, I'm on the second floor," Paul cautioned her, then took her in his arms and swung her around in a circle before setting her down and clasping Tom's hand in both of his.

"Good job," Tom proclaimed paternally. "Let's transcribe this thing onto paper and then decide what to do with the information." He looked at Mitchell. "This doesn't just belong to those of us in this room. Germán and Margarita have a say also. Let's say that all parties must be in agreement before we do anything. Can we all agree to that?"

Before Mitchell could answer there was a knock at the door. They all looked at Paul who frowned and shook his head no. He held his hands out open to the ceiling and lifted his shoulders in the universal I don't know gesture. The knock came again and a voice called out, "Paul, I can see the light is on. Let me in." It was Pam.

"Just a minute," he called. Why would all these people be here if not for the chip? "What should I tell her?" He whispered. There was not enough room to hide everyone in his tiny apartment.

Tom said, "Mitchell, get in the bathroom. I'll say I am here to get Polly and take her to my place for the night." They looked at Polly dressed in T-shirt and gym shorts, her hair still damp from her shower. Well there was nothing that could be done about that now.

Paul opened the door, "Pam, what are you doing here?"

"I thought you might be glad to see me, but I see I'm interrupting something."

"No," he replied guiltily, "Polly was just leaving with Tom."

Polly shot him a dirty look, and then smiled artificially at Pam. "Yes, Tom is taking me to his place to spend the night."

"You certainly do get around," Pam said cattily.

"Apparently you do too," she answered back tartly. Pam blushed.

"Why are you here?" Paul asked, trying to ignore the tension building up in the tight space.

"I'm looking for Germán. He is no longer living at the same place. I thought you might know where he is. Veronica's chip destroyed itself when we opened it. I thought Germán might have the original" She noticed there were two computers on the table. "Did you bring a computer with you, Tom?" She asked suspiciously.

"I have two computers," Paul lamely bumbled.

"I know that isn't true. You can barely afford one," Pam smirked unbecomingly.

Polly joined the fray, "It's mine. I'm lending it to Paul."

"What's going on here?" Pam searched the room with a quick gaze. "Do you have the chip?"

Polly and Paul blanched and looked to Tom for help. "We might be able to make a deal with you," he decided.

Hearing this and unable to bear being left out of the dealings, Mitchell burst out of the bathroom. Pam nearly fell over backward at the sudden appearance. "What's this?" She exclaimed and stumbled over to the sofa bed before her feet went out from under her. She eased herself into a seated position. The rest of the group stood between her and the computers like a human shield. "You do have the chip. I want to see it," she declared.

"We intend to use the technology for good," Polly chirped, nerves raising her voice into a higher register than normal. She looked to Paul for approval, but his eyes were glued to the woman on the sofa.

He peeled them away and said to Tom who stood on his right, "There is no reason Pam can't be part of our cadre is there?"

Tom did his best not to grimace. He imagined Margarita's solemn face in that tiny shack on the sparse little ranch she was ready to relegate the rest of her life to restoring. He saw those strong, slender fingers worn down to the bone, crooked with arthritis from a lifetime of unrelenting hard labor in the hot Texas sun. He wanted to save her from that. He wanted to make enough money off this chip deal to build her the farm she deserved with a nice flit to ferry them around when they wanted a break from the peace and quiet of farm life.

No matter how Paul felt about Pam, she was a corporate shill. He didn't know if she was working for Veronica or Bob or Binge directly, but she was not going to be satisfied with giving away the technology. Then again neither was he. Only Polly, Paul, Margarita and Germán would be satisfied with doing that and they were wrong. They needed to profit from this chip as much as any of them, maybe more. He didn't answer Paul's question.

"If we give it to Veronica, she will at least use it," Pam offered. "Binge is going to destroy it. Veronica will see that you all get what you deserve."

Who will see that you get what you deserve, Polly thought uncharitably.

"I need to talk privately to Paul and Mitchell for a minute," Tom finally said. "Polly, could you keep Pam company while we go outside?" She glared her answer.

"So are you interested in Paul," Polly came right to the point as soon as the men disappeared.

"You certainly are," Pam commented in bemusement. "The question is whether he is interested in you. He might have a future with me."

"What kind of future is that," Polly huffed. "The one where you're the boss of everything and he does what you say?'

"Something like that," she laughed. "I am a Vice President. What do you do for a living? Take handouts from friends? And to think that I was almost one of them. Don't expect a receptionist position with Veronica Industries."

Before Polly could say that she would rather starve than take anything from Pam or Veronica, the three men filed back into the room. Tom declared, "We do have the chip and we are willing to deal with Veronica in person.

Have her meet us at 1:00 tomorrow afternoon at Dempsey's Dive near Binge. She knows where it is. We'll be ready to make a deal with her then."

"I'll tell her," Pam said with a warning glance at Polly as she got up to leave. Paul caught the look and wondered what they had been discussing.

"And bring your father to represent Binge if you like," Tom added as she was about to close the door.

As soon as she was gone, Tom surveyed the group before him. What a motley crew they were: two computer experts, a retired English professor/spy and an out-of-work receptionist. All they needed to complete the team was an energetic teenager with a heart-of-gold and an undemanding woman who could cook and manage a farm.

"Germán messaged me that he is going back to the ranch. I told him to get Margarita and meet us at my place. There's more room and I can use my computer to help." With a secretive smile, Tom added, "Shall we let Polly in on our secret plan?"

Chapter 32: The Deal

Polly got the most sleep that night. She passed out about 2:00 AM in Tom's bedroom, no longer able to keep her eyes open, much less contribute. It was unclear if anyone else slept.

German's friend had let him borrow his aromatic truck to pick up Margarita. He promised to bring it back before the restaurant closed the next day. He also promised to help clean the kitchen once again.

Tom's place was twice the size of Paul's but they were still crowded together as they made their plans. Paul sat on a pillow on the floor at one end of the coffee table where he and Tom laid out computers and papers. Everything was set up and ready to go when German returned with Margarita. She and Tom shared the sofa once Polly shuffled off to bed and Mitchell got the large, overstuffed armchair. Tom didn't know exactly how his plan would work, but when he read through the precis that was included along with the formula on the chip he thought it was worth a try.

Binge was investigating the use of genetically engineered bacterium to replace silicon in solar cells. The beauty of the process was that it was self-replicating when fed the appropriate materials, mainly sunlight, and therefore less polluting. Solar cell manufacture was not as green as people liked to think. Batteries used for storing energy were both dangerous and dirty. This new process worked much like stingrays create an electric charge. Like stingrays, these bacteria produced electrolyte energy when stimulated by a sodium trigger. The sodium trigger could be used to start and stop the process when necessary. In the daytime when the trigger was off the bacteria stored energy, thus alleviating a need for battery backup.

The first chip that was purloined from the Binge mainframe server detailed this process. Told by Binge to stop there and forget about further research, the inventors had continued their work at home. What they had discovered was too simple and beautiful to let alone.

It was in the second chip, taken from the garage of the original inventors that the process of practical production was outlined. This was the chip that Veronica wanted so badly. It explained how to tap that energy in the form of electricity and included instructions for how to produce the bacteria in large quantities. More importantly, it was in the second chip that the genome for gene sequencing this magical powerhouse bacterium was contained. Even if Veronica's experts could figure out how to harness these little power plants, they needed the other half of the bio-formula to create them.

This was the trump card that Tom and his cadre held and he planned to make enough off its sale to take care of everyone. They didn't care who they sold it to. Let the bidding war begin. He had invited Bob to come bid for Binge. They were ready to hand over the chip as soon as they saw proof of transfer of funds. The trick was that they would hold the patent. Germán's friend at the restaurant was in the process of producing a test batch of bacteria.

It was time to meet Veronica and the Binge representatives for lunch to discuss the sale of the chip. Dank and dark though it was, it was a relief to enter the interior of the café away from the blinding heat of the early afternoon sun. Tom asked the waitress if it would be possible to put a couple of tables together for a group of twelve. Even though the lunch rush wasn't over she happily obliged, informing them that an automatic 15% tip was added to groups of over six. He told her to add 25% and she told him she would get them ice water right away. She motioned for the busboy to push the tables together in middle of the room.

"Let's order queso and chips while we wait," Paul suggested.

"And guacamole," Polly chimed in.

"I need a beer," Mitchell remarked and they all agreed that was a good idea.

While they were munching on the hors d'oeuvres, the rest of the group arrived. Veronica brought Ted and her body guard. Ted acted uncomfortable about appearing at the other side of the bargaining table, especially after Germán gave him a hard, unfriendly look while he was taking his seat. However, he was lunching at the bequest of the most beautiful and sophisticated woman he had ever met, thus rendering any dirty look from his former friend innocuous.

Tom suggested the six of them, the sellers, occupy one side and two ends of the table. The buyers would be lined up before them on the other side. This way the buyers could not readily see each other's reactions, while the sellers could. It would be harder for them to make an under-the-table agreement to keep the price low. Just because Bob said that he was working for Binge didn't make it so. As an independent he could change sides as it suited him. Pam had already gone over to Veronica's camp, instead of remaining faithful to her father's interests.

Seeing that the rest of the party had arrived, the waitress came back for their drink orders and brought some more menus. When they had ordered and she had disappeared back behind the counter, Veronica broke the ice. "Do you have the chip with you?"

"We should discuss the price first. If that can be agreed upon then I'll tell you where the chip is," Tom countered. It felt good to be on neutral ground. He had felt at a disadvantage in her hotel room with her armed body guard looming over him.

"So it is you six that I am dealing with?" She asked, surveying the group with a sharp, predatory eye, like a jaguar ready to pounce. Ted felt an involuntary shiver go down his spine. "I ask because the ownership of this chip moves around, does it not? Are you now in charge of it Tom?"

"The six of us have formed a consortium," Tom said. "Any payment will be split equally between us and conversely any agreement must be a consensus."

"I can work with that as long as I get what I want," Veronica agreed. Ted and the body guard maintained a blank, stony stare while the waitress brought beer, margaritas and water.

"We want 100 million creds each and a signed document stating that we are not liable for your satisfaction with the product you are buying, and we are exempt from any law suits or liability before or after the actions stemming from procurement and final delivery of the product. We sell you the chip, but password access, patents, whatever else is necessary to use, it is on you."

"I can deal with Binge and the missing inventors if that's what you mean. How does Bob fit into this? Are you here to accompany Pam or do you have something to say, Bob?" Veronica eyed him cynically.

"Binge will pay 101 million," Bob chimed up.

Veronica laughed, "Oh, I see, he is here to run up the price. In that case, let us skip the chase. What is your top offer, Bob?"

"One million above your top offer," he countered,

"My top offer," Veronica sat back and sipped her margarita. Lime and tequila blended on her tongue into a refreshing, cold and sweet-tart flavor that infused her brain with pleasant memories of tropical beaches and swaying palms. She sat it down and surveyed the group before her, ending with a glance to her left near the end of the table where Pam and Bob sat. "Bob, you have no loyalty. Your daughter works for me now and yet you bid against her. I do not judge, however. What we will do is take care of your debt to Binge. You will have your retirement restored. And, I will pay 100 million creds each to this fine consortium for the chip. Everyone will be happy."

Bob looked at his daughter. She nodded to him, willing him to take the deal. He looked at the group seated on the other side of the table. They appeared more interested in the food and drinks than in haggling. Finally, feeling that he was left with little choice, he agreed.

"Good," Tom declared as the first of their order arrived at the table. They had decided on hamburgers and fries. Considering the quality of the queso and guacamole they'd just eaten, they all agreed that this was not the place to get good TexMex. "I will bring the chip to your hotel room tomorrow afternoon where you can make sure that it is what you want. You will transfer the funds to our account at that time. No body guards. You by yourself."

"I have not cheated you so far," Veronica said. "And you have not disappointed me. It will be as you say. If you do try to cheat me, then that will be the last thing that you do."

"What will I tell Binge?" Bob stammered.

"Binge will survive," Veronica said. "You must be brave. Once they have lost, they will have no reason to kill you." He gulped audibly and Pam patted his hand under the table. "Now let us enjoy these fine, vat-cultured hamburgers, something that it is hard to make poorly even in a place like this."

Mitchell ignored the insult to his favorite hamburger joint. His mouth was stuffed with juicy beef, caramelized onions and spicy barbecue sauce thus making any utterance impossible. He was going to be a rich man. He even regretted treating the waitress badly last time he was here. From now on, he thought, he was going to be a better person.

As soon as Veronica and her entourage left, they got busy with their plan. Calling themselves Gaea Inc., they filed paperwork to incorporate and began the patent process for their new bacterium. There was much to do so they split into groups.

Germán's friend from the restaurant was already contracted to help them, and his truck was on semi-permanent loan to the group. Part of the restaurant kitchen was now a makeshift lab. With a few ingredients from the pantry and a nearby chemical supply store, he and Germán were going to cultivate their first batch of bacteria.

Polly and Paul were getting into the loaner truck when they spotted the Binge helicopter. "What are they doing here?" Polly asked tensely. "You don't think Bob told them do you?"

"It could be," Paul replied. "Bob didn't seem too happy about Pam making a deal for him with Veronica. How many do you see in the cabin?"

"It looks like two. Why would Bob double-cross Veronica? If he gives his loyalty to her, she will give him everything that he wanted from Binge as well as supporting his daughter and her career."

"Do you think Bob's pride would let him be obliged to two women?"

"I guess you're right. Anyone with Binge would have to be a male-chauvinist," Polly sighed. "What are we going to do?"

"We need to buy time until tomorrow. How do you feel about being tortured for 24 hours?"

"I'd rather not. Any other ideas?"

"We need to create a distraction. You go back inside and tell the others what we are going to do. I don't trust that our comps aren't being monitored. Tell Tom to take Margarita back to his place. I don't think he would mind entertaining Margarita all evening." They both laughed knowingly. "And warn Germán to go out the backdoor. I'll tell you the rest of the plan on the way."

Germán's friend had filled the tanks so there was plenty of fuel. They headed out of town toward the hill country. Polly peered out the back window to make sure the helicopter was following. "It's following us," she affirmed. "They might send a flit after Tom and the others, but I guess they will have to come up with their own plan in that case. Which reminds me, what's our plan?"

"Our plan," Paul answered sagely, "is to come up with a plan between now and when we get to Germán's *pequeño rancho*."

"Well at least we know where we're going," Polly said hopefully.

Evening was presaged by the slanting golden rays of the lowering sun as they drove the last dusty miles to the ranch. A fox ran across the road in front of them and disappeared into the overgrown gully skirting the gravel covered lanes. Foxes were one of the few wild animals that had survived human transgression. The grey fox of the hill country was the most common of all the foxes and could climb trees like squirrels. This one headed across a field of dead grasses that had been reborn in the lustrous light of the evening sun. No longer a dull and dirty brown, now soft hues of yellow-orange and rose transformed the broken stalks into visions reminiscent of their living splendor.

Polly took a deep breath as she departed the old pickup, silently watching Paul hunt under the doormat for the key. Finally she said, "You know they left a window open over there. We could just go in that way."

"I found it," Paul said triumphantly. He let them in. "See if you still see the helicopter."

The helicopter did not find it necessary to be sneaky. It had hovered a short distance behind them the whole way. Now it seemed to be circling, no doubt looking for a place to land. The surroundings were hilly and densely forested, but there were a few open spots, like the field they had just passed. They didn't have long to initiate their plan. They could hear the helicopter landing close by as they headed out the back door.

"Which way?" Polly asked.

"That way," Paul pointed left to where Germán had said there was a creek. A deer trail created a narrow path overhung with limbs high enough for deer to pass under but face and chest height for humans. They had to walk bent over half the time. Paul went ahead and tried to hold the branches up so that they didn't lash back into Polly's face. The going was slower than optimal.

Polly wished she was wearing long pants. Brambles and branches slashed her bare legs as she ducked under branches and stumbled after Paul. At least she had exchanged the flip flops for her sturdy boots. They could hear their Binge pursuer searching the house behind them. "I don't think I can outrun them," Polly panted.

"We need to hide," Paul agreed.

They reached the creek where flowing water had cut crevices and hollowed out the dirt around tree roots to create natural shelters. "They don't strike me as the types to have experience at tracking. If we hide we can buy some time at least." Paul decided.

"Much better than buying time with torture," Polly agreed, "although this comes close. Do you think there are snakes?"

"Of course there are snakes," Paul assured her and slid down the bank as gently as possible so as not to obviously disturb the plants and soil. He reached up his hand to assist her descent and they tucked under a large exposed root. Above they heard the slashing and tearing of undergrowth as the Binge security guard tore through habitat. It sounded like there was only one. He had to know that they couldn't have gone far, but he passed them and continued on.

"We need to go back up," Paul whispered. "He is sure to come back this way and see where we slid down the bank."

They ascended as quietly as they could, but when they reached the top of the bank the guard was standing before them grinning as if he had just hit a homerun. He was wearing a Kevlar vest but no helmet and in his hand pointing at them was a Glock 17. "Well, this is convenient," he gloated. "Looks like you will both die in a hunting accident."

"Hunting with a Glock? You can't kill us in cold blood and get away with it," Polly reasoned. "They'll trace your gun and your shoe prints. You must have touched something in the house, too."

"Oops, looks like the new occupants started a fire and burned their new house down. That's city folk for you. But thanks for reminding me to sweep away my boot prints. Too bad you have to die. Maybe I won't kill you if you give me the chip."

"It's in the house," Paul said. "Take us back there and I'll get it for you." Polly gave him a surprised look and he shook his head. "I'd rather live as a poor student than die a hero, Polly."

They trudged back to the house with the gun pointed at their backs. The back porch stood off the ground by a height of three steps. The gunman waved them up ahead of him, but Polly hung back.

"I have something in my shoe," she whined and stopped to bend down at the top step. "It's slicing into my toes. I have to get it out." She plopped down on the top step to fiddle with her boot lace.

"Get it out later," the gunman grunted. Sweat poured down his face from all the exertion. Kevlar in the Texas heat was hardly efficient attire, especially when you're chasing down prey.

"Paul," she cried, ignoring the command. "Come help me. My boot is stuck. I think my foot is swollen. Something must have bit me, a snake maybe."

Paul turned back from the door and went back down the steps to a position below Polly and next to the gunman. "This will just take a minute," he assured the guard. "Don't worry you'll get your chip."

Before he could reach for her boot or the gunman could order him to move, Polly slid down the steps on her butt causing Paul to step aside. Before she hit the bottom, her booted foot kicked upward. The gunman was busy looking at Paul who was no longer in front of the gun and in fact was uncomfortably close and off to his right. He was turning the gun toward Paul to wave him back up the stairs when the boot made contact with his gonads. Paul saw him lurch forward in pain but quickly recover enough to train a deadly expression on Polly and begin to move the gun in position to shoot her. He didn't have time to think. He aimed a sideways karate kick at the killer's arm hitting him in the ulnar nerve that stretched over the elbow, also called the funny bone. The hitman's grip loosened but he did not drop his weapon. In an instant, Polly jumped up off the bottom step and grabbed the gun as it fired.

The cartridge whizzed by her foot tearing the leather of her boot on one side. Blood began to trickle out. She seemed dazed and the gunman made a grab to regain his weapon. Paul whirled around and kicked him again in the side of his knee. He crumpled to the ground.

"Polly, you're hit. Let me have the gun," Paul commanded. He took it from her without a struggle and pointed it at the man on the ground. "Take off your shoe and see how bad it is."

Polly did as she was told. There was a shallow, if painful, gash along the outside edge of her foot. "My boots are ruined," she said tearfully looking up at Paul with an expression of anguish.

"We'll get you a new pair," he soothed, wishing he could take her in his arms and hold her against his chest. She had disarmed a trained thug and then an instant later was crying like a little girl with a broken toy. "Go inside and wash your wound and see if you can find any Band Aides. I'm going to tie this guy up."

Through sniffling sobs she managed to nod begrudgingly, "my foot will heal itself, but how am I going to get a new pair of boots without any money? These aren't cheap boots. I have a high instep so I have to have good shoes."

"I told you, I'll buy you any pair of boots you want, I promise," Paul jerked his head toward the door with a strained look. "Tom will chip in if it comes to that. Your foot might not heal itself without some help. Go inside and take care of it." He motioned with the gun for the Binge guard to enter the house after Polly.

The gunman sat sullenly in a kitchen chair with the gun trained on him while Polly cleaned her wound. Paul handed off the gun to her when she was finished and searched the boxes in the living room for something with which to tie him. If only I had some duct tape I could tape him to a chair, he fumed. The long, sleepless night and Polly's close call had shortened his fuse. He had to tear one of Margarita's sheets into strips to make rope.

"Chip or not you aren't making it out of here alive," the guard said before Paul stuffed a sock in his mouth and tied it in place with a strip of sheet.

"He's right," Paul told Polly, "this is a ghost gun. It's untraceable. The frame was built from a polymer frame kit so there's no serial number. Binge sent them here to kill us and leave no trace. Binge doesn't care about the chip. They just don't want it in use. They intended to destroy it anyway. If they kill all of us then no one will know where the chip is and they have accomplished their goal.

"What about the others?" Polly gasped.

"Let's take care of the helicopter pilot first," Paul decided, "and then we'll contact Tom and see how he's doing."

They headed down the road in the direction of the earlier helicopter noise, walking until they spotted the chopper in the field of dead grass that the grey fox had crossed. Paul motioned downward with one hand and Polly joined him in the ditch.

"He's probably armed," Paul said, "but now I am too. I'm going to sneak up behind him while you create a diversion in front. It's almost dusk, so that works in our favor. I can blend into the shadows."

She looked at him in amazement. "You want me to walk into the jaws of the tiger as a diversion."

"Unless you want to switch and take the gun. Are you ready to shoot if you have to?"

"Who kicked the other guy in the balls and sustained an injury taking the gun?"

"You did," Paul smiled, "so I know how brave you are. Don't take him out. Just make some noise so he doesn't hear me coming."

She frowned irritably, but agreed. She wished she had some duct tape to cover the gap in her boot where the bullet had torn the leather. Her Band Aides were slipping off and dirt and debris had begun to aggravate the wound. Limping up out of the ditch she continued ahead, walking in middle of the road, while Paul crawled along in the bushy trench beside her. When they drew level with the helicopter and Paul had time to crawl out into the brush toward the chopper, she picked up a hand full of gravel and began to throw the individual pieces in the direction of the aircraft.

The pilot was sprawled out inside the helicopter cabin with the door open. When he heard the noise from the gravel, he hopped down from his seat and began to advance toward her. She stood for a moment staring back at him and then began to move forward. He was armed, but had not drawn his weapon. She waved and walked more quickly in his direction. "Can you help me?" she called to him. Pulling up her T-shirt, she pointed at her belly and wrapped her arms around herself as she bent forward. "Please help me," she cried painfully.

He was beginning to look suspicious. He peered around the field, but did not see Paul creeping toward him. The wind moved across the field in erratic patterns, gusting here and there but not sustained, so it was hard to pick out a particular movement. "What's wrong?" he asked. He was about 50 feet from her now.

"It's my stomach. Can you take me to the hospital in that helicopter? I called for an ambulance ages ago. I heard you land and thought you might be airlifting me out? But you never came." She moaned and bent over again peeking out from under her hair to gauge his reaction. He didn't look convinced. His hand went toward his holster, but the girl was obviously unarmed and he didn't want to scare her away. He thought he recognized her now that she was closer.

He made a snap decision. "Sure," he said, "I'm not an ambulance, but I can take you to the hospital. Let me help you in." He started to move closer.

She backed away. "I don't understand," she said, "who are you? I need an ambulance."

He came forward more quickly. He was no more than 20 feet away when he heard a rustling in the dried, broken stalks on his left. Polly inhaled sharply and held it. This time he did draw his gun and pointed it in that general direction. A grey fox bounded out of the weeds. The fox froze for a moment then pounced head first back into the brush. Mesmerized by the sudden graceful movements, neither one could look away as she reemerged, ignored them completely and ran away toward the road with a fat, brown field mouse in her jaws. Their eyes followed her as she crossed the road and disappeared into the woods on the other side.

"Don't kill it," Polly cried. "I'll go with you, but please put that thing away, you're scaring me." The man lowered the weapon but did not holster it. He was holding it down at his side when Paul came up behind him.

"Drop your weapon," Paul ordered. "I have your friend's gun pointed at your head and if I pull the trigger and clean off the fingerprints no one will know who did it." Polly didn't hesitate. She grabbed the gun from the man's hand before he could strategize. "Get into the helicopter, please," Paul ordered.

"Oh look," Polly cried with delight as they rummaged inside the cabin for something that could be used for tying him up. "He has duct tape! This is going to hurt when it comes off."

They taped his mouth and hands and feet, and then wrapped it around his body and the cockpit seat to secure him in place. Polly saved out a bit to use to repair her shoe. "I wish non-assassins who don't work for Binge could get this stuff," she sighed. "Do you think Binge has a secret supply somewhere that they are hoarding?"

"How would you like to make duct tape for a living?" Paul suggested. "We'll have plenty of money when we sell that chip and we could power our plant naturally with a bio-engine and make the backing out of hemp instead of cotton. It's easy to grow in Texas and takes a lot less water to irrigate."

She looked at him thoughtfully. "It would be a service to humankind for sure. I might consider it. Right now let's contact Tom and warn him that Binge is making its move."

Paul pulled his comp out of his back pocket and typed in, "Binge means to kill us".

Once back at the house, Paul insisted on washing and disinfecting Polly's foot. It wasn't any worse than a bad scrape but a bullet has lead in it and he didn't want to take any chances. After cleaning it with soap and pouring hydrogen peroxide over it, he filled the tub with hot water and salt and made her sit on the edge to soak it.

As she sat with her back to him he picked bits of leaves and debris from her frizzy, sun-streaked tresses. In the single bright overhead bathroom light it glowed like a halo. "You might be growing a tree out of your head," he laughed, exhibiting a twig he had disentangled.

His gentle touch was soothing, but she worried that he must be exhausted too and turned to tell him that she could get the rest out when she showered. Their eyes met and the tenderness they held for each other flowed between them like a magnetic force. Paul slowly bent toward her. His hands still in her hair, he pulled her face to his and their lips met. She melted into the kiss and the world flowed and ebbed around her and into her. It was only a moment. Polly started to lose her perch on the slippery tub and Paul pulled back and moved his hand to her back to support her.

"I better shower now, so you can get cleaned up," she said nervously.

"Yeah," he answered, "do you have towels and shampoo and a change of clothes?"

"I found some things in the unpacked boxes. I hope Margarita doesn't mind that I went through her things."

"I'm sure she won't," he said, backing out of the room, unable to take his eyes off her. "I'm going to sacrifice another one of her sheets to mummify that security guard we tied up in the kitchen. I don't want him getting loose after we leave."

"I won't take long," she said.

"Take as long as you like," he answered. "I'm not going anywhere. We have all night to drive back into town." He closed the door and stood outside in the hallway for a minute wondering what had just happened and what it meant. Maybe it's the stress, he thought, we both did almost die.

Chapter 33: Ted

Ted left with Veronica, but they'd gone hardly a block when he asked to get out because he left his sunglasses at the restaurant. "Don't bother waiting for me. I'll grab an auto-flit back to my place." Veronica shrugged and ordered the pilot to continue back to the hotel.

His sunglasses were safely in his pocket. Instead of returning to the restaurant he grabbed an auto-flit from a nearby stand and hovered just above the ground in an alley next to the restaurant waiting for Germán's exit. Veronica might be satisfied with the deal she had made, but Binge certainly wouldn't be. Binge wanted this whole natural energy thing shut down and they were willing to pay way more than 100 million creds to get what they wanted. Besides, no one had thought to give him a piece of the deal. Veronica had yet to even offer him a job. Once he was rich he would have a hundred Veronicas lapping at his feet.

Germán finally left by the back door that exited the kitchen. If Ted hadn't been in the feeder alley he wouldn't have seen him. He headed down the main alley toward the crossover to the east side of town on foot. Ted followed above at a discreet distance, trying to blend in with the rest of the traffic and the rooftops. Lots of flit traffic went to the crossover this time of day so it wasn't too difficult.

Surprisingly, Germán went to another restaurant. Surely he wasn't still hungry, Ted thought, so this must have something to do with the chip. He needed a disguise if he was going to get close enough to figure out what Germán was up to.

Luckily, there was a One Credit Store next door to the restaurant. Ted abandoned his ride at a nearby stand and went in. Just covering up with a hoody was not going to be enough, so he purchased a backpack and some cheap combat boots. He bought the hoody in a size too big, put his shoes in the backpack and put it underneath the sweatshirt. The resulting hump gave him a nice Quasimodo effect. Hoping he hadn't missed anything he hurried back out to rub some filth into his new clothes and scuff the shoes so they didn't look brand new. It was too warm for a sweatshirt, but he didn't have much choice.

Thus disguised, he entered the restaurant and took a seat near the window. A waiter took his order for a cup of coffee and a donut. Germán was nowhere to be seen. Then just as the waiter brought him the hot drink and greasy dessert, Germán came out of the kitchen and rounded the counter with another man. They headed for the door. "Damn," Ted cursed, "check please."

The waiter gave him a strange look, but shrugged and dropped a ticket onto his table. "Pay at the register," he instructed.

By the time Ted paid and rushed out the door, the two men had disappeared. "Hell," he kicked the pavement in frustration, then ripped off the suffocating hoody and dropped the backpack to the ground. He could go back into the restaurant and pump the workers for information, but they would most likely tell Germán. He wasn't going to be able to find them now on the auto-flit. He decided to wait in the shadow of a nearby awning behind a pillar for a while until he came up with a better idea.

Waiting turned out to be a good plan. Less than an hour later a flit-cab deposited the two men in front of the restaurant. They each carried large, lumpy bags. What they contained Ted could only presume, but he presumed it was something to do with the formula. As they passed the alley, he saw on one of the bags the words Capitol Chemicals. "Gotcha," he gloated.

They would need the formula if they were planning to make the much sought after product. Therefore, all he had to do was to sneak into the kitchen and grab it somehow. He wasn't going to get back there dressed as he was, so he would have to revise his disguise. He could make a delivery.

No sooner than he decided this than a delivery truck pulled into the shopping center and followed the road around to the back of the stores. Ted jogged along behind. They were making a delivery to the One Credit Store but no matter. Accosting the driver before he could open his door, Ted waved his credit card in front of his face and offered him a day's wages for his cap and a box of something edible. With nothing to lose since the cap and the goods belonged to the company and stuff went missing all the time, the driver agreed. After making the transaction over their respective comps, Ted knocked on the back entrance to the restaurant wearing the cap pulled down low and the oversized hoody.

The kid who opened the door looked confused, but let him in. "Wait here until I get someone to take delivery," the kid said. "I just bus tables."

"Not a problem," Ted agreed. Once the kid was out of sight he left the box on the floor and quickly stuck the cap into his back pocket. He grabbed an apron hanging from a nearby hook and thus attired, headed into the main kitchen area.

The cook was busy flirting with a waitress and the busboy was nowhere to be seen. The dishwasher noticed him and favored him with a sour smile before turning back to his work. There were sounds coming from a storeroom off to the left where the door hung half open, but Ted couldn't see what was causing them. He supposed it was Germán and his friend.

Germán's friend was also a mentor like Pam who worked with high school students. Unlike Pam it wasn't for credit. Juan was a first generation high school graduate and college graduate who wanted to help others. He had triple majors in biology, chemistry and mechanical engineering and worked at his family's restaurant during his breaks from school where he assisted one of his former professors. The bio-truck was his master's thesis.

When Germán contacted him early on the morning after they copied the code from the chip, he offered to run it through the DNA software at the university lab to transform the code into a simple formula of readily available chemical compounds.

Now they were going to make the bacteria in the restaurant kitchen. This wasn't the first time that Juan had used the family property in creative ways. None of the employees paid him any heed. His family wondered when all that education would pay off, but he was good about helping them whenever he had free time so they humored him. Since the lunch rush was over, they had the kitchen to themselves for a few hours.

"We'll set it in the yogurt maker for a few hours and then see what we have," Juan said as he and Germán pushed open the storeroom door to enter the kitchen. Ted ducked back into the corner and pretended to be looking for something. "You'll want a prototype even though it is not necessary to patent it."

Maybe I can grab the yogurt maker when they leave, Ted thought, or what's in it. He glanced at the pair to see what they were talking about. It was right behind the cook who still stood flirting with the pretty waitress. "Get a room already," Ted breathed but it had no effect on them. They were enjoying the chase.

"Let's grab some drinks from the front," Juan suggested and he and Germán went into the dining room through a pair of swinging doors.

As soon as they disappeared, Ted sidled closer to the countertop where his prize incubated. It would be impossible to grab it and get away behind the cook's back, but the chip might be in the storeroom. He turned and headed that way.

He made it inside just as Juan and Germán reappeared, iced teas with lemon wedges in hand. The tea looked refreshing and Ted realized how thirsty all the spying had made him. No time for that now he told himself licking his parched lips and he began to methodically peruse the area in front of him. Shelves full of boxes and cans lined two sides of the small room. On the third side was a desk next to a bookcase filled with plastic filing containers. On the desk lay an open book and several papers along with some canisters, glass jars and a gallon of distilled water. He flicked off the lid of the water jug and took a long drink.

"Can't do my best work when I'm thirsty," he told himself. A few drops of water fell onto one of the papers. It contained letters and numbers in a diagram that looked similar to those on the open page of the book. Below the illustration in the book was written "Chemical formulas of common DNA". "Bingo," Ted softly proclaimed snatching up the loose papers near the book and tucking them into the pocket of his hoody.

Mission accomplished, he peaked through the open edge of the door. Luckily, Germán and his friend were no longer in the kitchen. The cook was making something at the grill, while the waitress prepared a couple of plates for the food. They glanced up as Ted was going through the backdoor, but neither one acknowledged the intruder. To them he was just another delivery guy or busboy. He was home free and soon would be as wealthy as he ever dreamed.

Chapter 34: Binge Wants You Dead

When Tom received the text from Paul, "Binge wants you dead," he already knew that he was being followed. Two auto-flits hovered outside the restaurant when he and Margarita exited. Suspiciously, the same two followed their flit-cab back to his apartment.

Once safely inside, Tom grimly informed Margarita of the text from Paul and that they had been followed. He had hidden the original chip. If Binge could get rid of them, no one would know where the chip was. It could all stay hidden forever, it didn't matter to Binge. They needed a plan, and soon.

"It won't be long before those two Binge thugs who were following us are knocking at the door," Tom told her. "We need to prepare before that happens."

"Maybe Veronica could help us," Margarita suggested.

"Asking her for help would weaken our position. At this point, we can't give her what she wants. We've already set our plan to patent in motion and we'd lose everything if we turn back now. I think we'll have to figure this one out on our own."

"Is there a back door?" she asked.

"Yes," Tom said, "but there are two of them. I am sure they have both exits covered."

"Not the fire escape," she countered.

"It would be easy to see us climbing down the building on the fire escape, but that gives me an idea," Tom replied. "It might cause some panic, but then we aren't in a crowded theater."

"Are you intending to start a fire?" Margarita frowned disapprovingly.

"You are quick. Only a few small, harmless ones I assure you," Tom affirmed with a disarming grin. Margarita's handsome, solemn face broke into a lopsided smile. Tom was not such bad company and her life had become more exciting since meeting him.

"A trashcan fire should do the trick," Tom decided. "We need the smoke to create confusion. If we just triggered the fire alarm it would get turned off before we got our chance. We'll need to set up fires on several floors and create as much smoke as possible."

"Rubber and plastic make a lot of smoke," Margarita suggested.

"I have some plastic in my recycling bin," Tom said. "Let's get started setting up our fires. We need to act quickly."

"What do you have that is metal? We can't actually set the building on fire." Margarita insisted.

"My recycle bin is metal and I have a chimenea on that miniature balcony off the bedroom. We will need to create more smoke than that though. There are dumpsters in the back alley. Once we get the smoke going inside, we'll exit out the back entrance and set those on fire too. That should create enough confusion for us to slip past one guard."

"We need bottles with combustible fuel and cloth wicks," she said. "What combustible liquids do you have handy? We can set the dumpsters on fire with Molotov cocktails."

"You amaze me," Tom admitted, "are you a revolutionary? There might be some kerosene under the sink. And I have some strong liquor. This rum is 151 proof." Smoothly opening his desk drawer, he held up a bottle retrieved from inside. Margarita smirked. "It was a gift," he added sheepishly.

Tom went online to find out how to make Molotovs while he set Margarita to the task of cutting up some of his towels for wicks and rummaging through his cabinets for bottles. With the kerosene, liquor and bottles they had available, they assembled three bombs, two for Tom and one for Margarita to deploy. Tom gathered up a couple of lighters and a box of kitchen matches for ignition. He put his bombs in a satchel that he swung across his chest. She carefully deposited hers in the bag full of essentials she always carried

Next they stuffed the chimenea and metal trash bin with paper and plastic. Tom sprinkled a little kerosene on for good measure. They didn't know how long the guards would wait before they decided to close in. It was time to set their plan in motion.

Tom's apartment was on the 3rd floor, but since smoke would travel upward, they decided to start the fires on the first two floors. Handily, there was an intake HVAC vent at the end of each hallway near the exit at the back. They positioned the metal can and chimenea under these. Tom took up a position on the 2nd floor by the chimenea and Margarita took the 1st floor. The plan was for them to leave the building with the other occupants and toss the lit Molotovs in the trash bins in the alley as they passed by. Tom would meet her at the 1st floor exit as soon as he got his chimenea going and in the ensuing smoke and confusion they would elude their pursuers. Since they would have to wait indoors by the smoking containers for the apartment dwellers to start evacuating, Tom provided N-95 respirators. He had purchased a box when he spray painted an old frame for his Hatch Print Festival poster.

It took longer than they had planned for the residents to notice the smoke and for the fire alarm to sound. In the meantime, the guard at the rear of the building had illegally parked his auto-flit in the alley and was leaning against the wall smoking. He threw it on the ground at his feet when headquarters contacted him with orders to eliminate the problem using extreme prejudice. Attaching a silencer to his unregistered weapon, he prepared to enter the building. The other guard was doing the same on his end.

Tom was just joining Margarita when the handle of the exit door jiggled. Residents used a key card or punch code if they lost their card. It was rare for someone to forget both. When the guard shot open the lock, they were already on the alert. Even so, for a moment they were too stunned to do anything. Tom was the first to react as the door was pushed inward and the guard appeared in the doorway. He did not expect them to be standing right inside, so they had the advantage of surprise. Tom picked up the smoking metal trash can and threw it into the man's face. Margarita was slow to react at first, but snapped out of it in time to grab the gun before it went off.

"Hell," Tom declared, "what are we going to do with him? His partner will be here any time now."

"I'll use the gun," Margarita declared.

"Are you going to kill him?" Tom stammered. "We can't kill him." Still he didn't attempt to get the weapon.

She pointed it at the man's instep and fired. He bent over in pain and shock and she struck him with the gun butt on the back of his head. He wasn't unconscious but did not appear interested in completing his mission. "Let's go," she ordered.

"You are a revolutionary," Tom proclaimed. "Remind me never to get in your way."

He followed her to the series of dumpsters and they lobbed their lit grenades into each one, leaving the lids open for best effect. The smoke inside the building was finally causing alarms to sound and the occupants began to leave. As they turned the corner at the end of the alley, they saw the gunman stagger out and down the stairs helped by a young couple.

"Keep an eye out for the other guard," Tom ordered.

"Tom, your hands," Margarita exclaimed, noticing him holding them away from his body. "You burned them with that trash can."

"Not badly, I will be okay," he assured her. "We have to find a safe place for the night. I think this is as good a time as any to pick up the chip. I put it in the office fridge of my former TA. He gave me a copy of his key card. In fact, that might be the best place to hole up for the night. It might not be comfortable, but Binge doesn't know about it. We'll take turns keeping watch."

It was dark outside and with the smoke and confusion they would be difficult to see. An auto-flit leaned against the front of the building, but they didn't see the driver. His partner had probably contacted him and he was heading to the other side. They crossed Guadalupe Street and entered the gloom of the empty campus.

"My friend grows aloe in his office and there should be some ice too," Tom said touching Margarita gently on the shoulder. She turned fiercely toward him and he quickly took his hand away, but then she relaxed and favored him with a tight smile.

"You should not touch hot things with your bare hands," she chided. "I will dress your hand and then keep watch. You will sleep." She hoisted her weapon to the dark sky threateningly.

By morning the two felt more weary than rested. There was still work to do before they went to see Veronica. Then there was the problem of getting the chip to the rendezvous without being stopped by the opposition. Margarita brandished her gun and declared, "Leave it to me. I will get it there."

"Not by force," Tom insisted, "it is too dangerous. You should not be using that gun anymore."

"Okay," she agreed. "We don't want to get arrested. I'll keep the gun in here for now," she indicated her ubiquitous bag.

"Assuming they do not know that we are here," he said, "we might get away with disguising ourselves."

"Good plan," Margarita agreed, "but how?" She looked around the room. There was a green cardigan sweater on a coat rack, a bookcase overflowing with books and papers and a desk with chair. It was lucky that the floor was covered with a thick, oriental carpet or the night would have been even more uncomfortable.

"We exchange clothes," he suggested. "You will dress as a man and I will dress as a woman. I'll shave my beard and maybe I could get my hair into a ponytail. You wear that cardigan and try to look like Mr. Rogers." Mr. Rogers was a famous kid's show host of whom Margarita had never heard.

"My TA kept scissors and razors in his desk drawer because he was always running late to class." He went to the desk and pulled out the necessary items. "It is still early. I doubt there will be students in the restrooms yet." Indeed the sun wasn't up.

Tom grabbed the shaving gear. "I can shave myself, but you might have to help me with my hair."

When he came back from the restroom, Margarita had tied her hair into a tight bun and covered her head with a scarf from her bag. She was still wearing khaki's but had rolled them up into shorts and she covered her Tehuana-style embroidered shirt with the cardigan. The incongruous combination made her look like a crazy person. People would definitely give her space.

"Not bad for a gringo," Margarita teased Tom about his new, clean-shaven appearance. "Let me fix your hair." By the time she was finished Tom didn't even recognize himself in the mirror. He decided the change was drastic enough without trying to look like a woman.

"You look nice," Margarita smiled coquettishly. He rubbed his face and grinned. "How do we proceed? We have to get to the downtown offices to complete our paperwork before we see Veronica. It's already getting light."

"The safest way to go is by Yooter," Tom suggested. "Will you be able to ride one?"

"One of those floating scooter things?" Margarita queried. "I am not very good, but I tried one when they first happened. I was curious when my grandson was interested."

"Of course you did," Tom acknowledged smiling. "You carry the chip. We'll take it slowly." Margarita's omnipresent large tote could easily conceal a small bag of ice to chill the original chip which might still send a transponder signal.

"We follow each other but not too closely. Stay within sight. There is a stand nearby and this early there should still be a couple of Yooters available."

Chapter 35: Finalized Plans

Polly and Paul found a parking garage for the pickup and spent the night curled up inside it. They were already at the court office complex when Tom and Margarita showed up. Polly complimented them on their disguises, while Paul affected indifference. Then after a few minutes, he burst out laughing. Tom humorlessly glared him into silence.

"I'm sorry," Paul apologized. "You both look lovely…inside," then he laughed again.

Much to Tom's chagrin, instead of insisting that he was handsome, Margarita said, "appearances are not important."

With their paperwork finalized, it was just a matter of making it to Veronica's room without incident. At this point, they decided to order a flit-cab. Mitchell, Germán and Juan were going to meet them there. Four people could just squeeze into a double bench sedan.

The drive to the hotel was uneventful. They found the others relaxing in the lobby when they arrived. It was after one o'clock, so they took the elevator up to the 21st floor. Tom experienced déjà vu knocking on the door.

Veronica opened it and ushered them in with a palm out hand gesture. Strangely, Pam and Bob were there sitting on the sofa.

"What are you two doing here?" Tom asked as the door closed behind them revealing an armed man who had been concealed behind it. His gun was pointing at Veronica. They had walked into a trap.

Paul stared accusingly at Pam. "I thought you were working for Veronica?"

"My dad is all the family I have, Paul. With what Binge is paying us I won't have to work for anyone."

"So much for good causes and helping the disadvantaged, I guess," Paul spat the words.

"Don't be so emotional. That was always your problem. You never could separate your feelings from your actions," Pam countered. "I need someone strong enough to stand up to me *and* alongside of me. Or do you want to change your mind and come join us? I could put in a good word with Binge. You could still go into technical administration."

"Enough," Bob declared, "where is the chip?"

Tom removed the bag of ice from Margarita's tote and handed it over to Veronica. She took it into the kitchenette and emptied it into the sink. The chip was securely sealed in plastic wrap inside. While she unwrapped the tiny package another gunman appeared from one of the bedrooms. "The threat has been neutralized," he told his companion. Paul figured that meant Veronica's body guard wasn't going to come to their rescue.

"I suppose you want me to check to see if this is the correct chip," Veronica said, holding it up between two beautifully manicured fingers.

"If you don't mind," Pam purred, "we'll use your equipment, but I am sending it to Binge."

Veronica inserted it and hit send while Pam looked over her shoulder. "It appears to be password protected," she said. "This will take a few minutes. Would anyone care for something to drink while we wait? I could send out for room service."

"Not a good idea," Bob objected. "Binge is well equipped to break a password. I think it best everyone stay seated and wait quietly. We all want to get out of here alive. Right?"

It didn't take long. Pam's comp buzzed and after a brief conversation with someone on the other end, she ejected the chip and dropped it into her purse. Nodding to the two gunmen, she and her father got up to leave. The gunmen covered their departure. When father and daughter had disappeared into the elevator, the gunmen slowly backed out with a warning that they were not to be followed.

After the door closed behind them, Veronica rushed to the bedroom where she found her bodyguard tied up but unharmed. Tom helped her untie him and they all went back into the living area. Veronica collapsed onto a chair, her expression dark with anger and disappointment. "You can't expect me to pay you," she told them. "I know that you delivered the goods, but without that technology it will be impossible for me to come up with the sums you were promised."

"You can still pay us," Paul said, ignoring her evil glare. "You can still pay us because you are still getting the technology."

"What do you mean? Was that not the chip? Did you make a copy?"

"It can't be copied," he answered. "It is failsafe protected and that was the original chip, but they are going to have a hard time opening it. It's locked tight now that it's been opened twice already."

"Then I don't understand. What are you saying?"

"We copied the formula down on paper and we are patenting the process. In fact, we've already applied for a patent. Our date stamp will precede Binge's if they try to use what they took and if they destroy it that makes no difference." He paused to enjoy the expression of relief and amazement on Veronica's normally unreadable face.

"So our deal still applies. You will have to wait a few months for the paperwork to go through, but I have no doubt that our application will be approved. You will be able to run your factories on the new energy source. You won't be allowed to sell the process, however."

This last information took her ebullience down a notch. She quickly recovered. "You couldn't patent it without the other half."

"I made a copy of the other half before I sold it to you. It came directly off the Binge mainframe so it wasn't failsafed," Tom explained.

"We will have to make a new contract," Veronica said with a smile of appreciation for Tom's cleverness. "I thought I would have all rights when I agreed to the previous sums." Mitchell started to protest, but Tom held out a silencing hand.

"Of course," Tom agreed. "In fact, we intend to use the technology ourselves. Perhaps we can provide your plants in the south with some business."

"I am not doing business with the maquiladoras," Germán interjected vehemently. Margarita said nothing. She would talk to her grandson later.

Chapter 36: All's Well That Ends Well

Six months later a new energy company named Gaea Inc. signed contracts to allow Veronica's factories to use the new technology for a period of seven years. It was enough money for everyone involved to pursue their individual dreams. Other companies were interested in using the new technology as well. By the time all the contracts had been signed and payment made, the founding members of Gaea were wealthy indeed.

Margarita and Tom went in together to purchase land adjacent to Germán's rancho to raise goats, chickens and hemp. It was a large spread and they were able to hire workers and pay them well. It turned out that goat and chicken waste was a wonderful medium on which to culture the bio-engine bacteria.

Germán's friend from the restaurant covered a car in the bacteria and was thinking of going in with Veronica to mass produce bio-battery powered trucks and cars. Bio-cell vehicles covered in the reddish-green material absorbed carbon dioxide and sunlight, cooled the planet and made oxygen at the same time. He asked Germán if he would like to join him in the venture.

Tom's hair had grown out into a real ponytail and Margarita kept it trimmed in a way that she liked. They shared a house and a business, but Margarita was slow to let him completely into her life. They were business partners. They had separate bedrooms.

In other ways she was like a wife. She made dinner in the evening after they tended the farm and checked the work of their employees. Though they hired people to do most of the labor; Margarita liked to do her own cooking and gardening. Tom was always beside her with a shovel and a hoe so she didn't work too hard.

One evening they were sitting on the porch watching the sunset over the little farm when Margarita took his hand in hers and said, "I can no longer imagine being without you. This must be a strange life for an English professor. You are the best friend I ever had and an excellent business partner."

Tom turned to tell her that he felt the same when he suddenly blurted, "I love you Margarita. Will you marry me?"

They were both taken by surprise. She laughed and he looked hurt. "Oh, I probably will," she answered. "Perhaps in the meantime we should sleep together tonight. What if I snore?"

"I will wear earplugs," he promised and they kissed. It was a beautiful sunset, a violet crown, but they forgot to look.

Paul and Polly didn't start their duct tape factory. They were happy enough when Veronica promised to make it in one of her apparel factories using hemp from Mexico and Texas. She told them they were welcome to tour the factory if they came to visit sometime. They assured her that they would.

Ted tried to make the energy bacteria from the plans he stole from the restaurant storeroom, but when he had dripped water while drinking from the jug on the desk a bit of the code got blurred. The chemist he hired to cultivate the bacteria using the incomplete plans blew up his yogurt maker and charged Ted for damages to his lab and to his face. The purloined paper with the formula on it was totally destroyed in the disaster.

Paul wanted to continue his computer studies. He decided to go to MIT and study robotics, since now he could afford to do whatever pleased him. He asked Polly to go with him, but it wasn't her thing. She had a restless spirit and wanted to let it take her where it would. They promised to see each other during holidays.

As they parted at the airport before she took off on her first trip around the world, Paul chided, "You still haven't solved the traffic problem. We almost didn't get here before your flight boarded."

"You're right. I guess I'll have to serendipitously work on that one next. At least we solved the duct tape issue and pollution to boot." They both laughed and hugged each other.

Mitchell blew a large part of his fortune building a huge house near the one owned by Pam's father. It even had an infinity edge pool with a view over the lake. He joined the same country club where Pam played tennis and sometimes watched as she played doubles with former Binge executives and women from the club. She was still living with her father, since it was only her father Binge paid for retrieving the chip. Veronica changed her mind about hiring her.

Binge was not happy that the formula was patented and that they could neither use it nor destroy it. Bob was no longer in debt but he had lost favor with the company. If Pam didn't find a rich husband soon, she was going to have to use her social worker degree to make a living.

Once a year the members of Gaea Inc. met at dank little Dempsey's Dive a few blocks away from Binge Headquarters where the jukebox continuously droned out classics by Willie Nelson, Waylon Jennings or sometimes Stevie Ray Vaughan's "Texas Flood". "Well there's floodin' down in Texas. All of the telephone lines are down," Tom would sing along.

Until the patent expired, they were all still pulling in creds selling the rights to the bio-cell technology. Afterwards, they'd still be rich. When they met at the restaurant, they told the waitress to add 25% and if the service was really good they doubled it. The waitress didn't mind at all if they came during lunch rush.